VALERIO MASSIMO MANFREDI

THE LOST ARMY

Translated from the Italian by Christine Feddersen-Manfredi

MACMILLAN

First published 2008 by Macmillan
an imprint of Pan Macmillan Ltd
Pan Macmillan, 20 New Wharf Road, London N1 9RR
Basingstoke and Oxford
Associated companies throughout the world
www.panmacmillan.com

ISBN 978-0-230-53065-2 HB
ISBN 978-0-230-53067-6 TPB

First published in Italian 2007 as *L'Armata Perduta* by
Arnoldo Mondadori Editore S.p.A., Milano

3 5 7 9 8 6 4 2

A CIP catalogue record for this book is available from
the British Library.

Typeset by SetSystems Ltd, Saffron Walden, Essex
Printed in the UK by CPI Mackays, Chatham ME5 8TD

To my mother

If the venture of the Ten Thousand was extraordinary, that of the women who followed them was nothing short of incredible.

W. W. Tarn

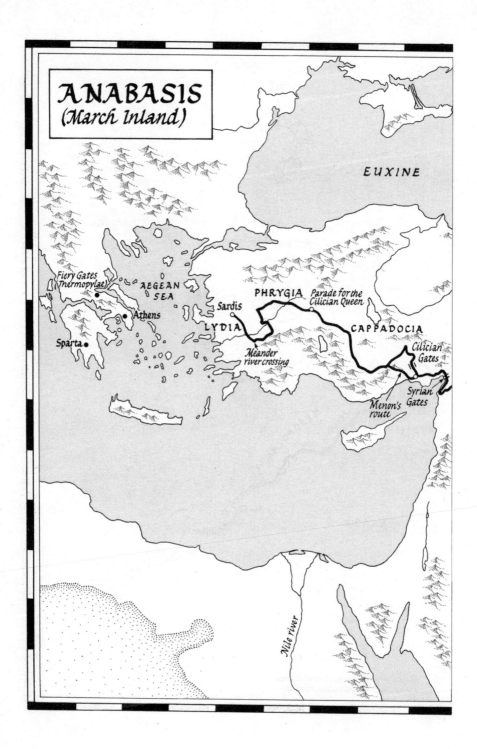

ANABASIS
(March Inland)

EUXINE

Fiery Gates
(Thermopylae)

AEGEAN
SEA

PHRYGIA   Parade for the
                 Cilician Queen

Sardis

Athens   CAPPADOCIA

LYDIA

Sparta   Cilician
                                               Gates

                 Meander
                 river crossing
                                                        Syrian
                                                        Gates

                                        Menon's
                                        route

                                                Nile river

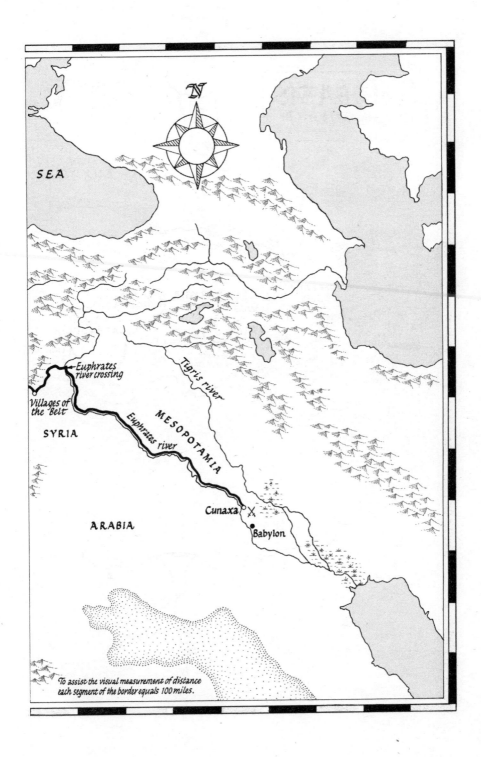

N

SEA

Euphrates
river crossing

Tigris river

Villages of
the Belt

MESOPOTAMIA

SYRIA

Euphrates river

ARABIA

Cunaxa ○ X
● Babylon

To assist the visual measurement of distance
each segment of the border equals 100 miles.

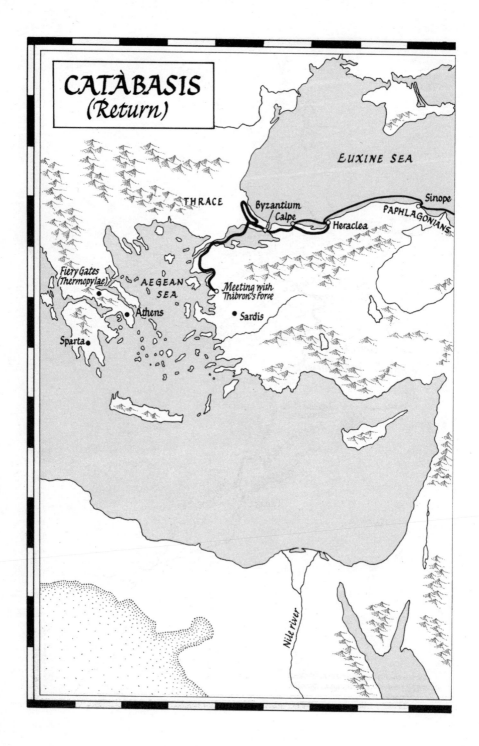

CATÀBASIS
(Return)

EUXINE SEA

THRACE

Byzantium
Calpe

Heraclea

Sinope

PAPHLAGONIANS

Fiery Gates
(Thermopylae)

AEGEAN
SEA

Meeting with
Thibron's force

Athens

Sardis

Sparta

Nile river

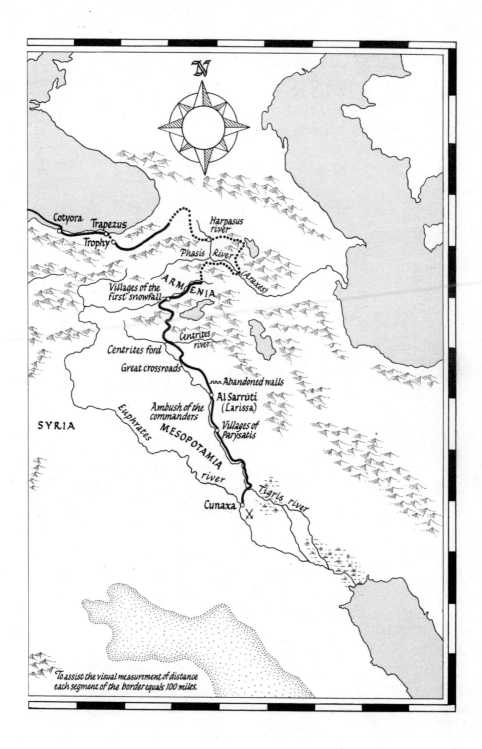

Cotyora
Trapezus
Trophy

Harpasus river

Phasis River

(Araxes)

ARMENIA

Villages of the
first snowfall

Centrites
river

Centrites ford

Great crossroads

Abandoned walls

Al Sarrùti
(Larissa)

Ambush of the
commanders

SYRIA

Euphrates

MESOPOTAMIA

Villages of
Parysatis

river

Tigris river

Cunaxa

To assist the visual measurement of distance
each segment of the border equals 100 miles.

Main Characters

Abira *is the novel's narrator*
Abisag – *one of the girls who saves Abira*
Agasias of Stymphalus (the Stymphalian) – *Greek army general*
Agias of Arcadia (the Arcadian) – *Greek army general*
Anaxibius – *Spartan admiral stationed at Byzantium*
Archagoras – *Greek officer*
Ariaeus – *commander of the Asian contingent of Cyrus's army*
Aristonymus of Methydria – *valiant Greek soldier*
Artaxerxes – *the Great King, Cyrus's brother and Emperor of the Persians*
Callimachus – *Greek soldier*
Cleanor of Arcadia (the Arcadian) – *Greek army general*
Clearchus – *Spartan commander of the mercenary expeditionary force*
Cleonimus of Methydria – *valiant Greek soldier*
Ctesias – *Greek physician to Artaxerxes*
Cyrus – *second son of the King of Persia, governor of Lydia*
Demetrius – *young Greek soldier*
Dexippus – *Greek soldier*
Durgat – *Persian prisoner, one of Queen Parysatis's ladies in waiting*
Epicrates – *Greek officer*
Eupitus – *Proxenus's second-in-command, from Tanagra*
Eurylochus of Lusia (the Arcadian) – *young Greek soldier*
Glous – *one of Ariaeus's cavalrymen*
Lycius of Syracuse – *cavalry commander with Xeno*
Lystra – *young prostitute following the army*
Masabates – *Persian eunuch*
Melissa – *one of Cyrus's concubines*

Menon of Thessaly (the Thessalian) – *Greek army general*

Mermah – *one of the girls who saves Abira*

Mithridates – *Persian general*

Neon of Asine – *officer in Socrates's battalion and Sophos's field adjutant*

Netus (Sophaenetus) the Stymphalian – *Greek officer*

Nicarchus of Arcadia – *young Greek soldier*

Parysatis – *Queen of Persia, mother of Artaxerxes and Cyrus*

Phalinus – *messenger in the Great King's service*

Proxenus of Boeotia – *Greek army general, Xeno's friend*

Seuthes – *barbarian king of Thrace*

Socrates of Achaea (the Achaean) – *Greek army general*

Sophos (Chirisophus) – *only high-ranking regular officer of the Spartan army*

Timas (Timasion) the Dardanian – *Greek army general*

Tiribazus – *Armenian satrap and 'eye of the Great King'*

Tissaphernes – *Artaxerxes's brother-in-law and general in his army*

Xanthi (Xanthicles) of Achaea – *Greek army general*

Xeno (Xenophon) – *young Athenian warrior who enlists in Cyrus's mercenary army to write the diary of the expedition*

1

The wind.

That ceaseless wind that blasts like the breath of a dragon through the craggy folds of Mount Amanus and then beats down on our plains, withering the grass and scorching the fields. All summer long.

And for most of the spring, and the autumn.

If it weren't for the stream that trickles down from the high Taurus peaks, nothing would grow here. Nothing but stubble for herds of hungry goats.

The wind has a voice, but it's always changing: sometimes a long lament that seems never to find solace, at other times a hissing that penetrates at night into every crack in the walls, into the gap between a door and its frame, letting in a thin haze that envelops everything, reddening your eyes and parching your throat even as you sleep.

Sometimes it's a roar that carries the echo of the thunder of the mountains and the snapping of the nomads' tents in the desert. A roar that gets under your skin and makes every fibre of your body tingle. The elders say that when the wind roars that way something extraordinary is about to happen.

Our land is made up of five villages: Naim, Beth Qadà, Ain Ras, Sula Him and Sheeb Mlech, with no more than a few hundred people in all. Each one stands on a little rise made up of the remains of other villages destroyed by time, built and then abandoned and then built up all over again in the same place, using the same sunbaked mud. But the administrators of the

Great King call them the 'Villages of Parysatis' after the Queen Mother.

They're also called the 'Villages of the Belt', because all of the labours of all the people who live in our villages, everything we produce and manage to sell, except for what we need to survive, is earmarked every year for buying a single precious new belt for the Queen's gown. At the end of each season there's a richly garbed Persian who comes escorted by numerous bodyguards to collect everything that our parents have managed to scrape together in a whole year of hard work. We're left with the risk of starving and the certainty of hardship so that a belt can be bought for a woman who already has dozens and surely doesn't need one more. But they tell us it's an honour for us and that we should be proud. Not just anyone can say that they are able to contribute to the wardrobe of such an important member of the royal family.

I've tried hard to imagine that family, that home, but I just can't. You hear so many stories about such a fabled dwelling. Some say it's in Susa, others in Persepolis, still others in Pasargadae, on the vast high plains. Maybe it's in all of those places at once, or maybe in none. Or perhaps it stands in a place that is equally distant from all those places

I live in a house with two rooms, one for sleeping and one for eating our meals. The floor is beaten earth, and maybe that's why everything we eat tastes of dust. The roof is made of palm trunks and straw. When we go to the well to draw water, my friends and I, we'll often stop and dawdle. We talk on and on and daydream out loud, at the risk of catching a hiding if we're not home in time.

What do we dream about? About finding a handsome, noble, lovable young man who will carry us away from this place where every day is like the next, knowing full well that such a thing could never happen. I'm happy, all the same, happy to be alive, to work, to go to the well with the other girls. It doesn't cost anything to dream, and it's like living another life: the one we'd all like to have and never ever will.

One day, as we were making our way to the well, the wind hit us full force, making us feel dizzy as we leaned forward to stay on our feet. We knew that wind all right: the wind that roars!

All the objects around us were obscured by a thick fog of dust. The only thing we could see distinctly was the disc of the sun, but it had taken on an unreal pinkish shade. It seemed to be suspended in nothingness, over a wasteland without edges or definable shapes, a land of ghosts.

An indistinct shape appeared in that dim cloud. It was moving, fluttering in the air.

A ghost.

One of those spirits that come out of the ground at dusk so they can slip away in the dark as soon as the sun drops below the horizon.

'Look,' I said to my friends.

A body was taking shape but the face remained invisible. Behind us we could hear the usual sounds of the evening: farmers returning from the fields, shepherds urging their flocks towards their pens, mothers calling their children home. Then, all at once, silence. The roaring wind fell quiet, the gloom slowly dissipated. To our left appeared the group of twelve palm trees that encircle the well, to our right the hill of Ain Ras.

Between them, a woman.

We could see her quite well now: her body, her face framed by long dark hair. A young woman, still beautiful.

'Look,' I repeated. As though that apparition were not already at the centre of everyone's attention. The slender figure advanced slowly, as though she felt all those stares upon her, weighing her down, as each step brought her a little closer to the edge of Beth Qadà.

We turned around and could see that many men had gathered at the entrance to the village, lining up as if to shut her out. Then someone shouted something that we couldn't grasp the meaning of, but the words we understood were terrible ones, laden with a violence we'd never known. Some women started running up as well, and one of them shouted: 'Get out! Leave now while you can!'

But either she hadn't heard or chose not to listen. She kept on walking forward. Now she was burdened by the weight of their hate as well and her steps were even slower.

A man picked up a stone from the ground and threw it. He only just missed his target. Others gathered stones as well and hurled them at the woman, who struggled to keep walking. A stone hit her left arm and another her right knee, making her fall. She rose to her feet with difficulty and continued on towards the village. Her eyes scanned the ferocious crowd, seeking a single friendly face.

I shouted out this time, 'Leave her alone! Don't hurt her!'

But no one listened. The rain of stones turned into hail. The woman swayed and fell to her knees.

Even though I did not know her, even though I knew nothing about her, I realized that her stubborn approach towards the village was something like a miracle, the kind of event that had never before happened in our forgotten corner of the Great King's empire.

The stoning went on until the woman showed no signs of life. Then the men turned around and went back into the village. They'll be sitting down at their tables soon, I thought, breaking bread for their children and eating the food their wives have prepared. Murder with stones, from a distance, doesn't stain your hands with blood.

My mother must have been among the crowd, because I suddenly heard her voice, calling out to me, 'Get over here, you stupid thing, move!'

We had all been frozen by what we had seen; none of us could ever have begun to imagine such a thing happening. I was the first to snap out of it, and I started walking towards my mother, towards home. As frightened as I was, I walked as close as I could get to the body of that stranger, close enough to see a trickle of blood coming out from under the stones, sinking into the dust and staining it red. I could see her right hand and both of her feet, which were bloody. I looked away and walked off quickly, swallowing a sob.

My mother greeted me with a couple of slaps, almost making me drop the jug of water I still held. She had no reason to hit me, but I guessed that she needed to vent the tension and anguish she'd felt at seeing a person stoned to death at the gates of our village, a person who hadn't harmed anyone at all.

'Who was that woman?' I asked without acknowledging my own pain.

'I don't know,' replied my mother. 'And you shut up.' I knew right away that she was lying and so I asked no further questions, but started to make dinner. My father walked in as I was putting the food on the table. He ate without lifting his eyes from his plate or saying a word. He went into the other room and soon we could hear him snoring. My mother joined him as soon as it was dark enough to warrant lighting a lamp, because we couldn't afford one, and I asked if I could stay up for a while in the dark. She said nothing.

A long time passed. The last glimmer of dusk faded and night fell, a dark night with a new moon. I was sitting next to the window, which was half open, so I could look for stars. The dogs were barking: maybe they could smell the blood or feel the presence of the stranger's body lying out there all covered with stones. I wondered whether the villagers would bury her the next day or just leave her there to rot.

The wind was still, now, stunned into silence by the crime, and everyone was sleeping in Beth Qadà. Everyone but me. I knew I would never fall asleep while the troubled spirit of that woman was wandering through the streets of the sleeping village, seeking no doubt to pass her torment and suffering on to someone else. Unable to bear the agony of sitting cooped up in the dark waiting for her to find me, and unable to even think about resting on the mat rolled out in a corner of the kitchen, I went outside, and the sight of the vast vault of the starry sky gave me a sense of peace. I took a deep breath and sat down on the ground, leaning back into the warmth of the wall with my eyes wide open in the darkness, waiting for the beating of my heart to calm.

I soon realized that I wasn't the only one in the village unable to sleep: a shadow slipped by, quiet as could be, but her gait was unmistakable and I called out to her, 'Abisag!'

'Is that you? You nearly scared me to death!'

'Where are you going?'

'I can't sleep.'

'Me neither.'

'I'm going to see that woman.'

'She's dead.'

'Why are the dogs still barking, then?'

'I don't know.'

'Because they can feel that she's alive and they're afraid.'

'Maybe it's her ghost they're afraid of!'

'Dogs are not afraid of dead people. Only men are. I'm going to see.'

'Wait, I'll come with you.'

We walked swiftly down the street together, knowing that if we were found out we'd surely get a beating from our parents. The house of our friend Mermah was on our way; we knocked at the window sill and called her name softly. She must have been awake, because she opened the window at once, and as she was leaving the house her sister joined us as well.

We crept along close to the walls until we had cleared the village, then quickly reached the spot where the stranger had been stoned. An animal ran off as we drew near; a jackal, probably, attracted by the smell of blood. We stopped short in front of that jumbled heap of stones.

'She's dead,' I hissed. 'What did we come here for?'

The words weren't out of my mouth when a stone shifted and rolled down on the others.

'She's alive,' breathed Abisag.

We bent over her and started taking the stones from her body one by one without making a sound, until she was completely free. It was so dark we couldn't even make out her face. It was a swollen mess anyway and her hair was clotted with blood and dust. But her jugular vein was pulsing and a low moan was coming from her mouth. She was alive, all right, but it looked as if she might die at any moment.

'Let's get her away from here,' I said.

'Where can we take her?' asked Mermah.

'To the hut by the river,' Abisag proposed. 'No one has used it for ages.'

'How can we get her there?' asked Mermah again.

I had an idea. 'Take your clothes off. No one can see us anyway.'

The other girls did as I asked, realizing what I had in mind, stripping off until they were almost naked.

I laid out our clothes and knotted them together to make a kind of sling that we laid on the ground next to the woman. We gingerly eased up her arms and legs and shifted her onto the cloth. She gasped when we pulled her off the ground; her limbs must have been shattered. We lifted the sling as gently as we could. That poor thing was as thin as could be; she wasn't even heavy for girls like us, and we managed to carry her to the hut without much trouble, stopping every now and then to catch our breath.

We made a bed for her, using a mat and some straw and hay. We washed her with cool water and covered her with sackcloth. She wouldn't catch cold, because the night was warm, but that was the least of her problems anyway. None of us knew whether she'd live through the night, or whether we'd find a corpse the next day. We decided there was nothing more we could do for her then and that the best thing to do was to get back before our parents realized we were gone. We washed our own blood-stained clothes in the stream and took them back home with us, hoping they would dry before morning.

Before splitting up, we made a plan for helping our protégée, if she survived. We'd bring her food and water in shifts until she was able to take care of herself. We swore that we would tell no one our secret. We would not betray her for all the gold in the world, and would protect her with our very lives.

We hadn't a clue what this actually meant, but an oath was an oath, and must contain solemn promises. We left each other with long hugs; we were tired, worn out by the emotions that we'd experienced that day and that night, yet so excited that we were sure we would never get back to sleep.

The wind started blowing again during the night and continued until dawn, when the crowing of the cocks woke the inhabitants of Beth Qadà and of the other four Villages of the Belt.

The first thing everyone noticed as they made their way to the fields was that the stoned woman had disappeared, and this threw them all into a panic. The strangest rumours spread from one person to the next, most of them terrifying, so terrifying that no one dared to investigate further: it was better to forget the bloody deed that had tainted them all. Their superstitious fear would make it easy for us to look after the woman we'd saved from certain death, without anyone noticing, we hoped.

We were just past our girlhood but what we'd done was much bigger than we were. Now we were frightened of the repercussions. Would we be able to keep her alive? We didn't know how to heal her wounds, nor how and where we could get food for her, if she did manage to survive. Mermah had an idea that got us out of this fix. There was an old Canaanite woman who lived all alone in a kind of den dug out of the embankment that kept the stream from overflowing when it was in flood. It was said that she gathered herbs to prepare unguents and potions that she used to cure burns, coughs and malignant fevers in exchange for food and the rags she dressed in. She was called 'the mute' because she couldn't talk, or maybe didn't want to. We went looking for her the next night and took her to the hut.

The stranger was still breathing but it truly seemed that every breath might be her last.

'Can you do something for her?' we pleaded, crowding around. The mute woman seemed to take no heed of us, but instead leaned closer to the dying stranger. She took a leather sack from her belt and poured its contents into the bowl hanging from her cane, but then she stopped. She turned towards us and rudely waved us away.

We looked into each other's eyes as if to consult about the wisdom of this move, but when the old woman raised her cane and shook it at us we ran out in a flash. We waited outside until we heard a loud scream coming from the hut, so loud we were petrified. None of us made a move; we stayed put where we were, sitting on the ground, until the old woman came out and beckoned us to enter. We peeked in the door and could see that the stranger was sleeping. The old woman signalled that we should come back the next day, and bring some food. We nodded and left reluctantly, stealing backward looks at the hut. The mute woman wasn't following. We thought she would probably stay there with the stranger all night.

The next day we came back with some goat's milk and barley soup. The old woman was gone but the stranger opened her swollen eyes as we came in and the look she gave us was intense and full of suffering. We helped her to eat the little food we'd brought and stayed there watching her long after she'd fallen asleep again.

Days passed like this, with the mute woman coming and going, and we never opened our mouths the whole time. We kept our secret and were very careful not to do anything that would make our families, or the other people in the village, suspicious. The stranger was healing very slowly, but we could see some improvements. The swelling had gone down, the bruises had paled and even her wounds were starting to scab over.

She must have had a number of broken ribs because she took very short breaths and could never seem to fill her lungs. There was probably not an inch of her body that didn't hurt, that hadn't been hacked by those cruel stones.

I WAS ALONE with her when she opened her eyes one morning in mid-autumn, at the first light of dawn. I'd brought her barley soup and some pomegranate juice we'd made for her. She said something. It was 'Thank you.'

'I'm so happy you're better,' I answered, 'I'll go to tell my friends. They'll be as happy as I am.'

She sighed and turned her head towards the window where a little early sun was streaming through.

'Can you talk?' I asked her.

'Yes.'

'Who are you?' I asked.

'My name is Abira and I come from this village, but you may not remember me.'

I shook my head. 'You're from here? Why did they stone you, then? Why did they try to kill you?'

'Because I did something that an honourable girl should never have done, and they never forgot. They recognized me, judged me and condemned me to death.'

'Was what you did so terrible?'

'No. I didn't think so. I don't think I hurt anybody, but there are laws that everyone accepts and we've managed our lives by those laws for a long time now; it's not right to break them. Especially us women. The law is always harder on us.'

I could see how tired she was, so I didn't ask any more questions then, but little by little, as I could see she was getting better and regaining her strength, my friends and I would come and listen, day after day, to her story. Her adventure.

A number of curious circumstances had led her far away

from home, and she'd met people from all different walks of life, but it all started because of a young man, handsome and mysterious, the very one we'd dreamed of as we loitered at the well. She had met many men and women who told her what they knew or what they had learned through the course of their turbulent lives, and so many stories flowed together in her that they had joined to become one great, terrible story, as when in the rainy season every dry stream bed becomes a torrent and all the torrents rush into the river, which swells and roars and finally breaks its banks and spills over into the countryside, sweeping everything away, houses, people, herds . . .

Her story thrilled us as she told of danger and wonder, of love and of death, of exploits that had stirred up thousands and thousands of people and had completely overturned Abira's own existence, tearing her away from the tranquil, unchanging life of Beth Qadà, her village and ours, one of the five Villages of the Belt. But at the beginning, that story, so grand and so compelling that nearly the whole world was soon caught up in it, was only . . . the story of two brothers.

2

'WHY DID THEY want to stone you?' I asked her one day after she'd regained her strength.

'Was it because of those two brothers you told us about?' Abisag chimed in.

'It was my own fault,' she answered. 'But it wouldn't have happened if it weren't for the two brothers.'

'I don't understand,' I said.

'Back then,' she began, 'I was just a little older than you are now. I worked for my family in the fields, took the sheep to pasture and went to the well to draw water with my friends, just as you do now. Life was always the same, the seasons came and went. My parents had already chosen a husband for me, a cousin of mine. His hair stuck out all over and his face was full of pimples. But we had our clan to think about, and we had to earn a living. I wasn't at all upset by the idea of getting married, and my mother had already told me what would happen afterwards, after the wedding, that is. I'd keep working as I always had done, and my cousin would make me pregnant and I'd have his children. That didn't seem so terrible, after all; it was what women do, nothing to fret over. Once, one of the very rare times that my mother was in a good mood, she told me a secret: that there were women who felt pleasure when they did that thing with their men. This other feeling was what people called love, which usually didn't happen with the husband your family chose for you, but could happen with other men that you liked.

'I really didn't understand what she was getting at, but as she spoke her eyes lit up and seemed to be chasing distant, long-lost images.

'"Did that happen to you too, Mama?" I asked.

'"No. Never to me," she answered without looking me in the eye, "but I know women it happened to, and from what they say it's the most beautiful thing in the world, and it's something that can happen to anyone. You don't have to be rich, or noble, or be educated, all you have to do is meet a man that you like. That you like so much you're not ashamed to take off your clothes in front of him and when he touches you you're not disgusted. Just the opposite. You desire what he desires and his desire joins with yours and liberates a powerful energy that's more inebriating than wine. It's a sublime feeling, an ecstasy that might only last a few minutes, or maybe just a few instants, but it makes you feel like an Immortal. It's worth years and years of a dull, monotonous life."

'I realized that my mother was trying to tell me that even the life of a woman could – at certain moments, if only for a very short time – be like the life of a goddess.

'Those words filled me with longing, but also with a very deep sadness, because I was sure that my cousin with the pockmarked face could never make me feel those emotions, not in a whole lifetime. I knew I'd have to put up with him anyway, because that's the way life was. Nothing more, nothing less.

'The day that would unite me with him for the rest of my life was getting closer, and the nearer it got the more I felt distracted; I just couldn't seem to concentrate on the everyday tasks I had to do. My mind was somewhere else. I couldn't stop thinking about the man who could make me feel the way my mother had described. The man I would want to show my body to instead of hiding it, who I wanted to hold me in his arms, who I'd like to find lying next to me on my mat when I woke up, licked by the light of the dawning sun.

'I would cry, sometimes, because I desired this man so much and I knew that I'd never meet him. I looked around, thinking that he must be hiding somewhere: maybe one of the many boys who lived in our villages. But I wasn't too sure about that. How many young men could there be in the Villages of the Belt? Fifty? One hundred? Certainly no more than one hundred, and every one of them that I saw or met stank of garlic and had chaff sticking out of his hair. I finally became convinced that the whole thing had just been dreamed up by women who were tired of the same old life, pregnancies, giving birth, toiling day after day, getting beaten to boot.

'But then it happened.

'One day, by the well.

'First thing in the morning.

'I was alone. I'd lowered my jug and was pulling it up on its rope by leaning on the other end of the pole. I was shifting a big stone to get the pole to stay down when I felt the weight of the jug being lifted at the other end and I raised my head.

'He looked the way I'd always imagined a god to look. He was young, handsome, smooth-skinned. He was broad-shouldered, muscular but harmonious, his hands strong and gentle at the same time, along with a smile that was just enchanting. It blinded me like the rays of the sun rising behind his back.

'He took a drink from my jug and the water ran over his chest, making it shine like bronze, then he looked intensely into my eyes and I didn't look away. I looked back at him, with the same intensity.

'Later I would learn that you can live the life of a beast or of a god; it depends on the place that destiny has chosen for you to be born. The same place you're likely to die, when fate has humbled your desires and denied your hopes. A good life can nourish your body with athletic contests and with dancing and illuminate your gaze with the passion of dreams and adventures. That was the light I saw in the eyes of that young man with the jug in his hand, at the well of Beth Qadà, one late summer morning in my sixteenth year, but at that time I thought that the energy I saw sparkling in his eyes and the beauty that shone from within him could only belong to a divine being.

'Yet here was the man my mother had been talking about, the only man I could desire and want to be desired by. At that moment, as I stood up and let go of the pole I knew that my life was changing and that it would never be the same. I felt immense excitement and great fear at the same time, a giddy sensation that made me gasp.

'He came closer and managed with a great deal of difficulty to pronounce a few words in our language as he pointed to the horse standing behind him, hung with his weapons. He was a warrior and he was the first of a huge army advancing behind him at a few hours' distance.

'We could only speak with looks and gestures, but we both understood. He touched my cheek with his hand, and brushed my hair, and I didn't move. He was so close I could sense what he was feeling, like a vibration that ran through me at that quiet hour of the morning. I tried to tell him that I had to go, and I think the expression on my face let him know how sorry I was about that. He pointed to a little palm thicket near the river and drew some signs in the sand that were his answer: he would wait there for me in the middle of the night and I already knew that I would be there at any cost, no matter what happened. Before accommodating my cousin and his stink of garlic into the intimacy I was so jealous of, I wanted to know what making love was really like and – even if just for a few moments – find out what it felt like to be immortal, in the arms of a young god.

'The army arrived as night was falling and the sight left everyone stunned: old people and young, women and children. I dare say that the entire population of the five Villages of the Belt had run to see what was happening. No one had ever seen the like. Thousands of warriors on horseback dressed in tunics and long trousers, carrying sabres, pikes and bows, advancing from the north and heading south. At the head of every division were officers wearing the most extravagant outfits, their weapons glittering in the setting sun. At the head of them all, surrounded by bodyguards, was a tall, slender young man with olive skin and a black, well-groomed beard. I wouldn't learn until later who he was, and I'd never forget him: he was one of the two brothers I told you of. Brothers and enemies. Their bloody struggle would overwhelm the destinies of countless human beings, sweeping them away like logs in a raging river.

'There was one division of that army that struck me most of all: men dressed in short tunics with bronze breastplates. They held enormous shields made of the same metal and wore red cloaks over their shoulders. I would later learn that they were the most powerful warriors in the world: no one could stand up to them in battle, no one could hope to beat them. They never tired and were heedless of hunger and thirst, heat and frost. They advanced on foot with a cadenced step, singing softly to the rhythm of flutes. Their commanders marched alongside them, and the only way you could tell them apart from their men was because they walked outside the ranks.

'New divisions kept arriving, hour after hour, and when the first had already pitched their tents and eaten, the last were still on the march towards their rest stop: our peaceful villages.

'This unfolding of events made my crazy plan possible: the village men were so overcome with curiosity that no one wanted to return home for dinner; they had their women bring the food to them so that they wouldn't miss an instant of what was happening. No one noticed when I slipped off, or maybe my mother did, but she said nothing.

'The moon was out that night and the chorus of crickets sang louder and louder as I drew further away from the villages and the vast camp that continued to expand in every direction, gobbling up any free, open space. I had to keep far away from the well because there was an unending line of men, asses and camels laden with jars and skins, waiting to quench the thirst of that huge army. I could see the palm grove in the distance by the river, its fronds swaying in the evening breeze. The water glistened in the moonlight, hurrying to join the great Euphrates, far to the east.

'Every step that brought me closer to that place made me tremble with emotion. I was filled with a sensation I'd never felt my whole life: an anxiety that took my breath away and a heady excitement that made me so light-footed that I might take flight at any time. I ran over the last stretch that separated me from the palm trees and looked around.

'No one was there.

'Maybe I'd imagined the whole thing, or maybe I had mis-interpreted what the young man had wanted to say with his gestures and signs, in those few words spoken in a language that wasn't his own. Maybe he wanted to trick me and was hiding behind the trunk of a palm tree and would pop out and frighten me. I looked and looked but there was no sign of anyone. I couldn't believe that he hadn't come. I waited. I don't remember how long, but I watched the moon sink towards the horizon and the constellation of the lioness disappear behind the distant peaks of the Taurus. No use waiting any longer. I'd been wrong about him and it was time to go back home.

'I sighed and began to start back when I heard the sound of galloping to my left. I turned and in a cloud of dust shot through with moon beams I distinctly saw a horse ridden by a young man urging him forward at great speed. In a moment he was there before me. He pulled on the horse's reins and jumped down.

'Perhaps he too had been afraid he wouldn't find me? Maybe he felt the same apprehension, the same desire, the same restlessness that poured through me? We ran into each other's arms and kissed with an almost delirious feverishness . . .'

Abira broke off, remembering that she was talking to young girls who had never known a man, and she looked down, confused. When she lifted her head she was weeping with heartfelt abandon, eyes misting over then spilling with tears as big as raindrops. She must have loved him more than we could even imagine. And suffered, tremendously. But a wave of modesty seemed to have come over her, and stopped her from telling the story of her passion to such inexperienced, innocent girls. We sat there and watched her for a long time, not knowing what to say or how to console her. At last she raised her head. She dried her eyes and returned to her tale.

'That night I understood what my mother had meant. I knew that if I stayed in the village, if I gave in to my destiny and married an insignificant man, undeserving of a spirit as passionate as my own, I would end up being offended by the mere thought of him, and intimacy would be absolutely unbearable. I understood what it meant to be loved, swept away by another's passion, our bodies and souls vibrating with the same intensity. This young warrior had made me touch the face of the moon and ride the back of the torrent.

'We loved each other every night, for those few days that the army stayed encamped, and with each passing hour my anguish grew at the thought of how soon we would part. How could I live without him? How could I resign myself to the goats and sheep of Beth Qadà after mounting that spirited steed? How could I bear the sleepy lethargy of my village after knowing the heat that sets your flesh on fire and injects the light of folly into your eyes? I wanted desperately to talk to him, but he couldn't have understood me. When he talked to me in his language, so smooth and soft and sweet, all I could hear was music.

'Our last night.

'We lay on the dried grass under the palms watching the myriad stars twinkling between the leaves, and I could feel the need to weep welling up in me. He was leaving, and would soon forget me. His life would oblige him to forget me: he'd see other villages, other cities, rivers, mountains, valleys and many, many other people. He was a warrior, betrothed to death, and he knew that every day could be his last. He would enjoy other women, why shouldn't he? But what would become of me? How long would the memory of him torment me? How many times would I leave my bed on a hot summer night, dripping with sweat, awakened by the wind hissing over the rooftops of Beth Qadà?

'It seemed that he could read my thoughts, and he put his arm around my shoulders and drew me close, filling me with his warmth. I asked him what his name was, but he answered with a word so difficult I would never even be able to remember it. I told him that my name was Abira and he repeated it easily, "Abira."

'I remember every instant of that night, the rustling of the leaves, the babbling of the river. Every kiss, every caress. I knew I'd never have anything like that again.

'I was home before dawn, before my mother woke, when the wind still covered every other sound.

'As I slipped under the rugs I heard a strange noise: the muffled pawing of thousands of horses' hoofs on the cobble-stones, a low neighing and snorting, and the drumroll of the war chariots. The army was striking camp! They were leaving!

'I opened the window a crack in the hope of seeing him one last time. I watched and watched as thousands of infantry and cavalry men marched by, with their mules, asses and camels. But he was not among them!

'My eyes searched the ranks of the mysterious red-cloaked warriors, but their faces were covered by strange-looking helmets that only let their eyes and mouth be seen, like a grotesque mask. If he were one of them, I'd never be able to recognize him. I gathered my courage and went outside. I leaned against the wall of my house, hoping that even if I couldn't recognize him, he would recognize me and look my way, stop to say a word. Even a small gesture would enable me to keep him in my sights until he disappeared completely.

'Nothing happened.

'I went back to lie on my mat and I wept in silence.

'The army filed by for hours. The people of our villages lined up on both sides of the road so as not to miss a moment of the spectacle. The elderly would compare this vision to others from their youth, the young would remember it as long as they lived and would tell the story to their grandchildren when they were old. I couldn't care less about the parading troops. Of all of those thousands of men, only one was important, no, vital, to me.

'Where was that army going? Where would they wreak death and destruction? I thought of how terrible men are, of how cruel, violent and bloodthirsty they can be. But the young man I'd known had a gentle look, a warm, deep voice: he was different from the rest, and the idea of not seeing him again knifed through me.

'Would I forget him? Would this pain ever end? I would find other reasons to live, I tried to tell myself, I'd have children one day who would love me and keep me company and give meaning to my life. Did it matter who I had them with?

'When the soldiers were gone the wind stirred up a dense cloud of dust and the last traces of the army dissolved into the mist.

'I felt my mother's eyes on me all that day, suspicious and cross. She must have sensed trouble in the way I was acting, in my look, in my dishevelled appearance, although what had happened was beyond her imagining. She asked me once or twice, "What's wrong with you?", not to have an answer but to gauge my reaction.

' "Nothing," I replied. "There's nothing wrong with me." But the very tone of my voice, hinting that I might burst into tears at any moment, belied my words.

'The wind calmed towards evening. I took my jar and went to the well to draw water. I went later than usual so I wouldn't have to put up with my friends' chatter and their curiosity. When I got there the sun was nearly touching the horizon. I filled my jar and sat on the dry stump of a palm tree. The solitude and silence gave me some solace from the turmoil of my emotions. I couldn't stop hot tears from falling, but it was good for me to cry, I told myself, I needed to let myself go so I could heal. Cranes were soaring overhead, a long line of them, flying south and filling the air with their cries.

'How I wished I were one of them.

'It was getting dark. I lifted the jug onto my head and turned around to go back to the village.

'He was there in front of me.

'At first I thought it was a hallucination, a vision I'd created out of my longing, but it was truly him. He had got off his horse and was walking towards me.

' "Come away with me. Now," he said in my language.

'I was amazed. He'd said those words without a moment's hesitation, without a single mistake, but when I answered him. "Where will we go? And my mother, can I go to say goodbye?" he shook his head. He couldn't understand me. He'd learned those words in the right sequence and the right pronunciation because he wanted to be sure I'd understand him.

'He repeated them again and I – who would have done anything just a few moments earlier to hear them, who was so desperate about his departure – was afraid, now, to make such a drastic, sudden decision. Leaving everything – my house, my family, my friends – to follow a stranger, a soldier who might die from one instant to the next, at his first skirmish, his first ambush, his first battle. What would happen to me then?

'But my fear lasted just for a moment. The agony of never seeing him again rushed to take its place and I replied at once, "I'll come with you." He must have understood because he smiled. So he'd learned those words as well! He mounted his horse then gave me his hand so that I could get on behind him. The horse set off at a lope, heading towards the path that led south, past the villages, but soon we were spotted by a girl walking towards the well with her jug. She recognized me and started shouting, "A soldier is kidnapping Abira! Run, hurry!"

'A group of farmers returning from the fields ran towards us, waving their tools in the air. My warrior pushed the horse into a gallop then, and managed to rush past them before they could form a closed line to bar our way. They were near enough by then to clearly see that it was me holding on to him and not the other way around. It was no kidnapping; I was making my escape.'

ABIRA FELL SILENT again and let out a long sigh. Those memories seemed to weigh on her heart; just talking about them was opening old wounds that had never healed. Now we understood why she'd been stoned upon her return to Beth Qadà. She had abandoned her family, her clan, her village, her betrothed, to run off with a stranger whom she'd given herself to shamelessly. She'd broken all the rules that a girl like her could possibly break and her punishment had to serve as a lesson for all the others.

She stared straight into my eyes then and asked, 'My parents, are they still in the village? Are they well?'

I hesitated.

'Tell me the truth,' she insisted, and she seemed to steel herself to hear bad news.

Strange, I thought, that she'd never asked us about her parents before. Maybe she had a feeling that she didn't want us to confirm. Whatever she was thinking, there was still something about her I couldn't quite figure out; a mysterious, enigmatic quality that must have had something to do with surviving her own murder. She'd crossed the thin line that separates life and death, I thought. She had taken a look beyond that line and had seen the world of the dead. Her question was more than a premonition; as if she were seeking a truth that her soul was already sure of.

'Your mother is dead,' replied Abisag. 'Of malignant fever. Shortly after you left.'

'My father?'

'Your father was alive when you returned.'

'I know. I thought I saw him throwing stones with the others. Dishonour weighs more heavily on men.'

'He died on the night of your stoning,' I said. 'It was a sudden death.'

Upon hearing those words, Abira stiffened. Her eyes became glassy and unseeing. I'm certain that behind that vacant stare was a vision of the Underworld.

Abisag put a hand on her shoulder, trying to bring her back to the real world. 'You told us that your adventure – your running off with the soldier, the passage of that great army through the Villages of the Belt, everything that happened later – started with the story of two brothers. Tell us that story, Abira.'

Abira started with a shiver and pulled her cloak tighter around her shoulders.

'Another time,' she sighed. 'Another time.'

3

SEVERAL DAYS PASSED before Abira felt like talking with us again. In the meantime we'd found her a little work that she could do in secret, and make a living for herself. We couldn't keep sneaking food from our homes; someone was bound to notice sooner or later. All the same, any time we were sent out to tend the flocks we tried to take enough lunch with us so that some would be left over for her.

We helped her to fix up her shack so that she could spend the autumn and winter there and we visited every time we brought water back from the well. We learned a lot of things from her. The man she'd fallen in love with had such a complicated name that she always called him Xeno. She stayed by his side for the whole of their grand adventure. It was he who had told her the story of the two brothers who would change the history of our whole world. Other parts of the story she gathered from the many people she met during that endless journey.

She confirmed for us what we'd heard from our parents during long winter nights: that one of those two brothers was a prince of the empire. He was the one leading the army through our villages when Abira met her love. The story that had swept through so many lives and had been on the lips of countless people poured out in the words of that fragile, frightened woman whom we had freed from under a heap of stones. We learned the story from her, starting at the end of that autumn. Three fifteen-year-old girls who had never seen anything outside our villages and would never see any more than that in our whole lives.

THE QUEEN MOTHER, Parysatis, had two sons. The elder was Artaxerxes, and the younger was called Cyrus, like the founder of the dynasty. When the Great King died, he left the throne to his firstborn as was customary. But the Queen Mother was vexed at this, because Cyrus was her favourite: he was more handsome, more intelligent and more charming than his brother and he greatly resembled her; he had the same fluid grace that she'd had as a young woman, when she was forced to marry a man she detested, the man who was the image of his first son, Artaxerxes. The Queen had procured the governance of a very wealthy province, Lydia, located on the shores of the western sea, for her son Cyrus, but in her heart of hearts she had always hoped that some day she'd be given the chance to raise him up higher.

Powerful women are capable of acting in a way that normal women would never even dream of.

She was well practised at disguising her thoughts and her plans; she used her influence covertly to achieve the objectives she had set for herself. Intrigue was her favourite pastime, in addition to playing chess, a game she had mastered. Belts were her passion.

Every day she wore a different exquisitely woven and embroidered belt. Belts of silk, of byssus, of silver and of gold, adorned with superbly crafted buckles from Egypt and Syria, Anatolia and Greece. It was said that she wanted silver only from distant Iberia because of its matchless milky tone, and lapis lazuli only from remote Bactria because of the great number of golden flecks it contained.

Cyrus arrived in Lydia when he was but a boy of twenty-two, but his innate shrewdness and sharp intelligence led him to grasp at once what moves were required on that compli-cated chessboard where the two most powerful cities of Greece –

Athens and Sparta – had been fighting for over thirty years without either of them gaining the upper hand.

He decided to help the Spartans for a single reason: they were the most formidable warriors existing in the known world, and one day they would take up arms for him. They were the warriors of the red cloaks and bronze mask-like helmets who struck fear into any opponent. Athens, on the other hand, was the Queen of the Seas, and to defeat her it was necessary to commission a mighty fleet and load it up with archers, slingsmen and expert crews led by the best commanders. Eighty years before, those two Greek cities had united against the Great King Xerxes and defeated his fleet, the greatest of all times. Now Cyrus knew he had to set them against each other, goad them into wearing themselves out in an exhausting conflict until the moment came when he could tilt the scales in favour of the Spartans. Beholden to him, Sparta would support him in the venture most dear to his heart: seizing the throne!

Thanks to his support Sparta won the war and Athens had to bow to a humiliating peace agreement. Thousands of men from both sides found themselves in a devastated land where they saw no hope of a livelihood.

That's how men are: for some mysterious reason they are seized, at regular intervals, by a blood frenzy, a drunken violence that they can't resist. They deploy themselves on vast open fields, lined up one alongside another, and wait for a signal. When that trumpet sounds, they charge the enemy formation, which is full of other men who have done absolutely no harm to them. They hurl themselves into the attack, yelling with all the breath they have. They're shouting so loudly to quiet the fear that grips them. In the moment before the attack many of them tremble and break out into a cold sweat, others weep in silence, some lose control of their urine, which flows warm down their legs and wets the ground they stand on.

In that moment they're waiting for death. Black-cloaked

Chera swoops down among their ranks and her empty sockets eye those who will fall first, then those who will die later and finally those who will suffer for days from their wounds before dying. The men feel her eyes upon them and they shudder.

That moment is so unbearable that if it were to last for any length of time it would kill them. No commander prolongs it any more than is strictly necessary: as soon as he can, he unleashes the attack. They cover the ground that separates them from their foes as quickly as they can, running, then crashing against the enemy like the surf on cliffs. The collision is terrifying. In those first moments there is so much blood shed that it soaks the ground beneath them. Iron sinks into flesh, skulls are bludgeoned, spears pierce shields and breastplates, cleaving hearts, lacerating chests and bellies. There is no fending off such a storm of fury.

This horrible butchery can last for only an hour or little more, before one of the two formations breaks down and starts to withdraw. The retreat often becomes a disorderly rout, and that's when the bloodletting becomes slaughter. Those who flee are massacred without pity for as long as the victors' strength endures. At dusk representatives of the two sides meet on neutral ground and negotiate a truce, then each side gathers up its dead.

There you have it, the folly of men. Episodes like the one I've just described, which I saw myself with my own eyes time and time again, were repeated endlessly during the thirty years of war between Sparta and Athens, mowing down the flower of their youth.

For years and years the young men of both powers – and their fathers too! – did one thing only, fight, and those who survived all those years of war knew no other way of life but combat. Among them was the man I fell in love with as I was drawing water from the well at Beth Qadà: Xeno.

When we met he had already covered over two hundred parasangs with Cyrus's forces, and by then he knew exactly where the army was heading and what the aim of the expedition was. And yet he was not a soldier, as I had imagined when I saw the weapons he carried. Not then, not at the start, at least.

The night I ran off with him, I knew my people would disown and curse me. I had betrayed the promise of marriage with the boy I was betrothed to, I had broken the pact between our two families. I had dishonoured my mother and father. But I'd never known such happiness. As our horse raced over the plains illuminated by the last glimmer of dusk and then by the rising moon, all I could think about was the man my arms were holding and of how beautiful my life would be alongside my love, who had come back for me. No matter how short a time my bliss might last, I would never regret my decision.

The force and the immensity of the feelings I experienced those first days meant more than years of dull monotony. I wasn't thinking about any difficulties to come, of what I would do if he left me, where I would go, how I could survive. All I thought about at that moment was being with him, and nothing else mattered. Some say that love is a kind of disease that hits you out of the blue, and maybe that's true. But after all this time, and everything I've been through, I still think that love is the most noble and most powerful feeling that a human being is capable of. I'm also sure that love makes it possible for a person to overcome obstacles unimaginable for anyone who has not felt its power.

We caught up with the army that night after dark, when everyone had finished eating and was preparing for the night. Everything was new for me, and difficult. I wondered how I could hold on to a man I couldn't even talk to, but I planned to learn his language as soon as possible. I would cook for him and wash his clothing, I would look after his tent and I would never complain. Not if I was tired, not if I was hungry, not if I was thirsty. The fact that he had felt the need to learn even just a few phrases in my language meant that he cared very much and didn't want to lose me. And I told myself that I was beautiful, much more beautiful than any woman he'd ever met before. Even if it wasn't true, the thought gave me confidence and courage.

Xeno loved the way I looked. He'd spend hours watching me. He'd ask me to move my body in a certain way and he'd look at me from various points of view, moving around me. Then he'd ask me to move a different way. To stretch out or to sit or to walk in front of him or to let down my hair. At first he'd use gestures, but then little by little, as I learned his language, he'd use words. I realized that the poses he asked me to take corresponded to works of art that he had seen in his city or in his land. Statues and paintings, things I had never seen because there were no such things in our villages. But I'd often seen children moulding mud into little figures and letting them dry in the sun. And we'd make dolls as well, which we'd dress with scraps of fabric. Statues were something like that, only much bigger, as big as a person or even more so. They were made of stone or clay or metal and they were used to adorn cities and sanctuaries. Xeno told me once that if he were an artist – that is, one of those men capable of creating such images – he would have liked to portray me as one of the characters of the ancient stories told in his homeland.

I soon discovered that I wasn't the only woman following the army. There were many others. A great number were young slaves, most of them owned by Syrian and Anatolian dealers who leased them out to the soldiers. Some of them were very pretty; they got enough to eat and had nice clothing and wore make-up to be attractive. But their life wasn't easy. They couldn't refuse their clients' demands, not even when they were ill. Their only advantage was that they didn't have to walk; they travelled on covered wagons and they weren't made to suffer hunger or thirst. That was something in itself.

There were others of the same trade who met with only a few men, or even only one man alone, if he was very important: the commanders of the army divisions, noble Persians, Medes and Syrians, or the officers of the red-cloaked warriors. That type of man doesn't like to drink from the same cup as everyone else.

The red-cloaked warriors didn't mix with the rest. They spoke a different language and had their own habits, their own gods and their own food. They didn't speak much. When they stopped to rest they would always polish their shields and their armour so that they shone, and they would practise fighting. They seemed to do nothing else.

Xeno was not one of them. He came from Athens, the city that had lost the great thirty-year war. When I was able to converse in his language, I understood the reason why he was following the expedition. It was only then, when I learned the Greek of Athens, that his story became mine. The accident of fate that had torn me from my village was woven into a much bigger destiny: the destiny of thousands of individuals and of entire peoples. Xeno became my teacher as well as my lover. He provided everything I needed: my food, my bed, my clothing, in a single word my whole life. I wasn't just a female for him, I was a person to whom he could teach many things and from whom he could learn many others.

He spoke rarely of his city, although it was clear how curious I was about it. And when I insisted that he tell me why, the unexpected truth came out.

After Athens had fallen into the hands of the enemy, she'd had to accept being ruled by her conquerors: the Spartans, the warriors who wore the red cloaks!

'If they defeated your city, why are you on their side now?' I asked him.

'When a city is defeated,' he began, 'people are divided, each side blaming the other for the disaster. As they say, victory may have many fathers, but defeat is an orphan. This dissension can grow so profound, so visceral, that the two sides attack each other with weapons in hand. That's what happened in Athens. I sided with the wrong faction, the one that lost, and so I – and many others like me – were forced into exile.'

So Xeno had fled from his city, from Athens, the same way I had fled from Beth Qadà.

He had wandered Greece from one end to the other without finding the courage to leave. One day Xeno received a letter from a friend asking to meet him at a place beside the sea because he wanted to talk to Xeno about something important: a great opportunity to win glory and riches while experiencing a thrilling adventure. They met one night at the end of winter at a fisherman's wharf, an out-of-the-way place that wasn't very busy. His friend, whose name was Proxenus, waited for him in a small house out on an isolated promontory.

Xeno arrived a little before midnight, on foot, leading his horse by the reins. He knocked at the door but there was no answer, so he tethered his horse, unsheathed his sword, and went in. There was nothing inside but a table with an oil lamp on top and a couple of chairs. Proxenus's chair was set back, beyond the halo of light, but Xeno recognized his voice.

'You entered without knowing what you would find in here. Risky.'

'You summoned me here,' retorted Xeno. 'Why would I expect danger?'

'Not too smart, are you? Danger is everywhere these days and you are a runaway. A wanted man, even. This might have been a trap.'

'That's why I've got a sword in my hand,' replied Xeno.

'Sit down. Not that what I'm about to tell you will solve your problems.'

'I wouldn't have thought so. Tell me what all this is about.'

'First of all, what I'm going to say must remain between you and me.'

'Trust me.'

'All right. At this moment there are five commanders in various regions of this country looking to enlist men who are ready for a good fight.'

'So what else is new?'

'This is very new. The official reason is that they're trying to muster an expeditionary force to crush certain barbarian tribes in Anatolia who are making trouble in Cappadocia, raiding and sacking the villages.'

'But the true reason is . . .'

'My gut feeling is that there is another explanation, but no one's talking.'

'Why does there have to be another reason?'

'Because their task is to recruit from ten to fifteen thousand men, all from the Peloponnese, as many as possible from Laconia; the best going. Doesn't that seem a little too many to put down a bunch of chicken-thieving oafs?'

'Curious, to say the least. Is there more?'

'The stipend is generous and guess who's paying?'

'No idea.'

'Cyrus of Persia. The brother of the emperor, Artaxerxes. He's waiting for us at Sardis, in Lydia. And the word is that he's recruiting troops as well: fifty – but some say as many as one hundred – thousand men.'

'That's a lot of men.'

'Too many for such a mission.'

'You're right there. So what are you thinking?'

'I think there's a much bigger game at stake. An army of this size can have only one purpose and one aim: to conquer a throne.'

Xeno fell silent, too taken aback by what his friend was implying to venture any hypothesis of his own. In the end he said, 'So you're in on this?'

'Wouldn't miss it for the world.'

'But what have I to do with any of it?'

'Nothing. You're not a fighting man, are you? Then again, an expedition of this sort might offer a lot of opportunities for someone like you. I know that you've got yourself into a bit of trouble – they say that your fellow citizens want to bring you to trial. Come with us and you'll be in the inner circle, you'll have access to Cyrus himself. He's young, ambitious, intelligent, as we are. He can recognize talent and determination and maybe give you the chance you deserve.'

'What would I do? Is there any alternative to joining a combat unit? I'd need a mission, a role, wouldn't I?'

'You'll be my personal adviser. And you can keep track of everything that happens, keep a diary, a chronicle of the expedition. Think about it, Xeno: the Orient! Incredible places, dream cities, beautiful women, wine, perfumes . . .'

Xeno sheathed the sword he'd laid on the table and got to his feet, turning his back to his friend. 'What about the Spartans? How much are they involved in all this?'

'Sparta knows nothing about it. That is, the government either doesn't know or doesn't want to know. There's not one regular Spartan officer in the entire force. It's obvious they want to stay clear of the whole thing. They want absolutely no involvement, and that confirms my suspicions. It means we must be talking about something big, otherwise why would they bother to be so cautious?'

'That may be. But it seems impossible that they're ready to let this happen without controlling it in any way.'

'They'll find a way if they want to. Well then, what do you say?'

'Yes,' replied Xeno. He turned to face his friend. 'I'll come.'

'Excellent decision,' commented Proxenus. 'I'll be waiting for you three days from now at the wharf. After midnight. Bring everything you need with you.'

XENO WAS NOT invited to spend the night, which meant that not even Proxenus, who was his friend, could take the chance of being associated with an outlaw, a fugitive. This strengthened Xeno's resolve to leave with the expedition. It was a bitter choice, but he had no other.

To the Greek way of thinking, your own city is the only place worth living. The Spartans are the only Greeks who have a king – no, two actually, who reign together. None of the other Greek cities is ruled by a king. The people choose to be represented by an individual, who can be anyone among them: a nobleman, a wealthy landlord, or even a person who is not particularly in the public eye. A tradesman, a doctor, a ship-owner, a merchant. Or even a carpenter or a shoemaker! Xeno told me that one of their greatest commanders, the man who had defeated the fleet of the Great King Xerxes at sea, was the son of a shopkeeper who sold beans.

This makes them feel free. Everyone can say what they like, can criticize or even offend those who govern the city. And if these governors don't do a good job, they can be kicked out of office at any time and sentenced to pay compensation, if the citizens have been damaged by their ineptitude. Every Greek thinks that his own city is the best, the most beautiful, the most desirable place to live, the most ancient and illustrious. The citizens of any given city are convinced that they have the right to the best property and the sunniest, most beautiful coastlines, and thus the right to expand their territory over land and sea. The result is that these cities are continually at war, forming alliances to fight against one another. Then once a coalition wins it starts to split apart and those who were allies become enemies and band together with the cities they have defeated.

At first it was hard for me to understand what made these cities so much more desirable than our villages like Naim or Beth Qadà. But then Xeno told me about places they call 'theatres' where people sit for hours or entire days watching other men who act as though they were people who lived centuries earlier, portraying their adventures and their trials and tribulations with such realism that they seem true. The people watching become incredibly emotional: they cry and laugh and get indignant and shout out their anger or their enthusiasm. It's as if they were allowed to live out other lives that they'd never have the chance of experiencing otherwise. So they can live another life every day, or even more than one! And this is truly an extraordinary thing. When would a man who was born in one of the Villages of the Belt ever have the chance to challenge monsters or outwit tricksters, overcome sorcerers or fall in love with women beautiful enough to make a man lose his mind, or to consume exotic foods or magical potions with unbelievable effects? In Beth Qadà, it's always the same life with the same people and the same smells and the same foods. Always.

Watching those events unwind before your very own eyes inevitably makes you a better person. You naturally take the side of good against evil, of the oppressed against the oppressors, of men who have suffered injustice against those who have inflicted it. You would be ashamed of acting out any of those wicked deeds that you've seen in places called 'theatres'.

That's not all. In their cities live wise men who walk around the streets and squares to teach others what they've studied or investigated: the meaning of life and death, of justice and injustice, what's beautiful and what's ugly, whether the gods exist and where you can find them, whether it's possible to live without gods, if the dead are truly dead or if they're living someplace else where we can't see them any more.

There are other men called 'artists' who paint marvellous scenes with vivid colours on walls or on wooden boards. Xeno says they can fashion images that have exactly the same shape and appearance as the gods or human beings or animals. Lions, horses, dogs, elephants. These images are displayed in the squares and temples or in private homes simply to give pleasure to those who live inside them.

The temples, I was saying. The temples are the homes of the gods. They are magnificent structures, built on marble columns which are painted, gilded, glowing. They hold up beams sculpted with scenes from their history and mythology. There are images on the façades as well, marvellous depictions of the birth of their city or other extraordinary events. Inside the temple is the image of the divinity that protects the city: ten times taller than a human being, made of ivory and gold, lit by shafts of light from above that make it shine in the shadows.

Thinking of all this makes you realize how hard and how sad it is for a man to forsake such a place and the people who live there, those who speak your same language, believe in the same gods and love the same things that you love.

Xeno left three days later from the wharf of that little town on the sea. Along with five hundred other men, fully equipped warriors who arrived at the port a few at a time, or in small groups, from different directions. There was a small fleet waiting for them, of boats looking like ordinary fishing vessels.

They weighed anchor that night without waiting for dawn. First light surprised them when they were already far out at sea and the familiar shores of their homeland had vanished on the horizon.

No one knew yet who would be commanding them, who was to lead them in the greatest adventure of their lives. An adventure which, they imagined, would take them to unknown places, magnificent cities, meeting peoples whose existence they could only have dreamed of.

Other groups of warriors had quietly gathered in other secluded spots and were now journeying towards the same destination, beyond the sea, where they would be joined by a young prince consumed by the biggest ambition that a man could have: to become the most powerful ruler of the entire earth.

In the meantime, the commander of the expeditionary force was being briefed in Sparta. He had been instructed to attend to Cyrus's orders and enable the Prince to fulfil his ambitions. In reality he would answer to his city – the city of the red-cloaked warriors – and obey her orders alone, but no one, come what may, was to know of this. For the common soldier he would be just another political exile, cast out of his city and unable to return. Officially he had been condemned to death for murder and had a pretty price on his head. He was a man as hard and sharp as the iron that hung by his side even while he slept. They called him Clearchus, but who knows whether that was his true name or another deceit, like so much of what was said about those warriors who had sold their swords and their lives for a dream.

4

CLEARCHUS WAS of medium height, about fifty years old. His hair was black, with a few white threads at the temples, and he was always well groomed. When he was not wearing a helmet he gathered his hair at the nape of his neck with a strip of leather. He always went armed: he wore his greaves and carried a shield and sword from the moment he got up until he went to sleep. It seemed that the bronze had become part of his body. He seldom spoke and never repeated an order. Very few of the men he commanded had ever met him before.

He appeared out of nowhere.

One morning in early spring he came forward before the assembled troops drawn up in the city of Sardis in Lydia. He leapt onto a brick wall to address them.

'Soldiers!' he began. 'You are here because Prince Cyrus needs an army to fight the barbarians in the interior. He demanded the best: that's why you were recruited from every part of Greece. We are not at the orders of any of our cities or our governments, but of a foreign prince who has engaged our services. We're fighting for money, nothing else: an excellent reason, I say. Actually, I know none better.

'Don't imagine that this means you're free to do as you please. Whoever disobeys an order or proves guilty of insubordination or cowardice will be put to death immediately, and I'll carry out the sentence myself. I promise you that you will soon be more afraid of me than of the enemy. Your commanders will bear full responsibility for any errors made while executing my orders.

'There are no troops anywhere better suited to accomplish this mission. No one can match you for valour, resistance and discipline. If you win you will be rewarded so generously that you'll be able to leave this work and live well for the rest of your lives. If you are defeated, nothing will remain of you. No one will mourn your passing.'

The men listened to those words without blinking an eye, and when he finished speaking they did not leave their places. They stood still and silent until their officers ordered them to break ranks.

Clearchus had no apparent authority for commanding that army, but everyone obeyed him. He was the very image of a commander: gaunt cheeks framed by a short black beard, eyes that were deep and penetrating, armour polished to a high sheen, the black cloak flung over his shoulders.

Like the men he commanded, he too was out of keeping with the mission: too harsh, too authoritative, too dramatic in appearance and behaviour. In all respects he was a man forged to carry out impossible tasks, certainly not to put down some trifling clash with troublemaking tribes from the interior.

No one knew whether he had a family. He certainly had no friends. He didn't even have slaves: just a couple of attendants who served him the meals that he always ate alone in his tent. He seemed incapable of emotion; if he had feelings he hid them well, apart from the occasional burst of anger that sent him into a rage.

Clearchus was more machine than man, a machine designed and built for killing. During our time together, Xeno would have several close encounters with him and witness his prowess in battle: the man struck down his enemies with unrelenting, unfaltering energy, never missing a blow, never showing signs of flagging. Every life he took from another seemed to feed into his own. It wasn't that he showed pleasure at killing, just the measured satisfaction of a man doing his job with method and precision. Everything about him inspired fear, but in the thick of battle his impassive ferocity and icy calm instilled a sense of tranquillity in the others, made them certain of victory. Under his direct command, he had all of the red-cloaked warriors. Everyone knew from the start that they were the best; no one could cross them without paying the consequences.

Xeno knew some of the contingent commanders personally. Proxenus of Boeotia was a friend, the one who had convinced him to join the mission in Asia. Proxenus was an attractive man, and very ambitious: he dreamed of winning wealth, honour and fame, but over the course of the long march he showed that he wasn't up to his position, and his relationship with Xeno started to deteriorate. It's one thing to meet up in the city square and stroll under the porticoes or sip a cup of wine at the tavern while making predictions about politics or horses or dog races and exchanging witty remarks. It's quite another to endure exhausting marches, to suffer hunger and fear, to compete for survival. Few friendships can withstand such trials and theirs soon failed, turning into wary indifference, if not outright dislike.

Xeno knew the other commanders of the large units, the generals, as well. There was one in particular who fascinated him at first and then ended up disgusting him deeply. I believe Xeno hated him and wanted him dead; he was so intolerant of him that I think he blamed him for things he had never done, vile acts that perhaps he had never committed.

This man was Menon of Thessaly.

I met him as well when Xeno and I were following the army and I must say I was impressed. He was a little older than Xeno, thirty, maybe, with straight blond hair that came to his shoulders and often fell across his face so that the only part that you could see were his blue-grey eyes. His look was so intense it felt as if it could cut through you. His body was lean and athletic and he liked to show it off. He had muscular arms, but his hands were more like a musician's than a soldier's. Yet when you saw those hands curled around the haft of a sword or a spear you could see what terrible power was in them.

I'd often notice him, in the evening, roaming our campsite with a spear in one hand and a cup of wine in the other, enjoying the admiration of both women and men. He wore nothing to cover his body; only a short, lightweight cloak, tossed over his shoulder and open on the right side. When he passed he left a trail of oriental perfume. But when the combat began he turned into a ferocious beast. That didn't happen until many months after the troops had mustered at Sardis.

I sometimes asked myself why Xeno hated Menon so. I know that the young Thessalian commander had never clashed openly with him; there'd never been a quarrel or a fight between them. In the end I became convinced that I was the unintentional cause.

One evening, when the soldiers were pitching their tents for the night, I went to draw water from a nearby stream, carrying a jar on my head as I would do back at the well of Beth Qadà. Menon appeared suddenly on the bank just a short distance away from me, and as I dipped the jar into the water he unbuckled the clasp of his cloak and stood there naked. I don't know if he was watching me because I dropped my head at once, but I felt his gaze on me, somehow. As soon as I filled the jar I started walking back towards camp, but he called me.

I could hear the water splashing behind me as he entered the river and I stopped without turning. 'Take off your clothes,' he said, 'come in with me.' I hesitated a moment. It wasn't that I desired the intimacy he was suggesting, but I was intimidated by his rank, his importance, and I didn't dare let him think that I wasn't listening.

I think that Xeno may have seen us. I wasn't aware of it; I'm sure that when I stopped to listen to Menon's words there was no one else around. But afterwards, Xeno seemed unsettled, suspicious. He never said anything – he was much too proud for that – but a lot of little things let me know that a certain tension had crept in between us that wasn't there before.

The rest of Cyrus's troops – the bulk of the army – had pitched their tents not too far from us, in a separate camp. There were many thousands of Asians from the coast and the interior, infantry and cavalrymen. A haphazard, multicoloured host who spoke different languages and obeyed their own chieftains. Cyrus disregarded them completely; the only person he had contact with was their commander, a hairy giant named Ariaeus, who always wore the same leather tunic. He had waist-long hair that he wore in long braids.

He gave off a horrible stink and he must have realized it, because whenever he talked to Cyrus he always took a few steps back.

Menon of Thessaly spent a lot of time with him; he was often over at the Asian camp, for reasons I was unaware of. Xeno always said that they had a physical relationship, that Menon was Ariaeus's lover. 'He's having it off with a barbarian!' he would jeer. 'Can you believe it?'

He wasn't at all scandalized by the fact that Menon was going to bed with another man, it was the barbarian part that got to him. 'So am I a barbarian,' I protested. 'But when you come to bed with me you seem to like it.'

'That's completely different. You're a woman.'

'How illogical!' I thought to myself. I just couldn't under-stand, but then with time it became clear to me. For Xeno and those like him it was totally normal that two men could be making love. But both of them had to be Greek; it was degrading to do it with a barbarian. That's what he was accusing Menon of: of going to bed with a man who stank, who didn't wash every day, who didn't use a strigil and a razor. It was a question of civility. But I think that he was insinuating that Menon was playing the woman for that hairy, rank-smelling goat. He wanted to cut down Menon's virility in my eyes because he thought of him as a rival.

I was not attracted to Menon, although he was the most beautiful man I'd ever seen in my whole life, because I was so in love with Xeno that I had eyes for no one else. But I was curious about Menon; he fascinated me. I would have liked to talk to him, ask him some questions, perhaps. That world of men built and brought up only for killing gave me the shivers. From a certain point of view, Menon and Ariaeus were very similar to each other, identical, really. Maybe that's why they made love together. I thought that their shared vows of savagery, the job of inflicting death, made them special somehow, so unique that they couldn't tolerate someone in their bed who might attempt to stand in the way of their life's work. A woman, for instance, a woman capable of giving life rather than taking it away.

But perhaps this was only a fantasy of my own making. Everything was so strange, so new and different for me. And that was only the beginning.

There were others who commanded the contingents of that great army. One of them was Socrates of Achaea. He was about thirty-five, powerfully built, with brown hair and beard and thick eyebrows. I would see him in formation every time Clearchus reviewed the troops. He was always on the left. Every so often he had supper in our tent and I overheard some snippets of his conversation with Xeno as I brought the food or cleared the table. I thought I heard he had a wife, whose name he mentioned, and some little children. When he spoke about his family his voice would grow quiet and you could see sadness in his eyes. Socrates had feelings then, a family he was fond of. Maybe he was doing this work because he had no choice, or maybe he'd had to obey someone more powerful than he was.

He had a friend, another of the generals: Agias of Arcadia. I'd often see them together. They had fought on the same fronts, in the same theatres of war. Agias had once saved Socrates's life by covering him with his shield when he'd fallen with an arrow in his thigh. He'd dragged him to safety under a hail of darts. They were very close to one another; I could tell from the way they

43

talked and joked and exchanged experiences. They both hoped that the mission would be over soon without much damage so they could return to their families. Agias had a wife and children too: a boy and a girl, five and seven years old, who were being cared for by his parents, who were farmers.

It made me cry to see that even the most relentless warriors were human beings, with the same feelings as other people I'd known in my life. I realized as time went on that many of them were like that. Young men whose breastplate and helmet were hiding a heart and a face like all the boys I'd known in my village, boys who were afraid of what was coming and yet who'd had the courage to join up in the hope of radically changing their existences.

Be that as it may, Socrates and Agias were simple men, and rather reserved. They got on well with Xeno, but there was no personal friendship because Xeno wasn't part of the ranks. Xeno answered to no one; he took no orders but gave none either. He was there because there was nowhere else he could be; because his city didn't want him.

'Do you miss it?' I asked him once. 'Your city, I mean?'

'No,' he answered. But his eyes said the opposite.

Xeno set about his work scrupulously. Every evening, when the army had encamped, he lit a lamp in our tent and started writing. Not for very long, if the truth be told; by the time I had prepared dinner he had finished. Once I asked him to read me what he'd written and I was disappointed. Terse, brief notes: the distance covered that day, the point of departure and the point of arrival, whether we'd found water and could stock up on food, the cities we'd passed. Not much else.

'But we've seen such beautiful things!' I'd say, and remind him of the fast-running streams, the colours of the mountains and the fields, the clouds inflamed by the setting sun, the monuments of ancient civilizations corroded by time. Not to mention what he must have seen before he met me while crossing the vast Anatolian highlands that I'd heard about from those in my village who had been there.

'Those are my own memories. What I'm writing here will be passed down as the memory of all of us.'

'What difference does it make?'

'It's simple. The beauty of a countryside or a monument is in the eyes of the beholder. Something that's beautiful for me can be insignificant for someone else. The distance between one city and another is a valid, unquestionable fact for everybody.'

That was certainly true, but sad, as far as I was concerned. I didn't understand then that he had a particular reason for writing and that emotions didn't come into it. He meant for the diary that he was writing to be used by anyone who wanted to follow the same path in the future.

What I was most struck by, however, was the writing itself. No one in our villages could write. Stories were handed down by word of mouth, and everyone retold them however they liked. I was sure that the passage of Cyrus's army and my flight from Beth Qadà had already been worked up into a good story, or very different stories, told by the village elders, some of whom were well practised in the art – not unusual in such small communities where hardly anything ever happens to satisfy people's natural curiosity.

I loved to watch Xeno, although I was always careful to stay out of his way: how he dipped his pen in the small jar of ink, how he moved it rapidly over the white papyrus paper. Those scrolls were precious, more costly than food or wine, than iron or bronze. That's why Xeno usually wrote on a white stone tablet first, using a charcoal stick. Only when he was perfectly sure of what he wanted to set onto the page did he pick up his pen and recopy. He wrote in a very small, close hand to take up as little space as possible, and his script was extraordinarily precise, so that he formed a sequence of perfectly straight, well-aligned marks. Once those marks were drawn on the page they could become words any time he looked at them. It was marvellous! He could see how interested and fascinated I was by his writing. I knew that in the temples of the gods and the palaces of kings there were people called scribes, but I'd never seen anyone carry out that activity. Many of those warriors, if not most of them, actually, could write and I'd often see them draw marks on the sand or on the barks of trees. Their writing symbols were simple, like the aleph-beth used by the Phoenicians on the coast. I thought it couldn't be too difficult to learn, and so one day I plucked up my courage and asked Xeno if he'd teach me.

He smiled. 'Why do you want to learn to write? What would you do with it?'

'I don't know, but I like the idea that my thoughts would remain alive even after my voice has disappeared.'

'That's a good reason, but I don't think it's a good idea.' And that was that.

But Xeno's art fascinated me, so that I started drawing marks anyway, on sand or wood or rocks, and I knew that some would be rubbed away by the wind and others by water, while others, perhaps, might still be there years, even centuries, from now.

After the army left Sardis we travelled up the Meander river until we reached the high plain, stopping in a beautiful place where one of Cyrus's summer palaces was located. There was a spring inside a cave there where you could see a skin hanging, the flayed hide of some wild animal. Xeno told me a story then that I'd never heard before.

In that cave had lived a satyr, a creature that was half man and half goat, called Marsyas. He was one of the creatures of the woods who protect the shepherds and their flocks, and he would often sit alongside the stream to play his flute, a simple reed instrument. The melody he coaxed from his flute was sublime, deeper and more tender than a nightingale's song. A melody that evoked shadowy recesses and moss with a strain that recalled the burbling of a mountain spring, a harmony that blended with the wind rustling the leaves of the poplar trees. He became so enamoured of his own music that he believed no one could play as well as he could, not even Apollo, who was the god of music for the Greeks. Apollo heard his boasting and appeared before him suddenly one afternoon in the late spring, as radiant as the light of the sun.

'You challenge me?' he demanded in anger.

The satyr did not back down. 'That was not my intention, but I'm proud of my music and I'm not afraid to measure myself against anyone. Not even you, O Shining One.'

'Challenging a god is not something you can do without putting yourself at great risk. If you won, your glory would know no bounds. Your punishment in case of defeat would have to be proportionate.'

'And what would that be?' asked the satyr.

'You would be flayed alive. I myself would strip you of your skin.' Thus saying he drew a razor-sharp dagger made of an unfamiliar, blinding metal.

'Pardon me, O Shining One,' said the satyr then. 'How may I be certain that your judgement will be impartial? You risk nothing. I risk death, and an atrocious one at that.'

'The contest will be judged by the nine Muses, the supreme divinities of harmony, of music, of dance, of poetry, of all the highest manifestations of human and divine nature. The only beings who can join the world of the mortals with that of the immortals. Nine is an odd number, so their verdict will favour one of us.'

Marsyas was so intrigued by the idea of vying with a god that he thought of nothing else and accepted the terms of the challenge. Or perhaps the god, jealous of his art, fogged the satyr's judgement.

The contest took place the next day, as evening was falling, at the peak of Mount Argeus, still white with snow.

Marsyas was first. He put his lips to his reed flute and blew into it the sweetest and most intense of melodies. The warbling of the birds ceased, even the wind subsided and a profound calm descended upon the woods and fields. The creatures of the forest listened enchanted to the song of the satyr, the rapturous music that blended all of their voices, all of the sylvan moans and whispers, the silvery tinkling of the waterfalls and the slow trickle of the caves, the trill of the skylark and the screech of the owl, the symphony of April rain on leaves and branches. An echo reflected the sound, magnified it, multiplied it over the crags of the huge, solitary mountain and through her ravines until mother earth vibrated down to her most hidden depths.

Marsyas's flute let out a final long piercing peal that softened into a deeper, darker note, then into a tremor that faded into dazed silence.

It was Apollo's turn then. The outline of his figure could barely be made out in the flaming radiance of the aura that surrounded him, but a lyre suddenly appeared in his hand, his fingers plucked the strings and the instrument burst into sound.

Marsyas knew the sounds that a lyre could make and he knew that his flute was capable of more mood and more colour, more notes high and low, but the god's instrument had all of this in a single string and much, much more. He heard Apollo's fingers unleash the crash of the sea and the roar of thunder with such power that Mount Argeus trembled all the way down to its roots, raising whole flocks of birds from the treetops in a concerted rustling of wings. And then, as soon as that roar died down, another string vibrated and then another and another still and their vibrations mixed and cascaded in a breathless race, uniting into a chorus of wondrous clarity and majestic power. The shrill notes chased one another at an ever swifter pace with iridescent splashes of silvery outbursts, dark echoes of horns, luminous flares of dazzling sound which surged out into solemn, vast resonance.

Marsyas himself was enthralled. His eyes filled with tears, his expression spoke of wonder and enchantment. And thus was he condemned. Nothing in his music had moved the impassive demeanour of the god; every note of Apollo's music, on the contrary, poured into the dark eyes of the satyr. The Muses had no doubts in awarding the victory to Apollo. All of them, except one, beautiful Terpsichore, the muse of dance. Distraught over the fate of the woodland creature, she did not join her vote to those of her companions, risking the wrath of the god of light. But her gesture did not prevent the cruel punishment of him who had dared to make such a sacrilegious challenge.

Two winged spirits appeared all at once at the sides of the god and put their hands on Marsyas, tying him to the branch of a large tree, securing his feet so he could not escape. He implored mercy, in vain. The god flayed him alive and screaming. Apollo proceeded with serene detachment, stripping the skin of man and beast from him and leaving him mangled and bloody to the wild animals of the forest.

No one knew how that dry hide ended up in the cave above the source of the river that bore his name, or whether it was another false relic stitched together craftily from the skin of a man and the hide of a goat. But the story was terrible and disturbing nonetheless, and it could mean but one thing: the gods are jealous of their perfection, their beauty and their infinite power. Anyone who so much as gets close to them will arouse their suspicion and push them to strike out with a vengeance so that the distance between man and god will always remain insurmountable. But if that were true it would mean that the gods fear us, that the spark of intelligence born of our fragile, perishable nature frightens them somehow, makes them worry that one day, maybe a long time from now, we could become like them.

On the high plain, stories blossomed and flourished like the poppies that painted the fields and slopes of the hills red. Many of them concerned Midas, the king of Phrygia, who had bid the god Dionysus to transform everything he touched into gold, nearly causing his own death by starvation. The god took back that ruinous gift, but he gave the king two donkey's ears to

49

remind him of his foolishness. The king hid them under a wide hat, and the only person to know about them was his barber, who the king had sworn to secrecy and threatened with death should he let the word out. This poor man could not keep such a huge, intolerable secret but was wise enough to realize that he must not confide in anyone, since anything he said would quickly get back to the asinine ears of the king. The poor man was dying nonetheless to tell his secret, so he dug a hole in the river bank and whispered inside, 'Midas has donkey's ears,' then filled it back up again and warily made his way home. But a bed of reeds grew where the hole had been and every time the wind blew, they whispered that phrase endlessly, 'Midas has donkey's ears . . .'

Further on, when we had nearly reached Cappadocia, the army stopped near a spring to stock up on water, and there we heard another story about King Midas. There was a satyr named Silenus who was a follower of Dionysus's. This creature was gifted with extraordinary wisdom, but it was practically imposs-ible to force him to share his knowledge unless he could be enticed by wine, for he was an insatiable drinker. Midas mixed wine with the water of the spring and the satyr drank so much that he became drunk and Midas succeeded in tying him up for long enough to compel him to reveal all his secrets.

This was obviously a very tranquil time for the army. No one was worried, there were no enemies in sight, the men were being paid regularly. So there was time even to tell fables. But over one hundred thousand men cannot move without being noticed. Soon the first worrisome events would occur, signals that the advancing army had awakened a huge, wrathful empire. The Great King, in Susa, surely knew we were coming.

5

I'VE OFTEN WONDERED how many stories populate the villages of the world, stories of kings and queens or of humble peasants or the mysterious creatures of the woods and rivers. Every cluster of houses or huts has its own, but only very few grow and spread and become known beyond local confines. Xeno told me many stories about his homeland during those long nights when we were stretched out next to one another after making love. He told me of a war that lasted ten years against a city in Asia called Ilium, and the story of a small king of the western islands who called himself 'no one', but who had journeyed over all the seas, defeating monsters, giants, enchantresses. He had even descended into the land of the dead. When in the end he came back to his island home he found his house full of pretenders to his throne who had devoured his riches and wooed his wife. He killed them all, except one: a poet.

He was right to spare the poet: those who sing tales should never die because they give us what we could never have otherwise. They see far beyond our horizons, as if they lived on the peak of the highest mountain. They hear sounds and voices that we don't hear, they live many lives simultaneously and they suffer and rejoice as if these many lives were real and concrete. They experience love, grief, hope with an intensity unknown even to the gods. I've always been convinced that they are a race unto themselves. There are gods, there are human beings. And then there are poets. They are born when the heavens and the earth are at peace. Or when a bolt of lightning flashes out in the deep of night and strikes the cradle of a baby but does not kill him, brushing him only with its fiery caress.

I liked the story of that wandering king and every night I had Xeno tell me a little more. I imagined myself in the part of his bride, a queen with a long unpronounceable name. She had waited twenty years for her husband's return, not out of servile devotion, but because she couldn't be satisfied with anything less than her hero with his multi-faceted mind.

'Bend this bow, if you are capable of it,' she had said to her suitors, 'and I will choose the one among you who succeeds.' Knowing that none of them could ever succeed. And then she had thrown herself into the arms of her husband who had finally returned to her, for only he knew the secret that united them: he had built their wedding bed nestled in the branches of an olive tree. How lovely to sleep in the arms of an olive tree, like birds in a nest. Only he could have had such an idea. How happy they must have been in that bed, the young prince and princess of a happy land, contemplating the future of their newborn son. And I shivered as I thought of the horrors of the war they had yet to experience.

I was certain that the same would happen to us. It was only a question of time.

The first ominous signs had already emerged before Xeno and I even met, when the army was crossing the vast highlands. The morale of the troops was low, in both the Greek and Asian camps. Xeno knew why: money. Cyrus hadn't been paying the men for some time. Strange . . . very strange indeed. Cyrus was immensely wealthy: how could he not have enough money to sustain the costs of an expedition against an indigenous tribe? Xeno thought he knew the reason, but the troops certainly didn't, nor did many of their officers. Some of the men had become suspicious and were spreading stories that were fomenting tension and unrest in the camps. Fortunately something happened that changed the mood of the soldiers, at least for a while.

One day the army had stopped at the centre of a huge clearing, surrounded by woods of poplar and willow. As evening approached, a great procession of warriors arrived at their camp, escorting a carriage covered by fluttering veils. Inside was a woman of incredible beauty. A queen. The queen of Cilicia. Cilicia was the land that bordered on my own, but it was much more fertile and luxuriant. It overlooked the foaming sea and was rich with olive groves and vineyards. Her husband, the sovereign of that beautiful land, must have been worried. Although Cilicia was theoretically independent, he was still a subject of the Great King, and his kingdom was on the direction of march of Prince Cyrus. At this point, it wasn't hard to guess at his objective. If the Cilician king opposed Cyrus's advance, he would be mown down. If he didn't stand up to him, the Great King would demand to know why he hadn't been stopped, and the Great King was not a man to quarrel with. He probably decided that it was best to face one problem at a time, and Cyrus's approaching army was the closest and most pressing. The only true weapon that the king had at his disposal was the beauty of his wife: an invincible weapon, stronger than any army. All it would take was a little money and a queen in the prince's bed and this problem, at least, would be solved. Money and beautiful women move mountains, and the two together would crumble any bulwark.

Cyrus was young, handsome, daring and powerful. As was the queen. She was also willing to satisfy him in any way he desired. She brought him a large sum of money on behalf of her husband so that he could pay his soldiers' salaries, and she brought him herself. For a few days, it seemed that the whole world had stopped. The army was encamped, its tents solidly pitched. The royal pavilion was adorned with the finest fabrics and the most precious carpets, with bronze tubs for her majesty's bath. The men whispered that Cyrus would watch as she undressed and sank into the hot, fragrant water and had herself washed and massaged by two Egyptian handmaidens dressed only in tiny loincloths. He would sit on a stool covered with the royal purple and caress a cheetah curled up at his feet. The sinuous forms of the feline must have felt like the curves of the queen languidly stretching her limbs in the bronze tub.

The third day he decided to offer her a stirring display of his military might, all decked out in full battle order. He asked Clearchus to draw up all of his red-cloaked warriors wearing their polished armour and carrying their big round shields. They were to march at a cadenced step, to the beating of drums and the music of flutes, and parade before the prince and his beautiful guest on their chariots. The effect was brilliant. The queen was happy, as excited as a little girl watching a show of street jugglers.

Suddenly the blare of a bugle filled the ears of the royal spectators, shrill and prolonged. The scarlet warriors slowed their pace, executed a long, perfect right wheel then, at a second bugle call, charged towards the Asian camp where Ariaeus's troops were housed, their spears low and ready. The attack was so realistic that the Asians ran off in every direction, overwhelmed by panic. When a third bugle call stopped them, Clearchus's warriors turned back, laughing and making fun of Ariaeus's troops, who had certainly not made a great show of bravery or resistance.

Strangely, Cyrus was pleased with the trick, because it proved what a disruptive effect a heavy infantry charge by the red cloaks had on the Asian soldiers.

The queen left the camp a few days later, after Cyrus had promised that her husband would suffer no damage or harassment from his troops, in exchange for their unchallenged transit through the pass known as the Cilician Gates. The gap was so narrow that two harnessed horses could not pass at the same time. In effect, a very few selected, well-trained troops posted at the point of passage could have prevented anyone – even the most powerful army of the earth – from crossing. But it seemed that the king of Cilicia had no desire to engage in conflict and preferred to let Cyrus pass rather than attempt to stop him. Whoever held the Gates had the whip hand, so Cyrus had no choice but to trust him. Soon his word of honour would be put to the test: the Gates were only days away from their camp.

The queen departed laden with precious gifts, and perhaps Cyrus made a secret promise to see her again in Cilicia. A beautiful woman – and a queen at that – can't be considered the object of a few nights' hurried amusement.

Some days later the army passed close to Mount Argeus where Marsyas was said to have been flayed alive by Apollo. It was a lofty, solitary mountain that loomed like a giant over the high plains. Many other legends were told about that place. They said that deep inside the mountain there was a titan fettered to the rock who from time to time would angrily shake his chains and spew forth flames from his mouth. Rivers of fire would erupt out of the mountain top then, incandescent clouds would form and the whole region resound with fearsome roars. But most of the time Mount Argeus was calm and peaceful, perennially capped with white snow.

Fifteen days or so passed without anything much happening until they reached a city called Dana. Before them loomed the imposing Taurus range. Up on those snowy peaks, Anatolia ended and Cilicia began. As the army made ready to ascend towards the pass, Cyrus imprisoned the Persian governor of the city and had him put to death. Another person, whose name was kept secret, was arrested as well and executed. It seems that neither one of them had ever done anything to deserve such punishment.

Xeno did not know Persian and there was only one interpreter who maintained contact between the Greek officers and Cyrus. The reason was clear enough: restricted conversations could not be heard by too many people, and in this case 'too many' meant more than one.

The only Greek to confer with Cyrus was Clearchus. The other senior officers – Menon, Agias, Socrates and Proxenus –

were invited to banquets every so often, and sometimes to war council meetings, but at such meetings Cyrus spoke personally to the interpreter, who repeated his words to Clearchus in a murmur. Clearchus passed the orders on to his officers, probably as he saw fit.

Anyone who approached this single interpreter would certainly arouse suspicion and attract the attention of unsavoury characters. All Xeno had to rely on were rumours and hearsay that were difficult to verify. It was very likely, nonetheless, that Cyrus wanted to hide his presence in the area as far as possible, since it was evident that he never should have been there in the first place. No one believed the story of an expedition against mountain tribes threatening Cappadocia any more.

Xeno was already convinced then that the march of such a huge army hadn't escaped the powers that be: Susa, for instance, and Sparta. But we wouldn't be sure of this until much later, when Xeno learned that something important had taken place in Greece, something that would influence the fate of us all.

SOMEONE IN SPARTA had already made a decision that might have shifted the balance of our world, but at that point he didn't know how to control the sequence of events that he had set off. The instrument was the mercenary army that was now crossing Anatolia, but how could the situation be handled? How to stay out of the game and be inside at the same time?

It was late at night in Sparta when the two kings were awakened one after another in their houses by a messenger: they were to report immediately to the council hall where the five ephors – the men who governed the city – had already joined for a special session.

They probably discussed the issue at length, attempting to establish, with the help of informers, where the army was at that moment and whether it was possible to intercept their march at the border between Cilicia and Syria.

It was evident by now that Cyrus's objective was the one

they had all imagined, although no one officially knew anything: he planned to attack the heart of the empire and overthrow Artaxerxes.

'Brother against brother,' someone observed. 'It's difficult to hypothesize any other possibility.'

A heavy silence fell over the council hall for a few moments, then the two kings exchanged a few words in a whisper, as did the ephors.

Finally the eldest of the ephors spoke. 'When we made the decision to accede to Cyrus's request we considered all the evidence scrupulously and cautiously. We feel that we made the right choice and acted in the best interests of the city.

'We could have turned Cyrus down, but he would only have looked for help elsewhere: in Athens, for example, or Thebes or Macedon. It was best not to miss out on this opportunity: if Cyrus is truly marching against his brother, there are only two possible outcomes. If he wins, he will owe us his throne and our power in that part of the world will have no limits. If he loses, the army will be destroyed, the survivors executed or sold off as slaves in distant lands. No one will ever be able to accuse us of having plotted against the Great King or of supporting the endeavours of a usurper, because none of the men recruited knows the reason for which Cyrus had ordered them to assemble at Sardis, except for one. And he will never talk. There is not one regular Spartan officer among them.'

Someone present there, perhaps one of the kings, or both, must have thought about how much things had changed in three generations. Then, Leonidas and his men had fought at the Fiery Gates, three hundred against three hundred thousand, the Athenians had done battle on the sea, one hundred ships against five hundred, all the cities of Greece had fought, together, on the open battlefield. Against Persia. Side by side they had fought for the freedom of all of Greece and defeated the largest, richest and most powerful empire in the world. Now the Grecian peninsula was an expanse of ruin and devastation. The flower of its youth had been mown down by thirty years of civil strife. Sparta had won hegemony over a graveyard, over cities and nations that were shadows of what they had once been. And in order to feed this ghost of power they were forced to beg for money from the barbarians, their former enemies. This expedition represented the point of no return. They had reached the limit, sending off a select corps of over ten thousand extraordinary warriors in a venture that was almost certainly doomed to failure, with a good chance that these men would be completely wiped out. What city was this that they ruled over? What sort of men were these five bastards called ephors who were responsible for governing Sparta?

Perhaps they were tempted to voice their outrage, they who were descendants of the heroes of days gone by, but they limited themselves to stating a more realistic appraisal: something might go wrong. Something unexpected might push the situation out of control. It was a possibility they had to consider.

The chief of the ephors admitted that the objection was well put and that they had already paid it heed. For this reason, a regular Spartan officer, one of the very best, was on his way to join the army, with precise orders that could not be revealed. A secret mission that must remain so at any cost. Only when the situation was resolved would the kings be informed.

The man chosen for such a delicate mission – which required courage but also intelligence and above all, absolute loyalty and obedience to his orders – would be leaving next day on a ship from Gythion. The kings would learn of his identity six days after his departure.

The session was ended at once and the two kings went back to their homes, distraught and disillusioned, in the middle of the night.

A few hours later the Spartan envoy was awakened by a helot and accompanied to his harnessed horse. The man mounted his steed, secured his bag and galloped off. The sun was rising from the sea when he arrived within sight of the first houses of Gythion. A trireme of the war fleet was waiting at anchor with a light blue standard flying aft: the signal that they were expecting him.

He crossed the gangplank and led his horse aboard the ship.

THE ARMY left their quarters in Dana at dawn. Before the bulk of the troops set off, Cyrus asked Clearchus to send a detachment of his men to another pass that gave access to Tarsus – the capital of the kingdom of Cilicia and the biggest city in the region – from the rear. If the Cilicians refused to admit him, the detachment could attack from the west and force a resolution to the situation.

Clearchus chose Menon of Thessaly and gave him orders to move his battalion towards a pass in the Taurus chain that opened on to the plains west of Tarsus, while the rest of the army would transit through the narrow Cilician Gates and arrive at the capital from the north.

Menon left when it was still dark, while Cyrus waited until dawn and then headed towards a rest stop at the foot of the mountains. From the moment when the road began its steep climb, there would be no opportunity to make camp until after crossing the pass; this was true not only for such a huge army as his but even for a mere caravan. It was thus necessary to divide the journey in two stages. After spending the night at the foot of the Taurus chain, Cyrus led his army towards the Gates. It was dawn, they would be there before dusk. The road was little more than a winding mule track often flanked by deep gorges.

If the king of Cilicia decided to oppose their march, he could easily pick them off one by one, or decide to hold them in check for days and days, perhaps even months.

Tension was high among the ranks. The soldiers couldn't help but look upwards, at the rocky, towering peaks that surrounded them. What really disturbed them was that the road – usually heavy with traffic, since it was the only route for caravans from Mesopotamia heading towards Anatolia and the sea, and vice versa – was deserted. Not a single donkey or camel, only a few scattered peasants hauling basketfuls of goods on their shoulders. Some of the locals gathered by the road to watch the passage of the incredibly long column. Surely the word was out that something dangerous was bound to happen along that route, and no one dared use it, nor would they until the whole army had passed.

Before venturing through the pass, which was cut into the solid rock and allowed the passage of a single pack animal at a time, the prince sent scouts forward to reconnoitre. They reported back that there was no one at the top but that they'd spotted a camp on the other side which seemed to be completely deserted. Perhaps there had been an early plan of resistance that was later abandoned. Cyrus and his men crossed the pass with no trouble and settled into the camp while the long column continued its climb, all night long. When the last man had arrived at the top, it was already time to set off again.

In the meantime Menon and his battalion were crossing the western pass. They were moving quickly and without much worry because their guide had assured them that the area was clear.

The pass was found at the watershed of two streams: one flowed towards the Anatolian high plains, the other descended towards the sea. The first part of their route climbed upwards with a rather constant, moderate slope. They were covering open countryside and the view was clear all around. But when Menon had crossed the saddle and reached the slope beyond, he could see that the valley of the second torrent was steep and rugged, a deep gully buried at the foot of high, craggy walls. The descent was much steeper, and the water raced much faster.

Everything seemed nonetheless to go well at first but then, little by little, as the battalion entered the ground flanking the gully, worrisome signs started to appear. First, a flock of crows rose suddenly from a copse, evidently startled by something. This was followed by a cascade of pebbles rolling down the valley. Menon had no sooner shouted 'Watch out! Take cover! There's someone up there!' than a volley of arrows rained down from above. Three of his men were hit and fell to the ground. More arrows followed in a dense, relentless hail, striking many among the ranks.

Menon shouted, 'Shields up! Let's get out of here, now! Out, out!'

His men raised their shields to cover their heads as they started to run, but the slope was very steep and the gully very narrow. Many stumbled and fell, those behind surged forward and pushed against those in front, causing both to lose their footing. As they struggled to advance, their path was strewn with the dead and dying. For a moment it seemed as though the lethal rain had stopped, but it was only the calm before the new storm. A huge crash was heard, and an avalanche of rocks and pebbles was unleashed from above, cutting down more and more men. When at last they were able to rally at a clearing beyond the enemy's range, Menon counted his men. Seventy were missing, killed by the arrows and stones.

'We cannot go back to gather our dead,' he said. 'More of us would fall. But we can avenge them.' And as he pronounced those words his blue eyes turned as cold as ice.

6

THEY DESCENDED on Tarsus unannounced.

They were just over a thousand but they seemed like one hundred thousand. They were everywhere at once, and then they were everywhere else. They attacked, burned, butchered.

What was most terrifying was their silence. They did not shout, they did not curse, they did not rage. They killed without ever stopping.

They came in, went out. Leaving only death behind them.

They looked all the same, seemed a single man. The ghostly mask of their salleted helmets, their bronze breastplates and black, silver-rimmed shields: they were the men of Menon of Thessaly avenging their dead, unburied comrades.

By the time they were done, the city was at their feet, bloodied and maimed. The king had fled to the mountains.

Clearchus arrived the following evening and entered through open, unguarded gates. He advanced with his men down the city's main street, stunned by the sight of countless dead bodies strewn outside the houses, or at the threshold, or inside. The Chera of death had been through here, brandishing the scythe that spares no man.

He expected to meet her, wrapped in her black mantle. He found Menon of Thessaly instead, sitting in the centre of an empty square, wearing only his white cloak.

'You're late,' he said.

Clearchus looked around in dismay. The city seemed dead.

Not a lamp, not a voice. The last gleam of sunset tinged the place with a red glow.

'What happened?' he demanded.

'I lost seventy men,' he replied as if he were talking about the weather.

Clearchus widened his arms and turned in a circle, gesturing at the devastation that surrounded them. 'And all of this? What does all of this mean?'

'It means that whoever kills Menon of Thessaly's men pays a high price.'

'I never gave you orders to take out an entire city.'

'You never gave me orders not to.'

'I should punish you for insubordination. You must do only what I command you to do. Nothing more.'

'Punish me, you say. I don't think that sounds like a good idea.' As he spoke he had risen to his feet and was staring Clearchus straight in the eye.

'Get your men out of here and set up camp near the river. Stay there until I tell you.'

Menon crossed the square. In the silence that weighed on the city the only sound to be heard was the wailing of an infant. It stopped, and the only sound left was made by Menon's boots. His steps rang out in the deserted square like the steps of a giant.

Cyrus arrived much later, after night had fallen, and he flew into a rage at the sight of the massacre, but when he discovered that all that damage had been done by Menon's battalion alone, his mood changed. If a single unit could accomplish so much, what would the whole contingent be capable of when the time came to unleash it? He then received a message from the queen asking to see him in private, and this further buoyed his spirits. They met at a villa not far from the sea where Cyrus arrived accompanied by a numerous retinue.

No one ever learned what was said in that encounter, although Cyrus had been escorted by his personal bodyguards. All that leaked out was that the queen was incredibly beautiful.

63

She wore a light, nearly transparent gown in the Ionian style, was made up like an Egyptian and wore a black pearl from India on a pendant between her breasts and a pair of exquisitely crafted earrings bought from a merchant from distant Taranto.

There is no doubt that Cyrus had one more reason the next morning for not being too harsh with King Syennesis of Cilicia, who had run up to the mountains to hide in his burrow like a rabbit.

Advised by a messenger that the danger had passed, the king descended to the valley and exchanged every manner of pleasantries with the prince of the empire. His face was evidently the only thing he had left to save.

The following night, the moon was completely covered by clouds when a warship bearing neither insignia nor standard approached so close to the coast that it nearly ran aground in the shallows near the mouth of the Cydnus river. The crew lowered the gangplank and a man walked over it, leading his horse by the reins. As soon as the steed's hoofs hit the water at the end of the plank, the man leapt onto his back and urged him to shore. In the distance the fires of a large camp could be seen, and the man headed in that direction at an easy canter, without making the slightest sound.

The ship withdrew the plank and, as silent as it had arrived, made its way out to sea, where it would join the squadron waiting offshore at anchor, all lights out.

CYRUS REMAINED a few days as the city's worst wounds were attended to, but he was ready to proceed. They had arrived at the sea. At this point the problem was no longer the Cilicians or the inhabitants of Tarsus. The problem was his 'Yauna' mercenaries, as he called them. The Greeks. He had kept his final plan a secret for as long as possible, but among the soldiers and officers there were a good many who knew what it meant to arrive at the sea from the Cilician Gates. Anatolia lay behind them and their journey was leading them south – straight towards the heart of the empire. All kinds of strange rumours spread among the men, and the strangest of all was started by Xeno himself when he confronted Proxenus of Boeotia, his friend Proxenus. Not in the intimacy of his tent but while he was eating his dinner, surrounded by his men.

He appeared suddenly in the halo of light cast by their campfire and he spoke loudly and without even taking a place among them. 'Do you have any idea of what is going to happen in the next few days?'

'What kind of a question is that?' replied Proxenus.

'You have no idea?' he repeated.

'I don't think it's my concern.'

'Oh, but it is. It concerns you most closely! You and all of your men!'

'Look, look who we have here!' exclaimed one of Proxenus's lieutenants, a man from Tanagra called Eupitus. 'The writer! Why aren't you in your tent giving your pen some exercise?'

Xeno paid him no mind and continued, 'We're walking straight into the lion's den!'

Many of them started laughing, others dug their elbows into those who were snickering, trying to get them to stop. Some of the men leaned forward to hear better.

'What the hell are you spouting off about?' said Proxenus, visibly irritated.

'I'm talking about the truth, and all of you should listen. Cyrus lied to us and so has Commander Clearchus, who is surely in on the whole thing. Off to fight the barbarians in Pisidia, are we? Pisidia has nothing to do with this expedition. We left it behind us ages ago. We're in the Gulf of Cilicia now. Do you know what's down that way?' he shouted, pointing at a spot behind him. 'Egypt, that's what. And do you know what's beyond that mountain range? Syria! And after Syria, Babylonia.'

'How do you know that?' asked one of the soldiers.

'Because I do. What I'm saying is true. And we're heading in that direction, I'm sure of it.'

'And who the hell told you we're going to head that way?' demanded another.

'My brain, idiot!'

'Watch who you're talking to!'

'You watch who you're talking to. If you don't know what you're saying, shut up and listen to someone who knows more than you do!'

A fight was about to break out when the officer from Tanagra stopped them. 'Enough! I want to hear what the writer has to say. Spit it out, then. I'm all ears.'

Xeno calmed down and started to explain. 'I thought some time ago that there had to be another reason for this expedition and that Cyrus had lied to us. At the time, a plausible hypothesis occurred to me: I imagined that the Great King had asked for his brother's help to conquer a land in the Orient. But from what I've heard, there's no love lost between the two of them, and so it didn't really make sense for Artaxerxes to ask his brother of all people to be at his side in such a difficult and ambitious endeavour. What's more, nothing was ever said about such a venture. So later I thought that Cyrus wanted to carve out a kingdom all for himself, I don't know, Egypt, for instance: Egypt would be easy to defend, easy to conquer, too, if you don't interfere with their beliefs. But then I realized that there was a much bigger game being played here. Cyrus is too ambitious, too intelligent, too crafty. He is convinced that he's much better than his brother and he'd never put up with submitting to him, living in his shadow. Men, Cyrus wants nothing less than the throne of Persia. Cyrus wants to lead us against the Great King!'

'You're mad!' said Proxenus. 'That's totally impossible.'

'Then you tell me what we're doing here in Cilicia. And why Cyrus executed the governor of Dana and his military commander when they were guilty of no crime. He had them put to death because he knew they were loyal to his brother. Maybe they asked him to account for what was happening, maybe they demanded to know what such a big army was for and where we were headed. They may even have managed to inform the Great King about this expedition. That's why they're dead!'

The argument had attracted other soldiers. Many were elbowing their way forward to hear what was being said. Others had begun to cry out, 'Our commanders have to tell us where they're leading us! We have the right to know! We want to be told what's happening. They can't keep us in the dark!'

Their indignation mounting, many of the men were determined to take the question straight to Clearchus. Just then Xeno noticed a man he'd never seen before, sitting on horseback, riding past the crowd of soldiers. He was armed and wore his hair long, gathered at the nape of his neck and pinned back, in the Spartan manner. He was heading towards Clearchus's tent.

Xeno turned to the men thronging around the campfire. 'Leave Clearchus alone for now,' he said. 'He's got visitors.'

The men glanced up in surprise, jostling to get a look, and a certain calm briefly settled over the gathering. But word was quick to spread that the expedition was marching against the Great King, the Lord of the Four Corners of the World, and disorders of every sort broke out in the camp. The commanders had a struggle to keep order, and the rioting and brawling went on all night. After two days of turmoil, Clearchus attempted to start moving the army again, as though nothing had happened, but the men stood up against him resolutely. Some even threw stones. Clearchus ordered them to cease all activity for the time being, until he could call an assembly, and went to Cyrus's tent.

'Prince,' he said, 'my men demand to know where we are going. They are furious because they say they've been deceived. Many want to turn back. The situation is becoming uncontrollable.'

'So this is the famous discipline of the Greek troops? Order them to return to their ranks and prepare to fall in.'

'That is simply not possible,' replied Clearchus. 'Discipline for them means holding their place in the battle line and executing orders during a campaign. But they are mercenaries, and thus everything depends on the rules of engagement. They were hired for an expedition in Anatolia, not for . . .'

'Not for what?'

'For a different mission altogether. They know full well that we're not in Anatolia. The rumour is that we'll be fighting against your brother. Against the Great King.'

'That's perfectly correct. We're going to challenge my brother. Don't tell me you didn't know that.'

'What I know is of secondary importance. My orders are to follow you.'

'Then convince your men to do the same.'

'It's difficult. I may not succeed.'

'You must. There's no going back now.'

'Listen. These are hardly things I can force upon my men just like that. I have to call an assembly.'

'An assembly . . . in an army? What are you saying?'

'That's the way we do things. It's the only way I can hope to convince them. I'll need your help: wait until I've begun speaking, then send me one of your men. He will interrupt me and say that you demand to see me immediately. He must speak loudly enough so that the men closest to me can hear him. I'll tell him what to do next.'

Clearchus walked out, his expression grim, and went to his tent. As soon as he arrived he called his field adjutant. 'I'm going to be calling the army to assembly. What I want you to do is to choose a few men; when I give them the liberty to speak, they will say exactly what I'm about to tell you. Listen well, because everything depends on how the next few hours go.'

'I'm listening, Commander,' replied his aide.

He left the tent soon after and slipped into the camp to contact the men selected to intervene at the meeting. Clearchus waited, pacing back and forth, practising the words he would say. As soon as his aide returned he had the fall-in sounded.

He knew it wouldn't be easy to address the assembled

soldiers. The men's faces were sullen; there was an undercurrent of grumbling and shoving. Stray voices shouted out as he passed. 'You've tricked us! We want to go back! We didn't come here for this.' But when Clearchus stood on the small platform set up for the purpose, silence fell over the troops. Their high commander stood before them with his head low and a stern expression. He could feel their eyes boring into him. Xeno's as well. Who knew where the writer was now? Lurking on the outskirts no doubt, observing what he'd set into motion. What did he have to lose?

'Men!' began Clearchus. 'This morning when I ordered you to march you refused to do so. You disobeyed me. Some of you even threw stones at me . . .'

Low muttered protests spread through the ranks.

'So you don't want to go on. This means I won't be able to keep my word, my promise to Prince Cyrus, that we would follow him in this expedition.'

'No one said we were going to have to follow him to hell!' came a shout.

'I'm your commander, but I am a mercenary,' continued Clearchus, 'as you are, all of you. I do not exist without you. Where you are is where I have to be. And what's more, I'm Greek. It's evident that if I have to choose between siding with the Greeks or with the barbarians I have no doubts. I'm on your side, men. You want to go? You refuse to follow me? Very well, I'm with you. You are my men, by Zeus! Many of you fought with me in Thrace. I saved quite of few of your skins, if I'm not mistaken. And at least a couple of you have saved mine. I will never abandon you! Do you understand that? Never!'

Loud applause broke out. The men were beside themselves with joy: they'd be going home, finally. The applause had not yet died down when a messenger sent by Cyrus showed up. 'The prince wants to see you at once,' he said loudly to Clearchus.

'Tell him that I can't come,' replied Clearchus in a low voice. 'He needn't worry, I'll settle this. But tell him to keep sending me messengers, even though I'll continue to refuse them.'

The man looked at him without understanding, but nodded and hurried off to report back.

'That man was a messenger from Cyrus, but I sent him away!' said Clearchus aloud.

Another burst of applause.

'Now we have to see how we can return home. Unfortunately, it's not a simple matter and it doesn't depend solely upon us. Cyrus's Asian army is ten times more numerous than we are . . .'

'We're not afraid of them!' came the shouted answer.

'I know, but they could do us a lot of damage. Even if we are victorious, many of us will die.'

One of Clearchus's men who had been planted in the crowd spoke up. 'We could ask him to let us use the fleet.'

'We could,' nodded Clearchus, 'but we won't.'

'Why not?'

'First of all, the fleet hasn't arrived yet and there's no saying it will be here soon. Secondly, it's clear that from now on we won't be getting a penny from Cyrus. How will we pay for passage? I know what you're thinking. That once the fleet has unloaded the food and supplies, it will be going back empty and we can ask for passage. But don't believe for one moment that they'll take us on board for free. How do you think Cyrus will feel about helping us once we've ruined all his plans? I know him well. When he wants to be – if you've earned it – he can be the most generous man on earth, but if you cross him he'll slaughter you. Let's not forget that he has soldiers, weapons, warships. And we're on our own.'

A buzz of discontent rose from the assembly; the men were unnerved.

'And even if he accepted, who's to say they won't abandon

us in the middle of the sea or even sink us, to cover up any trace of the expedition?'

Another man his adjutant had briefed now stepped forward. 'Let's ask him for a guide who will lead us back over land. We can send advance troops forward to guard the passes so they can't lay traps on our return route.'

'You'd trust a guide given us by Cyrus? Not me!' exclaimed Clearchus. 'A guide could take us straight into an ambush or lead us astray and then disappear. Where might we end up? How would we find our way home in the middle of people who don't speak our language? I don't want even to think about the trouble we'd meet up with. You want to set off on such an adventure? Fine. But don't ask me to lead you, to lead my men to certain death.

'What I can guarantee is that I'm ready to die with you. I'm ready to share the same destiny. If you want to elect another commander, I will obey him.'

This last option was of no comfort whatsoever. Clearchus had played his hand: it was now their turn to come up with a solution that would get them out of this fix. They were formid-able warriors, capable of withstanding any hardship, but they easily fell prey to discouragement when they felt they had no prospects.

The buzz died down into silence. The men understood only too well that they had no choice; that a retreat would leave them wide open to double dealing. Clearchus had used his oratorical skills to worsen their outlook on the situation. He discreetly scanned their faces to gauge the effect his words had had on them. As he looked around he noticed the person he'd met with the night before, riding slowly by on his horse, apparently disinterested in the whole affair. He was wearing a salleted helmet now, which covered his face, and a red cloak on his shoulders. A large shield hung from his steed's harness. No doubt about it; he had all the trappings of a man of high rank.

At just the right moment, another of Cyrus's messengers showed up, whispered something into Clearchus's ear and disappeared.

'Cyrus wants to know what we're going to do. Time is up. What shall I answer?'

The last of the three men Clearchus had primed for the encounter stepped up. 'Listen,' he said, 'it's clear to me that on our own we have no hope of making it back, and defying Cyrus is the last thing we should be thinking of. I say, let's send a messenger to the prince with a plain proposal: if he thinks he can convince us to stay, let's hear him out and evaluate his plan. If we can't come to an agreement, we'll ask for a pact that allows us to go our own way without risks or problems, without having to watch our backs. What do you think of that?'

'Right, yes!' shouted the men. 'We're with you!'

'Fine,' continued the same man. 'Then let Commander Clearchus himself go to deal with Cyrus and hear what he has to propose.'

Entrusted officially with this mission by one of the men he had personally instructed to achieve just that, Clearchus reported to Cyrus.

'What shall we do?' asked the prince when Clearchus had explained the whole matter.

'I'm afraid that if you reveal the true purpose of the expedition they will refuse to follow you. Remember that no Greek will distance himself from the sea. It's inconceivable, just the thought makes him feel dizzy, robs him of his breath. A Greek has blood mixed with seawater in his veins, trust me. Here they've got the sea right in front of them. They know that in one way or another they can get back home. But plunging into the heart of an enormous empire, tens of thousands of stadia away from their sea, that frightens them. Put them opposite an enemy ten times more numerous than they are and they won't bat an eye. But you put them in front of an endless stretch of land without cities or roads, and panic will overwhelm them like children in the dark.'

Cyrus said nothing and for some time measured the space in his tent by pacing back and forth as Clearchus stood still with his eyes staring straight ahead. Cyrus finally stopped and said, 'I think I have the right solution. Tell them that there's a man who has betrayed me. One of my governors, Abrocomas. Tell them he's camped on the Euphrates at twelve days' march from here. That's the mission of the expedition. Tell them I'll raise their salaries by half as much again as what they're earning now and that they'll be further rewarded if we succeed in defeating Abrocomas. Then they can go where they like.'

'Yes, I can tell them that,' retorted Clearchus. 'But afterwards?'

'Afterwards they'll have no choice. They'll have to follow me whether they like it or not. I'll assemble them and speak to them. I can convince them to carry out the mission, I'm sure of it.'

'That's possible,' replied Clearchus, 'but before I go, allow me to remind you of something important. My men are extraordinary soldiers, the best that you could have enlisted, without a doubt, but remember: they are mercenaries. They're fighting for money.'

'I'm well aware of that,' replied Cyrus. Clearchus made his way towards the exit.

'Wait,' said Cyrus. 'I know that the last Greek contingent will be landing at a short distance from here. Will they come as well?'

'One of them, an officer, has already arrived. He reported to my tent last night, and I thought I saw him riding through the camp a little while ago. If he is who I think he is, we should have no problems.'

Cyrus nodded and Clearchus went back to address the assembly.

The soldiers allowed themselves to be persuaded, in part because they had no real alternative, but many refused to swallow the new story; they continued to be convinced that they were marching against the Great King and muttered their discontent under their breath.

Some of them noticed that the stranger who had appeared in their camp on horseback had positioned himself so that he could overlook the entire scene, and they imagined that from his vantage point he could count one by one those who showed any disagreement. It turned out that he had no need to count anyone. No one broke away from the army of warriors who were now ready to march for twelve days until they reached the banks of the Euphrates. No one had ever seen that river, but they had heard it was as grand as the Nile.

The men watched as the stranger approached Clearchus and whispered something in his ear. The commander responded with a nod of his head. Who was this newcomer? That day and the following night many of the men took note of him and many asked themselves the same question. Xeno was the first to walk up to his lonely campfire, where he was toasting a piece of bread on the end of his sword. He had removed his helmet and shaken free a full head of black hair. His eyes were light-coloured.

'Who are you?' asked Xeno.

He replied by stating his name. A name so complicated that I couldn't even try to pronounce it. So I started calling him – and will call him for the rest of my story – Sophos.

'I'm a decent swordsman,' he added, without saying any more than he had to. 'If I've understood what your commander had to say, I've come to the right place.'

'How do you know Clearchus?'

'You're certainly observant,' replied Sophos dryly. 'I'm sure I don't need to tell you that anyone who has used his sword over the last ten years is either dead or knows everyone else involved in the trade, on his side and in the enemy camp. As for me, I fought with Clearchus for a few months in Thrace. What about you?'

'I was fighting on the wrong side when the democratic exiles returned to take control of the government in Athens. My name is Xenophon.'

'What unit are you with?'

'None. I'm with Commander Proxenus of Boeotia. I'm writing the diary of this expedition.'

'Man of the pen or man of the sword?'

'Of the pen, for the moment. Things didn't go so well for me with a sword. But if the need arises, I have all the basics with me.'

'I'd be surprised if that weren't so. Will you write about me?'

'Should I?'

'It depends. If you think I'm important enough. So . . . where is it we're going?'

'South. Towards Syria. But then, I think, towards Mesopotamia. Cyrus is marching against his brother, no one can convince me otherwise. He's heading for Babylon and from there to Susa.'

The stranger frowned. 'How do you know all these things?'

'I don't know them. I imagine them. The Euphrates is the only road that leads to Babylon.'

Sophos offered him a piece of his toasted bread.

'By Zeus! Marching against the Great King of the Persians, are we? You don't say! What an adventure we're in for then! By the way, have you heard the one about the fellow who got captured by the Persians and ended up with a stake up his arse?'

'No, I haven't.'

'Better for you,' replied Sophos. 'It wouldn't make you laugh.'

He got up then, laid his blanket under a tree and stretched out to sleep. Xeno returned to his tent.

The next day the army resumed its march. All was calm. Many of the units had loaded their weapons onto carts and walked fast without the burden of all that weight. A squad of scouts rode ahead, three or four more at the side and a couple behind the column. For many hours they proceeded along the seashore. They'd never seen a bluer sea, fringed with a wide edge of white foam breaking on the pebbles on the shore with a soft, steady lapping that kept them company. The soldiers walked in the water; a few of them even managed to spear the fish swimming in the water, so numerous were they. It seemed more like a stroll than a military expedition. The men were boisterous, joking and laughing.

Cyrus seemed content with what he saw, and said nothing.

Xeno noticed Sophos, the warrior who'd appeared out of thin air, riding alone at the end of the column. He would dismount at times and walk along the shore, leading the horse by its reins. There was something unreal about him. Although he'd arrived more or less with the new contingent, he had reported to none of the division commanders. He seemed to know no one but Clearchus.

7

THE ARMY CONTINUED to march along the coast; they crossed one river and then another whose name I can't remember, although Xeno took care to write down all the names, until they reached a place called Issus: a little city with a natural port. The fleet that had been expected arrived there. Xeno thought that the place initially designated for disembarking the men must have been Tarsus, but since the ships had been late to arrive, Cyrus must have decided to move on in order to gain time and wait for them at the next port.

The fleet, commanded by an Egyptian admiral, delivered about seven hundred Greek warriors, who brought the total number to thirteen thousand three hundred.

I could never understand why later, when they had become famous, everyone referred to them as the 'Ten Thousand'. In truth there were never ten thousand of them; perhaps there was a time when there happened to be that many, but no one would have noticed. Probably because ten thousand is a nice round number that sounds impressive. It gives the idea of a substantial, compact group, big but not too big, well proportioned, as all Greek things are.

From there the army continued until they reached an impasse at a place called the Syrian Gates, a fortress that completely blocked the passage between the sea and the steep cliffs that flanked it. It was a towering structure; an army determined to resist could hold out indefinitely behind its double line of walls. Instead the fortress fell without a blow being struck. The Persian general holding the garrison chose to retreat, although he had a powerful and well-equipped army at his disposal.

When Xeno told me this story, I asked him what sense there could be in the general's bowing out like that: if he had chosen instead to hold the fortress and push back Cyrus's army, wouldn't that have given him lustre in the eyes of the King?

Xeno answered that a man who took on such a great responsibility would be staking all his luck and his destiny on a single throw. If by chance he was defeated he would have to kill himself, because his punishment would be unthinkably worse. By retreating from the fortress and joining with the Great King he showed his loyalty but shifted the risk onto the shoulders of the sovereign in person. This must have been the general's thinking: by uniting his forces with those of his King he could shirk the responsibility of fighting the invaders off alone.

They thus arrived at another beautiful city on the coast, the last before they would cross the pass on Mount Amanus that separated Cilicia from Syria. From that moment on, the Greeks would leave the sea and no one could say how much time would pass before they saw it again.

The sea.

The Egyptians called it the 'Great Green', a marvellously poetic expression. When I first met Xeno at the well at Beth Qadà I'd never been there, and I knew no one in any of the five villages of Parysatis who had seen it, although more than one claimed to have heard it described by travelling merchants. Xeno painted a picture of the sea for me when I was finally able to understand his language: a liquid immensity, never resting. She had one thousand voices and infinite reflections which mirrored the sky and its galloping clouds. She was the tomb of many a bold navigator who had challenged her by venturing out in search of a better life, furrowing her illusory surface, chasing an evasive horizon. The sea: home to a multitude of scaly creatures, of monsters so huge they can swallow a whole ship, all subject to a mysterious, infinitely powerful divinity who lived in her deepest depths. A divinity who was herself liquid, green, trans-parent. Treacherous.

Xeno told me that when you look at the sea you feel fear but also an irresistible attraction, a yearning to know what's hiding under her endless vast surface, what islands and what foreign peoples are embraced by her waves. To know whether she has a beginning and an end or if she is a gulf of the great river Ocean that surrounds every land, beyond which no one knows what may exist.

The night they camped near the port, two officers of the Greek contingent deserted the army and fled on a ship. Perhaps they had known that soon they'd reach the point of no return. Perhaps they had been thrown into a panic by the only fear that could overwhelm such indomitable soldiers: the terror of the unknown.

Cyrus let everyone know that if he wanted to he could send his fastest ships out after them, or rout them out wherever they had thought they'd found refuge, or annihilate their families held hostage in their coastal towns. No, he would do none of this; let them go, he said. He would force no man to stay on against his will, but he would certainly remember those who remained faithful to him. An able move: this way his soldiers knew that there was a way out for them that wasn't exceedingly risky if they decided to abandon this adventure, which they worried would become more dangerous with each passing day. They were not fooled by appearances or idle rhetoric: they had no consideration of the Asian troops marching alongside and they trusted no one but themselves. And the idea that they might be marching against the Great King led them inevitably to conclude that it would be the thirteen thousand of them challenging the greatest empire on earth.

Accustomed as I was to the small size of my village, to the modest emotions and ambitions of its inhabitants – expectations for the harvest, fear of drought or late frosts, of diseases that might decimate the flocks, plans for the weddings and births and funerals that punctuated their lives – when I finally joined Xeno and his companions I was fascinated by the idea that those men were forced to look death in the face almost every day. How did they really feel? How could they bear the thought of not seeing the sun the next day or of having to face a long agony?

After they had crossed Mount Amanus and destroyed an enemy settlement, the army reached the little group of villages where I lived, and that is when I met Xeno at the well.

That is when I became part of that way of feeling, when I began to share in their extreme emotions, the midnight anguish and the sudden shocks. The world of the soldiers became my own.

When Cyrus decided to reveal his true plans, everyone had been expecting them for some time and had grown used to the idea, and so the revelation had a very limited effect on them. It was not difficult for the young, charismatic prince finally to convince them. He promised them immediate payment of a stipend equal to the value of five oxen, plus immense riches if they were victorious.

Five oxen. I knew those animals well, with their big moist eyes and heavy tread. For five oxen Clearchus's men bartered their right to live with their willingness to die. It was their job, their destiny; their life was the only thing they had to put on their side of the scale.

In truth it wasn't death they were afraid of. They'd seen death too often, they were used to it. They feared other things: the atrocious suffering and hideous torture they would have to withstand if they fell alive into enemy hands, or perpetual slavery, or disfiguring mutilation, or all of these things together.

How did they keep from going mad? I asked myself that question many times. How could they see the bleeding ghosts of their fallen comrades – or those they had slaughtered themselves in battle – in their dreams without losing their minds?

By staying together. One alongside the next. While marching, on the line of combat or next to a campfire. Sometimes, on certain nights, I'd hear them singing. A mournful song, something like a dirge, low and solemn. They'd sing all together, and the song would get louder as more voices joined in. Then they'd stop singing all of a sudden to create the silence from which a solitary voice would rise. The clear voice of one of them alone: the one voice – deep and powerful, vivid and vibrant – that best expressed their anguish, their cruel and hopeless courage, their aching melancholy.

Sometimes that voice sounded to me like Menon of Thessaly. Menon, blond and fierce.

THE VILLAGES OF THE BELT, also called the Villages of Parysatis. Was there ever an encounter more improbable than ours? In the days and months that followed I asked Xeno again and again what he felt when he met me, what struck him about me, what he thought we would do together, besides make love. The story he told me every time I asked shocked me and fascinated me at the same time. He hadn't thought, or reflected on, or calculated the possible consequences any more than I had. Maybe because I was a barbarian, and he could have sold me at the nearest slave market as soon as he tired of me, or handed me over to one of his comrades, or just maybe – and this is what I like to think – maybe because his passion and desire left him no other choice. But it was difficult to make him admit it.

I had to read it in his eyes, feel it in his caresses, understand it in the little gifts he gave me.

For me all of this meant love, but the Greeks had an entirely different way of reasoning about these things, complicated and hard to comprehend. In their country they married a woman and slept in her bed only until a male child was born and no longer. For me the fact that we made love so often seemed an unmistakable sign of his attachment to me. He was careful to do it in such a way that a child would not be born, and that was only right. We had a terrible trial ahead of us, a trial that would break men of the strongest temper. And I was sure that his being careful was another sign of his love.

I would often stop and think about my village, about my friends at the well ... about my mother and her dry, work-toughened hands. My heart told me that I'd never see her again but I told myself, I fooled myself into thinking, that sometimes your heart can be wrong.

The Villages of Parysatis marked the start of Syria, my land, and for the whole time we were crossing it, the sunny colours of the countryside, the aroma of baking bread, the scent of wildflowers and herbs made me feel at home. Then, as time passed and the landscape changed I realized we were entering a different land. We started to see wild animals: gazelles and ostriches that looked at us with curious eyes. The male ostriches had beautiful black feathers and they would carefully guard their flock of grazing females. The Greeks called the ostriches a name that meant 'camel-bird'. I could see why: their curved backs looked a little like camels' humps. The soldiers had never seen them before, apart from the few who had been to Egypt, and they pointed them out one by one as they marched, or would even stop to gawk at them.

One thing I hadn't known about Xeno was that he had a real passion for hunting. As soon as he saw the ostriches, he jumped onto his horse with a bow and arrows and tried to get within shooting range of a large male. But the ostrich burst into such a fast run that Xeno's horse couldn't gain on him. Xeno pulled him up short when he saw he'd lost sight of his prey. The Asian guides said that that apparently shy and harmless bird could be very dangerous; a blow of its sharp claws could easily crush a man's chest.

Xeno didn't come back from his ride empty-handed: he brought back an ostrich egg as big as ten hen's eggs. I remembered how once a merchant had come from the coast to our village with some fabric and modest ornaments to sell, marvels that he'd laid out on the ground to attract the attention of the inhabitants. There was also an ostrich egg painted with beautiful colours, but none of us had anything precious enough to barter for that useless but incredibly desirable object.

The egg Xeno collected had been freshly laid and we cooked it over the fire. It was good; with a little salt and some herbs and accompanied by the bread I'd baked on a stone, it made an appetizing meal. Xeno sent a portion as a gift to Cyrus, and was thanked for it.

The next day we met up with a group of onagers, a kind of wild ass. Xeno tried to hunt one down but was once again unsuccessful. The magnificent steed he called Halys was humbled in his race against those shaggy, ungainly animals.

When his comrades teased him about his failure, Xeno replied that he'd already thought up a way to capture one and that he'd put his plan to work the next day. All he needed was two or three volunteers on horseback. Three men came forward, two Achaeans and an Arcadian, and Xeno set about instructing them by drawing lines in the dirt and placing pebbles at a certain distance from one another.

The next day I was to learn what those stones meant: they were the stalking positions of the three horsemen. One began the chase, then, when his horse was worn out, the second stepped in and then the third, driving the exhausted ass towards the point where Xeno would be waiting, in the shade of a cluster of sycamore trees. When the onager arrived Xeno urged on his charger as fast as he could go and let fly. The first arrow fell short because the ass suddenly swerved and changed direction, heading back towards us. The second hit its mark but didn't bring the animal down. But now it was only a question of time.

Exhausted, wounded, the ass slowed down and finally stopped: his open mouth was sucking in air, his head drooped forward. His legs gave way little by little until he fell to his knees, seemingly waiting for the final blow. Xeno grabbed a javelin and plunged it between his shoulder blades so that it pierced his heart. The onager collapsed onto his side, his legs still kicking for a few moments before he stiffened into death. It was a male.

At a certain distance his groups of females looked on with a detached air certainly not fitting to the tragedy they'd witnessed, and as Xeno picked up his dagger and started to skin the animal, they began grazing again, nibbling here and there at the wild wheat stubble.

It made me sad to watch the scene, man's crafty victory over that spirited animal that ran like the wind, whipping the air with his bristly tail. It seemed brutal and unfair, and I was sorry I had seen it.

That day Xeno suddenly became very popular among the soldiers who had appreciated his public lesson in elementary cavalry tactics. He'd shown them he was a man of action. When that evening he invited a large circle of men to join him in feasting on the well-roasted meat – including Clearchus, Socrates and Agias with their adjutant and subordinate officers – his popularity grew even further. Menon, who hadn't been invited, was nowhere to be seen that evening. Sophos showed up late and cast a wary eye at the remains of the banquet.

'What does it taste like?' he asked, but then walked off into the dark without waiting for an answer.

Xeno muttered, 'To me it tastes like venison.' It was his way of saying that it had a gamey flavour, but having slain a male, it couldn't have been otherwise.

Sophos was still very elusive, although Xeno tried in vain to involve him in various conversations. He kept an eye on the newcomer, especially when he saw him approaching Clearchus's tent. I would watch as Xeno attempted a casual stroll in the vicinity, perhaps trying to listen in on whatever they were saying, but as far as I knew he never managed to hear anything worthwhile.

That night we heard the yelping of jackals fighting over the donkey's carcass. At dawn we set off on our journey once again and for the first time I was approached by some of the other women. They seemed to want to befriend me, or get to know me, but I couldn't understand what they were saying. Not yet.

The hills to the north got further and further away, and we could begin to see the green foliage of the trees bordering the Euphrates.

The Great River.

We camped on a slight rise overlooking the banks and that night I couldn't sleep. I sat on a palm stump and couldn't take my eyes off the glitter of the water in the moonlight. If I saw a branch or a log floating by I'd try to imagine where it was coming from, how long it had travelled before I'd caught a glimpse of it. Very few people in my village had ever seen the Euphrates – we called it *Purattu* in our language – and they had exaggerated its size until it became so wide you could barely see the other shore.

The next day the sun's light revealed the city located at the ford. It was the only point where you could cross that stretch of the river and a number of caravans were crowding around, waiting to pass from one side to the other. There were also ferries going across, but those who had large animals with them – like horses, mules, asses or camels – were crossing on foot. The confusion was incredible! The costumes, languages, colours, the shouting and braying, people fighting, even, arguing in loud, discordant voices. The caravans were led by men who had crossed mountains and deserts to bring goods of every description from the countries of Asia to the sea and the port cities where they would be loaded on ships departing for other destinations. The name of the city we could see meant 'ford' and it was populated mainly by Phoenicians who had made it their staging post towards the interior.

'Do you see that water?' asked Xeno, approaching me. 'See how fast it's flowing? In two days' time it will be under the bridges of Babylon. It will take us the better part of a month.

The water never sleeps, it travels by day and by night, it fears no obstacles. Nothing can stop it until it reaches the sea, which is its final destination.'

Again, the sea. 'Why do all rivers go to the sea?' I asked.

'It's simple,' he answered me. 'Rivers are born up high, on the mountains, and the sea is down low, in the cavities of the earth that need to be filled.'

'So all you have to do is follow a river, any river or stream, and you'll surely reach the sea?'

'That's right. You can't go wrong.'

Xeno's words struck a deep chord in me, I'm not sure why. Maybe certain phrases we pronounce are involuntarily prophetic, in one way or in the exactly opposite way, like oracles.

'Can I ask you another question?' I asked.

'Yes, if it's the last. We have to get ready to ford the river.'

'What about the sea? Is there one alone? Or, if there are many, do they flow into one another or remain separate like closed basins?'

'They flow into the river Ocean that surrounds the earth.'

'All of them?'

'I said only one question. Yes, that's right. All of them.'

I would have liked to ask him how he knew that all of them flowed into the Ocean, but I'd already asked one question too many.

From the top of the hill we watched the fording: the river was quite shallow even though it was the end of spring and the army crossed it on foot with no difficulty. First a group of scouts on horseback and then all the others. Again, there was no resistance from the other side. That seemed strange to me but I said nothing.

'Curious, isn't it?' a voice rang out behind me, as if my own thoughts had been spoken aloud. 'No resistance here either. General Abrocomas isn't looking for a fight. He's disappeared.'

Xeno turned and found Sophos at his back, appearing as suddenly as he had when we were camping near Tarsus.

'It doesn't seem so strange to me. Abrocomas simply doesn't feel up to tangling with Cyrus. That's all.'

'You know that's not true,' retorted Sophos. Then he spurred his horse down the slope towards the ford.

Once across the river, we continued our journey, heading south. The countryside was flat and level but when the sun sank into the horizon, becoming an enormous red sphere, that empty, arid, abandoned expanse was transformed. Under the midday sun, the steppe was white and blinding. After dark, it was transfigured. The tiniest rocks or salt crystals glittered with iridescent reflections. Wild grasses that were invisible by day took shape, their stems, touched by the evening breeze, vibrated like the strings of a lyre, and their shadows grew taller and taller as the sun descended, ready to flatten in a moment when it dipped beneath the horizon.

The further we got from my village, the more I felt prey to a panicky lightheadedness, a fear of the emptiness around me. When the feeling overcame me I would seek out Xeno, the only person I knew among the thousands and thousands that passed in front of me, that flowed beneath my gaze. But he too was like the steppe, arid and parched by day, no different from anyone else. I couldn't have expected anything different: no man in the Greek army would ever be attentive to a woman in the light of day, wary of his comrades' derision.

But after the sun had fallen, when night descended and the endless expanse of the steppe became animated with fleeting shadows, with the rustling of invisible wings, when a strange kind of serenity spread over the camp and everywhere the men sat around campfires conversing in dozens of different dialects, then Xeno changed as well. He squeezed my hand in the dark or brushed my hair with his hand or my lips with a light kiss.

At moments like this I felt that I wasn't sorry for having abandoned my family and my friends, the quiet summer evenings, the suspended, timeless atmosphere surrounding the well at Beth Qadà.

8

THE LAST FRESH MEAT we'd have for a long time was consumed during the first days of march along the Euphrates, and again it was thanks to Xeno's hunting skill. There were great numbers of birds as big as chickens which were rather easy to catch. They rose up in a brief, panicky flight and all you had to do was chase them for a while to tire them out and you could capture them with your hands. There were hundreds of them. At first I couldn't understand why they didn't fly away, didn't try to escape. Then I realized that they were all females with nests and that all their flapping and fluttering was meant to lure intruders away from their clutch. In other words, they were sacrificing themselves to save their chicks. Many of the soldiers followed Xeno's example and threw their weapons to the ground to run off after the birds. The less agile of them ended up empty-handed and in a heap, rolling in the dust; others ran like mad without succeeding in grabbing their prey. They had plenty of fun doing it, laughing and making a real racket. Each time that one of them managed to capture his bird, cries and shouts of jubilation came from the rest of the army as if they were watching a wrestling match or a race. They shouted out the name of the lucky man, who raised his trophy high over his head for all to see.

I was incredulous as I stood there watching them. The most terrible warriors of the known world, tumbling around like children in the dust. Some of them got too close to the slippery river banks and ended up in the water, or slid into the mud and came out covered from head to foot.

The meat was delicious. I was surprised that it was so tasty, considering the birds were nesting. But after that we had to go back to our supplies, to the flour, wheat and olive oil that every unit carried along. We even had a market travelling with us, but the foods you could buy there cost a lot.

The landscape was changing, becoming bleaker and more arid the further south we went. Even the banks of the Euphrates were barren. The river coursed through a deep bed of sandstone which left no space for grass to grow, let alone trees. The hay and fodder we were carrying were enough at first to feed the pack animals, but then the forage ran out and the animals began to die. They were butchered, then, and the meat distributed to the troops: it was tough and stringy, but there was nothing else.

Cyrus often showed his face and Xeno was able to speak with him more than once, along with Proxenus of Boeotia and Agias of Arcadia. The prince was usually surrounded by the noblemen who accompanied him and by his guard. They were young, vigorous men, splendidly decked out with golden bracelets at their wrists and golden-hilted and sheathed swords at their sides. Their eyes were constantly on their prince, to ensure that his every need was attended to. I remember how they reacted the day we happened to reach a bend in the river. There was vegetation there: grass, flowers and plants, and the column almost instinctively veered in that direction, seeking shelter from the brutal heat. But then one of the wagons got stuck in the mud. It was carrying an important load: javelins and spears, trappings for the horses, even money perhaps. There must have been something precious in those bags, from the way Cyrus frowned. At the merest wrinkle of his brow, all of the noblemen jumped off their horses, dressed as they were with their embroidered trousers and cloaks fringed with silver and gold, and dived into the mire to push the wagon back out, to stop it from sinking.

Day after day we marched, and the conditions grew harsher and more taxing, especially for the women. I travelled on a wagon drawn by a pair of mules because I was Xeno's woman, but almost all of the baggage animals had died, and I'd often see the others – the slaves and prostitutes – trudging through the dust behind their masters, and this troubled me. There were differences between them too. The prettier ones were on mule-back or on a wagon so they wouldn't wear themselves out, the others were on foot.

There was no relief until nightfall. Then you could bathe in the river, and although the stream beds were dry, they abounded in withered shrubs and bushes that could be used to start a fire and cook what little we had. The sky extended its black dome over the camp, dotted with an infinity of twinkling lights, and you could hear the cries of the night birds and the howling of jackals from the depths of the immense, boundless desert. Almost none of the men had ever seen the desert. They came from a land of small valleys and high mountains, of narrow coves and golden beaches, a land that changed at nearly every step of your journey, every day and every hour. The desert was always the same, they complained, as vast and flat as the sea in a dead calm. Even the air was unfamiliar, and disquieting. When the moon was full, the white of the chalky terrain and the dark blue of the sky were pervaded by an unreal azure light, still and somehow terrifying in its eerie strangeness.

The further we got from the sea, the more the men felt the need to sing together at night or to talk quietly, sitting around the fire until late. I didn't understand the words to their songs but I could feel the emotion. It was homesickness. Those bronze warriors ached for their families, for their children and their wives, for the villages where they hoped to return rich and respected, so they could talk about their adventures one day, as old men, tell their stories to children gathered around the hearth on a cold winter evening. The burbling of the river outside the camp and the low hum of the men sitting around campfires inside combined to form a diffuse, indistinct murmur, and yet the voice of the river was created by the ruffling of countless tiny waves and barely visible ripples, and the other sound was in reality made up of thousands of voices telling a myriad of different stories, the stories of each one of the Ten Thousand who had pushed themselves further than any man of their race had ever dared to venture.

SINCE THE START OF their mission, the army had never done battle, except for Menon of Thessaly's incursion at Tarsus, and for the time being the expedition still felt more like an excursion or an exploratory expedition than like a military endeavour. But every morning that the sun came up, every time the warriors took up their arms and started on their march, their eyes scanned the horizon along its entire breadth, looking for a sign, an indication of human presence, of movement of any sort from that vast, monotonous territory. When would the enemy appear? They had no doubts that it would happen. By day or night, at dawn or dusk, they would make their presence felt. Perhaps at their backs or perhaps face-to-face, barring their way. Perhaps with a swift cavalry raid. And yet the days passed and nothing happened. The dust, the sun, the suffocating temperature, the shimmering of the air on the earth's scorched surfaces, the mid-day dust devils: these were their constant companions. When would the enemy arrive?

That's what I would ask Xeno, and with the question on my lips I'd be gripped by a kind of quiet frenzy, as if I were one of those warriors preparing to face the most formidable trial of their lives.

Then one day a returning group of scouts reported that they had found a great deal of horse dung and traces of passage in an area of the desert near Cunaxa, a village not far from Babylon. They also said they'd seen a reconnaissance patrol passing through a grove of palm trees. Could this be the sign they'd been waiting for?

Cyrus ordered all his men to set off immediately in full battle order, armed from head to toe. Their shields alone would be transported by wagon, ready to be slung on at the last moment.

There was tension, a sense of spasmodic expectation. Groups of horsemen were coming and going continually, reporting, heading out, others riding in, exchanging terse words with their officers. Others were using their polished shields to send off signals, others still waved yellow flags.

The men marched in silence.

Xeno took up arms as well. He was wearing the armour that I'd seen hanging from his horse as he washed himself at the well at Beth Qadà. This time I looked at it closely: the bronze breastplate with its leather shoulder straps finely decorated in red, his greaves which were also made of bronze, smooth and polished. The ivory hilt of his sword extended from an embossed sheath. On his shoulders was an ochre-coloured cloak.

'Why are you carrying a weapon?' I nervously asked.

He didn't answer. The situation must have seemed so evident that there was no need for comment, but I was sorry he wouldn't speak. I was upset; I wanted to hear his voice. I realized at once that by nightfall everything would be lost – or won – by our warriors: riches, glory, honour, estates. But for me the stakes were much higher. If there was victory I would have more time with the man I loved, although I didn't know how much. If there was defeat there was no limit to the misery I might suffer. His voice interrupted my thoughts.

'Oh gods!'

I looked south. The sun was in the middle of the sky, above our heads.

A cloud of whitish dust veiled the horizon as far as the eye could see.

'It's a sandstorm,' I said.

'No. It's them.'

'That's not possible. It's too wide.'

'It's them, I'm telling you. Look.'

I could see black specks filling the white cloud and then as the distance shortened, I could see glittering. Arms. The tips of the spears, the shields.

Lightning bolts, inside a storm cloud.

'That's why we never met with any resistance. Not at the Cilician Gates, not at the Syrian Gates, not on the Euphrates at Thapsacus . . .' said Xeno without taking his eyes off the storm of dust and iron that was closing in with a roar, like the wind at Beth Qadà. 'Artaxerxes wanted to lure his brother here, here where he's massed all the forces of the empire, in this endless expanse with nowhere for us to take shelter, or build up any kind of defence. He means to crush Cyrus once and for all.'

'So this is the end,' I said softly and I lowered my head to hide my tears.

The bugles blared. Cyrus rode through at a gallop on his Arabian charger, shouting out orders in three or four different languages. Ariaeus had the horns sounded. Clearchus pulled up short on his horse in the middle of the plain and roared out, 'Men, stand to! Front line here to me! Fall in!'

Like the limbs of a single body the warriors ran in compact groups to take their places on the battle front. One block joined another, the line growing longer and longer, until it stretched all the way to the left bank of the Euphrates.

The enemy army was now in clear sight. There were warriors from one hundred nations: Egyptians, Arabs, Cilicians, Cappadocians, Medes, Carduchi, Colchians, Calibians, Parthians, Sogdians, Bithynians, Phrygians, Mossynoeci . . .

You could plainly see their armour, the colours of their garments, the weapons they held, hear the battle cries, muffled by the din of tens of thousands of galloping horses and hundreds of thousands of marching men. Beneath all this, deep and continuous, a metallic rumbling that seemed to accompany and exalt all the other sounds: it was coming from the flanks, where the cloud of dust was denser.

'Chariots!' shouted Xeno.

'Scythed chariots . . .' said a voice behind us.

Sophos.

He had appeared out of nowhere, as always. Xeno, who had been about to mount Halys, turned to face him.

'. . . with sharp blades extending from the wheel hubs, and more under the driver's seat. If you think you can save yourself by diving under the cart, forget it. They'll cut you into little strips, lengthwise. Ingenious and effective.'

I was horror-struck.

Sophos was armed. He was holding his helmet under his left arm and his shield was hanging from the horse's harness. He dug in his heels and headed towards Clearchus.

Xeno took my hand. 'Don't you ever move from here. Don't get off this wagon for any reason. The wagons, with all the food and supplies, will be taken to the centre of the camp and protected. I must go to Clearchus. Do as I say and we'll see each other tonight. If you don't do as I say, you'll die. Farewell.'

I had no time to say anything and maybe I wouldn't have been able to get any words out anyway, I felt so choked up and breathless. Only when he was too far to hear me did I yell, 'Come back! Come back to me!' The wagon's driver whipped the mules and took me to where the supplies were being gathered. Just a small hillock, really, slightly higher than the plain itself, but high enough to overlook the entire battle scene. I could see everything that was happening without missing a thing. A terrible, yet very privileged, place to be. I was the one who would tell Xeno later the details of the massacre that was to take place.

All of the army units were in motion by then. The Asians were to the left, covering three-quarters of the formation. Cyrus was at the very centre, splendidly armed and dressed, surrounded by his elite troops, archers and cavalry, protected by their shining gold and silver breastplates. They were a wonder to see, and were lightning-quick in their movements. Each of them bore a spear with a green standard flying from its shaft. Far to the right stood Clearchus and his red cloaks.

I saw Xeno break away from the massed troops and head in his direction. For a few moments he was alone in the middle of the plain, resplendent on his white horse. How could he pass unnoticed? What would happen to him before evening? My heart broke just thinking about it. I watched as he galloped, spun about, full of life and strength, and finally stopped his stallion before the high command.

Dreadful images filled my eyes, blinding me to the sight of that splendid young horseman: I saw Xeno falling to the ground with an arrow piercing his heart, covered with dust and blood, I saw him trying to drag himself to safety, wounded, dying, I saw him trying to escape on foot, pursued by enemies on horseback who finished him off. I wanted to scream. I realized that they'd reached the point of no return.

The two armies were about to clash. This was the moment in which the Chera of death passed among the ranks and files to pick her chosen ones.

From the mound I was standing on I could clearly see that the enemy formation was much longer than our own on the left, and it was easy to imagine that they would try to outflank us on that side. Where was Xeno at that moment? Where was his white stallion? Where was he? Where? Where?

I scanned the lines frantically but could not spot him.

The space between the two formations had narrowed to no more than three hundred paces. The centre of the enemy's army was beyond the far left of our own front line. There was Artaxerxes, standing straight and still on his chariot, resplendent as a star. I could see the red standard that accompanied him on the battlefield.

I saw Cyrus send a messenger to Clearchus. A brief, animated argument ensued, then the messenger rode back.

Two hundred paces.

Cyrus in person abandoned the formation and raced towards Clearchus. The prince seemed to be giving him an order, but nothing happened. Cyrus turned back. You could tell by the way he rode that he was enraged.

One hundred and fifty paces.

I could see everything that was happening in the rearguard of Artaxerxes's army. Why wasn't Cyrus standing where I was? From here he would be able to move his units like pawns on a chessboard. I knew why. The commander must show that he is the bravest of all. He has to be the first in the line of danger

Wrapped in a cloud of dust, the chariot squadrons moved invisibly just behind the front lines on the left wing and the right. They were about to charge Clearchus's men, about to charge Xeno! How could our soldiers survive the attack of such terrifying machines? I screamed out with all the breath I had in me, 'Watch your right!' But how could they have heard me?

One hundred paces.

A roar.

The Persian infantry lines suddenly parted, letting through the chariots, which swooped forward to mow down the red cloaks.

Unexpectedly, Cyrus charged forth with his guard at break-neck speed, cutting across the field and carving a narrow, diagonal path straight for the centre of the enemy formation. Cyrus wanted Artaxerxes! The two brothers, one on one, to the death!

Clearchus had the bugles sounded. The javelin-throwers and Thracian skirmishers ran straight for the chariots, hurling their pikes at the charioteers. Some of them hit their mark and the charioteers fell, leaving their driverless chariots to veer off course and tip over. Others, speeding forward, crashed into the wrecks and toppled over as well into a monstrous tangle of wooden splinters, shards of metal and human and animal flesh.

More mounted peltasts raced towards the chariots, hurling

arrows and missiles or jumping onto the chariots themselves to engage the drivers and the warriors in deadly duels. Those chariots that managed to forge on were greeted by more bugle calls: the Greek infantry ranks opened to leave a wide gap in front of each scythed chariot. When they had rushed headlong through the entire formation the archers in the rear turned and aimed their bows at the charioteers and warriors. The driverless chariots were carried off into the empty desert.

Fifty paces.

Clearchus had the bugles sounded again.

Meanwhile, Cyrus's squadron was engaging the imperial guard – the Immortals, the personal defenders of the Great King – in an ear-splitting explosion of violence.

The sound of pipes soared from the ranks of the red cloaks, who lowered their spears and advanced at a steady pace, in silence, against the enemy. Against the frenzy, the uncontrolled fury, the screaming horde.

In silence, their heavy steps accompanied by the drums and pipes.

The advance of Artaxerxes's Asian troops faltered, their lines wavered. Clearchus urged his own men forward with the cry of war:

Alalalai!

No one stood a chance against the red cloaks. The phalanx charged, crashing like an avalanche over the enemy front, breaking it in two. Plunging deep into the opening they'd made, they overwhelmed the entire Persian left wing, cut it off from the rest of the army and took off after the scattering soldiers in hot pursuit. Soon they were covered by dust and I lost them from sight.

The space they'd left empty was promptly filled by swarms of enemy horsemen. Great numbers of them were soon storming forward and lapping at the base of my hill. I was so frightened that I left the wagon, which was in a vulnerable position, as far as I could tell, to seek shelter in a more secluded area. Hidden, I hoped, by a copse of palm trees, I anxiously continued to watch the unfolding battle below.

As long as Cyrus and his crack troops stayed in the fight, most of Ariaeus's Asian troops held firm. Every now and then, I'd look at the sun, which seemed to be nailed like a burning shield into the empty white sky. The sounds of the gigantic battle raging below reached me muted and confused. Only the shrillest cries of terror or pain pierced the air so thick with dust, blood and sweat. When the wind changed, the whinnying of the horses and the screeching of the chariots ran through me like a sword.

The light of the sun slowly became redder and something happened, right at the middle of the enemy front, something that I couldn't understand because everything was wrapped in dense soot. But that was the moment in which Cyrus's army started to break down and was rapidly put to flight.

It was then that I glimpsed what I took for a group of our men on horseback along the banks of the Euphrates, and I thought I saw Xeno's ochre-coloured cloak in the middle of the galloping band. I took off at a run down the hillside. A foolhardy action indeed. Some of the Persian horsemen who had penetrated the ranks of Ariaeus's Asian troops spotted me and headed straight in my direction.

I turned around immediately and began running crazily back up the hill to reach shelter behind the circle of wagons. Impossible. They were already upon me. I threw myself to the ground and covered my head with my hands.

Time stood still. I breathed in dust and was enveloped in a cloud of terror.

Nothing happened at first and then, suddenly, a body fell on top of me, crushing me, and a trickle of blood seeped onto my clothing. I screamed and tried to get free. Someone had run through one of my pursuers with a javelin.

And he was galloping towards them now and towards me.

His face was covered by his helmet but I recognized his arms, his horse, his white cloak, spattered with blood.

Menon!

I remember it as if it were now. My eyes were so concentrated on him that each and every move he made was burned into my mind, moment by moment, and it looked to me as if he was advancing suspended above the earth in a space that didn't belong to me or to the rest of the world. I felt it again in the physical violence with which he burst into the pack that had taken off after me. He hurled a javelin and a second horseman tumbled to the ground. He brandished his sword, rearing up his horse. The steed's hoofs cleaved my attackers apart and Menon struck them down one by one with precision and deadly power. Then he took off his helmet, held out his arm, lifted me onto his horse and galloped off towards a spot which was far away from the battlefield and the circle of wagons, to a thick grove of tamarisks. There he lowered me to the ground. He smiled at me for an instant, with his white teeth, his wolf's teeth. He gave me a teasing, cryptic look, then rode back to the aid of his men, who were surrounded. He fought like a raging lion, but they were hopelessly outnumbered. Where were all the others? The daylight had become red as blood. Why was no one arriving? Why? What had happened?

One man alone, on horseback, galloped out of nowhere, brandishing a spear in one hand and a sword in the other, guiding his horse by the power of his legs alone. Powerful, massive, overwhelming. Sophos!

He hurled his spear and ran through the enemy commander from front to back and then broke into the fray sword in hand like a fury, striking left and right with awesome power. Menon and his men took a deep breath and were able to counter-attack with renewed vigour. They wiped out the remaining adversaries and then raced off across the plain headed south, perhaps to meet up with Clearchus's troops.

Only Sophos remained.

He cleaned his sword, sheathed it and sat still as a stone just staring into nowhere. He had no intention of fighting on, as if the whole ordeal had not touched him. But he was interested in the progress of the battle, which was drawing to an end.

The uproar continued for a while, but as the sun set everything quietened down until all noise seemed to cease.

Then Sophos reached my hiding spot and signalled for me to follow him to the top of the hill. I did. The scene that I saw left me speechless with horror. Before me was a vast expanse all strewn with the corpses of men and horses. Many animals were wounded or lamed, and they dragged on laboriously, snorting their pain from bleeding nostrils. In the distance I could see the dust raised by the winning army as they withdrew.

Human beings unrecognizable as such staggered through the slaughtered remains. Suddenly Sophos's gaze and my own stopped on a figure in the exact centre of our field of vision. It was a human figure, straight and still, with an unreal stillness. Sophos's seemingly impassive expression twisted into a grimace as he headed off immediately in that direction, leading his horse by the reins. I followed him over soil slippery with blood as we made our way through the fetid, sickening atmosphere.

It was Cyrus.

His naked body had been stuck onto a sharp pole that came out of his back. His head, almost completely detached from his body, was hanging onto his chest. I was sure that at any moment I would find Xeno's body too, buried among the heaps of corpses littering the ground. I started screaming then, completely out of control, screaming out all my desperation. I had never seen and could never have imagined such horror.

Sophos turned to me and snarled, 'Shut up, stop that!'

It wasn't to humiliate me; he was trying to hear another sound, which was becoming clearer, and closer. It was coming from the Euphrates. Troops, advancing and . . . singing!

'They're ours,' said Sophos.

'Ours? How can that be?'

'They chased the left wing all day and now they're returning. Menon and his men were ahead of the rest. Your Xenophon will be with them . . . if he's still alive.'

'Why are they singing?'

A red cloud was approaching now from alongside the river.

'They're singing the paean. They think we've won.'

We waited next to Cyrus's corpse until the officers riding at the front of the returning group saw us and raced in our direction. Clearchus, Socrates, Agias and Proxenus. Xeno soon arrived as well, his clothing and weapons so drenched in blood that I barely recognized him. It was all I could do not to run straight into his arms, I had to be content with the expression in his eyes that mirrored my own. Menon arrived as well, at the head of his Thessalian cavalrymen. I don't know if he could read the gratitude in my eyes when I sought his out.

Clearchus's face turned to stone. 'How did this happen?'

'And where is Ariaeus?' asked Proxenus.

Sophos pointed at a dark spot about half a parasang north of us. 'Down there, that's where he is. With his men. The bastard will already be negotiating with Artaxerxes by now.'

Clearchus gestured at Cyrus's body. 'What about him?'

Sophos answered with another question. 'What did he want from you when he rode over before the battle?'

'He wanted me to leave the banks of the Euphrates and charge the centre of the enemy formation where the Great King was.'

'Why didn't you?'

'It would have been suicide. The enemy line was already two-thirds longer than our own on the left; if we had left the Euphrates they would have encircled us on that side as well.'

'And that would have been the end.'

'That's right.'

'So what's this, then?' replied Sophos sarcastically, waving his hand over the field. 'Cyrus knew that he was greatly outnumbered, but he had a weapon that he believed in, blindly: your soldiers. Had you obeyed his order you would have broken through at the centre and overrun the King in person.'

Clearchus snapped back resentfully, 'In such extreme situations I only take orders from Sparta.'

Sophos looked straight into his eyes.

'I am Sparta,' he said. And walked off.

Meanwhile the song of Clearchus's soldiers was fading away as, little by little, they approached and were forced to take stock of the bitter truth. They thought they had won.

They had lost.

9

THE SUN WAS SETTING when two horsemen arrived at a fast gallop. It was the first time I'd ever seen them, but I would come to know them well, and once I'd also learned the language I would be able to pronounce their names. They were Agasias of Stymphalus and Lycius of Syracuse.

They jumped to the ground, breathing hard, and turned to Clearchus.

'Commander,' exclaimed Agasias. 'I thank the gods you made it back here. Artaxerxes's army is thirty stadia from here. We had no idea of what had happened to you. Our unit stayed with Ariaeus all through the battle We managed to hold firm and we didn't lose the supplies. Some of the Asians fled from their camp and took refuge behind our lines.'

'That's right,' confirmed Lycius. 'There were two women from Cyrus's harem as well. One is that beautiful girl from Phocaea. You should have seen her: as the Persians were closing in she ran out of Cyrus's tent stark naked and tried to cross over to us. She was being chased by a swarm of barbarians. So there we were, yelling and telling her to run faster. You would have thought we were at the stadium! As soon as she was close enough we opened our ranks to let her through then closed them again. The barbarians had to bugger off without their prize.'

Clearchus frowned. 'Never mind about the girl,' he said. 'What's Ariaeus up to?'

'He's retreated,' replied Lycius 'He abandoned the camp and

is hiding out in the desert. I know where he is. If you want, I'll take you there tomorrow.'

'Are any of our men with him?'

'A battalion. They stayed behind to keep an eye on things.'

'They did well. What about the King?'

'He's gone. He's left behind one of his generals. Tissaphernes, I think. What shall we do, Commander?'

'It's nearly dark; we won't go anywhere now. We'll spend the night here. Go and join your men at Ariaeus's camp while you can still see. Set up a double ring of sentries and keep your eyes open. If you have cavalry, send them out to patrol the territory. Tomorrow we'll regroup and decide what to do. Be careful of Ariaeus. I don't trust that barbarian.'

'We're off, then,' said Agasias. 'Good luck, Commander.'

They returned to their horses and rode off swiftly in the near-darkness. We set up camp for the night.

In reality, we had no tents, or cots or blankets. We had no water or food. The men curled up where they were, totally done in. The uninjured helped the wounded, improvising bandages. They had fought for hours, marched for many stadia, and in the moment that they desperately needed food and rest they had nothing but the bare ground and the cloaks on their shoulders.

We had wheat and salted olives on our wagon, but it was so dark that I couldn't find the key for the food chest. All I could find was the water skin. I remembered having seen plants that I was familiar with nearby: some of them hid tubers underground, others had a salty taste. I managed to dig up some of the edible roots and pick some of the leaves and I brought them to Xeno. It was not much of a dinner but it helped to still our pangs of hunger. Then I stretched out next to him under the same cloak. Despite the dangerous and completely precarious situation, I was deliriously happy to have him next to me. He was warm and alive, while the whole day I'd been terrified that I'd find a stiff, cold body at nightfall. It was a miracle, a gift from the gods, and

I thanked them in my heart as I kissed him, held him tightly, stroked his dust-covered hair.

'I thought I'd never see you again,' he whispered in my ear.

'I had nearly lost hope myself. So much killing, so much horror . . .'

'It's war, Abira,' he said. 'That's the way war is. It always has been like this and always will be. Sleep now . . . sleep.'

Even today, when I think back on that night I can't believe it. Ten thousand men lying on the ground all around us. Hungry, exhausted, wounded. A huge, menacing enemy army looming somewhere in the desert. Our comrades back at the camp wouldn't be closing an eye that night for fear of what they might expect from Ariaeus. And yet that was the most beautiful night of my life. I didn't think of what might happen the next day – actually the realization that there might not be a next day made me experience those few hours with an intensity of emotion that I'd never felt before. Perhaps I'll never feel that way again in my whole life.

That night I understood what it truly means to love someone with your whole self, for two people to become a single being. Adding your warmth to his, feeling your own heart beating in unison with the heart of the man holding you in his arms. All I wanted was for that moment to stretch into infinity. And that's what happened. By some unexplainable miracle, time spun out beyond imagining so that every instant lasted years and years.

I thought of my friends sleeping in their warm, clean beds in houses that smelled of fresh plaster, and I did not envy them, and I don't envy them now that they have sons and daughters, perhaps, and a husband who takes care of them, while I have no one. I don't envy them because I made love with the ground as my bed and the sky as my ceiling, and every kiss, every breath, every heartbeat made me fly higher and higher, over the desert, over the waters of the Great River, over the horror of that day of blood.

The light of the breaking day awoke us and the men seemed

reluctant to get up, sore all over and perhaps more tired than when they'd lain down. But their willpower and sense of discipline prevailed and soon they were donning their armour and taking their places in the ranks. Xeno took up weapons as well, and from that day on he always acted like a soldier, because that was what was needed.

Just then two horsemen arrived. One was a Greek who had been governor of a Persian province when Cyrus controlled Anatolia. The second was a strange character called Glous, whose shoulder-length hair was gathered at the nape of his neck with a golden pin. Ariaeus had sent them looking for us.

'I never thought we'd find you,' said Glous. 'What happened to you yesterday?'

'We were off chasing the Persians we'd routed, until night-fall.'

'Cyrus is dead,' the other broke in.

Proxenus was about to speak up, but Clearchus stopped him with a low gesture of his hand, and shot a look at all the others as well. He gave the messengers a deep nod.

'The army of the Great King is camped very close by,' continued Cyrus's cohort. 'You are in serious danger.'

'You say so?' retorted Clearchus. 'Listen, friend. We over-whelmed them and we ran them out like dogs. We sliced up quite a few of them and they're being careful to stay clear of us now. If they show up here, no matter how many there are, they'll get what's coming to them. If you want to know what I'd do, I was thinking of attacking them, because it's the last thing they'll expect.'

Glous looked at him as though he were mad. 'Oh right, there's no doubt about that. But wouldn't you say you're slightly outnumbered?'

'At the Fiery Gates eighty years ago we were one against one hundred. If we hadn't been betrayed we would have nailed them to the pass and kicked their sorry arses all the way home.'

'This is different,' replied Glous. 'Here it's flat and open and they have their cavalry. They'll wear you down. They can target you from a distance and pick you off one by one.'

Clearchus cut him off him with a tense gesture of his open hand. 'Go back to Ariaeus. Tell him that if he wants to try to take the throne we'll put ourselves at his service. Two of my men will come with you to lay out our plan . . .'

Sophos stepped forward without having been called. Clearchus scanned his men until he found Menon of Thessaly. Clots of blood smeared his hair and clothes, but there wasn't a single mark on his skin.

'. . . and him,' he concluded his unfinished thought, nodding in Menon's direction. Then his expression changed to a look of distress. 'I just need to feed my boys, understand? I'm like a father to them. I punish them harshly if they do wrong, but I worry about them eating and drinking and having what they need. Understand? My boys need to eat . . .'

Glous shook his head in bewilderment and exchanged a glance with the others. They remounted and rode off together.

Clearchus turned to his men. 'We're going back,' he ordered, and set off at a trot.

I couldn't understand why he wanted us back in that field of slaughter, but it turned out to be our salvation, at least for a while. I'd soon realize why.

He had the men gather all of the arrows and javelins scattered over the ground or protruding from the corpses and then, using the wreckage of the chariots, heap up enough wood to start a fire. Others skinned and butchered the carcasses of twenty or so mules and horses and spit-roasted the chunks of meat on the embers.

'Horsemeat builds blood,' said Clearchus. 'Eat, you'll need your strength.' He went about cutting up the meat and handing it out to his soldiers, as a father does with his children. But there wasn't enough for more than ten thousand men. He gave the last piece to an eighteen-year-old, without saving anything for himself.

They were just finishing when General Socrates rode up. 'We have visitors,' he announced.

'Again?' asked Clearchus, getting to his feet from where he had been sitting with his men.

'They speak our language,' replied Socrates, and let through a couple of men preceded by a flag of truce.

'My name is Phalinus,' said the first.

'I'm Ctesias,' said the second.

'Ctesias?' repeated Clearchus. 'But aren't you . . .'

The man who had claimed that name was about fifty years old, balding, and dressed in Persian garb. He nodded. 'Yes . . . I'm the doctor of the Great King, Artaxerxes.'

'Ah,' replied Clearchus. 'And may I ask how your illustrious patient is feeling?'

'He's well, but Cyrus nearly managed to kill him. He attacked his own brother like a bloodthirsty beast. His spear pierced the King's breastplate and cut through his skin. Luckily it was only a flesh wound and I was able to stitch it up.'

'Good job,' said Clearchus. 'I wouldn't mind a doctor like you myself, but I'm afraid I can't afford it. So tell me, what good fortune brings you here?'

'That's a question I should be asking you, actually,' replied the royal physician with an ironic smile.

Clearchus stared at him for a moment in silence. 'I imagine you know the answer to that quite well, Ctesias, but humour me, if you will: why has the Great King sent me his personal doctor? Does he think I . . . have a cold? Do you think a hot compress might do the trick? Or a nice infusion of hemlock?'

Ctesias pretended he hadn't heard: 'We're Greek. He thought that was reason enough.'

'Excellent, I agree, but allow me to remind you of a couple of things. We were engaged by Cyrus. Cyrus is dead. We have nothing against the Great King . . .'

'I believe you,' interrupted Phalinus, 'but that doesn't change matters. There are a great number of you, and you are armed. Go to his tent, now, wearing only your tunics. Implore his clemency, and I'll see what I can do for you.'

'Did I hear you right?' Clearchus retorted. 'Implore his clemency?' He turned to his commanders. 'My fellow officers, listen to this one! What a request! Would you mind giving these kind guests of ours an answer? I have to leave for just a moment.'

I was so surprised by his behaviour. Why would he walk away just then, at such a crucial moment? The generals turned to the messengers without batting an eye.

'You'll have to kill me first,' replied Cleanor of Arcadia, a formidable warrior with a voice that sliced into you like a sword.

Proxenus of Boeotia's tone was more accommodating, but not his words. 'In our tunics, right? Fine, Phalinus, but maybe you can tell me what will happen to my men if we do such a thing. Will they be . . . butchered? Impaled? Skinned alive? That's the way they do things here, isn't it? We've seen how he treated his little brother.'

Phalinus did not react. He only tried to make his request clearer. You could see he was a good negotiator. He was a big man, but very calm and attentive; he weighed his words and didn't waste a single one. 'The Great King knows that he's won because he defeated and killed Cyrus, and you were on his brother's side. What's more, you're in the middle of his territory and so you are his. You're surrounded. There are canals all around you as well as two wide, impassable rivers, one to your left and one to your right. You have no way out, and if you decide to go out fighting he will send so many soldiers out against you that you'd never be able to kill them all, not even if they offered you their throats for the cutting.'

Xeno in the meantime had pushed his way into the centre of the group of officers while I lingered behind. He listened to every word, and he even spoke up, despite the fact that he had no authority to do so. 'Listen, Phalinus, your demands are

ou can't ignore the fact that the Persians who
against us in the conflict were routed. You cannot
to negotiate as if we'd been defeated.'

art boy!' replied Phalinus. 'You sound like a philosopher.
you're delusional if you think you can challenge the greatest empire on earth by trying to reason your way around things. Forget it.'

'Wait a moment,' another officer broke in. 'Why don't we try to come to an agreement? You came to make a deal, right? We're excellent fighters. We've lost our employer, so we're back on the market. You've been having trouble in Egypt. Why don't you tell your King that we'll take care of things for him? I'm sure we could do that.'

Phalinus shook his head. 'You could take Egypt, all on your own? Oh gods, just who do you think you are?' Just then Clearchus reappeared and Phalinus turned straight to him. 'Listen, there's a lot of confusion here, everyone is saying something different. I need to talk to one person alone, one person who can speak for you all. So, Clearchus, do you want to tell me what you've decided? Yes or no?'

Clearchus drew up close. 'Listen. I know that we're up to our necks in trouble. But you're a Greek, damnit, there's no one listening to us. Except for the doctor, but he's Greek too, isn't he? Can't you just stop being an ambassador for a moment and give us some advice, from one Greek to another? One man to another? You know, if we manage to pull ourselves out of this shithole we'll never forget that you gave us good advice, and on the other side of the sea you'll always have ten thousand good friends to count on if the wind changes. You can never be sure of anything in this world.'

Xeno had returned to where I was standing. No one had noticed me because my hair was pulled up under a cap and I was wearing a man's cloak.

'What is he saying?' I asked.

'I think he's stalling for time. He's waiting for a signal from

Sophos or Menon about the situation at the Asian camp. He wants to know what Ariaeus is up to.'

A couple of men standing in front of us hushed us. 'Shut up, will you? We want to hear what's going on.'

Phalinus answered. 'If there were any way you could get out of this, I would tell you about it, I swear to you. But you can see for yourself that there's no way out. You can't head back and you can't go forward either. Surrender, and I'll try to put in a good word. You will too, Ctesias, won't you? The King will certainly listen to his personal physician, the man who saved his life.'

Ctesias nodded benevolently.

'See?' continued Phalinus. 'He'll put in a good word for you, you needn't worry. So, what's your answer?'

Clearchus got even closer and Phalinus instinctively took half a step back in order to stay out of arm's reach. 'I'd like to thank you for your advice, my friend, I truly appreciate it but, you see, I've thought this all through. Showing up in our tunics, on bended knee, begging for clemency . . . I'm sorry, that just doesn't seem like a good idea. In conclusion, there's no question in my mind: no.'

Phalinus could barely disguise his displeasure and he remained in silence a few moments to gather his thoughts. The sun was high and the buzzing of the flies attracted by thousands of rotting bodies was almost unbearable. Swarms of crows had appeared overhead, and several large vultures were circling above waiting for the chance to swoop down and begin their banqueting. Phalinus looked up at the vultures and then at Clearchus, while Ctesias maintained a detached attitude as if he had been sent merely to observe and not to get involved. In the end, Phalinus said, 'If that's the way things stand I have to warn you of what you're up against. As long as you remain here where you are now, a truce will stand between you and the King. If you move, that will mean war. What shall I tell him?'

Clearchus did not seem upset in the least. 'What you've just said,' he replied. 'If we stay here it's a truce, if we move it's war.'

Phalinus bit his lower lip in anger and went off without another word.

'It didn't go the way he thought it would,' observed Socrates.

'No. I'd say not,' replied Clearchus. 'It won't be pretty for him when he has to tell the King. In any case, we can't remain here. We have nothing to eat. Unless we stay strong we're dead.'

Just then Agasias and Sophos rode up. 'Ariaeus was wounded, but he'll pull through,' said Sophos. 'Menon decided to stay down at the camp with Glous.'

'What did Ariaeus say about my proposal?'

'No, he says forget about that – no high-ranking Persian would accept him as king, even if we won the throne for him. But if we join him, he says he'll lead us out of here. He said to come as quickly as we can if we decide to accept his offer. If we're not there by tomorrow morning, he's leaving alone.'

'I see,' replied Clearchus. 'Did you run into any trouble getting back here?'

'No,' replied Sophos. 'The whole area is very quiet. The Persians are staying out of sight.'

'For the moment,' Cleanor spoke up.

'For the moment,' Clearchus admitted.

He turned to the bugler and had him sound the call for a meeting of his staff. The generals who commanded the large battle units and the battalion commanders rushed over. Clearchus presided over the war council.

Xeno meant to join me, and was walking in my direction when he crossed paths with Sophos, who was heading towards the staff meeting.

'Come with me,' Sophos told him.

'But I'm not part of the . . .'

'Now you are,' replied Sophos curtly. 'Come on, then.'

Xeno followed without objecting. I sat down on the ground next to his horse Halys, his servant, his wagon and his bags. It was everything Xeno owned, and I felt it was best not to leave his things unguarded, given the circumstances.

The meeting went on until late afternoon. Xeno returned with Sophos and they stopped about twenty steps away from me. That was where they parted; Sophos took off and Xeno spoke to me.

'Get ready,' he said. 'We'll be moving at sunset.'

'Where will we go?'

'We're going to join up with the others and then, we'll see . . . Is there anything left to eat?'

'Yes, I can make some flat bread. There are still some salted olives and a little wine.'

'That will be fine. We'll eat early, before leaving.'

In truth there were more supplies in the wagon, but if I'd told him so, Xeno would have invited someone to dinner. Socrates or Agias or both of them. I didn't want to risk running out of food before we had a way to get more.

Of course I couldn't stop the aroma of the baking bread from wafting through the camp. Those poor boys were starving. They were twenty years old and had fought like lions the whole day before. Xeno didn't even need to tell me that: I offered what I could to those closest to us.

Xeno had nothing to write on and that left us time for conversation, especially after I'd poured him a little sweet wine.

'We're in terrible danger, aren't we?'

'Yes,' he replied.

'But there's something I just can't understand. The King's army is so much bigger than ours, why hasn't he attacked us?'

'Because he's afraid.'

'Afraid of what?'

'Of the red-cloaked warriors. Legend has them invincible. Eighty years ago a Spartan king named Leonidas deployed the three hundred men at his command at the Fiery Gates, a narrow mountain pass in central Greece. They held off an army of Persians that was even bigger than this one, for days and days.

They were outnumbered a hundred to one. These men here are made of the same stuff, and yesterday they overwhelmed the Persian left wing even though it was five times their size. The red-cloaked warriors are larger than life. The mere sight of them is enough to strike terror into their enemies. Cyrus was sure that this small contingent would be sufficient to defeat his brother, the most powerful sovereign on earth. He wasn't wrong about that. If Clearchus had obeyed his orders to attack the enemy centre, we'd be in a totally different situation right now.'

'Instead we're in trouble. What will we do?'

'I told you. We'll join the others and then look for a way out.'

I poured a little more wine so he'd forgive my insistence. 'So you think there is a way out?'

Xeno lowered his head. 'I don't know. We're at the heart of the Great King's empire. He fears us, but he's well aware that if we make it back, the world will know that a small group of men managed to get almost all the way to his capital without striking a single blow. Do you know what that means?'

'I think so. That one day a man with the courage and skill to repeat this endeavour could very well succeed. In conquering the Persian empire.'

'That's right. You know . . .' he said to me then, 'do you know that, if you were a man, you could become the adviser to an important person?'

'I don't want to be anyone's adviser. I want to stay with you, if you want me . . . for as long as you want me.'

'You can be sure of that. But you should know that you're joining your destiny to that of an exile. To a man who no longer has a house, belongings, a future. I have nothing.'

I was about to answer when the bugles sounded and Xeno sprang to his feet, grabbing his weapons.

At the second blare the men formed ranks. At the third they started marching. Evening was falling over the desert.

10

THE SOLDIERS MARCHED in silence for about thirty stadia in the dark, straining their ears at any suspect sound. Clearchus and his officers were well aware that by making the first move they had violated the truce and were at war with the Great King. They were trying to understand where he was and what he had in mind.

I was sure that he'd already struck camp and left. He'd won the battle, he'd defeated and killed his brother, and had no time now to worry about a small contingent of mercenaries trapped between the Tigris and the Euphrates.

I looked around from my place on the wagon, searching through the darkness for the shapes of the men passing, bent under the weight of their armour and by the terrible ordeal they'd suffered in the last two days. Their hunger had drained them of all energy, and if they were attacked en masse I didn't know how they would find the strength to react. It all depended on that brief space that separated them from Ariaeus's camp. Fortunately, absolutely nothing happened.

I watched Xeno, riding at a short distance; he showed no signs of apprehension. He was certain that the legend of the red cloaks would keep the enemy away. Maybe that was true, but later he told me something else that was important: the Persians never attack at night; they keep their horses tethered and unharnessed. Maybe he'd read that somewhere, but it turned out to be true, for the whole length of the expedition.

We arrived about midnight and straight away a meeting was

held between our officers and the Asians. Xeno was included for the second time and he found himself face to face with Menon, who had stayed behind with Ariaeus's troops. They barely acknowledged each other. I wandered through the camp pitched by Agasias's battalion, which had remained with the Asians throughout the battle. There were fires here and there, most of them going out, and a few lamps being lit.

I soon noticed a little group of soldiers who were pointing in the direction of a certain tent, and as I got closer I understood why. The lamplight was casting the shadow of a beautiful naked woman, who was bathing inside, onto the thin fabric of the tent.

'What's there to look at! Leave her alone and get out of here!' I exclaimed loudly, hoping they'd take me seriously. I knew instinctively what was about to happen. At first none of them seemed to have heard me; a few of them even started to approach the little pavilion, snickering under their breath. I knew that things were about to take a turn for the worse and thought I should start yelling, but after a few steps they stopped, exchanged a few words and headed off in different directions.

Perhaps they thought that if I'd told them to go away, I had the authority to do so.

I walked up to the pavilion and called out, 'If you don't put out that lamp, you'll be getting unexpected and very undesirable visitors.'

'Who's that? What do you want?' replied an alarmed female voice. My accent sounded strange to her, I'm sure, and she couldn't understand who I was, but she realized that I was a woman and this must have reassured her somewhat.

'I just wanted to warn you: you can see you're naked from outside and there was a group of men gathered here watching the show. I guess you can imagine what was coming next.'

'I'm getting dressed,' replied the voice.

'Can I come in now?' I asked.

'Yes, of course.'

I entered and saw one of the most beautiful girls I'd ever

seen, or ever would see, for that matter. She was blonde, her eyes were amber-coloured and she had the body of a goddess. Her skin was soft and silky, soothed by the rarest and most precious ointments, ready for the most aristocratic caress.

'You must be the one who escaped Cyrus's tent naked when the Persians arrived,' I said, observing her attentively.

The girl smiled. 'How do you know that?'

'The men were talking about it, and then when I saw your shadow projected onto the tent I remembered.'

'Who are you?'

'My name is Abira. I'm Syrian.'

'Are you a slave?'

'No, I'm here with one of the men taking part in this expedition. I came of my own free will.'

The girl looked at me slyly with a curious expression. 'Are you in love with him?'

'Is that so strange?'

'You are in love then,' she said, nodding. 'Sit down. You must be starving. There's something to eat here.'

I could tell she wanted company, perhaps female company in particular. It couldn't be easy for such a beautiful woman to find herself in the middle of a camp with tens of thousands of young, violent men, many of whom had already seen her naked. She opened a chest and offered me a piece of bread with a slice of goat's cheese.

I thanked her. 'You are very beautiful. You must have been the friend of someone very important . . .'

The girl looked down. 'You're observant, and clever as well.'

'Maybe even the most important.'

The girl nodded.

'Cyrus?'

Her eyes clouded. 'How horrible . . .' she said with a tremor in her voice.

'Were you his woman?'

'One of the many in his harem. But he'd often call me to

come and keep him company. He treated me with respect, with affection, maybe even with love. He gave me beautiful gifts, he liked listening to me. He'd always want me to tell him stories, fables . . . he was like a little boy, sometimes, but other times he was hard as steel, completely inscrutable.'

'What happened to you yesterday?'

'I was in the prince's tent when Artaxerxes's soldiers came. They were going wild: killing, burning, pillaging. Some of them burst into our tent and threw themselves onto the other girls. Two of them grabbed me by my gown, but I loosened the belt and the buckles and ran off, naked.'

'You managed to get to our garrison.'

'I ran like I've never run in my whole life. When our troops counter-attacked that evening and drove the Persians out, two of the other girls were found dead. They were raped for hours and hours, until they died.'

I couldn't stand that story, thinking of what an atrocious end those girls had come to. I got up and looked outside. Everything seemed quiet. We were safe, now. At the end of the field I could see a big tent, all lit up inside, where the staff officers were meeting. Xeno was there as well, and I kept asking myself why Sophos had insisted on getting him involved with the high command, Xeno, who wasn't even a soldier. Why had he accepted? Had Sophos promised him something in exchange? What, exactly? And in exchange for what? I wasn't allowed to ask, but I had to know and I would use any means necessary to find out.

I turned towards the prince's gorgeous concubine. The lamp-light cast a golden glow on her ivory skin, and her eyes reflected the flickering light with crystalline transparency, making her gaze so intense it was almost impossible to look at her. I asked her another question that had just occurred to me: 'You're still the most desirable prey on this side of the camp as well, and you don't have a man looking after you any more. How could you bathe in the nude without expecting someone to attack you? There was a group out there, just waiting to . . .'

'Do you think that it was you being there that drove them away? Do you think I would have risked bathing if I didn't feel safe?'

'Well then why . . .'

'Didn't you notice anything outside the tent?'

'It was dark, what was I supposed to see?'

The girl took her lamp and went towards the exit. 'Come here, look.'

I followed her and she lit up a corner of the doorway. There were the heads of two men stuck on spear shafts, with their testicles stuffed in their mouths. I backed away in horror.

'That's what keeps them away,' said the girl calmly.

'Gods, how could you . . .'

'You can't imagine that it was me who beheaded and castrated those two brutes.'

'Who did, then?'

'Well, as soon as I ran over to this side, one of the Greeks came up to me and covered me with his cloak. A group of Ariaeus's Asians tried to claim me for themselves, but the Greeks chased them off. They brought me to this tent and I finally caught my breath, but not for long. As soon as I lay down, two of those Asians managed to slip in here without making any noise at all. I tried to scream but one of them covered my mouth with his hand – it was as huge and hairy as a bear's paw! – and they dragged me out the back. I've never felt so wretched; I knew I'd either end up in the harem of one of those shaggy, stinking beasts or, worse, handed over to a mob of soldiers. But just then I noticed, about twenty paces to our left, a shadow going off in the opposite direction. I decided to give it a desperate try. I bit down hard on my captor's hand and then yelled 'Help!' as loudly as I could. The shadow stopped and in the firelight I could distinctly see a Greek warrior more handsome and powerful than Ares himself! He drew his sword and walked towards us, as calmly as if he were coming over to say hello. I can't tell you how it happened, but the men who had captured me tumbled over one after another like rag dolls. My saviour bent over them, chopped off their heads with two clean sweeps of his sword and stuck them there where you saw them in front of the tent. Then he sliced off their testicles and crammed them into their mouths. No one has bothered me since.'

'I believe it,' I replied. 'So did this warrior come back?'

'No, not yet. He went off without saying a word.'

'Was he one of ours? What did he look like?'

'He was built more like an athlete than like a warrior. Golden blond hair, straight, falling into his eyes. Eyes blue as a spring sky, but cold as ice.'

'Menon. Menon of Thessaly.'

'What did you say?'

'The man who saved you is one of the commanders of the biggest divisions of the Greek army. He's a formidable fighter, and a cruel exterminator.'

'But he's as beautiful as a god and he saved my life. I'm sure that there are other sides to his personality. Sometimes a gentle caress can bring out the most unexpected qualities in a man.'

'I understand. You need someone to protect you, and you don't want to fall into the hands of some repulsive, disgusting swine. But watch out if you're thinking of Menon: he's not the type of man you can tame. It will be like petting a leopard.'

'I'll be careful.'

'Right. I have to go now. What's your name?'

'Melissa. Will you be back?'

'I'll come again as soon as I can. Don't do anything silly, and if you leave the tent, cover yourself. Cover up well, even if it's not cold. Believe me, it's best that you do as I say.'

'I will, Abira. I hope to see you again.'

'Me, too. Sleep now.'

I went back to my tent. Xeno was waiting.

I asked him what had happened at the meeting with the Asian army chiefs. He said that they had sworn to stick together, and to help one another. Ariaeus was wounded, but not seriously so, and he was resolved to lead the two armies out of immediate danger. It was impossible to go back the way they had come. The expedition had been difficult enough until now, even with all of the supplies that the armies had set out with. To attempt a return on the same route without any provisions at all would be folly. It was better to take a longer route that would give them the chance to stock up along the way. The plan was to move out as quickly as possible and to force Artaxerxes to make hasty, and thus dangerous, choices. To keep up with them, the Great King would have to send out a smaller contingent, which would be very risky for him; if he chose to send the army that had overwhelmed Cyrus after them in its entirety, they would lose ground day by day.

'That seems like an excellent plan,' I said. That made him smile. The fact that a woman approved of the decision taken by the highest assembly of the army had no importance whatsoever, but I didn't mind that. I just wanted to express my own point of view. Before lying down I took the lamp and put all of our belongings inside the wagon so we would be ready to leave. All I kept in the tent was what we needed for washing: a jug that I always kept full of water and a damp sponge, so that even if there wasn't much water, both of us could keep ourselves clean. I would wash him first and then myself; it felt easier to rest after wiping away the day's dust; somehow it even made us forget about our hunger, which was getting harder to bear with each passing hour and day. Although we were fortunate enough to have some provisions, we tried to eke them out as much as possible, because no one knew when we'd be able to find more food and because we tried to share the little we had with those who had nothing.

I told Xeno about meeting Melissa, the girl who had run naked from Cyrus's tent to the Greek camp, and of the means of dissuasion that Menon had used to keep the others away from her tent.

Xeno said nothing. What could he say about such methods?

I've come to believe that Xeno's teacher had instilled such a deep sense of ethics in him that a being who was completely amoral, like Menon, provoked a sense of fear in Xeno that was even stronger than his repugnance.

THE RISING SUN and the last shift of sentries woke us and soon after that we were on the march. The landscape had changed considerably. The countryside around us was verdant and there were canals everywhere that irrigated the fields. Big palm groves announced towns and villages from afar.

We advanced all day, getting further and further from the battlefield. That evening we pitched our tents near a group of villages. They weren't very different from our Villages of the Belt. Small mud-brick buildings with palm-leaf roofs, pens holding donkeys, sheep and goats, a few camels, with geese and chickens everywhere.

Towards evening a group of scouts spotted a large herd of horses grazing, which could only mean one thing: the Great King's army was close by. Attempting to plunder the villages would be too risky, but Clearchus chose not to retreat; he didn't want the enemy to think the Greeks were afraid.

The night was fitful, continuously interrupted by bugle calls and false alarms. The smallest noise – the snorting of a horse or barking of a dog – had everyone scrambling to get up and put on their armour. All that pointless activity stirred the men up and greatly increased the strain and danger; the men were tormented by hunger, weary to the bone, tense with the anxiety of waiting for an imminent attack. They were reacting excessively and disproportionately to even the slightest threat, with the risk that a real attack would find them uncoordinated and confused, and unable to hit back effectively.

Xeno was even more worried about the fact that the men

hadn't been able to rest; their sleeplessness compounded the effect of their hunger. I realized that the only thing protecting the camp was the legend of the red cloaks. The reality was that our fearless warriors were afraid of the dark. There was no moon that night, no wood to build fires, no oil for the lamps. Those young men were afraid of the unknown.

Lined up on an open battlefield, in the light of the sun, against even a vastly superior enemy, they would face any danger, reacting with calm hearts and strong arms. Alone in the dark, in the heart of enemy territory, unsure of what direction death would be coming from, they were defenceless and desperate.

Clearchus was well aware of their state of mind. Around midnight he sent a herald through the camp to announce that a donkey had escaped and kicked up a fuss, and that there was no reason for alarm. The herald reminded the men that there was a double row of sentries posted all around the camp and that they could rest easy.

The voice of the herald was the voice of their commander, the man who stayed awake while the others slept, who suffered their same hunger and hardships, but who always had a plan for their salvation, a clear way out, a solution in reserve which could check their panic and dissipate the confusion.

Calm soon reigned over the camp. A few fires were even lit, and many of the men managed to rest.

I thought of Melissa. Where was she? Had her defender returned to her? Had she brought one of the severed heads along with her, planting it in front of her tent to ward off intruders? Certainly not. The heads must have remained behind, topping their iron poles on the abandoned field. No flash of desire had remained in their glassy eyes. Any resemblance to the men they had been ended precisely where Menon's blade had made its mark.

So where was Menon? Even his perfect body would be dirty and sweaty now. And Melissa wouldn't have her leopard to pet.

I felt Xeno tossing and turning in his sleep. He was thinking of tomorrow as well, perhaps wondering how long he would have to wait for death and how it would come.

I fell asleep beside him and slept enveloped in his warmth, as always. Death couldn't touch me and, even as far as Xeno was concerned, I was certain that my love would be sufficient to ward off any danger.

I knew that that was just wishful thinking on my part. My dreams might easily be swallowed up by the moonless night and by the dank, stagnant air rising from the ground. And yet, when the sun rose, a miracle happened. When Xeno woke me he was already armed, but there was an incredulous expression in his eyes. 'The King wants a truce!' he exclaimed.

It seemed impossible and yet it had happened.

'It was just after sunrise. Sophos and I were reporting to the commander to see if there was something we could do. We were talking when a soldier ran up announcing visitors.

' "Visitors?" Clearchus repeated.

' "Yes, commander," the soldier replied. "Ambassadors of the Great King who ask to be received."

'We were shocked and on the verge of saying "Tell them to come here," but Clearchus instead replied, "Tell them that I'm busy."

' "But you're not busy, Commander," said Sophos.

' "Yes I am," Clearchus retorted. "I'm thinking of how to receive them. It won't hurt to keep them waiting a little while. We don't want them to think that we're too eager to negotiate; they'd take that as a sign of weakness. But there's a bigger reason. I want my men in perfect order, their hair combed, their armour gleaming. The sunlight reflecting off their shields will be blinding. We want them to see seamless discipline, intact morale. The ambassadors won't report my words alone back to their King; they'll have to tell him what a Greek phalanx drawn up in battle order looks like. This will take a little time. I'll receive them when I'm ready."

'Then he goes back to chatting with us and tells us the story of the donkey that he'd had the herald proclaim to the camp, and there we were, all laughing, even on our empty stomachs. It's been nearly an hour since the messenger arrived and it seems he's ready to meet them now.'

He hadn't finished speaking when the bugles blared, sounding the assembly. The soldiers ran towards the centre of the camp.

Clearchus appeared.

He'd combed his hair and gathered it at the nape of his neck. His armour was polished to a high sheen and he held a spear in his left hand and a staff in his right.

'Men!' he began. 'A legation of the Great King has asked to be received. I want you lined up in perfect formation, four deep. They have to see an army, not a flock of sheep! Do you understand me? And now, my bodyguard.'

He started walking up and down the ranks, and if he saw a man who was too forward or too far back he gave him a tap with his staff, so that the line was perfectly straight. Then he chose eight men, the tallest and most brawny, to act as his personal bodyguard.

Another bugle blare was the signal to take up shields and close ranks. As the soldiers carried out the order with a harsh clang, he sent a man to summon the ambassadors.

The three legates came forward, and their stupor at seeing the phalanx in full battle array was immediately evident. The line-up was rigorous and impeccable, the soldiers' arms gleamed menacingly. Those boys were cramping up with hunger yet they stood straight and tall before the foreigners to demonstrate that they had not been conquered and were not fearful. On the contrary, they inspired fear. I saw Socrates of Achaea bareheaded at the centre of his unit, the eyes of his men perfectly trained on him. There was Agias of Arcadia, leaning on his spear like a statue of Ares. Menon was there, of course. Menon of Thessaly, bright as Orion, the star that portends doom. On his shoulders a cloak of the purest white – how had he managed that? And there were Agasias the Stymphalian, Lycius of Syracuse, and Glous.

They were standing ten paces in front of the front line, spaced precisely at the same distance one from the other like pawns on a chessboard. Sophos, that's who was missing. He always disappeared in such situations. He dissolved into the air like a mirage.

The ambassadors announced that the King was willing to call a truce but that he wanted Clearchus to pledge that there would be no sacking or aggressive actions on his part. Clearchus replied that before making any promises he wanted to feed his men. The Great King would have to arrange for this at once, or they would attack with all the force they could command.

As he said those words his eyes scanned the formation as if to demonstrate that he wasn't in the business of making idle threats and that his merest glance would suffice to unleash the red cloaks.

That must have been a signal to his officers, because they turned around to face the troops and what happened next seemed like an omen. From the first to the very last, one thousand warriors angled their shields one after another to catch the rays of the sun and reflect them forward. The move was so quick that it looked like a lightning bolt had set the phalanx aflame.

The Persians were speechless. They leapt onto their horses and were gone in a matter of moments.

It wasn't long before they were back, which led us to understand that the Great King must have been very close indeed. If not the King himself, someone who was authorized to act in his name.

They announced that the request had been granted. We should follow the guides and before evening we would reach a group of villages well supplied with food and drink.

We were saved.

11

WE WERE GIVEN GUIDES who would lead us to where we would find food. It was no easy journey. We encountered several canals full of water and each time had to find a way to cross. Clearchus was the first to act, grabbing an axe and chopping down tall palm trees to build footbridges over which the men, wagons and horses could pass. If there was not enough material handy to build a wide enough bridge, the wagons were dismantled. The wheels were rolled across the footbridge while the flatbeds were rope-towed across the water as if they were rafts, and then reassembled on the other side.

With Clearchus setting this example even though he was no youngster, the men pushed themselves as hard as they could to finish the job and shorten the time separating them from food and rest.

It wasn't the first time that I'd thought those men had already used up the last of their energy, but once again I witnessed the miracle of new strength and stamina pulled from exhausted bodies. I was beginning to believe in the legend of the red cloaks myself. It was true that each one of them was worth ten Asians.

Finally, towards nightfall, we arrived at the promised land: a group of villages scattered over a fertile plain. There were hundreds of palm trees richly laden with dates, dozens of granaries with their typical pointed-dome tops, brimming with wheat, barley and spelt, and jars full of palm wine. The officers had to give strict orders for the men not to gorge themselves on the food and drink. Modest rations were handed out, but many of the men became sick afterward nonetheless, with vomiting and headaches.

The doctors blamed that type of wine, which the men weren't used to, and the hearts of palm: the shoots of those plants were very hard and full of fibres that were hard to digest. But in any case, the men finally found sustenance and the opportunity to regain their strength.

I asked myself time and time again why the King had made such a mistake. All he would have had to do was bide his time or trick us in some way, and in the end hunger and exhaustion would have decided our fate. Why didn't he decide to wait it out? There's only one explanation: the King thought that there was no limit to the endurance of the red cloaks, was sure that nothing could bend them. It's also strange that he didn't think of poisoning the food and drink we were given. Xeno imagined it was because of his noble and sentimental nature; he assumed that the King admired their valour and courage and simply thought that men of their temper didn't deserve an unworthy death.

That may be. The fact is that the next day the ambassadors sent by the Great King arrived. It was quite a high-ranking delegation: there was the brother-in-law of the Great King himself, and one of the most brilliant generals of his army, Tissaphernes. He had greatly distinguished himself in the battle against Cyrus, and the King had awarded him the governorship of Lydia, the province which had been ruled by the late prince. They rode up on magnificent Nysean chargers harnessed with gold and silver trappings. They were sumptuously garbed in trousers made of the finest gauze and were escorted by a squad of horsemen from the steppe wearing leather helmets and cuirasses and longbows slung over their shoulders.

Xeno described the encounter as cordial: Tissaphernes and his companions shook Clearchus's hand, as well as those of all the high officers, in turn. Then negotiations started. Tissaphernes said that the Great King did not wish them ill and that he was willing to allow them to leave even though many of his advisers thought he was creating a dangerous precedent. But they would have to accept certain conditions.

Clearchus spoke then. 'We were unaware of the true purpose of Cyrus's expedition . . .' In saying that, he was lying, and yet he was telling the truth. He was lying because he had always known the true reason for the expedition, and he was telling the truth because the greatest part of the army had been kept completely in the dark. 'When, however, we found out about it, it seemed a cowardly act to abandon the man who had engaged us and who had provided for us until that moment, and so we fought loyally under his orders, winning victory at our battle position. But Cyrus is dead now and we are free of our obligations to him. We have no one to answer to but ourselves. Mark my words: we want one thing, and one thing alone. To return home. We have no interest in anything else here. As long as you do not hinder our return journey, everything will be fine. If you try to bar the way we will fight you to the last drop of blood. You know that I'll do as I say.'

The ambassadors looked at each other as the interpreter translated and then Tissaphernes spoke again. 'I've told you. You are free to return to where you've come from, but no pillaging and no violence. You will buy what you need in the markets.'

'And when we find no markets?'

'Then you can take what you need from the land, but only as much as you need and only under our strict supervision. What is your answer?'

Clearchus and his men withdrew in order to consult amongst themselves, but in reality the decision was already taken, seeing that the proposed conditions were reasonable.

'We accept,' was their answer.

'Well, then,' said Tissaphernes, 'we shall return to the King so he may ratify the treaty. As soon as we have his assent, we'll return here. We shall begin our journey to the coast together. The land I have been appointed to govern lies in the same direction. Do not move from here or, I warn you, the agreement will be cancelled.'

Clearchus looked him straight in the eye. 'I trust you aren't thinking of hemming us into a trap. That would be quite unwise of you.'

Tissaphernes smiled, revealing a double row of pearly white teeth under his thick black moustache. 'If we're going to be making such a long journey together, we should start trusting each other, wouldn't you say?'

Having said this he bade the commander farewell, mounted his horse and galloped off.

'What do you think?' Clearchus asked his men. Xeno replied that, seeing no alternative course of action, he would agree, but that the officers should decide. One by one, they declared their willingness to abide by Tissaphernes's conditions.

'Then we wait,' said Clearchus.

'We wait,' retorted Menon of Thessaly. 'But not for long.' He walked off.

Three days passed without anything happening and some of the men began to worry. Xeno accompanied me when I went to draw water because he feared a surprise attack. It seemed to me that the faith he had in the Persians' good will was probably beginning to falter. As time passed the tension grew because we'd had no news and no one knew what to think.

I went to visit Melissa, whom I hadn't seen for days. I found her well set up in her tent with two servants waiting on her every need.

'You've found a new friend?' I asked.

'I found the one I wanted.'

'Menon?'

Melissa nodded, smiling.

'Unbelievable. When did that happen?'

'The evening after the ambassadors arrived. He'd been consulting with the other officers, and he was heading back to his quarters when he happened to pass by my tent. I invited him to come in for a cool drink. Difficult to say no, with this heat. Palm wine with a little water and a touch of mint. I found a sweating jar at camp that I use to cool down the wine until it's nice and frosty.'

'How do you do that? What's a sweating jar?'

'It's simple. They're jars made of coarse clay and fired at a high temperature so they become porous. You just have to find a spot where there's a little breeze and wet the jar down continuously to chill the liquid inside.'

'I thought you'd seduced him with something else . . .'

'You mean this?' she smiled, touching her lap. 'Not so soon. Later . . . after he'd sat down, and relaxed, after he'd sipped that lovely, cool, refreshing drink. After I'd washed him with a soft sponge and dried him with fine, lavender-scented linen . . .'

'I don't think there's a man that can resist you. You could seduce the Great King himself.'

'I've had a little experience . . . Menon gave in to my caresses, but he never truly let himself go. He's incredibly wary and distrustful; something terrible must have happened to him in the past, but I couldn't get him to say a word about it.'

'Did he sleep with you?'

'Just one night. Naked, but with his sword at his side. The one time I got up to get a drink I found it at my throat. You were right: it was like sleeping with a leopard. The first thing you realize is that he could kill you as easily as he drinks a glass of water. Kill anyone, I mean, without distinction.'

'Be careful.'

'And yet there's something mysterious in him that fascinates me. His fierceness, so sudden and yet so cold-blooded. He's allowed this unchecked aggressiveness to grow in him, but I think it must spring from an experience of extreme suffering and terror. That night I heard him cry out in his sleep. It was just before dawn, when you dream things you can't remember when you awake. A horrible, inhuman cry.'

I truly admired Melissa just then; not only did she have a

perfect body and face, but such a rich range of emotions, such a sharp mind. She was one of those people who change the way you look at things, someone I never would have met had I remained at Beth Qadà,

'Do you have any idea of what we're in for here?' asked Melissa. 'Menon hasn't said a word and I don't dare ask him.'

'Xeno's troubled because nothing's happening. Too many days have gone by. The scouts say that we're shut in between the Tigris and a canal. Clearchus doesn't want to move because he's worried about violating the truce and giving Ariaeus an excuse to abandon us to our destiny.'

Melissa poured me a cup of her magical beverage and watched with a fond expression as I drank. 'Have you thought of what you'll do if things take a turn for the worse?'

'What do you mean?'

'If the army is wiped out by the Persians. If they kill your Xeno.'

'I don't know. I don't think I could survive without him.'

'That's nonsense. We have to survive, no matter what. A woman as desirable as you are can always find a way to survive. All you need to do is identify the most powerful male. He may be a king or a prince or an army commander; he'll protect you and give you everything you deserve in exchange for your favours.'

'I don't think I'd be very good at that. If you succeed, maybe you can protect me as well. I'm too stupid, Melissa. I'm one of those women who fall in love. For a lifetime. You are already a legend, the beauty who ran naked from Ariaeus's camp to the lines of Greek solders who were cheering you on. Not even cold-eyed Menon could resist your charms.'

Melissa sighed. 'Menon . . . I'm afraid he might be the one who does for me. You know, I've never fallen in love with anyone in all my life, but that heartless young man makes me tremble . . .'

I saw a shadow of doubt in Melissa's amber eyes and I left

then, so that I wouldn't have to answer the question she might have asked me next.

TWENTY DAYS PASSED before the ambassadors returned, and I think it was pure folly to wait so long without doing anything. I don't know why nothing happened, in the end. The Great King had accepted our terms and thus we began our return. That night Xeno and I made love because the fear of an imminent catastrophe was allayed and the warm, quiet night air, smelling of hay, urged us into each other's arms. Then we left the tent and sat on the dry grass to look at the starry sky. We could hear the buzz of the camp all around us; the low voices of the soldiers, the barking of the stray dogs that wandered among the tents. No one was singing, though. Everyone's thoughts were suffused with misgiving and a sense of gloom. The immense army they had faced at Cunaxa had given the men an idea of how vast the empire was, extending around us in all directions, and of how many obstacles stood in our way.

'Do you think we'll be taking the same road back?' I asked Xeno. 'Will we pass through my villages?' I felt deep dismay at the idea. If our route took us through the Villages of the Belt, the circle would close for me, and I'd probably be left behind so Xeno could take up his life again where he had left it, a life he was certainly eager to get back to.

'I don't know,' he answered. 'Wherever my mind turns, I have doubts and uncertainties. We have to follow the Persians, who hate us and will be watching everything we do. We're a foreign body festering inside their country. They're afraid to face us, but they know that in one way or another, we'll have to be destroyed.'

'Why should that be so?' I pleaded. 'The Great King himself has agreed to let us leave. He laid down his conditions and you gave your consent.'

'That's true. Everything seems perfect, nothing's wrong, and yet there's no logic in such behaviour. If we make it back, and tell everyone how easy it was to get practically all the way to one of their capitals, others could try to repeat the same endeavour. It's a risk the Persians cannot run. It's also true that the last word is never spoken, the paths of destiny are often inscrutable.'

'So if tomorrow your fears do turn out to be misplaced, what can we expect to happen?'

'Tissaphernes has been nominated governor of Lydia in Cyrus's place and so he has to make his way to his province. We'll be sharing the same road because we're going in the same direction, and this will allow them to keep an eye on us. We'll be travelling up the Tigris until we reach the base of the Taurus mountains. There we'll turn west towards the Cilician Gates, the pass that connects Syria with Anatolia, and we'll pass rather close to your villages, four or five parasangs, a day's march to the south.'

'So it would be easy for you to take me back to Beth Qadà, where we met.'

'Not of my own will,' he said. 'I'd miss you very much, too much ... You know, where I come from they tell stories of heroes who return after long journeys bringing a barbarian girl back with them ...'

'How do the stories end?'

'That's not important ...' replied Xeno and stopped talking all at once. My eyes followed his as they scanned the camp and stopped short at a figure on horseback, riding in silence in the tall grass.

Sophos.

WE STARTED OFF at dawn. After marching for two days we met up with a wall of mud bricks cemented together with asphalt and two days later we reached the banks of the Tigris, which we crossed on a boat bridge. Xeno recorded all of the place names and distances on his tablet and I could see him marking out the direction of our journey on the wax, based on the position of the sun. Beyond the river was a biggish city, encircled by another wall of mud bricks, like the ones we use to build our houses at Beth Qadà. There for the first time we went to a market. Our men yoked the mules to the wagons and went to buy what was needed to feed the whole army. I had never seen the quantity of food needed to satisfy the hunger of ten thousand men. It was an enormous amount, although it was made up of very few items, because they had to buy up what the market offered: wheat, barley, turnips and legumes, freshwater fish. The mutton, goat and poultry all went to the officers, like Proxenus, Menon, Agasias and Glous. Clearchus and his circle always ate the same things their soldiers did. Only one beverage was available, palm wine, but only for those who could afford it.

I noticed that the various units had put their money together and entrusted a single person to buy the provisions for all of them; he would provide an accounting of how the money had been spent and when it ran out they would contribute again to form a new reserve. The officers, except for Clearchus and his staff, sent their adjutants. Xeno had not lost his passion for hunting. When possible he would go out with a bow, arrows and javelins, and he nearly always came back with some prey: a wild rabbit, some ducks, a young gazelle, once, that stared at me with big, glassy eyes.

Ariaeus and his army who, in theory, were allied to us, joined Tissaphernes instead. They camped at a single site, all together, but our men took great care to pitch their tents elsewhere as we had from the start, at a distance of a parasang or even further. We wouldn't even have known where the Asians were, if it hadn't been for the smoke of their campfires.

This situation led to obsessive, pessimistic second-guessing: who knows what they've got in mind? Who knows what traps or tricks they're thinking up? That bastard Ariaeus was in league with them. Barbarians one and all, what could they have expected?

It is not difficult to imagine that the same kind of suspicions were circulating in the other camp and what had started out as a transfer of two army units in the direction of the sea soon became an undeclared war, both sides spying and jumping to conclusions, the tension spiralling out of control, day and night.

Fortunately, our men were level-headed enough to avoid direct contact, which would have inevitably resulted in skirmishes, but what they tried to avoid often happened by chance. Groups of our auxiliaries going out to gather forage often ran into Persian troops who were out for the same reason, and furious fights broke out, sometimes actual combat with casualties. It took Clearchus with all of his authority to prevent the officers from going out in full battle gear to avenge their dead and wounded.

The further north we advanced along the left bank of the Tigris, the tenser and more difficult the situation became, because the areas where forage could be gathered or provisions bought were becoming rarer and rarer, and competition for what was available was becoming more vicious almost step by step. Xeno was one of the few who had worried when things were going well, but events were proving him right now. What would happen when the tension built up to a real crisis? I would watch Clearchus as he carried out inspection at night, surrounded by his guard. At times he would venture out close to the Persian outposts. Their campfires extended over a vast area and gave the measure of the enormous discrepancy between the two armies. No one was fooled any more over where Ariaeus's loyalty lay: if push came to shove he would certainly do battle against us.

One night, around the second guard shift, I heard the sounds of a violent quarrel: it was Menon, who wanted to lead his men on a night raid into the Persian camp. He was sure he could cause a slaughter, and throw the entire army into a panic, after which an all-out assault by the rest of the Greek forces would wipe out the whole bunch.

'Let me go!' he was shouting. 'They're not expecting it. Can't you hear the row they're making? They're all half-drunk. We'll butcher them like sheep. They killed two of my men today! Whoever touches Menon's men is dead. Dead! Understand?'

He was crazed, like an animal who has scented blood. No one could have stopped him except for Clearchus, but I'm convinced that had he been set loose, Menon would have done all that he promised and more. He was so furious that his plan was being thwarted that I was afraid he would draw his sword against his own commander, but Clearchus's grim resolve stifled his rage and prevented events from getting out of hand. At least for the moment.

I noticed Sophos watching the scene silently from a distance. Lately I'd started seeing him with an officer of Socrates's battalion, a youngish man who didn't talk much but had the reputation of being a formidable combatant. He was from a city in the south, Xeno told me. He knew his name, Neon, but nothing else about him. The fact that they both had little to say seemed to be the only thing they had in common.

We crossed another river and sighted another city in the distance where we were able to buy provisions at the market, then we forged on into a barren territory where the only things growing were on the banks of the Tigris. Although it was late autumn it was still hot, and the long marches under a scorching sun put both man and animal to the test. Many days had passed since the day that Clearchus had met Tissaphernes and had signed the truce agreement, but since that time there had been no contact, no meeting, no signal.

Only once did a message arrive from the Persian camp. We were camped in the vicinity of a group of villages that reminded me of the place I was born and that I hadn't seen in so long. A Persian horseman appeared at dawn and waited, immobile, on his horse, until Clearchus approached him. The man told him, in stilted Greek, that as a sign of his good will, Tissaphernes was granting them permission to take what they needed from those villages.

At first, Xeno and the others thought that it had to be a trap, an invitation to plunder with the intent of scattering our men among the houses and down the alleyways of that small settlement, in order to unleash a surprise attack and finish them off. But Agasias, who had gone ahead to reconnoitre, reported that there were no Persians within a range of two parasangs and that this meant that they had no intention of assaulting us.

At this point, Clearchus posted several groups of scouts at a certain distance from the enemy camp and sent the others to sack the villages. By evening, little was left in those humble communities of farmers and shepherds, and the inhabitants would be exposed to the risk of starvation during the winter months. They'd lost their harvest, their pack and draught animals and their farmyard animals as well. None of the men who were sacking the villages of those poor wretches asked themselves the reason for such indulgence on the part of the enemy, but I did. There had to be a reason, and it wasn't hard to find. Those villages had the same name as mine: the 'Villages of Parysatis'. That is, they were named after the Queen Mother, and that authorized pillaging had to be an explicit insult to her majesty.

While our men were exploiting the opportunity they'd been given, I ran into a group of Persian prisoners who had just been captured by one of Socrates's units and tied to the trunk of a sycamore. There was a girl there who spoke my language, and until recently she had been in the service of Queen Parysatis. I asked Xeno if she could join us, because she might have interesting information to share. In fact, I learned a terrifying story from her, the story of the implacable hate between the two sons of Parysatis and of their mother's thirst for revenge after she had been so atrociously deprived of the one she loved most. Cyrus.

1 2

'WHAT'S SHE LIKE?' was my first question. It didn't seem real to me that I could be so close to a person who had looked into the face of a woman who seemed as remote to me as the stars in the sky. She'd even touched, possibly combed her hair . . .

'Who?'

'The Queen Mother! Tell me what she's like.'

The girl who spoke my language was called Durgat and she'd been one of Parysatis's servants until a few days earlier, in the Queen's summer residence on the high plain west of the central Tigris.

'She's tall and slender. Her eyes are deep-set and very dark and when they turn on you, you tremble. Her hair is very long and she wears it gathered at the nape of her neck. Her fingers are long and thin and make you think of claws. Her nose is . . . beaky, sharp. When she smiles it's even more frightening because everyone knows what gives her most pleasure: seeing people suffer.

'And yet she can count on the loyalty and even the devotion of all those who serve her. She inspires such terror that if she pays the tiniest bit of attention to you or gives you some small handout, you involuntarily feel immense gratitude, thinking that for this time around, at least, you've been spared the pain she's capable of inflicting.'

'What was she doing here, at this time of year?'

'She hadn't come to take her leisure, not this time. She wanted to be close to the conflict. To the duel to the death between her two sons.'

'How did you happen to be here, in these villages?'

'The eunuch in charge of the royal household sent me and some of the other girls, with a number of guards, to buy provisions for the palace. Your soldiers captured us.'

'I know, and I'm afraid you would have ended up in one of the soldiers' tents if it weren't for me. The man I live with is an important person. If you want to continue enjoying our protection, tell me what you know.'

She nodded and seemed relieved. The fact that I spoke her language made her trust me. She told me everything she'd heard or overheard from the Queen's chambermaids and from the eunuchs who had confided in her. She had a lot to tell, and we went on for days. The necessities of our onward march interrupted us, but we later managed to meet again and continue.

'In reality, Cyrus thought he had a rightful claim to the throne; he didn't think of himself as a usurper. He was younger than his brother but he was born when his father had already become King. Artaxerxes, his older brother, had been born when their father was a common man. Cyrus was a royal prince. His brother was nothing. There's a story I learned at the palace, but you mustn't repeat it to anyone. The Queen Mother would cut out your tongue, and mine.'

'What could be so terrible?'

'It's about Cyrus. The Queen Mother won't have him humiliated. So this is what happened. When Artaxerxes entered the Sanctuary of Fire for the royal investiture ceremony, Cyrus was hiding in a side chapel, waiting for his chance to attack. But Artaxerxes's bodyguards must have been tipped off, because they searched the place beforehand.

'They found Cyrus armed with a dagger and dragged him to the centre of the coronation hall so they could kill him then and there, before the eyes of the Great King. The Queen Mother screamed and threw herself in front of him just as the scimitar was about to lop off his head. She protected him with her own body and covered him with her cloak, imploring her elder son for mercy. No one dared to harm her.

'Everyone at court thought that Artaxerxes would find a way to take revenge but, little by little, the kind words and attentions of his mother won him over and instead of doing away with his brother, he was convinced by her to send Cyrus as far away as possible from court, to the furthest western province, Lydia, and make him governor there.'

I was moved by that story. The Emperor of the World, the King of Kings, the most powerful man on earth, was just a little boy to his mother, and he bowed to her will without a whimper. She was the one who fascinated me; what kind of a woman was capable of such conniving? Where I came from, we used to say that women like her had a 'womb of bronze'.

So, when Artaxerxes's army and all his generals started to mobilize their forces against Cyrus, she took up her entire retinue, her wardrobe and handmaids, and moved towards the battlefield. She wanted to be the first to know the outcome of their clash. Any mother would be crushed by the thought that she would certainly lose one of her two sons, but not her. She wanted Cyrus to win, knowing that this meant he would slay his own brother.

'You're right,' said Durgat. 'She deserved to be punished, and she was. It was Cyrus instead who was slain, and she was spared none of the gruesome details. In truth, no one knew who, exactly, had struck him down. Several witnesses declared that the two brothers met face to face and dealt out deep wounds, each one lashing out at the other, but no one could say exactly when and at whose hand the prince had died, whether it was then, at the start of the battle, or later on.'

'You know,' I reflected, 'our men weren't even on the field when this was happening. They had already routed the enemy's left wing and were in pursuit of the fleeing Persians; by that time they were far from the heart of the fight.'

'One thing is certain,' Durgat continued. 'King Artaxerxes was wounded in the chest by a spear that pierced his breastplate and penetrated more than two fingers deep into his flesh. The Greek doctor who was later sent to negotiate with you stitched up the wound and treated it, but before doing so he measured the depth of the lesion using a silver stylus.

'The Great King was informed of the death of his brother by a soldier from Caria, who showed him the blood-soaked caparison from his horse; he swore he had seen the prince's corpse. When it was all over, the King summoned this man to reward him, but the soldier evidently expected a greater sum, and he protested. He even boasted that he'd killed Cyrus himself, and that such a small prize was not equal to his deed.

'Artaxerxes was indignant, of course, and ordered the man's beheading, but the Queen Mother was present and she stopped him. So rapid a death was not a just punishment for one who had been so ungrateful and insolent. "Give him to me," she said, "and he'll have the death he deserves. No one will ever again dare to show you disrespect."

'Artaxerxes granted her request. Maybe his desire to believe that his mother loved him and truly wanted to punish the man who had been disrespectful to him made him turn over the poor wretch. Instead, she wanted the satisfaction of punishing him all for herself. All she wanted was revenge. A revenge worthy of the evil and cruelty of her soul.'

What Durgat told me then made me sick. There's nothing more terrible for any human being than to fall completely under the power of another human being who hates him, because there is no limit to the suffering he will endure. At that moment, the delight she took in her revenge was greater than any pain or grief she was feeling for the loss of her beloved son. She had the soldier from Caria strung up in the courtyard of her palace and she called in the torturers. She hand-picked those who most excelled at their skill; those who were capable of inflicting all the torment a body can stand without dying. Those who were capable of stopping a moment before death arrived to claim her due and end the suffering.

Every day she had herself carried out on a palanquin to the courtyard, where she sat in the shade of a tamarisk tree for hours and watched the atrocious agony of that poor creature. Since his screaming and moaning had been keeping her awake at night, she'd had his tongue cut out and his lips sewn up.

For ten days the abominable show went on until the man had been reduced to a shapeless mass of butchered flesh. The Queen let him die then, not because she felt any pity for him but because she was no longer amused; the diversion had begun to bore her.

She had his eyes plucked out and molten copper poured into his ears.

Durgat realized the devastating effect that her story had on me. My expression must have been eloquent, as I couldn't keep the terror from welling up in my eyes. I'd never heard of such savagery, growing up in my sleepy little village. She stopped for a while and took a look around, as if to reacquaint herself with the reality of the present. Then she went back to the past.

'There was another man who boasted of having killed Cyrus. His name was Mithridates. He had been given a handsome reward by King Artaxerxes: a silken gown and a scimitar of solid gold because he had actually wounded the prince with a javelin blow to his temple, although it had been the King, everyone said, who dealt the final blow, despite his own wounds. Others claimed that it was Mithridates, not the soldier from Caria, who showed up with Cyrus's bloody caparison, thus proving himself deserving of the King's gifts.

'One evening Mithridates was invited to a banquet secretly organized by the Queen. One of the eunuchs in her service was there as well. The wine flowed abundantly and when the guest seemed good and drunk the eunuch began to taunt him, saying that anyone could bring a bloody caparison to the King, without being a great warrior. That was all it took. Mithridates lifted his hand and shouted: "You can blather all you like, but this is the hand that killed Cyrus."

' "What about the King?" asked the eunuch.

' "The King can say whatever he likes. I was the one who killed Cyrus!"

'In saying this, he had accused the King of being a liar. In front of twenty or so witnesses. In other words, he signed his own death sentence.

'When they saw the eunuch's satisfied grin, the others understood what was in store for Mithridates. They dropped their eyes, and the master of the house said, "Such big talk! Let's leave these matters to others and worry instead about eating and drinking and enjoying ourselves tonight. No one knows what tomorrow may bring!"

'Mithridates's death was orchestrated by the Queen Mother who, once again, asked her son to allow her to avenge his offended honour. Mithridates's friends tried to get him out of trouble using the excuse that he was drunk, but the eunuch quoted the old adage about there being truth in wine, claiming that under the influence of drink one speaks the truth. None of those present at the banquet dared to disagree.

'Parysatis devised an even more perverse end for Mithridates: the torture of the two chests.'

At the thought of having to listen to more atrocities I begged Durgat to interrupt her story because I had neither the courage nor the strength to listen, but a voice I knew well rang out behind me.

'Well, I am curious to hear about it, and I know you know enough Greek to make yourself understood. I heard you speaking when our men captured you.'

Menon of Thessaly was standing behind me, and perhaps had been there for some time, although I hadn't noticed.

'Get out,' I said. 'Xeno could be back at any time and he won't like it if he finds you here with me.'

'I'm not doing anything wrong,' replied Menon. 'And I know you're a friend of Melissa's, that gives us something in common.'

He was holding a cup of palm wine in his left hand. The cup was made of fine ceramic, like those that the Greeks use when they take their meals. I've never been able to understand how he kept his cloak so white and how such rare, delicate items could travel with him without being damaged. The girl went on speaking in Greek: I had not expected that, and was really surprised. She must have been a precious commodity at the Queen's court. I turned to leave.

'Too tender-hearted or too weak-stomached to listen?' commented Menon sarcastically. 'You're not familiar with the torture of the two chests? I'll tell you about it myself. You know, before we left I had to brush up on the habits and customs of these countries, just so that I'd know what to expect if I was taken prisoner. This is what she's talking about. They take you out into the middle of the desert, someplace where the sun beats down all day long. They tie your hands and your feet and put you into a kind of chest, you know, the ones they use for leavening bread dough. Just big enough to contain you sitting down. Then they place another chest on top of that one, only this one has the end cut out so that your whole head sticks out of it. Then they spread a thick paste of milk and honey all over your face. That's just the thing for flies, wasps, horseflies, you name it. They come from every direction to enjoy the meal and so in moments your face is completely covered by those revolting insects. But that's not all. Spiders, centipedes and beetles all come to join in the fun. And ants, thousands of starving ants. You can't move because you're closed up in that wooden coffin, and once the honey is finished, the insects don't stop. They continue on your face and in no time at all, they've turned it into a bloody mask.'

'That's enough!' I shouted.

'Leave if you want,' replied Menon. 'No one asked you to

stay.' But I did stay. I don't know why but that horror had a strange effect on me, like a poison that slowly makes you drowsy yet torments you at the same time. I realized that human beings were capable of doing this, and worse. I couldn't walk away, it wasn't right. I had to be aware of everything that life may hold in store. Your existence can be totally serene, I thought, you might be blessed with children, a person who loves and respects you, a lovely house with an arbour and a garden, like the one I've always dreamed of. And yet something can happen that will make you forget about the happiness of a lifetime in a matter of hours, and make you sorry you were ever born.

Menon's voice continued, soft and low, telling his cruel story. '. . . And that's still not all. Every evening, when night and darkness liberate you for a brief time of those teeming hosts, dinner time comes around. They feed you, yes they do . . . can you believe that? Drink, too. Lots of it. They force it down your throat. If you won't open your mouth they pierce your eyes with pins, so that when you scream they can stuff more food into your mouth, and make you drink. So that after two or three days you are buried in your own excrement inside of that boiling coffin. The worms devour you alive, little by little. You can smell the stench of your own dying flesh and you curse your heart that keeps on beating and you curse your mother who brought you to life and you curse all the gods in the heavens that she didn't drop dead before she spat you into the world.'

I wept as I listened to his story. Such horror! I thought that even that poor wretch had been born of a mother who nursed him, held him in her arms and covered him with kisses and caresses, ensuring that his childhood would be filled with all the joy a child can have, not realizing that it would have been much better for him had she drowned him in a bucket as soon as he was born, before hearing his first wail.

It took Mithridates seventeen days to die.

The story wasn't finished. Durgat said that there was one more man who still had to pay his dues. The eunuch who had taken it upon himself to decapitate, maim and impale Cyrus's lifeless body. His name was Masabates and he was as wily as could be. He'd seen the way the other two had ended up and he realized that he was choice prey for that tiger. Not only was he careful to do no boasting, but he avoided any situation in which talk turned to Cyrus and shied away from any person who had had anything to do with anyone who had ever known Cyrus or even remembered him in any way. If the discussion strayed in that direction he simply left, alluding to one of the many tasks he was responsible for as a loyal and emasculated servant of the King. It seemed impossible to trap him, but the man-hunter was more cunning than he was. She let time pass, and began to behave as if Cyrus had never existed. She surrounded her surviving son with tenderness and solicitude, even making sweets for him with her own hands, or so she'd have him believe. She seemed sincere. She played the part of a mother resigned to the fact that only one son remained for her to shower her affection on. The one thing that truly melted the King's heart was the kindness and warmth the Queen Mother had begun to show for her daughter-in-law, Artaxerxes's beloved bride Queen Statira, whom she had never been able to abide. Parysatis even found time to join the King in his favourite pastime: throwing dice.

'I've never heard of anyone using loaded dice for the purpose of losing,' Durgat told us, 'but that's exactly what the Queen Mother did to achieve her goal. She bet one thousand gold darics and lost them all. She paid this enormous sum without batting an eye but requested a return game, which took place a few days later, one quiet evening after dinner in the garden of the summer palace. A fountain burbled softly and a nightingale warbled his song from the jasmine-scented hedges.

'This time around it was Parysatis's turn to name the stakes, and she decided they should play for a servant. A servant owned by whoever lost. Each of them could rule out five names, choosing from their most loyal and devoted servants, so as not to be deprived of a person close to their hearts.

'Parysatis has calculated well. Masabates was not among her son's top five. This time the dice were loaded to allow her to win, and when she claimed Masabates as her prize the King immediately realized that he had condemned a faithful servant to a horrible death, but a king's word is carved in stone, and can't be taken back.

'The Queen Mother had him flayed alive and ordered his skin to be hung from a reed trellis where he could see it. Then she had him impaled using three intersecting poles. His death was quicker than Mithridates's but no less painful.' This happened just a few days before Durgat had been captured at the villages with the other servants and their escort.

Durgat said that she had been present, with a basket of figs in her arms, when the King complained to his mother that she had inflicted a horrible death on a good servant. The Queen Mother shrugged and said, 'What a fuss over a worthless old eunuch! I didn't say a word when I lost one thousand gold darics in a single game.' Then she took a fig from Durgat's basket, peeled it with maddening slowness and bit into it, curling her lip just like a tiger does.

As Durgat was finishing her story Xeno appeared and found himself face-to-face with Menon of Thessaly. 'What are you doing here?' he asked curtly.

'Just passing through,' replied Menon.

'Pass some other way,' replied Xeno, frowning. I saw Menon's hand slip to the hilt of his sword and I shot him a look to stop him. He shook his blond mane and grinned. 'Another time, writer. Our day will come. While you're waiting, have your lady friend tell you a story or two. You'll find them interesting.'

He left, the wind billowing up under that absurd white cloak. Like the sail on a boat.

I ASKED DURGAT whether she'd rather return to the Queen or go on with us. 'You're free, if you want to be. You must decide for yourself. If you come with us, I think we'll be on the coast in a couple of months. There are incredible cities on the seafront, the climate is good and the fields are fertile. You might find a good man who will marry you, and raise a family.'

Durgat lowered her eyes for a moment without speaking. She was a pretty girl, with pitch-black hair and eyes and a dark complexion. She dressed with a certain flair and was even wearing ornaments: a drop of amber at her throat hung from a silver chain.

'You're very good to offer to take me with you, but I know I'm safe where I am now. You just have to close your ears and your eyes, obey always, even when you're not told to do anything, predict the Queen's needs and satisfy her every desire, and all is fine.'

I couldn't believe I'd heard the words 'all is fine' from a person who'd had a close encounter with the unimaginably ferocious acts she'd just told me about, a person who was at the service of a human beast who was capable of immense cruelty and of sudden, devastating mood changes. I realized that a person deprived of her freedom and her dignity can grow accustomed to anything and everything.

Durgat continued, 'You're doing this because you're in love, I can see that, and I understand you. I'm not used to this kind of life. But . . . that's not the only reason . . .' she broke off, looking straight into my eyes with an intense expression.

There was a message in her eyes, as there had been in mine when I silently implored Menon not to draw his sword against my Xeno. She wouldn't say another word; she had already warned me that she found it best to close her ears and her eyes. So, best not to hear and not to see . . . what? What was it that she knew but couldn't tell me? What Durgat had given me was a gift that I couldn't understand or benefit from. I didn't press her to say anything more because her expression was eloquent; it was impossible for her to go any further. She'd already given me what she could and the mere idea that she might be considered responsible for a prohibited revelation was more than enough to sew her mouth shut. Precisely because she'd decided to return to her cage.

'I'll ask Xeno to leave you here in the village. Your people will find you when they pass through, or you'll be picked up by Tissaphernes's men who are camped one parasang east of here.'

'I'm very grateful to you. Believe me, I would have liked to stay with you and become your friend. You're a lot like I am, you know? Maybe because we speak the same language and come from similar places. I'm from Aleppo.'

'Maybe,' I replied, and my gaze sought the point that had just caught her attention. Something up on a low hill, behind the villages: it was Menon's white cloak.

Xeno called me and I joined him, and began preparing our supper.

He realized that my mind was somewhere far away. 'What are you thinking about?' he asked.

'That girl that we found here, the one who had been captured,' I answered. 'I promised that you would free her.'

'I don't think so! You're too jealous to let another woman share our tent, and a pretty one at that. Am I right?'

'Of course you are.' I smiled. 'You know me well! Then can I tell her that she can go back to where she came from?'

'Yes, tell her that. Let's hope that nothing bad happens to her.'

'Durgat belongs to the Queen Mother Parysatis. She has only to say her name and her path will clear, even in the middle of a pack of wolves, believe me.'

'Fine, then.' But he continued to steal looks in my direction; he must have sensed that my mind remained elsewhere.

When evening fell a stiff wind came up, snapping the loose edges of the tent and rustling the palm fronds so loudly that I couldn't fall asleep. I couldn't get Durgat's enigmatic expression out of my mind, that intense look she gave me when she stopped talking.

There was something she couldn't tell me, something she knew but couldn't say. Why? Something dangerous, a threat that hung over our heads, something she'd overheard in the chambers of the Queen Mother or in the King's pavilion. What else could it be? But we knew we were up against danger every day; a sudden attack, an ambush, running out of food or water, poisoned wells . . . so many dangers lay between us and the sea. What threat could be more serious than the many we'd already experienced?

I tried to work out the sequence of what had happened to her, and how she must be feeling, in order to find an answer. She had heard something that concerned us, that had to do with our army, but perhaps she hadn't even completely understood it. Then she'd been sent to the villages to buy provisions and had been captured by our men. Xeno and I had protected her from the violence she might have suffered and she was grateful to us for this reason. What she had seen at our camp must have reminded her of something she'd heard in the royal palace, and she was trying to warn me. She was trying to say, 'There's something in store for you. I know what it is but I can't tell you because I'm going back to the Queen and if their plot is foiled it will be easy to trace the person who revealed their plans. And there's no limit to the suffering they'd inflict upon me. So you have to try to understand.'

Right, that must be it. If I couldn't understand now, I would be able to understand later, by being careful, keeping my eyes open, trying to take advantage of any clue or signal. Xeno pulled me close. He couldn't sleep either, with the wind.

'You know, in my village, the wind – in certain seasons or at certain times – makes a strange noise, like a roar,' I whispered into Xeno's ear. 'The old people say that when the wind roars like that something extraordinary is about to happen. We heard the wind's voice three days before your army passed through Beth Qadà.'

'So you think it's trying to tell us something now?'

'Maybe. But here we're too far from home for me to understand.'

The wind died down before dawn and I managed to get some rest. That night Melissa had slept alone, because Menon was out on patrol with his Thessalonians. He came back when the sun was high, having lost three of his own men and having killed ten or so of Tissaphernes's. The situation had continued to worsen day by day; there were constant skirmishes with the Persians but also with Ariaeus's Asians, who clearly had taken sides with Tissaphernes, openly spurning the oaths and promises they had made with the Greeks.

From then on, clashes of that sort intensified, usually without any apparent trigger. The strange thing was that Clearchus and the other commanders didn't seem overly concerned.

'They're provoking you,' I told Xeno. 'They want to goad you into doing something. Attacking maybe, and falling into a trap.'

'Clearchus doesn't think so,' Xeno replied. 'He doesn't see any pattern in the aggression. You see, the closer we get to the mountains, the less fertile land there is, and this means we're competing for the same scarce resources. Plus, we don't like them and they don't like us. That's all. We'll be on the road together for at least the next three months, so we'll have to put up with it.'

We resumed our northward journey three days later. Before leaving, I said goodbye to Durgat. She hugged me and gave me that same look again, as if to say: 'Watch out.' What she said was 'Good luck.'

'Good luck to you too,' I replied and got into the wagon.

We advanced with the rising sun at our right for about twenty days. The skirmishing continued between our army and small groups of Persian cavalry until we encountered another river which flowed into the Tigris from the east, which we crossed on a boat bridge.

Once we had reached the other side, Clearchus summoned all the generals and demanded to know if any of them had ordered his men to take the initiative against the Persian troops, but they replied that they had always obeyed his orders, that is, not retaliating unless they were attacked directly. Clearchus said he wanted to put an end to this problem, once and for all.

'How do you propose to do that?' asked Sophos, present with Neon, who had become his shadow.

'I'm going to ask to meet with Tissaphernes. A summit between their high command and ours.'

'And you hope to resolve something?' asked Sophos.

'I do. This situation is as damaging to them as it is to us. Tissaphernes knows that if this builds into a direct clash, they would take considerable losses, at best. At worst it would be a complete trouncing. Our men are in top form and well acclimatized. They're ready for an all-out attack. They'd welcome it, in fact.'

'How would you organize a meeting, if he agrees?' asked Socrates of Achaea.

'On neutral ground, halfway between the two camps. With a limited escort: no more than fifty men on either side. I want lads who are wide awake, and quick on the draw.'

'Leave that to me,' said Menon.

'Fine. Send out a group to arrange it today. They'll have to name a time and a place. I'll take care of the rest.'

That evening Socrates had dinner with us in front of our tent and told us all about their meeting. He was quite cheerful and seemed certain that all would go according to plan. I wasn't sure of this in the least. It was only after Socrates had gone that everything suddenly fell into place, or so it seemed to me, and I asked Xeno to listen to me, even if I was only a woman.

'This is what Durgat was trying to tell me: there's deadly danger looming ahead; we could be annihilated. She knew, but she couldn't tell me. Haven't you wondered why the attacks, the quarrels, the insults have multiplied of late without any precise reason? Our men are heading straight into a trap, I'm sure of it. You have to stop them.'

Xeno shook his head, perplexed. 'It's just your impression. That girl didn't say anything because she had nothing to say.'

'You're wrong. She spoke to me in the language of women, the language of intuition, of instinct. She knew that I would understand, that I would foresee the danger. It was her way of thanking me without putting her own life at risk. You must convince them not to go!'

Xeno seemed untroubled. I had tears in my eyes and was shaking. He tried to calm me.

'There's no reason for you to get so upset. All Clearchus is doing is setting up a preliminary contact. We don't even know if Tissaphernes will accept to meet or whether he'll be willing to negotiate. When we get his answer we'll talk about it.'

'Talk about it now. Go to Clearchus yourself, or get Socrates to speak to him.'

'And what am I supposed to say, that there was a girl who stared at you with a funny look in her eye? Come on now, try not to think about it. Sleep now, and tomorrow, when our envoys come back, we'll know whether the meeting is going to take place or not.'

I was expecting that. Who would ever take a woman's babbling seriously?

I didn't close an eye all night.

13

OUR EMISSARIES RETURNED next morning just after dawn, pleased at the positive outcome of their mission. Tissaphernes had not only agreed to the summit meeting, but declared that he welcomed the chance to put an end to all the difficulties and misunderstandings that had arisen. He had even chosen the meeting site: a pavilion at a short distance from the Tigris, at three stadia from their camp and from our own.

Clearchus decided to depart that very morning. The four generals accompanied him: Agias the Arcadian, Socrates the Achaean, Menon the Thessalian and Proxenus the Boeotian. Behind them were twenty battalion commanders and an escort of fifty of the strongest and bravest men. I tried to make Xeno understand the enormity of the danger they were headed for. 'Why all those men? Wouldn't a couple of representatives, chosen for their wisdom and intelligence, be sufficient? Why not Clearchus alone?'

'It seems that Tissaphernes insisted, he wants our officers to meet his. He's organized a banquet with an exchange of gifts. He wants to create a climate of mutual trust,' Xeno replied.

'I can't believe this! Seasoned men, with years of battlefield experience, can't understand that they may be walking into a trap? Just reflect for a moment and try to imagine what would happen if what I'm afraid of turns out to be true. Your entire army would be decapitated, in one fell swoop. The whole general staff, dead and gone.'

'Don't be ridiculous,' replied Xeno. 'Do you think it would

be easy to do in such formidable combatants? Clearchus is not stupid; he has taken all the necessary precautions. The terrain is perfectly flat, as you've seen; there's no place for a large force to hide. Clearchus's plan is intelligent: leave at once, so as not to give them time for any plotting. Believe me, to take out seventy-five of our men is no easy matter; it would take at least three hundred of them. More, if they wanted to be on the safe side. And where would all these men be hiding? Calm down, and don't say a word of this to anyone; you'll make me appear ridiculous.'

That's what he said to me, but I wanted to shout at them not to go, not to put themselves in such awful danger. I was sure that what I was feeling wasn't simply nerves, or some wild imagining, but a true premonition. I didn't say a word but I stood at the edge of the road with a water jug in my hands and I watched them go. They left on horseback. Clearchus rode first, clad in his iron armour decorated in gold, his black cloak on his shoulders. Behind him were Socrates of Achaea, with his embossed bronze breastplate, and Agias of Arcadia with breastplate and greaves in silver-plated bronze, both wearing light blue cloaks. Proxenus of Boeotia wore black like Clearchus, but his cuirass was made of white linen decorated with strips of red leather and a painted gorgon on his chest. The last of the generals was Menon of Thessaly. He shone in his polished bronze armour with highlights in gold. His greaves were trimmed with silver and he carried his white-crested helmet under his left arm. White, as always, was the long cloak elegantly draped over the rump of his stallion. Behind them rode the battalion commanders in rows of four. Alongside them, in two groups of twenty-five, were the guards.

When Menon passed I stared at him with such a distressed expression that he noticed, and answered me with a reassuring gesture, as if to say, 'Nothing will happen.' Then he turned his head and nodded to someone behind me and I turned in the same direction.

Melissa was standing there wrapped in a military cape that reached down to her knees. Her right hand was raised.

She had tears in her eyes.

TIME SEEMED to stand still. Tension flowed through the camp as if the future of the entire army depended on the outcome of that meeting, which was actually true. The men spoke quietly among themselves in small groups. Some of them climbed to the top of the knolls that rose alongside the camp to see if they could catch a glimpse of someone returning. Others, from below, cupped their hands to shout up asking whether they'd spotted anything. I wasn't the only person worried.

The sun seemed nailed to the centre of the sky.

I went to find Melissa.

'Did he say anything before he left?' I asked.

'He kissed me,' she answered.

'Nothing else?'

'No.'

'He didn't tell you what he thought of this mission?'

'No. He seemed fine.'

'Then why are you crying?'

'Because I'm afraid . . .'

'A woman in love is always apprehensive when she feels her man might be in danger. It's like a dizziness, you feel light-headed, empty-headed . . .'

'You're lucky. Your Xeno never has to fight.'

'That's not true. There are at least two full suits of armour on our wagon, and he wants to play his part. He fought at Cunaxa and he will again. The situation is worsening day by day and the moment will come when any man capable of using a sword will be indispensable. I'm just praying to the gods that all our men come back safe and sound. If they do, we'll have nothing to fear. We should try to keep our spirits up. Xeno says that Clearchus is a judicious man and he'll surely have taken every precaution. They'll come back and this nightmare will be nothing but a memory.'

Melissa fell silent, absorbed in her thoughts, and then sighed. 'Why does Xeno hate Menon?'

'He doesn't hate him. Maybe he's afraid of him. They're too different, they come from different worlds. Xeno was educated by great teachers in the art of virtue, Menon learned about life on the battlefield. Xeno dreamed of becoming a protagonist in the political life of his city, Menon has always only had to worry about surviving, about avoiding injury and death . . .'

'. . . Avoiding imprisonment and torture, you mean. That's what he's really afraid of.'

'I wouldn't have thought that Menon knew fear.'

'No, you're wrong. He's not afraid of dying. What terrifies him, although you'd never be able to tell, is falling into the hands of the enemy. Of suffering the horrible mutilations that he saw inflicted on Cyrus's body, of being disfigured by torture. He perceives the perfection of his body as an absolute, demiurgic work of creation that must not be spoiled.'

'What does "demiurgic" mean?' I asked.

'That it was made by the Divine Creator, the one who made us all.'

The blaring of a bugle interrupted us. The alarm!

'What's happening?' I asked.

Melissa glanced at me and in her luminous amber eyes I saw all her worst imaginings become reality.

We ran out of the tent and towards the southern limits of camp, where we could already see people gathering.

The bugle continued to sound the alarm, an insistent, penetrating din that tore your soul apart. We could already hear what the soldiers were saying.

'Who is it?'

'He's one of ours!'

'But he can barely sit up in his saddle!'

'You're right, look, he's bent in two, it looks like he's about to fall off.'

'He's wounded! His horse is covered with blood.'

Sophos appeared, as always, from nowhere, on his dark horse. Neon was right behind him and he was armed to the teeth.

'Whoever has a horse follow me! In battle order, form up immediately, in closed ranks! Surround the hill, in a semicircle, now, there's no time to lose!'

He hadn't finished speaking when a cloud of dust appeared at the horizon and in it the ghostly shapes of horses and horsemen in a frenzied gallop.

'Follow me!' shouted Sophos, urging his steed forward at great speed. Neon and the others were close behind, realizing his intent. They caught up with the lone horseman and flanked him, pressing against both sides of his horse. Sophos took the horse's reins and Neon rounded off the group at the rear.

Arrows began to rain out of the sky all around them and meanwhile the bugle had changed its tune. It was calling the men to arms. The warriors ran forth carrying their banners, as if they could hear, in that call, the voice of their commander Clearchus, who was no more. They drew up in closed ranks with their backs to a hill that stretched out like a promontory to the east, almost all the way to the banks of the Tigris.

The cruel reality of what had happened was now apparent. The Greek warrior on horseback had his belly slashed open and was holding his guts in his hands, drenched in blood. His face was a mask of pain and he would have certainly fallen off his horse if he hadn't been supported. Sophos yanked hard on his steed's reins to stop him, halting the horse carrying the wounded soldier as well. Four men jumped to the ground and encircled their comrade, lifting him by his arms and legs. They carried him behind the front line formed by our men, who opened and then closed their ranks again as they passed.

I could hear Sophos's voice shouting, 'A surgeon! Call a

surgeon at once!' Melissa and I ran in that direction, hoping to help the doctor who would be looking after the wounded man. Melissa kept asking me, 'Who is it? Have they recognized him? Who is he?'

'I don't know. It's no one we know, for certain.'

The Persians soon arrived at a gallop, but drew up short as they found themselves up against the closed phalanx, bristling with spear tips, impenetrable. They changed direction, racing back and forth and firing off clouds of arrows that fell without damaging the wall of shields raised in defence.

Melissa and I reached the foot of the hill. The surgeon was already bending over the wounded man and was laying his instruments out on the roll of leather he'd placed on the ground.

'Bring me water and vinegar, if you can find any,' he said as soon as he saw us. 'Hurry, or this man will die.'

We ran off to search for water and vinegar and as we were returning we saw Sophos on foot urging the phalanx forward against the Persian cavalrymen, forcing them back towards the Tigris.

The surgeon washed the terrible wound and gave the warrior a piece of leather to bite down on so he wouldn't scream. He ordered us to hold down his arms, and began to sew him up. He pushed the man's intestines back into his belly with his hands, then stitched first the membrane that held them in, then the muscles and finally the skin. The pain was so extreme that the soldier's face was contracted into the most awful grimace I'd ever seen.

One of the remaining high officers, Agasias of Stymphalus, arrived just then and asked, 'Has he said anything else?'

'No,' replied the surgeon. 'Does it look like he's in any condition to have a conversation?'

'He told Sophos that our men are all dead and the commanders taken prisoner.'

Melissa burst out, 'The commanders are still alive, then?'

She got no answer. The surgeon finished his stitching and

poured raw vinegar on the wound, extracting a final whimper of pain from his patient.

'The Persians are retreating!' we heard someone yell.

Agasias shot a look at the phalanx, then turned back to the surgeon. 'How long can he live?' he asked.

'A sword sliced through the muscles of his abdomen and the membrane, but didn't damage his intestines. He could live at least a couple of day, maybe more.'

'Keep him alive. We need to know everything he can tell us.'

The surgeon sighed and began to bandage the wound.

THAT POOR LAD was an Arcadian, his name was Nicarchus, and he'd endured unthinkable pain. He collapsed as soon as the surgeon's work was done, finally losing consciousness.

'Don't leave him,' I said to Melissa. 'I'll be back later.' I headed back to camp.

The sun had set and it was getting quite dark. The Persian contingent had withdrawn and disappeared. Since their surprise attack had failed, they must have returned to their base. They could not have hoped to break through the barrier of the phalanx. Once again, the mere sight of the red cloaks had paralysed the enemy. Sophos had gone out with a squad of scouts on horseback to patrol the area downriver, in the direction of the Persian camp, and for the time being showed no sign of return. It occurred to me that he might have gone to surrender, but I immediately discarded the idea: it was he who had drawn up the army, he who had saved Nicarchus of Arcadia, at least for the moment.

I went looking for Xeno, who I hadn't seen for some time, and when I entered our tent there he was putting on his armour. The most beautiful suit he had, made of bronze embossed to resemble the muscles of a man's chest, a sword in a sheath adorned with winged sphinxes, a silver mail belt, a Corinthian helmet with a flaming red crest and a pair of silver-plated bronze greaves with lion's heads at his knees. I was struck dumb by his appearance; he looked like another person. 'You frighten me,' I said, but I asked him no questions and made no comments because I knew that anything I said would irritate him. I'm sure that my look was eloquent enough; everything I'd warned him about had come true. What hurt me most was that all of this might not have happened had one of those great warriors listened to me, to a woman.

Xeno threw a grey cloak over his shoulders and left. I watched as he slowly walked across the camp.

What I saw was demoralizing. The men seemed to have completely lost heart. They were sitting here and there in small groups, talking in whispers. Others were sitting alone, their heads hanging low. Perhaps they were thinking of their homes, their brides, the children they would never see again. A sad tune wafted through the air, sung softly in some dialect from the north that I couldn't understand. Maybe they were Menon's Thessalonians, missing their white-cloaked commander whose strong, steady voice would no longer accompany their song.

Some of the men had built fires, others were preparing dinner, but most of them seemed to be in a trance, as if they'd been struck by lightning. They had no leader, they were surrounded by enemies on all sides, they didn't even know where they were or how to get home. But all at once Xeno jumped onto a wagon and shouted out, 'Men!'

In the sudden silence, his voice rang out like a bugle call, and many heads turned his way. Illuminated by the flames of a campfire, he looked like an apparition. He must have planned that move; he must have studied everything carefully and thought of what he would wear and the effect he would have on the men.

'Men!' he shouted again. 'The Persians have betrayed us! As you know, they have captured our commanders and massacred our comrades who had consented to meet with them, hoping for peace. They had sworn that we would march side by side all the way to the coast and that they would keep their promise so as to lay the basis for friendship and even alliance in the future. Ariaeus has betrayed us as well. He's been pitching camp with Tissaphernes's army, and has broken off every contact with us and with our command . . .'

As Xeno's discourse developed, the warriors started approaching the wagon, in small groups at first and then in entire units. Many had taken up arms and were wearing full battle gear to show that they were not afraid. As I continued to watch, I could make out in the darkness the shape of a horseman advancing at a slow gait. He drew up at the edge of camp and remained there to listen.

Xeno continued, 'We can't just wait idly for their final blow. We must react. Unfortunately, there's nothing we can do for our commanders. They may already be dead by now. We can only hope that death came rapidly, as is a warrior's due. But we, here and now, must think of the future. Of our return, of the long road that separates us from home . . .'

I heard one of soldiers close to me turning to his companion. 'Isn't that the writer?'

'Yes, it is. But if he has any idea of how we can get out of his inferno, I say we should listen to him.'

'At just a few paces from where we stand,' continued Xeno, 'lies a lad whose belly was ripped open. He's in the throes of death, and no one can say whether he'll be with us tomorrow or down in Hades. You saw him; he had the courage to make his way back here holding his guts in his hands, so that he could raise the alarm and save us from enemy attack. Such a sacrifice cannot have been offered in vain: we must prove ourselves worthy of such superhuman courage. I propose that we meet in assembly and elect new generals and new battalion commanders to replace those we have lost. You have seen me do battle at Cunaxa, but I do not belong to any of your units. I'm here only because Proxenus of Boeotia asked me to follow him. But I was a cavalry officer once and am well versed in the organization of such units. We'll need cavalry for scouting out the passes and occupying them when the army is in transit, for reconnaissance of the territory and for chasing off the enemy and making sure they stay away for good.'

The horseman I'd seen touched his heels to his horse's belly and slowly approached the wagon from which Xeno was making his speech. Who else but Sophos?

Perhaps he'd been waiting for his moment to speak. He actually seemed rather annoyed at Xeno's initiative; maybe he thought he belonged up there on the wagon instead of Xeno.

'And just where will we go, Athenian?' he asked, raising his voice.

Xeno took a look at him and understood. 'Where will we go? We don't have much choice. We can't turn back. We can't go east because that would take us further from home and straight into the heart of the Persian empire. We can't go west because that's where Tissaphernes's army is headed with that bastard Ariaeus. We have to go north, through the mountains. We can reach our cities on the Euxine sea; from there it will be easy to find ships that can take us back home.'

'Excellent plan,' nodded Sophos, dismounting from his horse and getting onto the wagon next to Xeno. 'Does anyone have any questions or objections?'

His sudden apparition was greeted by a widespread buzz. Up until that moment, Sophos had always stayed away from the action; he'd never taken a position and had rarely been consulted about his opinion. No one even knew whether he'd taken part in the battle of Cunaxa. I knew that he had. There were days when he seemed to have disappeared completely. But now he seemed to know that his time had come.

I had my own idea about what he was up to. He had been placed in the army's midst as an observer, with the task of reporting back to someone. But this someone had also put him there for another reason: in case events came to a head, or the whole endeavour went sour, he was the man who had the energy, the intelligence, the courage and the cunning to react, and to induce the others to do the same. You could clearly see that he'd done just one thing in his life: wage war. And there he was, on the wagon next to Xeno, covered in armour, with a black cloak on his shoulders. The signal was clear, and no one seemed ready to challenge him or claim leadership for himself.

One of the native interpreters came forward. 'I've heard that there's no way out to the north. The terrain is impassable, the climate is extremely harsh. You'd have to face one high mountain peak after another, raging rivers, vast glaciers. Those desolate lands are inhabited by savage tribes who are fiercely attached to their territory. They have never been conquered. They say that an army of one hundred thousand men was sent by the Great King into that region some years ago. Not one of them ever came back out.'

The interpreter's words put the hum of voices to an abrupt stop as the camp plunged back into dejection.

'I didn't say it was going to be a walk through fields of green,' replied Xeno. 'What I said was we don't have a choice. But if someone has a better idea, please step forward.'

Total silence fell over the gathering. Only the wild voices of nature, the jackals and the night birds, could be heard distinctly.

Sophos spoke.

'Men!' he thundered. 'You heard well, we have no choice. We're going north. We'll face whatever trials await us: we'll journey upstream and we'll climb the mountains, we'll occupy the passes with our quickest troops and we'll keep them open until every last man has passed. None of you will be abandoned, not even the sick or the wounded. Each man will be assisted until he regains his strength. No one will be left behind!

'We'll take what we need as we go: blankets and cloaks to protect us from the cold, and food. If they attack us, we'll fight back, and they'll be sorry that they ever tried! Men, there are ten thousand of us! We weren't defeated by the Great King, whose army was thirty times more numerous than ours. We certainly won't let ourselves be stopped by some wild mountain tribes.

'I am Chirisophus of Sparta and I ask you to entrust me with the command of this army in Clearchus's place. You will be able to count on me by day and by night, through heat and cold, whether you're healthy or ill. I will run every risk, I will face every threat and every danger and – by all the gods in the heavens and the Underworld – I'll take you home, I swear it!'

In any other situation, his words would have been greeted by a resounding roar of enthusiasm, but the men's uncertainty was too great, their doubts too many. The warriors realized what kind of hardships they would be up against and they knew already that many of them would fall. The Chera of death was already marking with black fog those she had chosen to drag back with her to Hades. Very few voices rose to acclaim his speech.

Sophos began again. 'I know what you're feeling now, but I swear to you that I will keep my promises. We shall vote now! Those in favour of my proposition come forward and touch the shaft of my spear. If the majority of you do not have confidence in me, I will gladly obey the man that you choose in my place. But before the third shift of guard duty begins, this army must have a commander or we'll be all dead within days.'

I was thinking of what Clearchus and Agias, Proxenus and Socrates must be going through. But I couldn't get my mind off Menon. He who had described the atrocity of the tortures used by the Persians with such frightening realism, he was their victim now. I felt terrible for him, I had a knot in my throat, a hole at the bottom of my stomach that made me shake. What colour was his pure white cloak now? What remained of his statuesque body?

Xeno was the first to touch the shaft of Sophos's spear. Next was Agasias and then Glous, and Neon, who looked him straight in the eye as he did. The other officers lined up and, one by one, did the same.

I couldn't bear to just stand there and watch that long line of men who were electing their new commanders. I needed to know more about the men we'd lost. I wanted to be able to tell Melissa, who must have been going mad with the uncertainty of not knowing.

I don't know how I found the courage but I managed to sneak off and to reach the banks of the Tigris. I stripped off, tying my gown around my waist, and slipped into the water, letting the current carry me off. The moon in the sky was almost full and the river glittered with myriad reflections. The water was warm and comforting. It didn't take long to reach the point where the pavilion stood. It was a large tent like the ones used by the desert nomads, erected on poles and a system of braces. There were no other structures as far as the eye could see; that had to be where the ambush had taken place. There were still people inside; I could see their shadows in the lamplight, and the sentries had lit a fire on the southern side.

I swam to the bank and crawled over the ground so as not to be seen, because there were large groups of Persian horsemen scattered around the tent for quite some distance. The progression of events leading up to the attack soon became clear to me. The riverbank was all trampled upon; there were what looked like hundreds of footprints and muddy tracks leading all the way to the tent. Alongside me were a great number of reeds cut to a length of about one cubit. They were strewn all over the terrain. I picked one up and blew into it: it was hollow.

I understood all at once where the ambush had come from: the river! The attackers were hiding under water, disguised by the floating water weed. They were using the reeds to breathe through. They must have leapt suddenly out of the water after our men had already gone into the tent. They'd killed the guards our commanders had posted outside, probably at a distance, using arrows. Maybe they were the same soldiers who were patrolling the territory now. I waited there, lying in the mud, for a long time, until the moon started sinking in the night sky.

Then I saw them come out!

There was a line of prisoners shackled together, and a Persian officer was securing the first man's chains to a horse's saddle. I couldn't recognize them because I was too far away, but I dared not go any closer. I waited until they had been led away and all the horsemen had disappeared, and then I crept up to the abandoned tent. Lying outside were the unburied bodies of our soldiers which had been mutilated by the Persians and left to the jackals. Soon the only thing left of those lads – who just a day before were so full of pluck – would be their bones.

I looked inside the tent, but the lamps were gone and I could see nothing but murky darkness.

I started walking back at a quick pace, keeping to the left bank of the river, and I reached our camp before daybreak.

Sophos had been acclaimed commander by the great majority of the warriors. The other officers who had fallen in the ambush were simply replaced by a show of hands: Agasias the Stymphalian, Timas the Dardanian, Xanthi the Achaean and Cleanor the Arcadian were chosen, in addition to Xeno. By the time they had finished the sun was rising.

No one had slept, no one had eaten. Those lads had nothing in them but a desperate will to survive.

14

MELISSA DRIED HER TEARS and tried to stop sobbing. 'Are you sure it was them?' she asked.

'I'm certain. It was too dark to see their faces, but there were five of them and they were wearing Greek military tunics. I recognized them from the way they were walking. Who else could it have been?'

'You didn't hear anything? A word, a signal?'

'No, I was too far away and I was afraid to get any closer. I stayed crouched down in the river mud so they wouldn't see me, but once they had left, I saw what they left behind. The horror that wounded my eyes will be with me in my nightmares for the rest of my life.'

'Did you see signs of torture?'

'I told you, it was dark. The inside of the pavilion was pitch-black.'

'If you had told me, I would have come with you.'

'It's better you didn't. You might not have been able to control yourself, and we both would have been in trouble.'

'Answer me honestly: do you think there is any chance that anyone has survived?'

'What I think doesn't matter. Fate has dragged us into events which are bigger than we are, and we're like bits of straw in a windstorm. But if you want to hear my opinion, I think there is very little probability that anyone survived, but if anyone managed, it would be Menon.'

Melissa's face lit up and I instantly felt badly for raising her hopes. 'Do you really think so?' she asked.

'I do, but I'm afraid what I think doesn't count. They're in a desperate situation. But Menon is the shrewdest and most intelligent of them all, and he never loses his head. The only way they'll get him is if they kill him right away and don't give him the chance to think his way out, or after he's already tried everything. If there is a single chance for him to save himself, he'll find it. Don't torment yourself so, and think about surviving yourself; it's not going to be easy for you either from now on.'

Melissa dropped her head. 'I know. With Menon gone, I'm easy prey again. You know, Abira, what I do in life and which arts I've perfected. But Menon defended me without asking for anything in exchange. I was the one who asked him to make love to me, to stay beside me in my bed. He almost seemed reluctant to accept.'

'Maybe because he loved you, and he knew how likely it was that he would die and have to leave you alone without protection. He wanted you to be free to use the only truly powerful weapon you possess: your beauty.'

I stayed with her until she fell asleep. As I walked back towards my tent, crossing behind the horse pen, I saw Sophos inspecting the guard when Neon came up and pulled him away, towards the pen. I stopped and stood stock-still; I had a feeling that something strange was about to happen. Neon was saying something. Sophos listened and seemed quite shaken; he reacted harshly and started to walk away, but Neon held on to his arm. I heard Neon shout, 'Those are your orders and you have no choice!' Then they started to quarrel heatedly in a dialect I couldn't understand. Neon left then and Sophos remained alone. He folded his arms on the fence and rested his head on them as if he were being crushed by an unbearable thought. I held my breath. He was so close I could hear him panting. Then he lifted his head suddenly and gave the stake a great punch, cursing. He walked off in long strides.

We set off as soon as we could, but all that day and the next we suffered continual attacks. The enemy wanted to see how easy it might be to wear down our resistance and to test the morale of our headless army. They soon realized they'd bitten off more than they could chew, but it was evident that we were vulnerable to attacks from their cavalry. As long as Ariaeus had been on our side, his horsemen had covered us, as had Cyrus's. They were the best of the ruling class, young men who were extremely loyal and courageous. But we obviously couldn't count on them now, and every time our warriors reacted to an attack, the Persians would swiftly and easily ride off beyond the range of our spears.

Sophos kept his promise not to leave anyone behind. Anyone who was wounded or fell ill was well cared for. I wondered how he'd be able to keep his word when there were dozens, or hundreds, of men injured. Nicarchus of Arcadia journeyed with us, stretched out in a wagon. His belly was as swollen as a wineskin and as hard as leather, but every time we stopped to rest the surgeon would probe his wound with a silver tube and drain the evil humours from his bowels. His fever was very high, and the heat of the sun added to that of his body made him delirious. All night he groaned, and many of his comrades found themselves wishing that he would die, to end his agony and their own. I was sure that somewhere, a long way away, there was a person hoping with all their heart that he would come back, praying every day to a god to protect him from the countless perils of his profession and bring him home safe and sound. Those hopes and prayers deserved to be answered, because they were like Melissa's thoughts for Menon, like mine for Xeno when he was not with me.

The idea of thwarting fate gave me great satisfaction, and I worked hard to help Nicarchus battle against death who, like a jackal, prowled around his wagon at night, eager to carry him off to the land of listless ghosts.

We crossed a river on a bridge of boats and proceeded in the direction of an abandoned city the locals called Al Sarruti.

I realized that there were quite a few women travelling with the expedition; a long line of them walked alongside the wagons being used for the wounded. They were all very young and scared to death in such a precarious situation. Some of them were pregnant, and I wondered how they would be able to make it through long marches and endure privation and hardships of every kind. The men who were their lovers or whose keeping they were in would certainly have preferred not to put them through such strenuous conditions, but the women had no choice, except for migrating to the enemy camp, which must have seemed altogether too dangerous.

The difficulties were beginning now, that much was clear. What we'd experienced until that moment was nothing; we'd had food and drink, at least, and we'd had our commanders, men who inspired courage and always made the right decisions. I knew that just because I was in love with Xeno, that didn't mean that he was equal to the task he'd set out to accomplish. Could he really lead his comrades to safety? Sophos impressed me as being up to the job, now that he'd come out into the open. But there was something he was hiding, something he wouldn't say. Maybe other men would emerge, others who had remained in the background until then.

One evening as I was cooking dinner with the little we had left to us, I told Xeno about the night of the ambush, how I swam down the river until I reached the pavilion and saw our generals dragged away in chains. I told him I'd discovered how the enemy had surprised them by lying in wait under the water, breathing through reeds.

My story upset him: he couldn't believe I'd done something that only a man could do to his mind. But what disturbed him most was the reason why I'd done it: to bring Melissa news of the man she loved, even though that man was Menon of Thessaly, whom Xeno despised.

'Are you going to write about your disdain for him in your diary?' I asked.

'Certainly,' he replied, 'every man will have the fame he deserves.'

'But you're the one who's deciding what kind of fame he deserves, and that's not fair. What do you know of his life? Haven't you ever thought that back in your city someone might be writing even worse things about you?'

Xeno seemed astonished, perhaps more because I was able to formulate such a statement in Greek than for the substance of what I'd said.

I told him about the other scene I'd witnessed, the quarrel between Neon and Sophos, but he seemed not to grant it any importance. It was nothing to fret about, he said, certainly just some minor difference in opinion. I couldn't stop worrying about it, though. I'd never seen Sophos in such a state.

I remained awake that night long after Xeno had fallen asleep. I was looking out towards the west, towards the land I'd come from, when I saw strange shapes passing in the darkness, shadows that quickly slipped away. I thought I could hear voices as well from somewhere in the distance.

There were boats on the Tigris.

I looked over at Melissa's wagon, covered by a tent, and wondered what would become of her. I listened to the shrieking of the night birds and imagined that I was hearing the cries of our commanders, tortured and killed, angry ghosts crossing the threshold of the night.

Then nothing.

I was awakened by a strange noise that I couldn't identify and I woke Xeno.

'What is that?' I asked him.

'I don't know. The wind can bring sounds from a great distance.'

The wind ... whenever I heard it blowing, I wondered whether it was the kind that merely raised the dust in Beth Qadà or whether it was the kind that roared and announced some extraordinary event.

'It's the sound of an army approaching!' exclaimed Xeno. 'Don't move from here.'

He put on his armour and went to find Sophos and the others.

The officers spread the alarm in silence. I watched as the men woke their sleeping comrades and before long the entire army was ready to march, while a small cavalry unit commanded by Xeno rode off in the direction of the noise, which was growing more and more distinct. A barely visible pallor was beginning to lighten the horizon to the east, behind a line of barren hills. In the meantime we resumed our journey; I had the mules yoked and the tent loaded on to the wagon. The servant was used to obeying me when Xeno was not around. Next to me was a girl on another wagon. She was pregnant.

'Do you know who the father of your child is?' I asked her.

She gestured at the long line of warriors winding before us in the darkness. 'One of them,' she replied, and goaded the mules pulling her wagon.

We soon arrived at the edge of a gully that intersected our path. It was a deep fracture in the ground, a splitting of the sandy rock that reached from west to east for a long stretch. The walls were steep and at the bottom lay huge boulders, scattered here and there as if tossed by a giant's hand.

It was completely dry, but during the winter it must fill up with muddy water dumped by violent storms back in the mountains; I'd seen that kind of sudden flooding often where I came from. The boulders must have been tumbled about by the raging flood waters.

There were only two or three points where crossing was possible, paths – trampled by the passage of herds of goats and sheep – which cut down the steep wall, crossed the bottom and climbed up the other side. Only one of the three paths would allow for us to cross in the wagons, but there was considerable risk in attempting it in that hour of darkness preceding the dawn. Two of the wagons tipped over and had to be pushed back upright using the tent poles for leverage and set back on track. The servants compensated for the unnatural angle of descent by using spear shafts to prop the top-heavy wagons up so they wouldn't take another tumble. The infantry and cavalry used the other two narrower paths.

Sophos, Agasias, Timas, Xanthi and Cleanor rode ahead, turning often to guide our passage. They rode at a distance of twenty or thirty paces and continuously called out to one another, but without raising their voices. They were all very young, between twenty and thirty, and strongly built, and they had taken their new assignments very seriously. But although I'd never strictly been a part of the military expedition, even I couldn't help but think of the commanders we'd lost.

Sophos kept his head turned and his eyes trained to the east, at the point where the sun would be rising. All at once, rays of light shone out from behind the hills and Sophos turned to the south. He was looking for something, and I looked the same way. A light flashed repeatedly on the plain, and Sophos exclaimed, 'It's Xeno! The signal, they're coming. We'll do as we've decided.'

Upon hearing his order, the officers on horseback rode fast to the foot of the gully and each one took position at the head of his unit. The men broke ranks at once and groped their way up the opposite bank any way they could. Our convoy, with the wagons, the pack animals, the women and the non-combatants, had reached the bottom of the gully and was starting to struggle its way up the other side. I began to think that the soldiers had forgotten about us and were leaving us behind. I saw two officers up on the opposite edge of the gully making wide gestures as if to hasten our ascent, but I didn't want to separate myself from the others.

As I was starting to climb up the slope I heard a galloping noise behind me and thought that all was lost. But it was our men on horseback, the scouts commanded by Xeno, who had given the signal and who were now racing down the path behind us at breakneck speed.

Xeno yelled, 'Abandon the wagons! Get up to the other side, now! Leave the wagons behind!'

The other scouts were shouting out as well. 'Move, run as fast as you can, leave the wagons behind, the enemy is at our heels!'

We all got out of the wagons and clambered as fast as we could up towards the outer edge of the gully. I saw Melissa stumbling and crying out with pain and rushed to help her. The fancy sandals she wore weren't suitable for climbing and her tender feet had never trodden jagged stones and splinters of black flint. She wounded herself with every step she took. I tried to lift her off the ground and drag her towards the top, but I couldn't do it alone. I was desperate and completely out of breath and I yelled as loudly as I could, 'Xenooo!' and there he was next to me, smiling behind the mask of his helmet. He knew I needed him, even before I called.

He pulled us both up to the top in no time as the other men were helping the other unfortunates in our company.

'Everyone behind the rocks!' shouted Sophos and we scrambled to obey him, as we could already hear the thunder of Persian horses galloping at our backs. As soon as we reached shelter, I looked back, panting, to the spot where Sophos and Xeno had gone and . . . nothing! There was no one to be seen.

'Where have they gone?' I exclaimed.

'They've left us alone!' whimpered Melissa. 'They've gone off and deserted us.'

'Don't be an idiot. They're on foot as we are, they can't have disappeared.' I hushed her because the Persian horsemen were emerging from the rim of the gully. They pulled up short in surprise, scanning the empty expanse of dry grassland. The profound silence was disturbed only by a light breeze that bent the tall grass and set white dandelion tufts adrift. But not for long.

A high-pitched, rhythmic battle cry burst out, followed by the clanging of metal on metal. Our men had been invisible because they were all crouched down in the grass and they rose to their feet all at once, in perfect formation!

Ten thousand shields joined in a wall of bronze, ten thousand spears jutted forward menacingly, thousands of red cloaks fluttered in the wind like standards. Their helmets covered their faces. I'd never seen them look like that and it was an awesome sight indeed. Behind their bronze helmets, all you could see were the eyes and mouth, and this transformed each man into an otherworldly being. Their faces disappeared but their eyes flashed in the dark and every movement of their heads was ominous. Their bare-faced adversaries could imagine any kind of ferocious power behind those metallic masks. Their faces were inscrutable, their bearing charged with dire intent.

The Persian horsemen tried to overcome their shock and they attacked at an order from their commander, but our men were too close and were already advancing. There was no room for the horses to gain momentum; the spears were upon them. The phalanx advanced like a machine, and nothing could stand in its way. The horsemen tried in vain to breach the line. At each attempt the ranks closed tight and the files doubled up so that the men behind pressed their comrades forward with their shields. Their spears cleaved the bodies of their enemies and the battle turned into a massacre. I watched in horror as men and horses fell headlong into the gully, tumbling over each other, leaving shreds of flesh and splashes of blood on the sharp stones and shards of black flint.

The phalanx opened then and let through the archers, slingsmen and javelin-throwers who showered the survivors with a hail of lethal darts. When we could finally approach the brink of the gully ourselves, the sun shone triumphantly in a pure blue sky but the ground . . . the ground was a slaughterhouse. The Persian cavalry squadron was reduced to a confused, atrocious pile of bloodied bodies and the excruciating groans of the dying broke my heart.

But it wasn't over.

Cleanor claimed that the scene was not terrifying enough. He wanted Tissaphernes's soldiers, when they arrived, to witness horror without end. They had to learn that they deserved to be punished for their betrayal. They had to see with their own eyes the fury that the red cloaks, deceitfully deprived of their commanders, were capable of.

There was a group of skirmishers accompanying the army from Thrace, fierce and primitive highlanders. They were ordered to mutilate the Persian corpses in any way possible, using axes, clubs and knives. I turned away and ran off to hide behind a boulder until Xeno started calling me because it was time to resume the march.

The wagons we'd abandoned were dragged up to the rim and the army began its journey under the noonday sun. I would turn back every now and then, and I'd see large numbers of vultures wheeling and circling in the air above the gully.

How could they sense the smell of death so soon and from such a distance? I wondered. But then I realized that I too could smell its stench. Xeno had it on him as he rode close by me and so did all the others. The Thracians looked like butchers, covered with filth from head to toe.

All day long we advanced without any further incident, and towards evening we reached the deserted city of Al Sarruti. It was ringed by a wall of mud bricks and at its centre was a pyramid-shaped tower that the inhabitants of those lands called a ziggurat. It too was in a state of ruin. The base was still covered by slabs of grey stone carved with images of warriors with thick curly beards and braided hair. The figures were painted in bold colours and were quite impressive. The whole building was crumbling, though, and some of the slabs at the base had collapsed so that the figures lay with their faces in the dust. 'That's how human pride ends,' I thought to myself.

Xeno entered to see if there was anything left inside and I followed him. As we went forward, the light of the entrance behind us became dimmer and dimmer, until all that was left was a faint glow floating with shimmering dust. At a certain point, I felt something alive under my foot and I screamed. My jerking movement and my shriek awakened a huge flock of bats who were sleeping inside the tower and the air instantly filled up with them. I could feel those revolting creatures brushing against me all over and I lost control and started to scream so loud that Xeno had to slap me to stop me. Xeno covered my mouth and nose with his cloak and held his breath as he dragged me out as quickly as he could. He knew that we could have died in there. The fast fluttering of their wings had raised a cloud of dust so dense it would have choked us. As soon as we got outside I slumped to the ground and gulped in the fresh evening air avidly.

'See how easy it is to die?' said Xeno, panting. 'Even without making war.'

'You're right,' I said, still gasping for air. 'If you hadn't slapped me I would have totally lost control and I would have choked and died.'

I lifted my eyes to the top of the pyramid and saw a number of people of every age. They were the inhabitants of the region who had sought shelter there, trying to put themselves beyond the reach of the armies moving through the area. Some of our men had climbed to the top as well, trying to catch a glimpse of Tissaphernes's approach, but they saw no one. We camped among the ruins and for most of the night I could hear the crying of the children who were on the top of the tower with their mothers. The women didn't dare descend and mix with us, and they had nothing to feed to their children. I was consoled by the thought that the armies would soon move on and the people would be free to return to their homes and their work.

We pushed on the whole next day until we reached another ruined wall that must once have encircled a powerful city. Our foes hadn't caught up with us; perhaps the carnage in the gully had served its purpose and scared them off for good. We hoped so, but it was hard to believe. They were surely camped somewhere on the plain, biding their time and regrouping for a fresh attack.

We saw the Tigris. It was magnificent. The current was fast, and every so often it carried strange boats, round as baskets, that would spin around at each bend or whirlpool in the river but never ran aground. I began to hope that we'd put enough distance between ourselves and our pursuers, and in the evenings I'd go to visit Melissa and help her with her wounded feet, massaging them and applying salves.

I was wrong about the enemy. On the seventh evening they reappeared. A multitude; as always, they greatly outnumbered us. Too many to take on.

They were sending ahead their cavalry squadrons, although for the time being they kept their distance. They had understood our weak point. They knew we had no cavalry and that Ariaeus wouldn't come to our aid: why should he? I was a little surprised at myself; I was starting to think and reason like a soldier.

At a signal from the lookouts, the alarm sounded and our soldiers drew up in marching order with a rearguard in battle formation. Our men countered every attack of the enemy cavalry, but our javelins never met their mark because the assailants would simply melt away. Their own arrows were deadly, on the other hand. Even as they were retreating they would twist around and let fly with extreme precision, armed with the double-curved bows used by the horsemen of the steppe. Our men had never seen this tactic before, and were wounded in large numbers; they were rescued by their comrades and carried to shelter in the wagons. That night a large tent was raised and eight surgeons went to work. I'd never seen anything of the sort, especially not so many doctors working together.

Each had his own razor-sharp instruments, needles, forceps, scissors and other tools that I was unfamiliar with. By the light of oil lamps, they cut and sewed, and where the wounds were ragged, they would snip off strips of skin with their scissors as though they were pieces of cloth.

What really struck me was the endurance of the wounded in dealing with the pain. Each of them could see that the others weren't moaning or weeping or screaming and so they were somehow forced to follow suit. They'd bite down on their strip of leather, lips curling and teeth bared as if they were dogs. A groan might escape them, but they'd never let their voices be heard. They breathed fast, clenching their teeth. In the end, all their pain was concentrated in their eyes. I'll never forget those looks of fierce suffering and agony.

Some died because the doctors couldn't stop the bleeding. I sat next to one of them until he expired. He lay naked in a lake of his own blood. His cot was soaked through and the blood kept dripping onto the ground. I held his hand to help him pass the last threshold; I didn't want him to have to face the darkness of death alone. Blood and filth could not completely mask his beauty, and it seemed impossible to me that such a perfect, powerful body would soon be a slab of still, cold meat. What I remember about him was his feverish gaze and the way the pallor of death ran so rapidly across his face and his limbs. Before he breathed his last breath, he had a moment of lucidity and he looked at me intensely. 'Who are you?' he murmured.

'Whoever you want me to be, child. I'm your mother, your sister, your lover . . .'

'Then,' he said, 'give me water.' And he fixed the sky with lifeless, staring eyes.

15

OUR MARCH HAD grown insufferable. The warriors were forced to move in tight formation and, what's more, wearing full armour from sunrise until after sunset. Attempting the journey in any other way would have meant certain death, but pushing on under those conditions was unsustainable. Tissaphernes's cavalry attacked us in continuous waves, letting fly with bows and slingshots to sap our defences; as soon as our spearmen tried to react the Persians slipped away until they were just beyond their range. There was always a fresh supply of horsemen, so the skirmishing never let up.

Only darkness would bring relief, because the Persians were afraid of us, and camped a long way off to avoid being surprised by a night raid.

One night Xeno asked to meet with the other commanders because he had an idea to propose. Sophos, Xanthi, Timas, Agasias and Cleanor arrived one after another at our tent and I served them all evening, bringing them palm wine mixed with water. Xeno had thought up an ingenious plan.

'We have to act at once,' he began. 'If we don't get them off our backs we'll never be able to stock up on provisions. The men will end up losing morale and strength and that will be the end of us. The enemy have learned their lesson well: attacking us frontally means getting cut to pieces, and so they won't do that again. They want to burden us with a growing number of wounded and disabled warriors and prevent us from eating and drinking. If they stopped us from sleeping – which is something they could do, actually, with little effort – it would be all over for us in three or four days at the most. Thankfully they haven't thought of that.'

'So,' interjected Sophos, 'what is your proposal?'

'We have to act at night.'

'You want to attack them? I don't think that's feasible,' interrupted Xanthi. 'They surely have posted sentries; we'll never manage to approach their camp.'

'No. I want to get free of them. Listen: it must be tomorrow, or we'll never have another chance. You'll have noticed that when we pitch our tents there's a group of horsemen watching at two or three hundred paces. They make sure we set up camp and then ride off to tell their commanders that all is well. What we'll do is pretend to stop for the night, set a few fires to make it look like we're cooking dinner, and as soon as they turn around we'll start marching again. With our armour on the wagons, so we can travel lighter and faster. We'll muffle the horses' and mules' hoofs so we can move in absolute silence. We'll eat and drink as we walk and we'll make very few stops, just long enough to rally, then off again. Brief sleep periods, while the others keep watch.'

The commanders listened attentively. The writer, who would have guessed! That young Athenian seemed to know what he was talking about. I could have told them why. Xeno had often told me how his teacher had taught him to reason and to draw on experience.

'Our Thracian skirmishers,' continued Xeno, 'have told me that when they are transferring their herds from the mountain pastures to the plains they have to stop as little as possible to avoid being attacked by other tribes and despoiled of their livestock. The way they rest is by sleeping often for a very brief period, sometimes even leaning against a tree, so that in reality they never stop. Their bodies become accustomed to these short rests and they recuperate enough energy to push on. Sleep is short but very deep and, ultimately, relaxing.

'What I'm saying is, we won't stop the day after, nor the day after that. They'll end up thinking that we've taken a different route, and they'll split up their forces to look for us. In the meantime we'll have reached the foothills, where the Persian cavalry won't be able to move as swiftly and easily as they do on the plain. At that point, we'll decide how to proceed.'

Sophos approved of the idea. 'If everything goes according to plan, we should be able to shake them off. On the other hand, we have no choice. They have clearly demonstrated their intentions. They have eliminated our commanders and now they want the rest of us dead as well, down to the last man. Neither Artaxerxes nor Tissaphernes wants a single one of us making it to the sea and boasting how easy it is to get all the way to Babylon without losing a man.'

That was the truth, then. It wasn't a question of revenge. It was a question of not letting out information that was vital for the survival of the empire.

Sophos turned to the other commanders. 'Pass these instructions on to all the men. Each fighting unit will organize guard shifts and all the rest. I'll decide on the stops; my signal will be relayed verbally down the line.'

'There's something else,' Xeno continued. 'We need a cavalry unit, even if it's a small one. I'm not saying we should take on the Persians, but it would be helpful for close observation of the enemy or for scouting out suitable passes.'

'Where will we get the horses?' asked Timas.

'We'll take them from the wagons,' replied Xeno, and at those words the jug I was carrying nearly fell out of my hands. He was talking about eliminating our means of transport.

'We'd have to give up the wagons at the base of the mountains anyway,' he continued calmly.

I thought of Melissa's feet and of my own and I got a lump in my throat. Would I be able to keep up? I thought of that pregnant girl I'd seen on her wagon, what would become of her? And all the others who were in her condition? Sophos had promised that he wouldn't leave anyone behind, but he was talking about warriors. I was afraid he wasn't including the women. But they'd already decided. The choice I made so instinctively when I decided to run off with Xeno was now starting to reveal its real consequences.

The commanders got up to leave and return to their own units. Sophos had changed since he'd come out of the shadows. He had managed to get himself elected by the assembly of warriors without opposition and had stepped into Clearchus's shoes without difficulty. He had imposed his presence, the tone of his voice, the flash of his eyes. He had the attitude of a man who knows what he wants and how to get there. There was an instinctive self-assurance about him, a flow of energy that had connected him with his men from the start. As he was leaving our tent he put a hand on Xeno's shoulder and said: 'This is just what we needed. A magician who could make an entire army disappear, just like that!' snapping his middle finger against his thumb.

He even had a sense of humour.

'You pulled off the same trick, Commander,' retorted Xeno. 'At the gully, when you hid the warriors in the tall grass.'

The others started to laugh, a swaggering, bold, disdainful laugh that didn't want to end.

'I can still see their faces when they saw us stand up with our shields in place,' said Xanthi, the long-haired Achaean with the neck of a bull.

'Like they were looking death in the face!' exclaimed Agasias, dark of skin, hair and scowl.

'And knowing they'd lost the game!' added Timas the Dardanian, lean as a leopard, with his olive complexion and short pointed beard.

'If they think they can sing victory, they've got another think coming,' concluded Cleanor, and he might have been staring down the enemy with his grey falcon's eyes. Cleanor was a bundle of nerves and muscles. He was built on two thighs as thick as columns and seemed impatient to show the world that he was up to his task. 'If they want us, they'll have to come and get us,' he said again, 'and to do that, they'll have to get off of their horses.'

They left the tent snickering and their voices soon faded in the distance.

Xeno washed and stretched out on the mat and I lay down next to him. We made love with a passion that I hadn't seen for ages. We were in danger, relentlessly pursued and hunted down, and yet he was at the height of excitement and energy. He – the writer who'd had to put up with so much irony and sarcasm during our long march – had thought of a way to lead ten thousand of his comrades beyond the grasp of death. And he had the courage to carry it out. When he finally lay back and closed his eyes, I took his hand and asked him the question that had been nagging at me for so long.

'The Persians want to wipe us out, but do you think there's anyone back in your country who wants this army to return?'

'What do you mean by that?'

'I'm not sure. It's an intuition, a sensation. But I'd like you to give me an answer, if you will.'

Xeno's response was a long silence.

'If you don't want to talk it doesn't matter.'

'This army is composed of mercenaries . . .'

'I know.'

'Except for two men.'

'Sophos . . .'

'Right.'

'And you. And the whole expedition was kept secret at your departure. I don't think that what was secret then can be announced openly now. Who is Sophos?'

'An officer of the Spartan army. Probably of very high rank.'

'Can I ask you how you know that? Did he tell you?'

'By the wicker bracelet he wears on his left wrist. Inside is his name and the number of the unit he commands. The soldiers wear it on their right. It's a custom of the Spartan army. When a man falls in battle and his body is not recovered immediately by his comrades, the enemy will strip it of anything precious. A twig bracelet is worth nothing and for this reason it is never stolen. But it bears the identity of the fallen man. Inside that bracelet it says Chirisophus.'

I tried to pronounce the name the way Xeno did but it was too long for me. 'I think I'll keep calling him Sophos . . . So, what is his role? Why did he appear so suddenly?'

'That I do not know.'

'Do you think he'll tell you?'

'I think not.'

'Will we survive?'

'I hope with all my heart that we will, but it is difficult for a man to change his destiny once the Moira has spun it out.'

I didn't know who this Moira was, who spun out the fates of human beings, but I was frightened nonetheless. In our villages they talked about women with long black hair, dressed in black, with deep black rings under their eyes who roam about at night and snatch the living and carry them away to the kingdom of the dead where the air is dust and the bread is dry clay . . .

'But as far as it's in my power, I will leave nothing untried to take these men to safety. They are extraordinary fighters and they have replaced my homeland, seeing that I can never return to Athens.'

'Do you really mean to leave the wagons behind?'

'We have no choice.'

I didn't ask him anything else. I fell silent, overcome by anguish. He must have understood. He held me tight, and whispered into my ear, 'I won't abandon you.'

The next day was no less hard than the ones before. The attacks were relentless and the army was forced to proceed in closed formation with the wagons at the centre, shields held high. It was an enormous strain, because each shield weighed as much as a bushel of grain. I tried to imagine what our formation must have looked like from above: like some kind of enormous metallic porcupine advancing laboriously, tormented on every side by a myriad mounted huntsmen shooting clouds of arrows and darts of every sort at us.

The darts stuck into the shields and made them even heavier to carry. Every so often our skirmishers attempted a counter-attack. Lying in wait behind some rise in the terrain, they would let fly with bows and slings, succeeding in downing a certain number of the enemy. Xeno told me that the slingsmen from Rhodes could hit a man in the middle of his forehead at fifty paces.

After passing a couple of hillocks we came to a place where we could camp, and that was where we carried out the plan. Campfires were lit, a certain number of tents were pitched, and sentries posted. As soon as it grew dark, the Persians who checked us every evening rode off towards their camp and we set about dismantling everything. The evening star sparkled above, not far from a perfectly curved crescent of moon with its points turned upwards. The ground was light in colour, making it easy for us to pick our way. The darkness would protect us in our night-time march. The men struck the tents and ate hurriedly and then, at a signal from their commanders, who were obeying an order from Sophos that was passed by word of mouth, the army set off without a sound.

We marched all night in silence, at a good speed. The warriors had left their shields on the wagons, in order to quicken their pace, but each man knew exactly where his shield was, and the quickest way to reach it if need be. All orders passed swiftly from man to man in a whisper.

The first stop was very short. The men lay on the bare ground and slept for a brief time, and then were back on their feet.

I'll never forget that journey through the night. Nothing happened, actually. There were no battles, no assaults, no ambushes. No one died or was wounded. All we did was cross the night from one end to another. In silence, in the dark. Through a thousand mysterious scents: the fragrance of dried amaranth, the dust – and the flint – giving up the heat that had scorched it during the day, the stubble on the plains and the distant hint of broom blossoming on the mountains.

Every now and then, the solitary song of a night bird would burst out of nowhere, or we'd be surprised by a sudden fluttering of wings as we passed by a bush. We watched as the evening star slowly sank into the horizon. There was a sense of magic all around, in the turquoise sky, in the sharp silver crescent of the moon. The long line of men crossing the threshold of the night seemed an army of ghosts. At times I thought I saw white manes tossing in the wind and the silhouette of a horseman standing out against the sky, but I realized that I was giving shape to my dreams or perhaps to someone else's. The only reality was the heavy step of those men trying to escape annihilation.

At a certain point, I slipped off to sleep in the wagon, because I knew that soon I'd lose that privilege, that I'd have to march through the burning sand and cold mud like all the others. Before I closed my eyes I thought of Nicarchus of Arcadia, of his torn belly. I hadn't seen him in a while and I wondered whether he was still alive or whether they'd dumped him somewhere along the road without burying him.

I was really half awake, because the swaying of the wagon and clanging of the wheels stopped me from falling into unconsciousness. Once I saw looming before me the powerful figure of Cleanor of Arcadia, who was pressing his enormous thighs against his horse's flanks to force the reluctant animal not to baulk at a difficult passage cut into the hillside. Shortly thereafter I saw the crest on Xeno's helmet waving in the breeze. The new commanders were leading the troops with a firm hand.

The second rest stop was no longer than the first, and the march resumed a bit more slowly. Fatigue had begun to set in. Finally, the glow of the dawn whitened the horizon and the five commanders plus Xeno regrouped on a small rise in the terrain and cast a look around. They were silent, grim, their jaws clenched and their hands tight on their spear shafts. The warriors stopped as well and looked in the same direction, there where the enemy might well appear on horseback. They waited a short time and then let out a cry of exultation.

'We've lost them!' shouted Xeno.

'You're right, we're rid of them!' yelled Xanthi.

'We did it!' the others rejoiced. But Sophos cut them short. 'Not yet,' he warned. 'It's too soon to know and we can't let up now. Take a short rest, those of you who still have food can eat something, but then we're on the march again. Do you see that high ground over there? That's where the mountains begin. When we're there we can say we're safely beyond the threat of the Persian cavalry. At my orders, we're back on the road.'

The sun was beginning to blaze on the horizon and soon grew hot and pitiless. The men kept turning their heads, fearing that they would see at any moment a white cloud announcing the hammer-blow charge of the horsemen of the steppe. Instead, nothing happened. Xeno led a group of scouts up and down the column, riding off at a distance at times with the evident intent of forestalling an attack.

Towards afternoon the countryside became a little hillier, and at a certain point, from a stretch of high ground, we could see a green hill in front of us which stood out against the brown of the surrounding terrain. Around the hill were a number of villages, and at its peak was a fortified palace. It was a stupendous sight, a combination of shapes and colours so fascinating that it seemed the stuff of dreams. Birds with huge wing spans soared over the castle, allowing the evening breeze to hold them aloft. Lengths of blue and yellow cloth fluttered over the towers, and the grass, incredibly green, moved in waves, keeping time to the wind, changing colour and light at every moment.

The castle turned out to be abandoned, while the houses were full of peasants apprehensively awaiting an all-out attack. Since they had nowhere to go, they had decided to remain with their wives and children. They were hoping that the war would pass like a sudden storm and then disperse in the distance.

The army loaded up all the provisions they could find, all the grain that had already been set aside for the winter. They needed it to survive, but so did the farmers who had harvested it. Without it they would die, perhaps, or they would see their children die, the little ones first. Their food was taken by those stronger than they were.

I walked through the castle alone. I'd often dreamed of such a building as a child, imagining it inhabited by a magical being, a man capable of transforming stones into gold and of taking flight by night from one of the towers, like a bird of prey. I went from one room to the next, looking all around, and saw for the first time what Xeno called 'works of art'. Figures carved in relief, others painted on the walls, others still carved into the wooden doors. I stared open-mouthed at winged monsters, lions with the head and beak of a bird, men fighting panthers and tigers, other men being pulled on a chariot by two yoked ostriches. I knew that nothing of the sort could ever have existed and that those images had been created by men, like the stories invented by narrators that had never happened. Because no one is content with the life they have; people always want some other life that is different and more exciting. Hadn't that been my problem? But I had actually abandoned my village, my family and my betrothed to run off on a crazy adventure.

Whoever had lived in the castle had taken everything with them. There was not a piece of furniture left, not a bed, not a carpet. The only thing I found, at the far end of a bare room, was a little clay doll with jointed arms and legs, dressed with a scrap of grey wool. I picked her up and took her to camp with me, feeling as if I'd found the last survivor of some awful catastrophe.

We didn't sleep that night either. Sophos and the other commanders were keen to carry out Xeno's plan: we had to put as much space as possible between us and the Persians so we wouldn't find them suddenly upon us with their rain of lethal arrows. The men rested for an hour. I saw one of the men measuring the time by planting two poles in the ground and waiting until the moon covered the space between them. They were truly tired now, even though the food they'd taken and eaten had given them energy and the drive to continue. But their faces were grim, they cursed at the slightest problem and grumbled when they received an order. Only Xeno was absolutely tireless. He was no longer 'the writer'; he was a commander, and it was evident that he wanted his deeds to be remembered, and that he desired the esteem of his comrades. He was altogether absent at times, in another world, and this gave me a cold feeling.

When we were halfway through the night, the sky darkened. Low, fast-moving black clouds veiled the crescent moon and galloped eastward. Here and there I could see sudden flashes of light illuminate the huge dark clouds from the inside, setting their tattered edges on fire. Bolts of lightning snaked their way from sky to ground, followed by the distant rumbling of thunder. The season had begun to change; the days were getting shorter and the mountains were harbouring storms. We were heading towards a world which was getting stranger and less familiar with every step.

When dawn cleared the sky the next morning, the first mountain buttresses appeared. The plain ended and led into a harsh, very different territory. It looked foreboding, impassable, and yet everyone was rejoicing. They were warriors: all they wanted was an even fight.

The sun was barely visible. Dim it was, and pale, behind a curtain of thin cloud. In front of us a tall hill loomed up over the crossing of two large roads. From what I'd understood we would be heading north, where the cold winds that numb your limbs are born.

The five commanders held a meeting without dismounting

from their horses. It was a curious sight: the rumps and the tails of the animals at the outside of the circle, their muzzles in the centre so that they were continually pushing their snouts at one another. They were ungelded stallions and each one wanted to be on top of the others. I wondered whether it was the same for the horsemen who mounted them.

The council was over quickly; just enough time, I suppose, to exchange a few opinions. Xeno immediately detached a group of infantrymen and sent them towards the top of the hill to guard it and defend our passage, but no sooner had he given the order than another group emerged from the opposite side: Persians! They were on foot as well, because the slopes of the hill were too steep for horses, but they were lightly armed and running fast. Xeno urged his Halys uphill nonetheless to encourage his men to move faster. I heard one of them shout back, 'Hey, you! It's easy for you to give us a lesson from the saddle of a horse. You try hauling this shield and let's see how fast you can run.'

I couldn't make out what Xeno said back, but I saw him leap off his horse, grab the shield away from the man who'd complained and head uphill with it, taking the lead himself. More Persians were arriving as well, the advance guard of their army, and the warriors on each side were exhorting their comrades to get to the top first. It was grotesque, actually: a war mission was turning into a foot race before our eyes, with the spectators cheering on their favourites.

Our men, led by Xeno, arrived first and they formed a tight circle. The others didn't even try to drive them off the top: they were red cloaks, better left alone. The pass had been occupied, and our army could now cross the Great Crossroads and make for the mountains by travelling up the valley of a small river.

The bulk of the Persian army arrived a few hours later and they drew up some way off. Our five commanders took position at the entrance to the valley on their steeds, one alongside the other, and I saw Xeno shining like a star in his silver-trimmed armour. His plan had been a great success and he had won the respect and admiration of all.

I heard a voice behind me ask. 'Do you think they'll attack?'

'Melissa! What are you doing here?'

'Will the enemy charge?' she repeated.

'I don't think so. Why should they? We've taken the high ground and our passage will be well defended. The sides of the valley will protect us as well. They're stuck here in the plain and that puts them at a total disadvantage. They've accomplished their goal, after all; they've succeeding in pushing us towards a desolate land that no one has ever returned from.'

Melissa bowed her head. 'I want my Menon back,' she said with tears in her eyes.

'No one can give him back to you,' I replied. 'But you're safe now. No one will hurt you.'

'Is it true that we'll have to leave the wagons behind?'

'It's true,' I answered. 'We can't climb those mountains pulling them along.'

'But I'll never make it,' she said in a tremulous voice.

'All you have to do is walk. It won't be so terrible. You'll get blisters at first and they'll break and bleed, but then you'll get calluses and your feet will get used to it.'

'But I'll be disgusting!' she wailed.

I realized that Menon wasn't quite so present in her heart as she'd have you believe. I comforted her as best I could. 'You won't lose your other charms. When the men turn around to look at you, I've never seen them starting from your feet.'

Melissa dried her tears. 'You never come to see me any more.'

'Neither do you. I'm sorry, I've been busy. But I'll be there for you when you need me. You can count on me. I won't leave you behind.'

The words that came out of my mouth were the same I'd heard from Sophos and from Xeno, and when I pronounced them I felt like a commander of sorts myself, because in our group there were certainly those weaker than I was, Melissa for one.

She hugged me and thanked me and then moved on. As she was walking away I saw Cleanor of Arcadia eyeing her, and Timas the Dardanian as well. Neither of them was looking at her feet.

That night, Sophos addressed the troops drawn up in formation.

'Men! We've managed to reach a territory where our enemy's cavalry will no longer be able to harass us. I'd like to tell you that the worst is over, but I can't because it's not true, and you've already heard enough lies. The worst is yet to come. Our route is marked out for us: if we went east we'd be headed into the heart of the Persian empire. We've already been south and you all know what lies in that direction. To the west there's Tissaphernes and his army, who managed in the end to catch up with us and would like nothing better than to annihilate us. And so we have to head north, towards the mountains, where he won't follow. Do you know why? Because no one has ever returned from up there. It's a steep and rocky land, studded with ice-covered peaks that pierce the sky, inhabited by fierce, wild tribes. But that's not all: we'll be facing the winter, the worst of our enemies. We'll have to journey up narrow valleys and down rugged paths. We'll have to break our path with our weapons, face violent storms, blinding lightning, hail and blizzards of snow. You can well understand that the wagons could only be a hindrance to us under these conditions. We'll load everything onto the animals, and we'll burn the wagons. We'll be faster and lighter. I told you when they murdered our commanders that they would not get the better of us and I repeat that now: they will not be able to stop us! Burn the wagons.'

The men obeyed. They unloaded the provisions, the tents and the weapons and piled all the wagons up in a single place. There was a moment's hesitation, then one of the soldiers whom

I'd never seen before took a brand from the fire and tossed it onto the heap. The flames caught almost at once, swept by the wind, and the dry, seasoned wood kindled instantly, crackling with little blue flames and bursting quickly into a gigantic bonfire that our enemies could surely see from afar. The intense light illuminated the warriors who stood in silence all around and seemed dazed as they watched their world catch fire.

None of them at that moment could have imagined what would happen when the flames turned to ash.

16

WHEN THE FIRE had begun to languish, another appeared at the foot of the mountains in the plain stretching out in front of us, a blaze of such size that the burning of our two or three hundred wagons seemed insignificant in comparison.

'Look at that, Cleonimus!' said one of the soldiers close to me. 'What is it?'

'I don't know,' grumbled his comrade, a thickset, swarthy lad.

Xeno was watching it too. He approached Sophos and the two of them spoke briefly. A couple of scouts rode off on horseback soon after, headed towards the site where the fire was burning. In the meantime the men had begun to walk off a few at a time, returning to the spot where the provisions had been unloaded so they could claim their own. Their weapons and tents, especially. There was still an abundance of food.

It was a difficult moment. They had all been accustomed to storing their belongings on a wagon; they always knew where and how they could find what they needed. Now they were forced to bundle them up roughly so they could load them onto an ass or a mule. Their quarrelling and cursing soon quietened down. The situation unfolding to the north was so spectacular that they were mostly struck dumb: looming above the mountains were masses of clouds, as black as pitch. Swollen and menacing, they hung over the immense chain, discharging blinding bolts of lightning which twisted and turned like serpents, as the roar of thunder tumbled down to the valley, rebounding off the dark craggy cliffs. I knew what the men were thinking. 'That's where we're bound for.'

The land we were leaving behind us was hostile, true, but it was a land dominated by light and the heat of the sun. We were headed towards the kingdom of the night and of endless storms. If we turned south we could still feel the tepid breath of the land between the two rivers that caressed our faces. Looking north we could sense the distant, threatening air of the tempest. We stood between two enemy lands, but one held only the hostility of men, the other the hostility of the elements as well.

The scouts returned to report on the fires blazing down on the plain. Tissaphernes had burned down the last villages along the river so we could not stock up on provisions. The two horsemen had met up with hundreds of desperate farmers fleeing with their families, their shoulders bearing the burden of what little they had managed to save.

I tried to imagine what those people must be thinking. They had probably lived in peace since they were born, eking out the same poor, monotonous existence as the folk in the village I came from, but having everything they needed, food and shelter. All at once they no longer had anything. The fire had cancelled their past, present and future.

War.

When Xeno came to lie beside me, I asked, 'What will we live on?'

'What we find,' he answered.

I asked no more questions. I understood well what he meant. From that moment on, we'd be consuming the resources of the territories we were crossing, like a flock of crows, like a swarm of locusts, leaving a desert behind us. All the men were sleeping now, thinking perhaps of the wives and the children they'd left at home, but tomorrow they would once again become the Ten Thousand, the demons of war, hiding the humanity of their faces behind the mask on their helmets, because from now on, every day and every night, for many days or months or even years, they would have to fight and win, or face death.

The next day there was just smoke rising from the plain, and Tissaphernes's army was drawn up to defend the Great Crossroads. They thought we would try to turn back! But none of us could even begin to contemplate a direct clash with the most powerful empire on earth.

We set off on our way, leaving the Great Crossroads behind us. The road we travelled flanked a torrent that swirled and foamed as it rushed towards the Tigris. One of the warriors tried to test how deep it was, but his spear disappeared completely under water without touching the bottom.

Xeno and I had loaded our baggage on the backs of three mules, tied together to form a little train. I was at the front, pulling the first by its halter. I scanned the crowd trying to spot Melissa, but couldn't find her. The path was not very wide, and the bulk of the army preceded us in a long line which was beginning to unwind at the end of the valley in the direction of a pass that we could now see clearly ahead of us, whenever the rays of the sun broke through the cover of dark clouds and illuminated the mountain peaks.

We started our climb up the mountain road which was strewn with sharp stones. At times the path would jut out above the valley or slope steeply over the raging torrent below, its water boiling with white foam, coursing over the gigantic boulders that poked out of the river and loomed at its edges. The mountainside was covered by forests full of age-old trees with enormous gnarled trunks.

The march was very tiring but exhilarating at the same time: I had never walked uphill for such a long way and I was suffering from the strain, from the scrapes to my arms and the cuts to my feet, but I was excited by the sensation of going higher and higher with each step.

I was used to travelling long distances, but always with the same field of vision, always surrounded by the flat, endless expanse of the steppe and the desert. But this was magnificent, the view changing constantly at practically every turn of the road. I was wonder-struck.

At a certain moment, I turned around and my attention was attracted by two different scenes, one in the distance, where Tissaphernes's army was moving off westward like a long black snake slithering over the desert sand. The other was much closer: there was the pregnant girl I'd seen on her wagon.

The Persian general was leading his army towards Anatolia and towards the sea, to take possession of the province in Cyrus's place. He was sure we'd all soon be dead amidst the steep mountains and precipitous peaks of the north, the region where the roaring wind was born. The girl, on the other hand, was lying at the side of the path, frantic, unable to move. For her, and for the child she carried, there was no tomorrow. No one stopped. The warriors marched past her, leaning on their spears, their cloaks sometimes brushing her face, but there was not one of them who reached out a hand.

I slowed down, taking advantage of the fact that Xeno was far off, bringing up the rearguard with his horsemen, and then I stopped. I tied the leading mule to a small oak tree and approached the girl.

'Get up now,' I ordered her.

'I can't!'

'Don't be stupid! Do you want to be devoured by the beasts of the forest? They'll eat you alive, a little at a time, and then they'll start on that little bastard you're carrying in your belly. Get up right now, you idiot, or we'll fall behind and it will be all over for both of us!'

I was convincing, and with a little help the girl managed to get to her feet and follow me to where I'd left the mules.

'Now hold on to the tail of the last mule and let him pull you. Don't you dare let go, or I'll beat you to death myself. Are you listening?'

'I'm listening,' she answered.

'All right. We're moving on, then.'

I wondered where Melissa was, and I was afraid that she wasn't much better off than that girl holding on to the tail of my third mule. I wondered too what had happened to Nicarchus the Arcadian, the boy who'd saved us all by overcoming the agony of his torn gut to raise the alarm. I would have liked to ask the surgeons what had become of him. They surely knew, but I was afraid of getting an answer that I didn't want to hear, and this stopped me. I'd already understood that certain things you're better off not knowing.

We soon reached the pass, a saddle between two forested peaks. The army had already started down the other side. When it was our turn to cross, I caught a glimpse of several villages nestling in the folds of the mountain, built of the same stone as the cliffs. It was difficult to distinguish them from the surrounding countryside. The atmosphere was strangely calm. At first there was birdsong and then not even that. Perhaps they'd been hushed by the imminent storm, announced by the dark clouds gathering at the peaks. We finally reached the valley and entered the villages.

There wasn't a living soul.

Our men looked around in bewilderment. It was clear that those houses had been inhabited until just a few hours earlier. There were animals in the pens, pots on the tables, fires going out in the hearths. I brought the pregnant girl into one of the houses so she could warm herself at the fire and get something to eat. It was very cold outside.

The soldiers started to sack the houses but Sophos stopped them. He climbed up onto a rocky spur and spoke out. 'I want no one to touch anything here! Listen to me: we take only what we need to eat, nothing more. They'll understand that we don't have hostile intentions; let's hope that will suffice to hold them back. Look around you: we have to cross all these mountains, using passes like the one we just came through. They're waiting somewhere, and they can tear us to pieces if they want to. They know every inch of their territory. They could be anywhere, and we wouldn't even know it; they could easily strike at any moment. Our strength is in the phalanx, standing shoulder to shoulder on open ground. Strung out in long lines we are completely vulnerable. We have to do all we can not to make enemies.'

The men grumbled a little, but obeyed. I'd come to understand, that in that army, the orders were carried out, but the soldiers had to be convinced first by their commanders that they were doing the right thing.

They searched the villages and gathered all the provisions they could find at the centre of a little square, calculating how many animals we could bring along to guarantee our survival as long as possible. As they were searching they realized that there were women and children in some of the caves, hastily hidden behind the vegetation. They were rounded up and put under guard. Maybe they had refused to follow their men up to the mountains, perhaps there hadn't been time. It was an important find, and the commanders were cheered: they had hostages now, who could be exchanged for our unhindered passage. But I did not share their enthusiasm, and I didn't think the inhabitants of those villages would bend so easily.

THE COLUMN OF our men on the march was so long that when the last ones arrived it was already getting dark. They didn't bring good news. After crossing the pass, they'd been attacked from behind by the natives. They'd lost four of their comrades, felled by a hail of arrows and stones, and they were carrying about ten wounded with them. Their welcome into that wild land.

Xeno and his rearguard had captured a few prisoners: shepherds who hadn't wanted to abandon their flocks.

At that point, everyone looked for shelter for the night. Competition was fierce. The officers were first, and settled in the houses. The others scrambled to find a space in the remaining structures. No one wanted to sleep outdoors because it was very cold and the night promised to be damp. Obviously, the buildings could not house even a quarter of our soldiers. Those who had managed to locate their tents pitched them, others built make-shift shelters using leafy branches and mats or settled under the canopies meant to protect the animals.

I wondered what would become of that poor pregnant girl the next day, and whether I'd be able to drag her along to the next pass hanging on to the tail of my mule.

Xeno had the servants pitch our tent and I even managed to cook something for dinner. He hadn't given up writing. By lamplight he opened his case, extracted a white scroll, fastened it to the edges of the cover, as if it were a table top, and proceeded to trace out letters in his language. I wanted so badly to know what he was writing, but he'd already told me what he thought; that it 'wasn't necessary' for me to know. There were times, when he was in a good humour or after we'd made love, that he read me what he'd written. Many of the things he talked about I had noticed myself, but I'd seen them with different eyes. Actually, I'd seen and noticed much more than what he'd thought to write, things he took no account of. I would tell him about them, precisely and with an abundance of details, but I knew they'd never be included on the white scroll that he unwound a little nearly every day, filling it up with tiny, regular marks, perfectly aligned. That's the way he thought, after all: precise, organized, and in a certain way predictable, and yet here and there I saw a leap, a stumble, a sudden quickening of the characters, and I thought, that's where he's expressing emotion.

I went outside before lying down to rest and I looked around. I wasn't alone. There were many others looking northward because the mountaintops were studded with fires: our enemies were observing us from up above. I called out, 'Xeno!'

'I know,' his voice answered calmly. 'There are fires on the mountains.'

'How do you know if you don't come out to see?' I asked.

'I can hear the talk of those who are outside watching.'

He was so absorbed in what he was writing that he wouldn't be persuaded to leave his white scroll. I started back in, but something attracted my attention: a figure wrapped in a shawl approaching the house of one of our commanders, Cleanor. I thought I recognized a certain swing of the hips under a rather close-fitting gown, but it had become dark and I couldn't completely trust my eyes.

When Xeno extinguished the lamp I was already half-asleep, in that torpor that lets you hear and feel what's happening around you but won't let you move. For a long time, I continued to hear the calls of the sentries, who were shouting out their name and unit in order to stay alert, then fatigue overcame me and I sank into silence.

WHEN I OPENED my eyes Xeno wasn't there. In no time, the tent was struck and folded by our two servants and I stood there alone under the open sky swept by darkening clouds. The wind had started to blow furiously and I could hear a distant roll of thunder. Up high on the mountains I could see white columns of rain descending from the heavens and the oaks bending under the raging wind. I gathered all our things together as quickly as I could and loaded them onto the mules, making sure that the case with the white scroll was secured.

Xeno was with the other commanders who were meeting with Sophos to decide on the day's business. I soon saw a group of our men departing with one of the prisoners, heading towards the pass. They were going to negotiate, to ask for free passage in exchange for the hostages. I didn't think success was likely.

Our envoys soon returned. One of them had been wounded by a flying stone, and was limping. They hadn't even been allowed to get close.

The only thing we knew about our enemy was their name. They were called Carduchi, Kardacha in their own language, and they considered themselves enemies of the Great King. From what I could see, they certainly were. The fact that we were also his enemies made no difference at all to them. At the end of their meeting, Sophos gave the orders that had been decided upon. All disabled animals would be abandoned and the prisoners freed, except for a few of them. To make sure that his orders were respected, he put a dozen officers along the road. Any of the soldiers caught trying to sneak off with a pretty girl or, depending on their taste, a good-looking boy, chosen from among the prisoners, was immediately stopped and forced to return them to the villages.

I saw that the dealer who hired his prostitutes out to the soldiers had left three or four of the girls behind. A couple of them were limping; they must have twisted an ankle on the rocky path we'd taken and they were certainly in no shape to continue climbing. A couple of the others weren't well; they had caught some kind of fever. That bastard could have allowed them to ride on one of his mules, but he was evidently more worried about the animals than the women, given the situation. As much as it vexed me, there was nothing I could do. I was already saddled with one of them, and Xeno certainly wouldn't have allowed me to help anyone else. He cared about the mules as well.

Sophos had shown the natives that he did not have hostile intentions, seeing that he hadn't taken hostages, hadn't allowed rape or violence, and not even plunder, forbidding the men to take any of the many bronze objects they'd found in the houses. But his show of good will had not helped in the least. Those savages were convinced of one thing alone: whoever set foot on their land had to die.

The army began to ascend towards the pass, and I ensured that the pregnant girl was hanging on to my mule's tail and was tagging behind us. Every once in a while I'd call out to make sure she was still there, well aware that if she stumbled, no one would stop to help her.

Each of the warriors wore his full war gear. I could tell why they all had such big, muscular legs: ever since childhood, they'd practised walking for days at a time with the weight of their arms upon them. Their strength was impressive: they advanced with an enormous shield on their arms, chests covered with a shell of bronze, a heavy sword slung over their shoulders and a long, solid spear held tight in their fists as if it were all just a part of their bodies.

The army had a voice of its own, that changed with changing situations. It was a confused sound made up of all their voices and all the noises that accompanied them. On the plain, the roll of the drums and the wail of a flute helped measure their steps, but in the mountains it was different. They marched on as best they could, slower at times, or faster, and there was no room for drums or flutes. The silence was filled by the thousands and thousands of voices of warriors on the move. The sound they made was quite strange: the sum of many words, of sudden shouts, of braying and whinnying, of clanking metal at every step. There was no common beat, no harmonized chord, and yet the sounds united in a single voice. That voice could be suddenly hushed, at times, or turn gloomy. The jangling of the weapons might grow dominant and then the army spoke with a cutting, metallic voice, or the utterances of men might prevail, and be expressed as a buzzing or a deep grumbling, in a sound like mounting thunder or in a screeching as keen and sharp as the mountain peaks towering above us.

The path was getting steeper and steeper and yet our march continued unobstructed. But the sky was black with bloated clouds and it soon started to rain hard, a cold, dense, heavy rain that completely drenched me. I felt a trickle of water slipping between my shoulders and down my back and my hair was plastered to my forehead. My clothing clung to my legs and even made it difficult to walk. I was terrified of the lightning: rivers of fire that gashed the leaden sky and tore through the big black clouds that galloped dishevelled across the sky, enveloping the peaks in a thick, dark fog. The claps of thunder were so loud that they made my heart tremble inside my chest.

The warriors did not seem perturbed by the fury of the storm. They continued to advance at an even pace, planting their spears to mark their stride. They had lowered their helmets over their heads and with every flash, every bolt of lightning, their gleaming armour sparkled with bright bursts of light.

I turned around to look at the girl, who seemed to be totally depleted; I was counting the steps until she would certainly drop. She was thin and pale, livid with the cold, and her belly seemed huge and impossibly heavy. All the warmth she had in her body was defending the child within her, but soon he too would feel the cold, and that would be the end. She slipped and staggered and her utter fragility contrasted with the powerful stride of the bronze-covered soldiers. Whenever she stumbled her hand shot forward to protect her belly and she was continually cutting and wounding herself on the sharp rocks. I kept thinking of how long and difficult our journey was sure to become.

The clouds grew closer and closer. Ever since I can remember, the clouds I'd seen were high in the sky, tiny and white, but now I wondered what it might soon feel like to touch them. The path took a sharp turn to the left and I watched as the entire column paraded before me. There was Cleanor, not too far away, cutting an imposing figure even in this rain. He was followed by his horse and two servants, and then by a strange apparatus: two mules, one in front of the other, harnessed together carrying two long beams on which a makeshift carrier had been fashioned, covered with tanned hides. A shelter of enviable wellbeing given the miserable conditions we found ourselves in.

What treasure was guarded in the litter swaying with the gait of the mules? I did not doubt for an instant that the treasure was Melissa, with what she kept warm between her thighs.

At that same moment I heard a cry and a group of Carduchi charged at our advance guard. The bugles blared and the warriors ran towards the head of the column, scrambling up the slippery slope, until they could draw up in frontal formation. The attackers lunged against a wall of shields, were impaled on the spears pointing forward, and many of them fell at first impact. The others were surrounded by our skirmishers and massacred. The march resumed under the pounding rain.

When it came my turn, I passed by the fallen and could see them for myself; their bodies were scattered over the terrain and among the rocks. Most of them were piled up on top of each other along the same line, the others were on higher ground, where our scouts had encircled and killed them off as they tried to flee. They were shaggy-looking men, with long hair and beards, wearing tunics of coarse wool and tall rawhide boots. Their weapons were large knives like those used by butchers. Poor people who were defending their land and their families against invincible warriors. I thought of how much courage it must have taken to attack automatons of bronze and iron, all of them faceless and looking exactly the same, looking like the creatures that populate nightmares, creatures born of a non-human seed. I imagined the moment in which their bodies would be returned to their huts, greeted by the wailing of widows and orphaned children.

Perhaps they hadn't understood that all we wanted was to pass through and that we would never come back. They hadn't even gone back to their villages, to see for themselves that we'd taken only food and touched nothing else. I was sure that those dead bodies would kindle hatred and the thirst for revenge. There would be more battles and more ferocious clashes, more dead and more wounded. Crossing that land would be an ordeal. Not only the men, but the very earth and sky, were against us.

Much later I saw Xeno bringing up the rear of the column with his horsemen on foot; I could tell it was him by the crest of his helmet. I could see that he was constantly putting himself in harm's way and I trembled for him. I took another look at the pregnant girl who was limping along, clinging tight to the mule's tail. I knew what a docile animal he was, used to dragging a weight that wasn't his. But it would have taken nothing more than a single kick of his frightful hoofs to cut short two lives at once.

I really couldn't understand what energy was holding her together. I thought of the mysterious force that impels each creature on this earth to preserve his own life and his children's. I thought of how many lives I'd seen cut short since I'd set off with Xeno and how few I'd helped to save. Death had certainly taken no notice of my efforts; the lives she had snatched for herself greatly outnumbered those I had tried to wrest away from her.

An idea came to me. I was still reflecting when I saw the head of the column being swallowed up into the swollen cloud that covered the mountain peak.

And disappear.

17

THERE'S NOTHING all that strange about entering a cloud. From far away it looks like something that has a shape and a consistency, but the closer you get, the more its shape goes away and it just becomes a mass of denser air, a kind of fog that envelops and surrounds you. Sounds are muted, voices are lower, figures fade into one another and become confused. Sometimes you can't tell things apart. Our men looked like shadows come up from the Underworld. The swaying of their cloaks seemed a natural phenomenon like the rustling of the leaves or the waving of the tall grass on the mountain's slopes.

When we finally arrived at the crest, we heard shouting and the clanging of weapons coming from the rearguard and I felt panic-stricken. Xeno was always out there, ahead of all the others. How would he be able to fight off the enemy hidden in the fog, lurking among the trees or behind the rocks? Would I ever see him again?

The clouds opened in front of us, revealing a terrain which was even steeper and more impervious than what we'd left behind: a rocky ridge crossed by a path that rose towards the top of the mountain. I realized that on this kind of terrain you can never be sure of arriving anywhere. After one peak you find another, even higher than the first. What looks close can be very far and what seems far away can in reality be relatively near to you. You had to continuously adapt your gait to the ever-changing ground.

Luckily, the storm had calmed and only a few occasional

drops were falling. But you still could be pelted suddenly when the stiff wind shook the tree branches above you. All at once, something happened that really alarmed me: the speed of marching suddenly picked up. The men were advancing faster and faster, for no reason that I could understand. Although you could never know what was happening at the head or at the end of such a long column, each one of us had to adapt to the movement of the army as a whole, in front and in back of us, just as every muscle in the sinuous body of a snake contributes to making him glide forward.

The path was rising steeply and walking was very strenuous, and yet the army was moving faster. We women wouldn't have been able to keep up such a fast pace for long and I was stupidly making it even harder for myself to breathe by urging on the pregnant girl, encouraging her not to give up. Out of the corner of my eye I could see the awkward, desperate jerks of her body as she strove to keep her balance; I could hear the yelps of pain escaping her at every step. Wasn't there anyone at all who could help me? We were invisible to them, all they cared about was the mules. The mules were precious, we didn't even exist. Xeno was too busy with his new duties as a commander, in showing off what he was worth and how wrong everyone had been about him. The man who everyone had sarcastically called 'the writer' was now charging about on his horse with extraordinary mastery, striking with great precision, killing and wounding, attacking and falling back, utterly tireless and always mindful, with every move he made, with every sway of the crest on his helmet, of the effect he was having on the others.

I, and the girl I was dragging along behind me, were dirty, soaking wet and covered with mud. There was nothing beautiful or fascinating about us, nothing that would attract attention. We just didn't matter, and the army was completely indifferent to whether we survived or succumbed. This made me so angry that when I saw the girl shoved and knocked roughly to the ground by one of the soldiers rushing forward, I grabbed him by his cloak as soon as he got close enough to me and shouted, 'Listen, you bastard, why don't you look where you're putting your feet? Can't you see that girl with the big belly you just crashed into? Her cunt isn't worth anything now, is it? Less than spit, damn you, and if she dies no one gives a fuck, but if there hadn't been someone like her carrying you around for nine months, you wouldn't even exist now. If you're in such a hurry, you bastard, you can rush off and fuck yourself!'

To my utter amazement, I'd pronounced words that under normal circumstances I would have blushed just thinking about. But the man stopped and took off his helmet, revealing a double row of pure white teeth. 'If we don't rush, we'll die, woman! We're rushing because we've got to get somewhere quick. When we're there, and if I'm still alive, I'll come back and find you and give you a hand. Try to hold out.'

I couldn't believe my eyes or my ears: that youth was Nicarchus of Arcadia, the hero who'd succeeded in raising the alarm with his guts in his hands. I stammered, 'But you . . . but I . . .' No use. He was gone, he'd stuck that helmet back on his head and had turned back into a mask of bronze, like the others, one of Ten Thousand.

It was a miracle, I thought. If he had made it, so could we. 'We have to push on,' I yelled to the girl. 'Grit your teeth and don't give up. I know we can do it!'

The clouds cleared and I finally understood what was going on at the head of the column. The Carduchi had occupied the pass and a great number of them were deployed in a compact formation up above. They carried enormous bows, so tall that I could even see them at this distance, and they had gathered up huge piles of rocks, ready to throw at us.

The column stopped short.

Just then, I saw Xeno riding by at a fast clip. He drew up alongside Sophos at the head. I could imagine what they were saying.

'Have you gone completely mad? You let us fall behind without saying a word, exposed us to continuous attacks.'

'Can't you see? Up there, take a look. I was trying to seize the pass before they did.'

We were stuck. I could tell that Sophos had no intention of doing battle in such a highly adverse situation.

At least we could catch our breath. The girl had let go of the mule's tail and had sat down. She was taking in great heaving gulps of air. I tied the leading mule to a tree and went to help her. She had deep black rings under her eyes and was as pale as death; her breath was coming in short gasps now. A little pool of rainwater had collected in a hollow of the rock near us.

'Drink,' I told her. 'And wash your hands, they're covered with mule shit. I have something for us to eat.' I gave her a piece of bread which she wolfed down. I couldn't remember the last time I'd eaten.

Xeno was still protesting, because he wanted to be informed when there was any danger, and he was also badly shaken because he'd lost a couple of his best men. Basias of Arcadia had been hit by a boulder rolled down from above which had crushed his helmet and smashed his skull. The other had been pierced by an arrow that had transfixed both shield and breastplate and entered his side. The heavy, deadly arrows used by the Carduchi had big pyramid-shaped tips.

But what disturbed him most was having to leave his men behind unburied. Xeno was religious, and the idea that their bodies could be violated or maimed, that their spirits would not find rest or peace in the other world without funeral rites, tormented him. On the other hand, in the battle of the gully they'd horribly mutilated the bodies of their fallen enemies, merely to scare off the Persians. Apparently it was a religion that counted for Greeks only.

Given the general indecision, Xeno proposed a solution: in the clash, his rearguard had taken two prisoners; they could be questioned to find out whether there was another passage that could be transited by the baggage animals as well. We had an interpreter, two, actually. The first knew Persian and the Carduchi language, the second knew Persian and Greek. Who knows where they'd found them! Evidently there was someone in the army who took care of such things. But they had surely joined us after the commanders had been captured and we'd decided to start marching north.

The first prisoner would not say a word. Neither threats nor blows to his face and body served to loosen his tongue. Cleanor struck him with the hilt of his spear shaft, hard in the stomach, making the man bend in two, and then struck again even harder on his back. The man crumbled to his knees, but would not talk. At this point Sophos signalled to one of his men, who drew his sword and ran him through from front to back. The prisoner collapsed like an empty sack, his blood spilling into a pool on the ground.

Xeno was surprised by that gesture, but then understood that it had been the right decision, because the other man burst into speech. He said that yes, there was another passage, wide enough for the mules and pack animals, leading to the summit. He hadn't spoken earlier because he was afraid that his comrade would report him to the tribal chiefs.

'What else do we need to know?' Sophos asked, speaking calmly while the man who'd been run through writhed on the ground in his death throes.

'Well . . .' gulped the surviving prisoner, looking away. 'There's a rise overlooking the pass. You'll have to occupy it in advance, otherwise you'll be trapped again and no one will be able to help you.'

The sky in the meantime had cleared and the setting sun inflamed the clouds with streaks of red and gold, spreading an aura of peace and serenity through the countryside. You could hear birds singing and the rustling of tall trees that I'd never seen in all my life. Some of them had enormous trunks and foliage so vast that they could give shade and shelter to over a hundred men. Others came to a pointed shape at the top and were a deep green or an intense bluish colour. Water flowed everywhere. It frothed and rumbled over colossal boulders at the bottom of the valley, and on the sides of the mountain it spilled in white columns of foam from one cliff to another, spreading iridescent halos in the refracting light and mist left behind by the storm. In the forest it dripped from the branches and trickled from the leaves, dotting the stems of flowers with beautiful translucent pearls. Coming from the arid steppe, all this wealth of water was inconceivable, but it was also the mark of a nature so vast and so unfriendly that I felt our very lives were threatened by it.

Organizing the operation was quite challenging, because the two passes, the one seized by the Carduchi and the one our army intended to occupy, were in plain sight of each other. The officers decided that two operations would be launched at once: Xeno would launch a front attack on the Carduchi who held the pass, to make it look as if we wanted to force our passage. This would distract their attention from the main operation: a party of volunteers would follow the prisoner under the cover of night and occupy the rise that commanded the other pass. At dawn, a trumpet blast would signal to the bulk of the army that they could attempt the crossing. At this point, the enemy were bound to realize they'd been tricked and would attack the second pass. Our party there would have to counter-attack and hold their position at all costs to allow our army to cross. When Xeno's rearguard caught up, they would cover the party's withdrawal.

It was Xeno who explained all this to me, so clearly and effectively that I had no trouble understanding. I'd been living with soldiers for so long that I'd grown accustomed to military tactics and could even come up with my own ideas in certain situations.

'When will the operation begin?' I asked.

'Now.'

'Did you actually offer to lead the diversionary action by assaulting the pass?'

'Yes.'

'Why? You've already had to fight today, you lost two of your best men. Someone else could go in your place; no one would blame you.'

'Because I'm the best at this type of operation. And because Agasias will be leading the other operation, the march towards the second pass, with the native guide. He's the best after me.'

'What about Sophos?'

'He's beyond any comparison with the rest of us.'

'He's beyond the rest of you, you're right about that. Maybe that's why he always shows up in the right place at the right time.'

'What do you mean by that?'

'No, nothing. It's just a feeling. Xeno, I miss you. Ever since we've left the plain I only see you from far away, if at all. I'm terrified that something will happen. Death is hiding behind every tree in this land.'

Xeno brushed my cheek with rough fingers. 'From the moment we come into this world there's a death sentence hanging over our heads. The only things we don't know are when and how.'

'I see things differently.'

'I know. You fight death. You think you can change the course of events, you presumptuous little barbarian,' he teased.

'I have done so. Do you know who I saw today? Nicarchus of Arcadia.'

'Yes, I'd heard that he made it through. He's in Agasias's unit, with the other Arcadians. That lad has a tough hide.'

'Don't expose yourself to danger needlessly. Dying for no reason is stupid.'

Xeno did not react. He looked over at the pregnant girl. 'Do you think you can save her?'

'Her, and her son.'

The sun was setting behind the mountains. Xeno donned his helmet, took up his shield and left me Halys, his horse. He was an extraordinary animal. His coat was white and his eyes were big and expressive. He had hocks of steel, powerful muscles and a thick mane that Xeno combed every evening while the servants were currying him.

'Promise me you won't stray from the others,' he said. 'They have arrows they can shoot at quite a distance. I want to find you in one piece when I come back. Him, too,' he added, slapping the horse's rump. Halys whinnied in approval.

I tried to smile and nodded my head as he walked away.

Meanwhile the other contingent had already gathered under Agasias's command. They had the guide with them, his hands tied behind his back. They were waiting in the forest for Xeno to launch the attack and draw all the enemy's attention and fury down onto him.

The Carduchi. A hard people, and fierce as could be.

They weren't satisfied to let us leave their country, they wanted all of us dead just for having dared to enter. Not one of us was to survive. I thought that such vehemence and determination must be motivated by something deeper than the mere defence of their territory, but if there was a secret behind their aggression, it was very jealously guarded.

I ordered the girl to find a sheltered place and not to move from there, hid Halys behind a group of century-old trees, and went to look for a vantage point high enough to watch from.

Xeno was ascending the trail; I could see his white crest waving in the stiff wind. The sun had disappeared and the valley was flooded with a pale, unreal light. The men following him were fanned out in formation behind their shields.

The pass was already covered by storm clouds constantly lit up from within by lightning. A heavy rain poured down almost at once, carried on violent gusts of wind. Xeno shouted to be heard over the roar of the thunder and led his men into the assault. But as soon as they started to climb the slope, a noise even more threatening than the thunder exploded up high, sounding as if the mountain were cracking apart.

An avalanche of boulders crashed down the mountainside, making a tremendous commotion. The stones collided with each other, ricocheted off the craggy rock, shattered into fragments that shot out in every direction, pulling other stones along with them in their fall. Xeno shouted even louder, his voice rising over the menacing din, and his men ran fast for cover.

Those who weren't close enough to any of the big rocky outcrops just lay flat on the ground and covered themselves with their shields.

The storm blew stronger, and with every lightning bolt or flash I could make out the armour our men wore, shining under the pouring rain as if it were ablaze.

There must have been some barrier between our men and the Carduchi position. I couldn't see anything, but Xeno had stopped and was trying to get first up one side and then up the other, without making any headway. Each time they tried to advance, the enemy rolled big stones and boulders at them and the violent barrage set off further landslides of stones and pebbles and rock splinters which were carried off by the turbulent streams of water formed as the rain pelted down on the mountainside. It was a terrifying sight, made even more sinister by the sudden flashes of lightning. A big bolt directly hit a colossal tree which fell to the ground with a huge crash and then caught fire all at once like a torch, spreading a haze of vermilion light over the entire valley.

Xeno waited until the worst of the fire had died down, and then continued to launch one assault after another, keeping the enemy busy till late that night. He finally returned to camp because his men were exhausted and couldn't see a thing. Many of them had not even been able to get a bite to eat, and they didn't have a single spark of energy left in their bodies.

I watched them coming back and my heart felt as if it would

break. They were covered in mud, many were bleeding from gashes and cuts, others were leaning on their comrades and trying to stop the blood seeping from their wounds. The expression in their eyes was difficult to describe but impossible to forget.

Xeno arrived last, after all the men who had gone out with him had already returned, and reported to Sophos to find out if there had been news from the other group.

By then Agasias and his bunch should have reached their destination and seized the rise from which they could control the second pass. Perhaps the next day we'd be able to escape the vengeful Carduchi. I looked at the pregnant girl and thought that she'd be getting her last rest. As soon as we got the signal, we'd have to march at the same speed as the men, face the same risk of finishing up under an avalanche of stones or being targeted by their archers. Our men had brought back several of their arrows: they were two arm's lengths long and looked like javelins. When they fell from the sky, the effect was deadly.

There was a solution, I thought, but I'd have to make it a surprise attack, a word that made me smile in view of what I was planning. Xeno left to join the others for a meeting. I went to take care of the girl, bringing her blankets and something to eat.

'What's your name?' I asked, realizing that I didn't even know that much about her.

'Lystra.'

'What kind of a name is that?'

'I don't know. It's what my owner always called me.'

Her Greek was worse than mine and she spoke with a strange accent, using words cobbled together from many dialects and jargons.

'Where are you from?'

'I don't know. I was very little when he bought me.'

'So you don't even know how old you are.'

'No.'

'And do you know how soon your child will be born?'

'No. What difference does it make anyway?'

I couldn't argue with that.

'Listen well. Eat now, and get some sleep. Try to get as much rest as you can. Look, you can lie down under that spur, so that if it starts raining again you won't get wet. It's stopped now but you can never tell around here.'

The girl started eating without my asking twice.

'Tomorrow will be the worst. If we manage to get through tomorrow, I can't promise you we'll rest easy, but at least we won't have to be scared to death all the time. Tomorrow anything can happen, and each of us will have to take care of herself. We can't expect help from anybody. I don't know if it will be better or worse than what we went through today, but you just hang on tight to that mule's tail. If you have to let go, yell for me and I'll try to give you a hand, but there's no saying I'll be able to.'

Lystra looked at me with that frightened-animal look of hers.

'I'm not saying that we're going to die, we might make it. But you can't count on anyone, not even me. Do you understand?'

'I do,' answered the girl without changing her expression.

I gave her another piece of bread. It was stale and hard, but it was still bread.

'Keep this for tomorrow, and don't eat it until you know you can't go any further. No situation is so bad that it can't get worse. Do you understand?'

'I do.'

'Go to sleep now.'

I turned to walk away and nearly bumped into the iron breastplate of a young soldier.

'So I've found you then! Sorry I couldn't get here any sooner, there was a fight to be seen to. But I can see that you're both all right and I'm happy about that. I didn't mean to knock her down.'

'Nicarchus of Arcadia. Who would ever have guessed? You know, I helped take care of you when you were more dead than alive.'

'I was thinking you looked familiar.'

'Try not to get your belly slit open again; it wouldn't be easy to sew you up the second time around.'

The unwitting hero gave me the broad smile of an overgrown adolescent, then went off to join his unit.

I had the tent set up and started a fire. It wasn't easy, because all the wood I could find was damp. But there were slaves in every unit that kept a fire burning, day and night, inside a jar that everyone could draw from. I finally managed to build up a steady flame that wasn't too smoky and I cooked something hot for us, barley soup flavoured with olive oil. I still had a small reserve that Xeno guarded like a treasure. I was very careful to use it as little as I could. I even brought Lystra a little.

Xeno came back from the meeting with the other commanders. They had planned out every stage of the next day's operation for each of the units.

It felt as though we were suspended in a strange, still atmosphere. Unintelligible noises wafted down from above, shouts and cries in a language none of us understood. Every now and then the sound of cascading pebbles let us know that someone was out there in the dark, keeping an eye on us.

Our sentries were on the alert. They were calling out to each other constantly and this spread a sense of apprehension that was almost tangible. All at once there was a loud whistle, and an enormous arrow struck the trunk of a nearby tree with a dull thud. It would have gone straight through a man.

And soon one did. Another whistle, followed by a scream of pain. Then Xanthi's voice, shrill as an eagle's shriek: 'Take cover! Everyone take cover!'

An ear-splitting roar tore through the night air: the sound of hundreds of arrows piercing the air. Xeno jumped to his feet and covered me with his shield: one arrow hit the rim, a second was deflected by the boss and fell to the ground. Shouting every-where, utter confusion, calling and screaming.

We wouldn't be able to count the dead and the wounded until the next morning, when the sun came out. So many had fallen!

We were encircled by an invisible enemy who had been caught by surprise once, but then instantly adapted to our style of fighting, our weapons, and were striking back with all the strength and courage they were capable of.

The coming day would bring even greater challenges. I shud-dered to think of how many obstacles they'd put in our way, of the superhuman energy and valour our men would need to defeat them. Everything was at stake, and if, at the end of the day, our forces had succumbed, the survivors would have no choice but to fight to the last breath and the last drop of blood, or be massacred like animals in a slaughterhouse.

The surgeons were already at work to save our wounded.

Xeno had taken off his armour and laid down his sword, and was writing by lamplight.

18

As we tried to get some rest, our contingent was still advancing, led by the guide they'd captured, along a path that led to the second pass. They moved in silence, careful not to make a sound or to set stones rolling. They arrived at the top of the hill as the enemies who guarded it were preparing to turn in for the night. They were taken by surprise and slain; the few who managed to save themselves ran off. But mountain terrain is deceptive: the point they'd reached wasn't the one that overlooked the whole valley. They realized that there was another rise in a higher position with another group of Carduchi guarding it, but it had become too dark to attempt an assault and our men stopped.

At dawn they started out, as we too had begun our march, and headed towards the second hill. A damp mist had risen during the night, like the clouds we had walked through the day before, but coming from the ground rather than the sky. It slid ghostlike into the ravines and hovered over the gorges, letting only the tops of trees and craggy cliffs emerge. Our warriors made their way through this milky, billowing veil without being seen. By the time the enemy saw that they were there, our forces had come so close that they mowed them down without a fight.

The fog had perhaps been sent by one of the gods who protected the red cloaks, as they moved at will through the most hidden reaches of the sky.

That was when we heard the trumpet blast calling us to the peak. I had slept very badly and everything hurt. That shrill sound pierced my ears, but it gave me the burst of energy I needed to forge on. The second blast sounded more like a cock's crow announcing the rising of the sun to a sleepy village.

Lystra, my pregnant friend, had woken up early and was bravely tagging along after the mules. The sky was almost clear of clouds but the cold air quivered here and there with bluish shimmers.

Xeno was gone, and I hadn't seen his horse either. That was fine with me, I'd have more freedom to move at my own pace.

As we started our march, I realized what the plan of action was. Most of the men, led by Sophos, were climbing the slopes straight up towards the rise that our men had occupied. I could see the other commanders – Timas the Dardanian, Xanthi with his long hair, Cleanor gleaming with sweat – seeking other paths to scale the steep mountainside. They were urging on their men, who were pulling each other up using their spears.

We stayed on the wide path that allowed the baggage animals to pass as well.

At last I saw Xeno. Behind us, like a sheep dog with his flock, he was making sure that no one was left behind or got lost.

We were protected on the right and from behind, and the enemy arrived from the left: groups of screaming Carduchi armed with their gigantic bows. Xeno yelled out as well, calling his men to him. They immediately lined up in parallel columns and attacked the rise on which the enemy had appeared. They drew off the enemy's arrows and stones so we could continue to ascend in our long, winding train. He could have deployed his columns in a pincer formation but he didn't do so: it was evident that he wanted to leave the enemy a way out if they decided to retreat. In a certain sense he made war while offering conditions for peace, which seemed like a contradiction. But the Carduchi did not understand this benevolence or, if they did, refused to accept it.

As we climbed, I never lost sight of Xeno and the manoeuvres he was conducting, and my mind wandered to the interpreters who'd got us into this situation. I remembered having thought that someone had managed to find them. That was ridiculous, I realized. Who could have done that, where had they been found, and how? When had there been the time? The Persians had always been on our heels and now it was the same with the Carduchi, who gave us no respite, not even now that we'd left their villages. If I'd been a man, one of the generals or the captains, I would have demanded to know more about those interpreters. But no one had ever taken my warnings seriously, not even Xeno when I told him how worried I was about our commanders meeting with Tissaphernes. And we'd lost all five of them . . .

Before we'd arrived at the third bend in our path, Xeno had occupied the rise and routed the enemy. The road to the pass was free. And the sky was still clear. Just a little cirrus cloud now and then, light as a tuft of wool, floating off behind the peaks. Xeno maintained his formation halfway up the hillside with the peltasts in front and the heavy infantry behind. He didn't dare return his men to the rearguard.

He was right: soon we were attacked again from another rise. I was afraid that this would never end, that they'd attack us again and again without ever letting up, materializing from every gully, pouring out from behind every cliff. There would be no end to their attacks, we would never have peace as long as a single one of us was left alive.

A third attack, then a fourth. I soon lost count. At every turn in the road, at every saddle between the hills, they'd appear out of nowhere and let fly with clouds, no, storms of arrows, whistling on their way up and falling from on high like murderous hail. And stones, an endless rain of stones as well.

I glanced back at Lystra and could see that she was panting hard. I called out, 'Grab on to the mule's tail!' but maybe she had become afraid of the animals, who were agitated and skittish because of all the uproar. She was stumbling along on her own, trying not to fall behind.

We laboured on, and each time that Xeno took another position he left troops behind to defend it and moved on to occupy the next. But we knew that we had to reach the others, or we would be cut off and left at the enemy's mercy.

Xeno launched his third attack against a rise occupied by the enemy and succeeded in driving them away. It seemed that an end to our struggle was close at hand, when a couple of our warriors ran towards Xeno, shouting to get his attention. Xeno galloped towards them. 'What's happened?' he asked, even before he'd reached them.

'The enemy has retaken the first hill,' one replied, gasping for breath. 'There were thousands of them, we couldn't hold it. We lost many of our men, others are wounded. Look, they're up there.'

Xeno turned towards the hill, where the Carduchi were raising their war cries, celebrating their victory with shrill, syncopated shrieks, like the sounds made by a bird of prey.

Xeno scanned the troops until he saw his adjutant and called him over with a whistle. 'Bring me an interpreter,' he ordered as soon as the man approached.

The interpreter soon arrived.

'Go up there,' Xeno ordered him, 'and tell them I'm requesting a truce so that we can gather our fallen.'

Xeno never failed his convictions: he made war, he wounded, he killed just as the others did, but he observed certain rules, certain rituals, that made him feel like a human being rather than an animal. The last rites for the fallen were especially important to him. Leaving a comrade unburied pained him exceedingly, and could torment him for days.

While those negotiations were going on, a great number of enemies joined those who had seized the hill, and the two branches of our army – those who had occupied the pass and those struggling to make their way up – were trying to join forces. But accepting our offer to negotiate was apparently just a ruse on the part of the Carduchi. They suddenly attacked en masse, letting out wild yells and rolling huge boulders down the slope. I ran towards Lystra and pulled her to the ground beyond the edge of the path.

'Your head!' I shouted. 'Keep your head down!'

A stone struck one of our mules full-on and knocked him down. I watched as he tried laboriously to get back up onto his feet and I realized that his backbone was broken. I'll never forget the look of panicked terror in his staring eyes. One of the warriors passing alongside planted his javelin at the base of his skull with a clean blow and killed him. It put him out of his misery and allowed the column to press on.

As soon as the stones had stopped flying I raised my head and saw Xeno in the middle of the field leading his men in a counter-attack. He was racing madly towards the top of the hill on foot, enjoining his men to charge. There was no limit to his courage! He was ahead of them all, heedless of the volleys of arrows pounding into the ground all around him.

All at once, the roar of the avalanche sounded again as the Carduchi released more boulders and rocks against our men. And Xeno was shieldless! Moving so quickly to lead the attack, he had left it hanging from his horse's back. I watched as a huge stone struck a rocky cliff and broke into four deadly projectiles. One of the men was hit full in the chest and hurled twenty paces away from where he was standing; another had his left thigh completely crushed. He fell to the ground howling in pain, but his cry was soon extinguished as the blood gushed out of his mangled limb in a matter of instants.

I could feel my heart bursting as I scanned the hail of stones and arrows for Xeno's white crest. There it was, waving reck-lessly in defiance of the ministers of Death who were trying to sink their fangs into him like rabid dogs.

'He's going to fall,' I said to myself. 'Now,' I thought, at every stone that brushed his helmet, every arrow that penetrated the ground a palm from his foot or that flew between his neck and his shoulder, not even grazing his skin.

I suddenly focused on a single arrow. It was sparkling, caught by a beam of sunlight, and I could perfectly make out its trajectory. My heart sank, this time I knew it would be the end of him, and of me, and Lystra and all those young combatants charging fearlessly up the hill behind him. The arrow sought Xeno's chest, rushed towards it with whistling speed, but ... never plunged into his flesh. It ricocheted, at the very last, off a plate of metal! A shield had been held out to cover him. A barrier of bronze, offered by a young hero to deflect the arrow, which thudded into the ground. Then, side by side, both of them protected by the gleaming shield, they made their way up behind the others. And the contingent that had occupied the pass the night before arrived to succour them as well. The ranks were drawn up in compact order, their red cloaks flaming in the midday light, their shields held high to blind the enemy.

As they closed in on the Carduchi, the brutish faces of the enemy showed signs of terror. They were no longer the dark phantoms of the night, mysterious spirits of the peaks loosing avalanches. They were shaggy shepherds covered with hides who were fleeing in every direction, stumbling over the dead and wounded. I watched as Timas of Dardania urged his men on, waving a red standard on his spear shaft. There was Cleanor raging like a lion at the head of his Arcadian battalion. Xanthi's long locks bounced on his shoulders with his every leap. The sound of flutes marked the cadence of their advance as they marched on and roared out their war cry, 'Alalalai! Alalalai!'

It was over. Beyond the pass the valley opened up and the men all stopped, leaning on their spears, to take a deep breath and realize they were still alive. I saw the white crest and forgot all about my pregnant friend. I yelled as loudly as I could, 'Xeno! Xenooooo!' and I raced towards him and threw my arms around him. I knew it would embarrass him, there in front of all the others, but I didn't care in the least. I needed to feel his heart beating, see the sparkle in his eyes and the beads of sweat in his hair under the salleted helmet.

He held me close for a few moments, as if we were all alone, in front of the well at Beth Qadà. Then Sophos sought him out and he responded. But as soon as he could, he looked for the lad who had saved his life. His name was Eurylochus of Lusia, and he was very young indeed; he couldn't have been any older than eighteen or nineteen. He had the feckless, open gaze of an adolescent but the shoulders and arms of a wrestler.

'I owe you my life,' Xeno told him.

Eurylochus smiled broadly. 'Don't mention it. Those sorry goats sure took a trouncing and we saved our skins, at least for the moment. That's all that matters.'

We encountered another group of villages, all abandoned as well, and the men were able to rest and to shelter from the damp and chill of the night. There were provisions there for the taking and even some wine. One of Xanthi's men found it hidden inside some cisterns which had been cut into the rock and internally coated with plaster. There was enough to make half of the army drunk, and Sophos immediately ordered it to be placed under surveillance. He couldn't rule out that the natives had left it there deliberately: such strong wine, and so much of it, could be as effective as any weapon in this situation. No one was fooled by the apparent tranquillity of the evening. By now they knew what to expect from the Carduchi.

When the men were preparing to rest, Xeno's adjutant arrived with the interpreter, bearing news that left us all speechless.

'They've accepted, Commander,' he said.

'What?' asked Xeno.

'A truce to gather the fallen.'

Xeno stared at him incredulously. 'On what conditions?'

'We gather our dead, they gather theirs.'

'Nothing else?'

'They also want . . .' he looked around until he spotted the guide who had led Agasias and his men to the pass, '. . . him.'

'The guide? That's fine with me.'

BUT IT WASN'T fine with him. When he realized that he was being turned over to his fellow tribesmen, the man was desperate. He wept and implored, prostrating himself before each of the commanders, who he'd learned to recognize by the crests on their helmets and their richly decorated armour, and clutching at their hands. Pushed away by one he knelt before another, embracing his knees, begging with such impassioned pleas that he could have moved a heart of stone. They knew what atrocious punishment awaited him, and he knew even better. When he had caved in to their threats, he'd probably thought they'd keep him with us, finding it useful to have someone who was familiar with the landscape, and that he might well be let go when they no longer needed him. Maybe he'd worked out a plan of who he would turn to then, relatives or friends in some remote village where no one would ever learn of his betrayal.

He could never have imagined that, alive, he would be traded for the dead.

They dragged him away, but as they were taking him to his destiny, he turned to me. I don't know why, towards a woman who counted for nothing. Perhaps he'd seen compassion in my expression. And I saw in his eyes the same panicked terror as I'd seen in my mule when, hit by a boulder, he knew instantly that half of his body was already dead.

Our men climbed up the path on which they had fought just hours ago, carrying lighted torches to illuminate their way, followed by porters with makeshift stretchers. They returned late that night with the bodies of our fallen.

There were at least thirty of them, mowed down in the full of their youth. They had survived the great battle at the Gates of Babylon only to meet with an obscure, insignificant death in a barbarous land. I looked at them one by one and could not quell my tears.

The sight of a twenty-year-old boy pale with death, his filmy eyes locked in a blind stare, truly breaks your heart.

Xeno officiated over the ceremony. An army battalion was drawn up to render last honours while the flutes played a tense, high-pitched music which sounded itself like a cry of pain. The bodies were burned on three large wooden pyres. The earthenware pots in which the ashes were collected were sprinkled with wine and the names of the fallen were shouted ten times as the men jabbed their spears towards the sky. As the light cast by the flames reddened their shields and breastplates, the swords of the fallen were plunged into the fire until they were red-hot and then ritually bent so that no one could ever use them again. The swords were buried with the urns.

The men's voices joined then in song, in a dark, melancholy dirge like those I heard during the warm nights in Syria under the starry desert sky. I almost thought I could hear Menon's strong, singular voice rising above those of his comrades. But he was gone, like the young lads who'd just burned in the fire. To think that I'd seen them only that morning, clambering up those steep slopes, helping each other up with the shafts of their spears, calling back and forth by name to keep up their courage, to chase off the death that was sniffing at their trails like a starving wolf. The sad, powerful song of their friends accompanied them into the other world, that blind world where the air is dust and the bread is clay.

THE NEXT DAY we set off again and we soon realized that any illusions we had of peace were mistaken. The enemy was even more aggressive, the path steeper and more difficult. The territory we were crossing was the roughest we'd seen, an endless chain of high mountains where no truce could hold. Negotiating our way out was unthinkable: the savages at our heels wanted us all dead, from the first to the last.

Their relentless attacks began again, hill after hill, peak after peak. Xeno was in the vanguard this time, on his horse, and Sophos brought up the rear. Big grey clouds scudded across the sky, as long and thin as the iron shafts of their spears, fleeing south against the direction of our march. Xeno would have interpreted that as a bad omen.

But he moved forward with incredible vigour and speed: each time we neared a height from which enemies might strike us or bar our way, he charged forward to occupy it, followed by his men. If the hill was already in enemy hands, he attacked with untiring ardour. But the Carduchi were quite astute; they would often leave a position before it was attacked and go off to hide or to occupy another position. It was easy for them to melt away: they were wearing hides and carried only a bow, while our men were clad in iron and bronze and carried a huge shield; every step cost them twice as much effort.

The Carduchi wanted to wear them down, to strip them of all energy and then, perhaps, to inflict the killing blow when they became too exhausted to take another step. But they didn't know the red cloaks. I watched Eurylochus of Lusia, the lad who had saved Xeno with his shield, fighting like a young animal. He would pick up the fallen Carduchi arrows and hurl them back where they'd come from like javelins, often finding his mark. And there were Agasias's dark arms, shining with sweat, striking out with tireless fury, mowing down men like blades of wheat, forging his way through blood and screams. Timas and Cleanor urged their battalions upwards, first one, then the other, so one group could catch their breath while the others fought on. Their bearing up under this immense strain, the wounds they took and the blood they shed, afforded us the protection we needed to go on. The long train of baggage animals, servants, and women advanced slowly, one step after another, towards a resting point that we could only imagine.

The day came to an end. The sun settled behind the foliage of the forests, the last screams died into death rattles or breathless panting, a falcon soared high up above, and then, suddenly, just before dusk, a wide valley opened up before us.

Our eyes rested on a vision of peace.

The vast plain was encircled by hills. The land rolled gently up and down and a slight rise sealed the opposite end. The valley was crossed from side to side by a crystal torrent. In the crook of this stream rose a steep hill which glowed red in the sunset and was topped by a village. Stone houses – the first we'd seen in a long while. Thatched roofs, small windows and low doors. A path cut into the rocky hillside descended towards the stream and a girl dressed in red and green, her black hair bound with bright copper rings, made her way down balancing a cushion with a jar on her head. Such silence greeted the sight that I thought I could hear the jingling of the rings she wore at her ankles.

We made our way up to the village and were finally able to sleep in a sheltered place, in one of the many houses. Others settled into the granaries or under the canopies that protected the animals.

Sophos posted sentries all around the village, and a second line at the foot of the hill that encircled the clearing.

Everyone hoped it was over.

No one believed it.

The girl we'd seen descending towards the river didn't come back. I found myself thinking of her graceful, proud bearing and wondering whether we'd seen a vision, a divinity of the mountains or the river, abandoning the lonely, deserted village to disappear into the forest or into the pure waters that flowed between rocks and sand.

The soldiers lit fires. It was clear that we were being watched, so we might as well enjoy some hot food, finally. Xeno invited Eurylochus and Nicarchus the Arcadians, together with Sophos and Cleanor, to our table. I wasn't sure whether it was meant to be their final supper. Would they promise to meet again in the Underworld, like that king of the red cloaks who, eighty years earlier, had dared to challenge the biggest Persian army of all time? Xeno had told me the story of that king named Leonidas, a man who had become a legend. A king who refused to wear a crown or a mitre or embroidered garments. He wore only a tunic of coarse wool and a red cloak, like the three hundred young men who died with him that day because they wouldn't surrender and give up their freedom, at a place called the Fiery Gates. When the Great King demanded that they give up their arms, Leonidas replied, in a rough soldier's dialect: 'Molòn labé.' Come and get them! A moving story, words I'd never forget.

I can remember what Sophos said then. 'Let us eat and drink . . . tomorrow . . .' A sudden wind came up just then, carrying away his last words. But Xeno completed them, because they were the same words spoken by the king who had chosen to fall with his men at the Fiery Gates, 'Let us eat and drink, for tomorrow we shall dine in Hades.'

When they had all gone back to their quarters, I brought Xeno a bowl of warm wine.

'What will happen tomorrow?' I asked.

'I don't know.'

'Will they attack us again?'

'As long as there's a single one of them left and as long as he's breathing.'

'But why? Why can't they just let us go? Can't they understand it would be best for them?'

'Do you mean that letting us pass would cost them infinitely less than trying to prevent us?'

'Exactly. They've lost many men, without counting the wounded, and they'll lose many more. What are they thinking? It's worth your while to fight if you want to stop an enemy from entering your territory, but we're already here and we want to leave and go somewhere else. They must know that a weapon that stays in your body will kill you, while a weapon that pierces cleanly from side to side will spare you if no vital organs are harmed. No one wants to die without a reason. How can you explain it?'

Xeno took a sip of wine and replied, 'Remember what the

interpreter told us? An army of the Great King invaded this land once and disappeared into nowhere. They've done this before and they're doing it again, with us. They simply want the world to know that any army that enters their territory will be annihilated. So no more armies will invade their territory.'

'What about Tissaphernes? He wanted to annihilate us too. For the same reason?'

Xeno nodded. 'The same. Whoever enters can't be let out.'

'But why didn't the Persians do it when they had us surrounded, without food or water? Why did they have to kill our commanders?'

Xeno shook his head.

'And what about the interpreters? Where do they come from? Who sent them?'

'I don't know.'

I had insinuated the worm of doubt, as I had tried to do before our commanders went to meet with the Persians.

'Take care, Xeno. Virtue can't win against deceit.'

'I hear you, but everyone is fighting with the same courage here; everyone is risking his life. Each one of my comrades, from the commander-in-chief to the last soldier, has my full trust. There's another thing: no one has anything to gain from betrayal. The only way that we can hope to save ourselves is by each person doing his duty, playing his part in the whole of the army.'

'That's true,' I replied, 'but tell me this: is there someone who wants this army to disappear? Is there someone who will be badly damaged if the army returns?'

Xeno caught my eye for a moment with an inscrutable look. As if there were an unspeakable thought there, like the look that the Queen Mother's servant girl had given me. I didn't insist. I didn't say another thing. It was something that he'd even listened to me. I helped him to take off his armour and went to fetch some water from the torrent so he could wash before he abandoned himself to slumber. I waited until he was sleeping to go and look for the pregnant girl. She was so tired she'd stretched out on the bare earth.

The wind was picking up, scattering pale white shapes across the sky. A horde of trembling ghosts, the dazed souls of those who were no longer with us.

19

'GET UP,' I told her. 'I'll give you a sheepskin, and a blanket.
You can use the mule's pack to lay your head on.'

She started to cry. 'I can't make it. I'm going to lose the
baby. Here, in these mountains, on these rocks.'

'No, you'll save him: he's a son of the Ten Thousand, the
little bastard, he'll make it. And you'll save yourself to save him.
Or her. It might be a girl.'

'It better not. Being born a female is the worst of fates.'

'Being born is hard on anyone. How many of these young
lads, yesterday, today, have lost their lives, how many will lose it
soon! You and I are alive. Tell me, have you ever loved anyone?'

'Loved? No. But I do know what you're talking about. I
would dream of him. I dreamed of a man who looked at me
with enchantment in his eyes and made me feel beautiful. I'd
wait for him to visit me as soon as I closed my eyes.'

'And now? Doesn't he come to visit you in your dreams?'

'He's dead. Death is the most powerful of dreams. Abira, will
they bury us when we die? If you can, cover us with dirt and
stones, don't leave us to the beasts of the forest.'

'Stop that. When someone dies they don't care about anything.'

I took the sheepskin and blanket and helped her to settle
down. I brought her the leftovers from our dinner that I'd hidden and a little wine to give her strength.

She dozed off and I hoped her young lover would come to
visit behind her closed eyelids.

The moon rose from the mountains and lit up the valley. It glittered, reflected in a thousand sparks of silver, in the torrent that splashed and flowed over a bed of clean sand.

All I wanted was sleep, to stretch out exhausted next to Xeno, but instead I watched the warriors assigned to sentry duty. They must have been tired as little children, falling asleep on their feet, and yet there they stood in their metal shells, wrapped in the cloaks that had become as black as the night.

I would have liked to know what they were thinking.

The others were already asleep, with the last echoes of combat still in their ears. What were they dreaming of? A mother's step, perhaps, carrying a fragrant, freshly baked loaf of bread.

There were stray dogs that had been following the army for some time, getting thinner and thinner because there was never anything left over for them. They howled sadly at the moon.

The wind blew from the coldest corners of the sky. It whipped lightly like a bird of prey rising from his nest among the snowy peaks, but the tent was tepid with Xeno's warmth, his body was soft under the wool of his cloak and I fell asleep, snug and secure, dreaming of other countrysides, other sounds, other skies. The last thing I saw before dropping off was the hanger that held his armour: in the dark it looked like a fierce warrior awake and contemplating massacres among a sleeping multitude. The last sound I heard was the voice of a big river, a river of seething waters, rushing over barren boulders and through rocky gorges. The wind . . .

The wind had changed.

I AWOKE BECAUSE OF the bitter cold gnawing at my feet. I could see that they were outside the blanket and I sat up to cover them. Xeno was gone, and the hanger that bore his armour was empty.

I strained to hear and was struck by a strange sound, a

confused buzzing and a distant neighing and snorting of horses. Then the long, mournful call of horns.

And dogs barking as they roamed starving through the camp.

I jumped to my feet, dressed and hurried out of the tent. A group of officers were galloping back and forth along the low ridge that covered the horizon to the north. At a short distance from where I was standing, the generals – Xanthi, Cleanor, Agasias, Timas and Xeno – were gathered around Sophos, fully armed, hands gripping the hilts of their spears, shields on the ground. They were holding council.

I saw the warriors pointing at something and turned to look: the peaks behind us were crawling with Carduchi. They were brandishing their pikes, and what I'd heard was their war horns blowing their implacable anger our way.

'They'll never go,' said one. 'We'll never be rid of them.'

'Then let's wait here for them and get this over with once and for all,' replied another.

'They won't come to us. They'll stay up high so they can strike at a distant, roll boulders down on us, stage ambushes. They've learned their lesson: they hit and run, we can't get a hook into them.'

'Look! What's happening over there?' shouted a third.

Many of the soldiers were rushing to the ridge where the officers on horseback had paused to watch something that was happening in front of them. I ran in the same direction, holding a jug as if I wanted to fill it in the torrent. What I saw when I reached the ridge made my heart stop beating: there was a river that crossed the valley from west to east; the torrent running alongside our camp merely flowed into it. On the other side of the river an entire army was drawn up!

And these were not coarsely garbed shepherds. They were warriors wearing heavy armour, infantry and cavalrymen with leather cuirasses and leggings, and conical helmets with black and gold horsehair plumes.

There were thousands of them.

Their massive steeds pawed the ground, snorting clouds of steam from their nostrils.

We were trapped. Caught between the mountain and the raging river, with a horde of implacable warriors at our backs and a powerful army facing us on the opposite shore. They had arrived just in time to cut off our passage, while the Carduchi – who we'd fooled ourselves into thinking we'd left behind – were right at our heels, more numerous and warlike than ever. How was such a thing possible? Who could have coordinated two armies from two different and hostile nations with such precision? A thousand thoughts and disturbing suspicions flooded my mind at once, and I was gripped at the same time by a feeling even more distressing than simple helplessness: even if our commanders were thinking the same thoughts as I was, there was no way out of this. No amount of planning or plotting would help. Only the gods – if they existed and if they cared about us – could release us from the plight that we found ourselves in.

I could overhear two of the officers on horseback, not far from me. Their cloaks were whipped by the wind, bright red against the muddy sky. They were scowling. Their words seemed no different from my thoughts.

'This time there's nothing we can do. It's over.'

'Don't say that! Do you want to jinx us? Who are those jokers anyway? They're not Persians, but they're not Medes or Assyrians either.'

'They're Armenians.'

'How do you know that?'

'The battalion commander said so.'

'Our weapons are better, and heavier.'

'But we have the Carduchi behind us. They're willing to fight down to their last man.'

'So are we.'

'Right. So are we.'

Timas arrived at a gallop.

'What shall we do, Commander?' asked the first of the two officers.

'It's not as bad as it seems.'

'It's not?'

'No.'

'Who says?'

'Commander Chirisophus.'

'Who has a certain sense of humour, that's what everyone says.'

'What's more, he's a Spartan. They're good at desperate situations. I'm not so optimistic.'

'Nor am I,' chimed in the other officer.

'Wait, listen to me,' said Timas. 'The Carduchi know that if they try to come down from those mountains we'll chop them to pieces. Actually, that's exactly what we'd like them to do: just let them try, and we'll finally be done with all their endless harassment. The valley is so wide here that they won't be able to roll any of their stones down on us. But then there are those over there. They're our real problem.'

'What about the river? I'd say that's a problem as well.'

'True,' replied Timas. 'The council has decided that the only way to go is to ford the river, attack them and force them into a rout before the Carduchi decide to come down. When we've got a river between us the savages won't be able to bother us any longer.'

'When?'

'Now. We have breakfast and then we attack. We'll need every bit of strength we've got.'

Timas turned his horse and headed back towards camp. The bugle sounded to call the men to eat.

'Right. So we have some breakfast, cross to the other side, cut them to pieces, then go on our way,' mused the first officer. 'What'll it take? Sounds easy. But wait, how deep is the water?'

'Let's see,' replied the second. He got off his horse and

walked towards the river. The other followed and covered him with his shield as they advanced towards the middle of the current. The Armenians kept their distance and didn't seem interested in what they were doing at all. Perhaps they already knew why.

I instantly imagined why myself. 'Careful!' I cried out, at the very moment when the first of the two lost his footing and was carried off by the current. The second tried to grab him, but he slipped as well, and I saw them floundering in the swirling waves, trying desperately to grab onto any handhold. The horses whinnied, pawed the ground and flew off down the river bank with their reins dangling between their legs, following their masters.

I started to shout, 'Help them! Over there, in that direction!' Some of the soldiers realized what had happened and galloped at breakneck speed along the bank, but they soon drew up short. They had to give up, powerless to still the hand of fate.

SOPHOS WAS SERIOUS about his intentions. As soon as they'd had breakfast the army drew up and formed ranks behind a front about fifty men long. They marched rapidly towards the river. A few remained behind to protect the camp and to guard from an attack from the rear by the Carduchi, who were still shouting and sounding their war horns. They seemed to be increasing in number.

Some of the men must have warned Sophos about the river after what had happened, but evidently there was no alternative plan and the army pushed forward. The head of the column entered the water, but the stones that covered the bottom were slick with algae and it was hard to keep their footing. They tried helping each other across, but they were not midway when the water had reached their chests, and the current was so strong that it became nearly impossible to hold onto their shields. Some of the men lifted them above their heads, but the Armenians immediately let fly with a volley of arrows and they had to lower them to protect their chests and stomachs. I watched wide-eyed as the army battled the river, but it was a losing fight. The violence of the swirling current was overpowering and the water was freezing cold. The trumpet soon sounded retreat and our men turned back, dragging the wounded behind them and calling out loudly for the surgeons.

We were trapped. All the enemy had to do was wait. The Carduchi began a slow descent. The Armenians held their ground.

Sophos sent units of peltasts, slingsmen and Cretan archers to stave off the Carduchi.

Nothing else happened that day but you could feel a sense of impotence – if not despair – weighing heavily on the camp.

Another night fell.

At least Lystra would be able to rest and regain some strength. But where had Melissa gone? I couldn't find her any-where, although, towards evening, there were plenty of the young prostitutes accompanying the soldiers hand in hand to their tents. The warriors knew what was coming, and if this was going to be their last night on earth, it would be a night of pleasure. Towards midnight a group of Thessalians and Arcadians gathered around the campfire and after having eaten, began to sing.

They were Menon's men. Their voices were deep and powerful, and they called up the valleys and mountains of their homeland. I couldn't understand all the words, but the harmony was so intense and heartbreaking that I felt tears coming to my eyes. Their song grew in intensity until all of their voices met in a single, thundering note, joining for a moment with the solitary cry of the bugle. They fell still, but their song echoed up the mountains with such force that I thought it would awaken the very cliffs from their rocky slumber. It was only when I got closer to the crackling flame and could see the faces of the soldiers in the red glow that I realized that their last note had been a call to the Underworld, raised with such power that he could hear it. Commander Menon, from the world of the dead.

I wandered around the camp with my head covered and listened to scraps of conversation, words overlapping other words, men groaning, calling, coughing. The voice of the army, the voice that from a distance sounded united and discordant, harmonious and clashing at the same time, broken down into the human and animals sounds that composed it. They cursed and swore, but their voices spoke of memory, of suffocated ire, of fear and melancholy. Mixed with animal sounds and the low panting of bodies clutched in the orgasm of a love that was beginning to feel like death.

I went back to my tent but it was still empty. Xeno kept vigil with the other chiefs as they racked their brains for a solution, even now that no solution was imaginable. The long march of indomitable warriors seemed to have reached an end.

When he came back, Xeno was scowling and depressed. From the few words he offered in explanation, I understood that Sophos seemed ready for a glorious death for himself and his men.

'But you have to give them the hope of victory! Not only the hope, the certainty that they will win. You're our commander, by Hercules!' Xeno had protested.

'Yes, of course,' Sophos had replied. 'That's what I'll do.'

None of the generals had any doubt that they were heading for death, not for victory.

Xeno curled up on his mat, silently awaiting sleep. I sat outside, sitting on a stone and thinking.

I thought, for an instant, that I'd seen, behind the trees, a white something fluttering, the ghost of a vague, fleeting figure, then nothing. The dead were coming to get us . . .

And yet, in the meantime, the unforeseeable happened.

As I learned later, the two officers – one was called Epicrates, the other Archagoras, and both had been among the men who had seized the first hill at the pass – had struggled hard against the whirlpools and vortices created by the fast-flowing current that tried to drag them under. At every bend in the river, there were huge boulders that parted the eddying waters and created even more turbulence. They had tried again and again to grab hold of each other, but the force of the current parted them every time. They sank deeper as the weight of their armour dragged them down; in no time their thick linen tunics would be completely soaked through, and there would be no hope. Tossed by the current right and left, they kept on colliding with boulders, stones, rocky outcrops, and were tormented by sharp stabs of pain and by cramps. The chill of the water penetrated deep into their bones and it became harder and harder to draw a breath.

All at once, when they were so exhausted they were about to surrender to the deadly embrace of the water, Archagoras spotted a trunk which had fallen into the river. It was a huge oak that was still rooted in the bank, but the water had gnawed at the roots until it seemed ready to carry off the felled giant. Archagoras headed that way with the last of his strength and managed to grab hold. He instantly felt something tugging at his foot: it was Epicrates, his comrade, who had also spotted their chance for salvation and was determined not to let it slip.

His weight nearly tore the first man from the trunk. Realizing what was at stake, Archagoras held on even tighter to allow the other to pull himself up along his body; Epicrates caught hold of his belt, worked up to his shoulders and finally got his own hold on the trunk. They helped each other to climb onto the bank.

The moment they were on land they heard a huge cracking sound as the oak broke free of its roots and was carried off in the roiling foam. They rested just long enough to catch their breath, then began to make their way upriver along the rugged bank so they could reach camp before the rest of the army gave up on them and moved on.

Once again, exhausted and on their own in a hostile land,

they had to win a fight against time. They marched on, gritting their teeth and ignoring the pain from the cuts and bruises they'd suffered from collisions with rocks on their long ride down the rapids. They marched on, overcoming muscle cramps and pangs of hunger. The stiff wind froze their wet clothes to their bodies. And yet their limbs refused to be paralysed, and somehow obeyed their staunch resolution to push on and reach their comrades.

The grey dawn finally lightened the mountains and the forests all around them. They could still hear the voice of the river raging from the bottom of the rocky gully at their feet. Archagoras and Epicrates leaned over to take a look and noticed that there was a point where the river narrowed, generating the gushing noise they were listening to, but that further upstream, the river bed widened into a broad pool where the water seemed quite calm; only at the middle was the current very fast. The ebbing waters had formed a deposit of sand and gravel which slowed the river's flow at the widest point between the two banks.

As they were resting, they saw an old man, a woman and two children on the other side, entering a cave overhung by a rocky spike. They seemed to be hiding bundles that perhaps contained their meagre belongings.

'If they can get across, so can we,' said Archagoras.

'Let's try,' Epicrates replied. They climbed down towards the bank, removed their armour, belts and swords, and lowered themselves into the water, each armed only with a dagger. The bottom was covered with sand and very fine gravel, and when they were at the middle, the water did not even reach their hips.

'Do you know what this means?' said Archagoras.

'It means we've found the ford. The army can get across and attack the Armenians from the rear.'

'Right. Let's hurry to catch up with the others before they do something crazy.'

They crossed back to the shore and after donning their

armour, made their way towards a hill that rose a short way off, covered by an oak forest. A path had been created by the passage of shepherds and their flocks, and the two officers followed it to the top of the hill, from where they could see the camp, as well as the entire valley crossed by the torrent. They could see that the army had drawn up in a column formation in full battle gear and were making their second attempt to cross the river and attack the Armenians, while the Carduchi were descending the hill behind them to attack from behind. Archagoras started to yell, 'Stop! Stop!'

'Shut up, they can't hear you. Let's try to reach them. Come on now, hurry!' replied Epicrates. He started down at a run, but no sooner had he taken off than an enormous bear emerged from the forest and blocked his way.

'Get out of here, damn you!' he shouted, trying to scare him off with a stick, but the bear became even more aggressive and he had to draw his sword to try to ward him off. The animal growled menacingly and opened his mouth wide, showing off his enormous fangs. He was standing on his hind legs, unsheathing his powerful claws. Epicrates tried to slip away to one side, but the beast was quicker than he was and bore down upon him. Archagoras shouted, 'Wait, stop. Back this way! Turn back!' But Epicrates could see his comrades down on the plain facing a deadly duel with the river and the enemies, and the last thing he wanted to do was turn back. A moment before the bear charged with all his might, Archagoras's hands grabbed him and threw him to the ground.

'What are you doing?' he cried out, jumping back to his feet, but he realized at once what had happened. The bear had calmed down, and was crossing the path in the direction of the river.

It was a she-bear and her cubs were playing on the brink of the ravine. She collected them and carried them placidly back into the woods.

Epicrates caught his breath. 'How did you . . .'

'I saw the cubs and I understood,' replied Archagoras. 'I'm

Arcadian, remember? I've been around bears since I was a child. The first rule is: if you put yourself between a cub and his mother, you're dead. Thank heavens I saw them and knocked you out of her way. Ready, then? Up for a run?'

They raced down the hill at breakneck speed.

TWO SENTRIES posted along the river spotted a couple of men approaching at a run.

'Stop!' they shouted. 'Or you're dead!' As one of them headed out towards the intruders, the other hefted his spear, ready to throw.

'Idiot, don't you recognize me?' they heard.

'Commander Archagoras . . . Commander Epicrates . . .'

'Run to Commander Sophos, hurry. Tell him we've found the ford. Look sharp, we're exhausted.'

The two youths ran swiftly as athletes, continuously overtaking each other. Archagoras and Epicrates slumped to the ground, completely done in.

The column was halted the moment before it plunged into the river.

Archagoras and Epicrates were taken to Sophos's tent. The war council was reconvened, only a few hours after they'd taken what they thought would be their last decision, to hear what the two officers had to say. Xeno's new friend, Lycius of Syracuse, was present as well; he was in charge of the small cavalry group that had been formed after the wagons were abandoned.

A detachment of two thousand men were sent to confront the Carduchi, who were taken by surprise and withdrew. The others remained in formation along the river bank.

'The trunk of a tree that had been uprooted by some storm had fallen into the river,' began Archagoras, 'and I managed to seize hold of one of the branches. Epicrates, who you see here by my side, grabbed onto my right leg and in the end we both managed to hoist ourselves onto the trunk. It was a miracle: we were frozen and close to giving up.'

'We climbed up to the bank,' continued the other, 'and set off right away. The current was so fast that it had dragged us downriver for stadia and stadia. We didn't want you to leave us behind . . .'

'. . . or to miss the party if you'd decided to attack,' the first joined in.

'Right,' Epicrates continued, 'but it wasn't until the sun rose that we realized where we were: at less than an hour's march from the camp. We were still trying to get our bearings when we heard some voices and hid. It was a couple of old people with two children who had just crossed the river and were on the other side.

'Right at that point there's a rocky spike that juts out over the water, and at the base of the spike there's a little cave, where the man and the woman were hiding some bundles. So, if two old-timers and a couple of kids could make it across easily, I'd say that we can cross as well.'

Archagoras told them about the bear, and their whole adventure seemed a miracle, willed by the gods, to get us out of that fix.

A new plan was drawn up at once: part of the army would feign another attempt to cross the river while the rest crossed at the ford further downriver and attacked the Armenians from the rear. One battalion would suffice to keep the Carduchi at bay.

Xeno asked me to bring wine, the last we had left, to offer to those two friends who had discovered the ford.

'Drink up! You deserve it.' The two men gulped it down and said they felt ready for anything.

'We'll move out now,' ordered Sophos. The bulk of the army set off down the river bank, following the officers who'd discovered the ford. Xeno, as usual, brought up the rear. In the middle were the pack animals with the baggage and the servants and women who followed the army. The women were all together, for once, and I was surprised at how many of us there were.

The battalion which stayed behind remained in part at the river and in part facing off against the Carduchi. But the Armenians couldn't help but notice that our men were moving downstream with the current, and they detached two squads of horsemen and sent them in the same direction. I stayed with the other women, along with Lystra, because it seemed the safest place in such a fix. I scanned the crowd for Melissa but couldn't find her. Where had she gone to?

Having reached the ford, our men began to cross to the other side, where the Armenian cavalry were already bracing for a fight. As soon as they'd passed the deepest point, the Greeks charged forward, yelling 'Alalalai!'

It was them again: the red cloaks. Inescapable, fearless, overpowering. The girls on my side of the river were going mad, cheering them on and yelling at the top of their lungs.

'Come on! Faster! Faster!'

'You show them who's got the balls!'

And other obscenities, even more brazen, that even I found myself yelling but that I wouldn't dare repeat. But it seemed to give the men a charge, to urge them on; they wanted to show us what they were capable of. At the same time, Xeno and Lycius plunged into the water with their cavalrymen, raising a cloud of spray and making straight for the enemy's flank.

The women were so sure of their men that they had already started to cross at the ford as well. Many were worried about getting their gowns wet, and lifted them up high so the men could catch a glimpse of the prize they'd be offered if they won. But at that moment, the warriors only had eyes for the enemy, and were looking nowhere but straight ahead.

I saw two Armenian horsemen on the brow of a hill, perhaps two commanders, turn their steeds and ride off flat out to the north. They must have known how the battle would finish. And sure enough, the Armenian cavalry soon folded under the unrelenting pressure of our attack. Finding such an unexpected way out, under such miraculous circumstances, had boosted the energy and courage of our men beyond measure. They had once again become the bronze avalanche that had swept away every obstacle from the Cilician Gates to the Tigris, and to the mountains of Armenia.

Sophos moved his infantry out from the rocky promontory standing over the cave and pushed on in a steady advance, but the enemy cavalry had retreated just enough to regroup, and soon flew at them in a fresh assault. This time they were deadly serious. Sophos was alert to the change and drew his men up to bear the brunt of the charge. He shouted, 'First row: kneel! Second row: close up! Third row: on your feet! Spears . . . down!'

I was so close I could hear his orders and I could see the Armenian cavalry attacking on their massive steeds. They broke into a gallop, hurled one and then another volley of javelins. But in the end they crashed into a wall of bronze. Our ranks did not waver, not in the least; the fourth, fifth and sixth lines buttressed their comrades with their shoulders and their shields. The Armenian horsemen and horses were gored by the protruding spears and many collapsed to the ground, causing the others to fall in turn. Once again, the cruel, bloody orgy that men so seem to love had been unleashed: the battle!

More than a battle, it became a murderous fray, a slaughter, the air thick with howls and shrieks, shouted orders, clanging steel.

Then the din stopped all at once and we heard the victory cry that the Greeks call their paean.

The battle was over.

The red cloaks had won.

Xeno charged off furiously with his horsemen to attack the Armenians still garrisoned at their camp, which was some way from the troops drawn up at the river. But the Armenians had witnessed the battle and could see Sophos's infantry advancing, victorious. Fearing that the Greeks might block their escape, they abandoned the position, fleeing along the road that led up into the mountains.

Lycius and his cavalrymen had hurtled off in pursuit of survivors, and they didn't stop until they reached the camp. It was unguarded, full of precious objects and provisions of every sort.

Xeno, realizing that he was no longer needed there, turned back with his men and raced downstream to cross the river again so they could join up with their comrades back at the first ford, still struggling against both enemy armies.

When he arrived, he saw that part of the battalion had actually succeeded in crossing the river and was attempting to establish a bridgehead on the other side. Behind them, to the south, the Carduchi had reached the valley and were drawn up for a frontal attack on the rest of the battalion.

They were counting on their numerical superiority; a single Greek battalion on its own seemed easy prey. The horn sounded the order to attack and the Carduchi surged forward, singing a hymn we'd never heard before.

Sophos had reached the Armenian infantry position on the north side of the river and quickly routed the remaining troops. He lined up his own men to protect the ford. In the silence that had fallen, we could hear the song of the Carduchi as well.

There was neither enthusiasm nor excitement in their voices, there was none of the belligerent, boastful shouting that makes men forget death. Theirs was a sorrowful chant with two tones: one was tuneful and harmonious and filled with melancholy, the other was dissonant and strident like the shrieking of hired mourners. It was accompanied by the deep rolling of a drum. They were marching unawares towards annihilation.

We watched the slaughter in silence. Our troops drew up in a wedge formation, lowered their spears and attacked at a run, shouting obsessively, 'Alalalai!' They sliced into their enemies like a knife through bread and they did not stop until they had wiped out every last one. For days and days they had seen their comrades crushed by boulders hurled from above, wounded by arrows raining from the sky, stabbed on watch at night by daggers flying through the air. Now they were settling their accounts, according to the laws of war.

When they were finished they turned back towards the river. They washed their weapons in the current and joined the song of their comrades who raised their voices in the paean. I wondered whether our enemies had finally understood that the Ten Thousand could not be stopped. Neither the armies nor the river had succeeded.

Xeno saw me and pushed his horse through the current to reach me.

20

THE VICTORY CELEBRATION was memorable. In the Armenian camp we found food, blankets, tents, pack animals, weapons and a great number of precious objects: cups, carpets, silver plates, even a bath tub. Xeno took some fabric for me. It was beautiful. I'd never seen anything like it in all my life, yellow and edged with golden threads. And he found a mirror so I could see myself as he draped it over me. It was a plate of polished bronze that reflected your image, a little like when you lean over and look at yourself in a pool or a well.

A sumptuous banquet was prepared, and many of the girls took part. They were all dressed up as well, and they looked incredibly attractive. It doesn't take much to make a young woman beautiful and desirable. Some of them even applied make-up; bistre on their eyes and rouge on their lips. I watched as they embraced and kissed the young warriors, passing from one to another to give each of them all the heat and excitement they were capable of. They were the lovers and the brides of those young men, and since it wasn't possible for them to love one of them alone, as they would have preferred, they loved them all as best they could. I realized that when I saw the girls cheering them on to fight and to win, urging them on with their shouts and applause, even with their ribald remarks.

The five commanders arrived decked out in their best clothing, and many of the ornaments they'd found in the Armenian camp. They really were impressive. Timas was the youngest: he didn't look a day over twenty. He was lean and well built, with white teeth and dark, expressive eyes. His boundless energy was astonishing; it was he who had led the last assault against the Carduchi. He was the point of the wedge that drove deep into their formation, splitting it in two and then overpowering both the left and the right wing.

I saw Agasias with two girls, one on each side, and Xanthi with his hair loosed like a lion's mane, holding another on his lap; she was half-naked, even though the evening air was chilly. The wine helped. And there was Cleanor. I expected to see Melissa with him, but she wasn't around. Then I understood why: she wasn't to be shared with anyone. That was her true talent: making herself indispensable and irresistible for the man she'd chosen, making him a slave to her beauty and her charms to the point where he'd do anything for her. Perhaps Menon had been different; he did what he wanted, and that was what made him special and aroused true feeling in her.

Sophos had joined the festivities, but he stayed lucid; he was drinking with moderation and not losing his head with the girls. He had no intention of losing control of his faculties and his hand never left the hilt of his sword.

Only Xeno was missing. Someone had to stay on watch while the others made merry, forgetting that not long before they had been looking death in the face. He had ordered a double ring of sentries, and named replacements as well, knowing that the others would be useless after their drinking and love-making. He was inspecting the sentries personally, going fully armed from one guard post to the next to check that everything was in order and that everyone was doing his duty.

I saw him sitting up on a hill scanning the countryside. It was a lovely night. The moon was almost full and it hung over the mountain peaks, lighting up the small swift white clouds passing above, streaking them with its pearly light. I approached him, walking easily up the slope.

'Beautiful evening, isn't it? It's not even very cold.'

'It will be tonight if it stays clear. Be sure to cover up well.'

'What a victory! Just when everything seemed lost.'

'I still can't get over it. I've offered sacrifice to the gods to thank them. I think that this was a miracle.'

'Do you really believe in the gods?'

'My teacher in Athens did. In his own way.'

The veil of clouds covering the moon drifted free just then and it lit up the valley lying before us almost as if it were day. The rolling terrain was traversed by another, widish river that crossed it from one side to another. There was not a living soul as far as the eye could see: not a village, not a hut, not a tent.

'No one lives here. How strange, it would be good for pasture.'

'They're afraid of the Carduchi,' replied Xeno. 'They must make raids on this side of the river as well.'

'So they're enemies.'

'Without a doubt.'

'But yesterday, the Armenians appeared exactly at the place and the time in which we could be crushed between two concerted attacks. As if they'd planned it together in advance.'

'Don't start up again with all your suspicions. What you're saying is simply impossible. Those two peoples hate each other.'

'Then perhaps someone else coordinated them. How did the Armenians know that we would arrive just then and attempt to ford the river?'

'Pure chance.'

'Chance, you say? What about their timing? You know, I can see how long it takes in the morning to get an army moving; to eat, to dress, to ready the animals, to don their armour, to take their places in the ranks. The Armenian army was bigger than ours is. For how long had they known that we would arrive here at the river yesterday? How did they manage to make it here at just the right time, with such precision?'

Xeno looked thoughtful as he watched the river sparkling in the valley below. 'This land is so rich with water! That's the

Tigris, and we'll be able to follow it upstream until we reach its source.'

'You don't want to answer my question.'

'Chirisophus is Spartan, I'm Athenian. Our cities fought each other for thirty years in a bloody, devastating war. The best of our youth was wiped out, fields were burned, cities sacked, ships sunk with all their crew aboard. Revenge, retaliation, rape, torture . . .'

'I know what war is.'

'And yet the two of us are friends. We cover each other's backs, we fight for the same cause with the same tenacity and passion.'

'So what is this cause?'

'Saving the army, saving the Ten Thousand. They are our common homeland. Each of us is the subject and the object of the fight. The men's valour, their courage. Understand?'

'I do understand, but I don't share your sense of trust.'

'This land we're on is Persian territory: does it surprise you that they're still trying to destroy us? The Armenians are commanded by Persian officers, and they obey a satrap. His name is Tiribazus. They won't let us cross in peace, mark my words. But we are ready for them.'

'All right. I may be an ignorant girl, but remember that women see things and hear things that men don't see or hear. When there are no more enemies willing to take you on, a new enemy will rise from where you least expect it.'

'What do you mean by that?'

'Nothing. But on that day, remember my words.'

I stood there next to him, watching the moon rise in the sky, listening to the racket coming from camp, the girls' squeals of delight, the calls of the sentries that echoed from one hill to the next, repeating the names of their comrades. They called to each other to ward off the darkness; so that the invisible, fleeting phantoms of the night would be warned that those obstinate men would not be caught slumbering.

The celebrating finally quietened, then died down completely. When silence had descended on the camp, the trumpet blared a solitary note and the second guard shift arrived.

Xeno took me to the tent and made love to me passionately but in complete silence. Not a sound, not a sigh. He could hear my words echoing like a gloomy prophecy and he had no words of this own to counter them, not even words of love.

Later I saw him get up. He took a silver cup full of wine to the banks of the river we'd crossed. He offered up a libation to the swirling divinity by pouring out the wine, because that day he had spilled blood and contaminated its pure waters.

The river which was as wild as a raging bull was called the Centrites, and the next day we finally left it behind us and began to cross the high plain which rose higher and higher, but very slowly, almost imperceptibly, until you realized all at once that the air had grown colder and thinner and that your breathing had quickened.

Even Lystra could walk now without much suffering. The ground was covered with dry grass that the flocks had grazed on, turning it into a thick, even carpet. Its hue was a yellowish-grey that varied with the changing light. Here and there were long stalks of oats with their tiny ears that shone like gold, and another plant with seeds the shape of little silver disks, like the coins used by the Greeks. The column advanced at a quick rate, and we travelled all day, from morning to dusk, without danger of any sort emerging. Xeno and Lycius kept the area under surveillance with their scouts on horseback, galloping back and forth from the van to the rearguard to forestall any possible attacks.

The landscape changed continuously. Looming before us were craggy folds of rock, soaring mountain chains, valleys as deep as gorges which the sunlight sculpted into dramatic forms. The days were growing shorter, the light was redder and more oblique, the sky bluer and almost cloudless.

The warriors explored the folds and crevices with their eyes as we climbed; never before had anyone of their race seen such wonders. The march had become so easy, peaceful, even pleasant, that I began to hope that we would soon reach our destination.

The sea.

An internal sea, to the north, enclosed by land. A sea that hosted many Greek cities, with ports and ships, from which we'd be able to get anywhere.

Even home.

Xeno had told me this, and Xeno knew everything about land and sea, mountains and rivers. He knew all of the ancient legends and the words of wise men and he wrote them down. He was always writing, every night by lamplight.

After several days we reached the source of the Tigris and I sat down next to the small stream that gushed from a cliff, as clean as the air after a storm. The river was like a child here: lively, reckless, fickle. But I knew what he would be like as an adult because I'd seen him: enormous, placid, majestic, so strong and so powerful that he could carry whole ships on his back, as well as those strange, round boats shaped like baskets.

I washed my face and legs in the freezing water and it gave me a magnificent sensation. I felt invigorated. I told Lystra to wet herself: it would give her child strength and bring her luck as well, because that water kept millions of people alive, giving them refreshment and sustenance, irrigating their fields so they could have bread, filling the fishermen's nets with fish. What a mysterious miracle sparkled in that stream, sang between the rocks and over the shiny black sand! I drank long gulps of water so pure that I could feel it flowing in me like my life's blood. Water must have been like this everywhere the day that the world was born.

Then we crossed another river that coursed over a vast high plain strewn with many villages. Here messengers reached us, sent by the Persian governor, saying that he had hired interpreters and wanted to speak with our commanders.

As soon as Xeno told me, I begged him not to go, but he just smiled. 'You really think we're so stupid? Don't you think we've learned our lesson? Rest easy that we won't let anything happen this time.'

And so the entire army went to the meeting, because the vast plain allowed it. Drawn up as in the days of Clearchus's command: in five rows behind a front two thousand paces long, in full battle gear, shields polished to a high sheen, crested helmets, greaves gleaming, the points of their spears seeming to pierce the sky.

Sophos, Xanthi, Timas, Cleanor and Agasias, on horseback, within calling distance of each other. Sophos slightly in front of the other four.

Ten paces behind them, in the spaces between them, were Xeno, Lycius, Archagoras, Aristonymus . . . and Neon.

Behind them, a small cavalry division, no less impressive than their commanders.

Facing them was a large contingent of Armenian troops, perhaps even those we had fought at the Centrites. At their head was the satrap, Tiribazus, in command of a magnificent cavalry squadron. His black beard was carefully curled and he wore a soft mitre on his head and a golden sword at his side.

The interpreter came forward. He spoke perfect Greek, a sign that he came from one of the cities on the shore of the northern sea. It must not be so distant, I thought hopefully.

'I speak in the name of Tiribazus,' he said, 'satrap of Armenia and the eye of the Great King. He is the man who lifts the Great King to his horse. Tiribazus wishes to tell you this: do not burn the villages, do not burn the houses, take only the food that you need and we will allow you to pass. You will not suffer further attacks.'

Sophos turned to consult his senior officers. He did not speak, but shot an inquiring glance to each of his men in turn. Each one of them gave a nod, and Sophos turned back towards the interpreter. 'You will tell Tiribazus, satrap of Armenia, eye of the Great King and his personal attendant, that his proposal is agreeable to us and we mean to stay true to our pledge. He will have nothing to fear from us, but should he fail to respect our pact, he should take a good look at the men lined up here and remember that all of those who have attacked them have suffered a harsh punishment at their hands.'

The interpreter nodded and made a bow, then went to report to the satrap. He soon gave another nod to indicate that the agreement was valid, and the Greek army made a perfectly synchronized wheel to the right to face north. The Armenians did not make a move, but later the scouts told us that they were following us at a distance of about ten stadia. They evidently didn't trust us.

We proceeded in this way for several days, climbing higher and higher with the Armenians still at our backs. One morning I woke up at dawn and the vista that opened before my eyes was spectacularly beautiful. The mountainous landscape stretched out all around me as far as the eye could see, but looming over the infinite ridges and peaks were three or four snowy white summits which stood out against the intensely blue sky. For a brief moment they were struck by the light of the sun and they lit up like crystals, like precious gems, sparkling over the vast mountain chain still immersed in darkness.

They shone with a rosy colour, so intense and clear that they seemed to be made of some heavenly substance unknown on earth. Titanic jewels carved by the hands of the gods! I noticed that there was also a group of young warriors contemplating the spectacle with the same wonder and admiration. Xeno was still sleeping, exhausted by the strain of ensuring safe conditions for the army's onward journey. The solitary gems of the land of Armenia would not make their way into his diary, into the dense, regular script that filled his scroll, which was becoming more voluminous day by day.

When he awoke I pointed them out to him, but the magic had vanished. He told me, 'They're simply mountains covered with ice. We have some in Greece as well: Olympus, Parnassus, Pelion and Ossa. But they're certainly not as high as these. The ice reflects the light as only a precious stone can. You might see it happen, if you're lucky.' But his tone held no enthusiasm or expectation.

One evening we arrived at a group of villages clustered around a large palace. Each one of the villages had been built on a rise, with thatched-roof houses made of stone. A wisp of white smoke rose from each of the chimney tops. The setting sun accentuated the smoke rising dense through the cold air, and made it take on a pink glow. There were hundreds of houses, scattered over a dozen little hills on the high plain. There was no sign of life coming from the palace.

The soldiers moved in to find shelter in all those houses and they found them full of every kind of treat: wheat, barley, almonds, nuts, raisins, aged wine that was strong and sweet, salted or smoked mutton, beef and goats' meat. It was a land of plenty.

I stayed with Xeno and his servants in a thick-walled building standing at the edge of the first hill we'd encountered. It was obviously used for storage and drying meat, but it was cosy and Xeno preferred it because it had a hearth and we didn't have to share it with anyone else.

I lit a fire and cooked our dinner. I'll never forget the sense of comfort, rest and tranquillity that I got from that simple dinner next to the man I loved in such a marvellous land. I had never imagined that such a magical place could exist. And then . . .

It snowed!

I had never seen it and I didn't know what it was. The merchants who crossed Mount Taurus in the winter had often described it to us when we were children, but there was nothing that could have prepared me for what I was seeing with my own eyes. I had opened the door and my surprise was so great that I was struck dumb. The reflection of the flames in the hearth radiated outside and revealed an apparition of astonishing beauty:

the manifestation of the greatness of nature and of the gods who inhabit this world and take on changing forms with the passage of the seasons.

Innumerable flakes of white fell from the sky in a soft, gentle dance, swirling through the air and alighting on the ground, which grew whiter and whiter with every passing instant. A light, downy carpet like the fleece of a newborn lamb. The smoke rising into the night sky from the chimneys in all the other houses seemed alive with the spirit of the flames inside. The snow, which was falling thicker and faster now, even took on a reddish cast as it tumbled in front of the smoke, before returning to its immaculate white nature. If filled me with a sense of dazed wonder, so deep and so vibrant that I can't describe it and I can't even recall it properly.

Even though it was night there was a barely perceptible light in the air – a soft, diffuse, omnipresent light, free of shadows – which would let you walk without losing your way, distinguishing each shape, each presence. It was the white flakes that had imprisoned the light inside and radiated it outwards from the ground and the sky.

I don't know why, but I found myself thinking that only Menon's immaculate cloak could blend into that whiteness, leaving no sign of his passage but his silent, empty footsteps. Footsteps that I could see . . . or couldn't see, had perhaps only imagined.

I could hear a dog barking; the howling of his wild brother answered him from the forests on the mountainsides, which had been transformed into slumbering white giants. I could hear the voices of our soldiers, the sentries calling out to each other, and then nothing.

The whole world was white, both earth and sky, and everything was swallowed up into that immeasurable silence.

I slept deeply, next to the burning fire. Xeno had found a big log that burned all night long, filling the room with a mild, agreeable warmth. Maybe it was the quiet and the soft, comforting atmosphere that helped me sleep, maybe it was knowing that I'd done the right thing when I chose to run off with Xeno. I'd lived intensely, seen enchanted landscapes and visions out of a dream. I'd experienced violence and delirium along with moments of aching sweetness.

Xeno was warm, too, next to me, and I could feel him moving now and then. Once he opened his eyes and his hand sought the hilt of his sword before his body relaxed again and drifted back into sleep. Outside under an awning, his horse Halys let his presence be known with snorts and soft neighing or by dragging his hoofs over the frozen soil. He was a proud, powerful animal, and he'd often saved Xeno from mortal danger. I loved him too, and in the middle of the night I brought him a blanket to protect him from the chill. He rubbed his snout against my shoulder: that was his way of thanking me.

The next morning we were awakened by an incredible din outside and Xeno rushed out with his sword in hand, but it was a false alarm. Our men were outside playing like children in the snow: they were tossing it at each other, burying their comrades in it, pressing it between their hands into balls which they threw or fired from their slings.

The inhabitants of the village had come out of their houses as well, and they watched smiling as the warriors come from afar amused themselves in such an inoffensive way. Some of their own children joined the fun before their parents could stop them.

The sun was shining, just coming up over the vast snowy expanse and setting off a magic sparkling effect all over the white mantle, as if it were full of diamonds or rock crystals. At the horizon I could see in the distance, at three separate points, the lofty peaks struck by the rising sun, turning them red as rubies. I wondered what they would be like when we'd got far enough to see them up close. Then all at once the air was full of cries of alarm and despair. Some of the houses had caught fire.

Sophos seemed furious and ordered the men to put out the

fires immediately. A score of them ran over with buckets and shovels to throw snow on the houses because the water had frozen. It was futile: they had roofs of wood and thatch, and were burned to ash in no time. The blackened ruins that remained were an insult to the blinding white of the village. The people who had lived in those houses were huddled together, and weeping.

Sophos had the assembly sounded and the men drew up on a level clearing outside the village.

'Who set those houses on fire?' he demanded.

'They just caught fire,' mumbled some.

'All of them? Fine. If those responsible for this act of bravado come forward and confess, they'll get off with a punishment. But if I have to find them out, and I will find them, I shall apply the maximum penalty: they will be executed. We have a pact with the Persians: they allow us to pass through, we do not burn their villages. Whoever was playing with fire today has jeopardized the lives of all his comrades.'

About twenty soldiers, heads hanging, took a step forward. One by one.

'Why?' asked Sophos.

'We thought we'd be leaving today.'

'And so you thought nothing of depriving these people of a roof at the height of the winter.'

No one said a word.

'All right. You've acted like idiots and you will have to learn at your own expense what it means to be without a roof in the winter. Tonight you'll sleep in the open, outside the perimeter guarded by the sentries. If you don't survive, all the better: I'll be free of a bunch of idiots. But first you'll help the inhabitants of the houses you've burned to repair the roofs and to put in new windows and doors.'

The men obeyed. When night fell they were escorted outside the watch circle and abandoned there, with a dagger, a cloak and a shield as their only means of survival.

21

I felt badly for them.

They had been irresponsible and stupid. They had burned down the houses of poor people who had never done them any harm. But wasn't it normal to have twenty dolts in a group of ten thousand?

After all, they hadn't killed anyone. And they risked paying for their bluster with their lives.

'If it stays clear, they'll die,' said Xeno.

'Why?'

'Otherwise they'll be killed by the enemy when they realize they're outside our sentry ring.'

'But why should a cloudless sky kill them?'

'Because heat escapes upwards: if there are clouds, they keep it down. It's like having a roof over your head.'

'Does Sophos's order hold for everyone?'

'It does for you.'

'But I'm not a soldier.'

'That doesn't change anything. Chirisophus's orders hold for everyone. He is the high commander, and what's more, they deserve this. It's right that they experience for themselves what it means not to have a roof in a land like this, in this season, at night.'

I tried to think of a way to carry out some blankets, but Xeno warned me not to do it. I settled into a chair by the window and every now and then I'd check the sky: I could see clouds drifting in from the west, but they were still very far away. If they didn't get here in time to cover the sky, those boys out there would be dead.

Xeno told me a story, one of those that they act out in their theatres. The story of a girl like me who disobeyed the orders of the king of her city out of the pity she felt for two young men: her brothers.

'The king of an ancient city of my land, called Thebes, had decided to leave his kingdom to his two sons, but he made them swear a pact. They would share the rule of the city by governing one year at a time, alternating with each other. At the end of the first year, the son who had been in charge would leave the city, and the other would enter and reign for that year. Unfortunately, their thirst for power won out, and when Polynices showed up to take his turn, the other, Eteocles, refused to leave the city. So Polynices contracted an alliance with six kings and laid siege to Thebes.

'The warriors on both sides fought furiously, stoked by implacable hate. The two brothers finally decided to face off in a duel, but their fight to the death left no victor. Both brothers died from their wounds.

'Their successor, whose name was Creon, decreed that the bodies should be left unburied, as a warning for anyone who went against blood ties or broke the faith of a sworn promise.

'The two brothers had a sister named Antigone, who was betrothed to Creon's son. She chose not to heed the will of the king, who had threatened to execute anyone who defied him. Antigone gave her brothers a ritual burial by tossing a few handfuls of dust onto their bodies. She was surprised by the king's guard and was brought to justice. Antigone proclaimed herself innocent, claiming that there was a higher law than that of the king and the government: the law of the heart, of pity for the dead, no matter how heinous a crime they had been guilty of. Every person had a moral obligation to provide funeral rites for his relatives: a law of the soul and the conscience, superior to any law established by man.'

As Xeno told me the story of Antigone, time had passed without my realizing it, and when I turned to the window I could see that the snow was falling thickly. The sky was white and every trace of human presence had been cancelled. The magical vision that enchanted me so – who could ever have imagined amidst the dust of Beth Qadà that a similar miracle could exist! – those marvellous white flakes, millions of icy butterflies suspended in a dance of love before surrendering to the light foamy blanket on the ground, did not let me forget that nature is always cruel, and that what for me was enchanting – sitting here by the warmth of the fire – could be deadly for others.

'So how did the story end up?' I asked, as if awakening from a dream.

'Badly,' replied Xeno. 'A long chain of deaths. So don't go getting any strange ideas. Sleep now. I'm going to inspect the guard corps.'

But I'd already made up my mind and Xeno's story only convinced me further – why else would he have told it to me? I would take fleeces and goatskins to those stupid boys out there in the snow protected only by their cloaks. But as I was gathering them up, a trumpet blare tore through the still atmosphere with a long alarm call. I dropped the skins and went outside. There were big fires burning on the mountains all around us, huge blazes shooting out red flares that formed a tremulous red halo in the falling snow.

The warriors left the houses they had occupied, armed and wearing their cloaks. Sophos and his commanders addressed the soldiers. 'It's too dangerous to lodge separately in small groups. They could surprise us in our sleep under the cover of night and massacre us in silence. We'll spend the night all together at the centre of the main village, armed and ready for combat! Anyone found hiding inside a house will be thrown out of the camp with only a cloak and a dagger.'

And so it was. The men scattered straw taken from the hay-lofts over the ground and lay down all together. Only the women remained in the houses. I joined Lystra, who I'd found cover for in a barn, where the body heat of the animals would protect her from the frost.

It snowed all night, and next morning we woke up to a thick white layer covering the ground. Our men were sluggish and sore, but the hay, straw and raw wool cloaks had protected them through the long night.

The twenty men who had been driven outside the ring of sentries seemed to have disappeared. Those idiots must have wandered off in search of shelter and got themselves killed.

'So much the worse for them,' observed Xeno. 'They should have thought about it beforehand.' But he hadn't even finished speaking when the blanket of snow erupted at various spots and the twenty warriors arose like spectres from the Underworld.

'Will you look at those bastards!' exclaimed Xeno. They'd survived by propping up their shields with dried branches and covering them with their cloaks, thus creating tiny but effective shelters that preserved their body heat. Curled up beneath their shields, they were protected from the cold all night long.

Xeno burst out laughing and the others had a chuckle as well at seeing their comrades returning unscathed to their units.

But now the soldiers had to be shaken from their lethargy before the enemy attacked.

Xeno set an example. He got to his feet, grabbed an axe and started splitting wood bare-chested. By then it was broad day-light, and although the air was cold, the sun's rays were warm. The daggers of ice that were hanging from the roofs of the houses began to drip as the sun got hotter. Inspired by Xeno's example, the others set to work as well and in no time the camp was full of concerted activity. They found some animal fat, as well as an ointment made from a plant that grew in the area. They set it over the fire to melt it, and the girls were called upon to grease and massage the chests and backs of the numb soldiers to help them regain a little energy. Since most of them were no older than twenty, that wasn't such a difficult chore.

Breakfast was prepared and the men were soon ready for action. A group of scouts was sent up into the mountains for reconnaissance and they returned towards midday with a prisoner who knew many things. Tiribazus was planning an ambush, at a choke point in the mountains up ahead.

It was starting all over again: a battle at every pass, an ambush at every bottleneck. There was a curse hanging over our heads, a fate that just wouldn't relent, poised to strike us again and again. But the Ten Thousand didn't seem concerned: as soon as they'd been informed of the situation, there was no hesitation. After their meal, they donned their armour and set off at a marching pace.

The sky was clouding over, but that made our trek easier: the glare of sun on snow was worse than in the desert. When the light was so blinding, you had to squeeze your eyes shut until they were mere slits.

The sight of the army moving through the snowy landscape was amazing: a long, dark serpent unwinding slowly over the clean white blanket of snow. I wondered how they could identify the road, since all the pathways had been covered up, but in this case, we had little leeway: our route headed straight for a line of mountains set across it, topped by a peak that was much higher than all the rest. After a couple of hours, a light infantry detachment struck out from the rest of the army and aimed straight for the pass, following a shortcut which the prisoner had indicated. They wanted to occupy the pass before Tiribazus's troops got there.

The peltasts were followed by a contingent of heavy infantry: the red cloaks with their heavy shields. The first group were to take the pass, the second were to defend it if the enemy counter-attacked.

Before evening our men had seized the pass and succeeded

in driving off the Armenians and other mercenaries who had been sent after them. They occupied Tiribazus's camp, which was full of every sort of bounty. If the satrap of Armenia had been planning to boast of this exploit to the Great King, he would have to think again. And I would just have to stop worrying so much. The dark thoughts that were obsessing me that morning had dissipated before dusk: there seemed to be no obstacle that our army could not overcome.

The losses we'd suffered up to that point had been limited. Three or four hundred men in all, including those who had died later of their wounds. I was shocked to realize that I had started to think like a soldier. Three or four hundred men dead in battle was a huge number, too, too many. Even if there had been one hundred, or fifty, or even one alone, it would have been too many. The death of any twenty-year-old was a tragedy, a disaster. For him, for the parents who had brought him into this world, for the woman who loved him, for the children he would never have. For everything that had been taken from him and that he'd never get back. And because ever since the beginning of our world, another man like him had never been born, and no one like him would exist until the end of time.

We reached the well head of the Euphrates, as tiny at its source as the Tigris. It seemed a sacred place to me, because the river was the father and the god of my land. Without it everything would be arid, the unopposed reign of the desert. When we crossed it the water reached nearly to our waists, and I can still remember that it was so cold it made my legs go numb.

The snow became deeper and deeper as we advanced, and whenever we stopped in some village the warriors would seek out lengths of cloth to cover their legs, which were customarily bare, and wrap their feet, but even so it was biting cold. As long as they kept walking it wasn't too bad, but when they stopped they had to stamp their feet on the ground so they wouldn't freeze.

We advanced in this way for several days, continuing upwards, passing along the slopes of soaring mountains of solid rock, standing out white against the blue sky or grey when it was cloudy. The air cut your face like a knife.

I realized that Lystra was flagging fast. Walking through the deep snow was incredibly laborious, and she was all stomach. She was close to giving up entirely. One day, as I was trying to help her to get up, I spotted the two mules carrying a litter that I'd first seen at the start of our trek across the Carduchian mountains, and I remembered a plan I'd hatched back then. I let go of Lystra and ran as fast as I could to stop the first mule. The servant leading the little convoy raised the reins to strike me with them, but I managed to dodge the blow.

'Get out of the way!' he shouted. 'Do you want to delay the whole column?'

'Forget it. I'm not leaving until I talk with the woman who's inside.'

'There's no one in there! Only provisions.'

'All right, then, I'll talk to them.'

A small crowd had gathered already. Out of the corner of my eye I noticed Cleanor glancing back in our direction with a nervous look. This confirmed my suspicions. 'Melissa, get out of there!' I yelled. 'I know you're in there! Come out, now.'

In the end, Melissa pulled back the drape that kept her hidden.

'Abira . . . I haven't seen you for ages.'

Meanwhile, the soldiers had slightly redirected their march, looping around us, so there was no longer any reason to hurry.

'You've been hiding for a long time,' I replied. 'I've always looked for you.'

'Well, now you've found me. What do you say we see each other for dinner this evening and talk then?'

'No, it's something we have to do now. See that girl over there, the pregnant one? She can barely take another step; she's about to collapse in the snow and die, along with her baby. I haven't fed and nursed her this far to watch her die now.'

'So?'

'You have to let her ride with you.'

'I'm sorry, there's no room.'

'Then you get out.'

'Are you crazy?'

'I went all the way to the Persian camp for you that night, because you were yearning for news about Menon. I risked my life, and you can't do this little thing for me? You are healthy as can be; you've got someone taking care of you. All you have to do is get out and walk while she rests and warms up. Then she can get out and walk for a while. For you it's nothing, but for her it's her life. Two lives, that is.'

Melissa was adamant. She simply couldn't conceive of forgoing her own comfort. Her situation seemed bad enough to her, and she had no intention of giving it up for something worse.

'I said get out.'

Melissa shook her head.

Lystra came close. 'Please, let her be . . . I can make it alone.'

'Hush now!'

Melissa tugged back the curtain. She had finished talking about it. That gesture made my blood rise. 'Open that curtain, you simpering whore! Get out of there now!'

I tore the curtain out of her hand, grabbed her wrist and pulled at her with all my strength.

'Stop that!' she cried out. 'Leave me alone! Cleanor! Help, Cleanor!'

Luck would have it that Cleanor was busy with something else: two mules loaded with provisions had fallen to their knees slightly beyond us and he and his men were trying to get them back on their feet.

I gave her a yank and made her fall in the snow. She started to scream even louder, but the soldiers were laughing; they were not about to interfere in a fight between women. She grabbed my foot and tried to pull me down, but I landed such a hard jab on her cheek that I knocked her flat, there on the ground. And while she was crying and snivelling, I helped the girl to get in. The mule-driver watched in dismay, not knowing which way to turn.

'What are you looking at, you nitwit?' I demanded. 'Move your arse, damnit, move!'

I don't know how or why, but he obeyed me. The way I had of cursing like a soldier must have surprised him, and I must have looked so enraged that he didn't even try to protest. The little mule train started up again with me following. Melissa, seeing that no one was paying any attention to her, got to her feet and started walking.

'Wait for me!' she whined. 'Wait up!'

I didn't listen. And I didn't even turn around when I heard her moaning. 'I'm cold! My legs are freezing. I feel ill, I'm going to faint . . . help, somebody help me!'

In the end she gave up her crying and complaining and began plodding along. When we stopped for a rest, I took care of her. I put some snow into a bandage and wrapped it around her swollen eye and cheek.

'I'm ugly! No one will want me.'

'Don't be ridiculous. You're beautiful, and if you keep some snow on it the swelling will go down in no time. I've seen the surgeons use it. What's more, you may even learn how to make do on your own. It'll come in handy, we're far from out of this mess yet.'

'You hurt me.'

'You hurt me too. We're even.'

She dried her tears with the back of her sleeve and I felt a little sorry for her. 'Look at that poor creature,' I said, pointing to Lystra. 'She could be having her baby at any minute. Imagine that you were in her situation. Try to hold out until evening. Then you'll be able to rest.'

And thus we went on and on and on, without stopping, without resting. As the sky grew dimmer and dimmer a stiff, cold wind came up, numbing our limbs and cracking our lips. We went on this way for days. Every so often Lystra would ask to get out so Melissa could ride inside, but this embarrassed Melissa and she usually refused. She was becoming a strong woman, deserving of respect. The other women struggled on bravely as well. Not a whine or a whimper out of them; if one fell, another helped her up. In the evenings, they took needle and thread and fashioned footwear to use on the snow or mended the holes in their garments and the men's. The cold had grown piercing and we had few opportunities to obtain provisions. Quarrels became frequent, especially between the men.

We were fighting a new, truly relentless enemy now, an enemy with no face but with a voice: the constant hiss of the wind. The winter.

Up and up we went. We had passed the first of the three towering peaks that I had seen glittering like diamonds from the hill beyond the ford on the turbulent river. It was the most impressive thing I had ever seen in my life.

Wide stripes of black rock that looked like petrified rivers descended from its sides. They stuck out of the snow, making me think of the backs of slumbering monsters, and they came all the way down to the path we were travelling on. Jutting from the sheer wall were black rocks, faceted and sparkling like gems; they were a little bigger than my fist. Perfect, extraordinary.

'That's a sleeping volcano,' Xeno told me. 'When it wakes up, it vomits rivers of red-hot rock that flow down its sides before they thicken and solidify into what you see there.'

'How do you know?'

'I heard about it from a friend who had been to Sicily and witnessed the fury of Mount Etna.'

'What's Sicily?'

'It's an island of the west that has a gigantic volcano that spits smoke, flames and molten rock which solidifies just like that. I'd like to go there one day and see it for myself.'

'Will you take me with you?'

'Yes,' he said. 'I will. We'll never be parted again.'

Tears came to my eyes when I heard him say that, but the wind nearly froze them as they tried to make their way down my cheeks. Xeno was an extraordinary man, and I'd done the right thing to trust him, and follow him on that adventure. Even if I died, even if our journey ended here on the desolate icy expanse we were crossing, I would have no regrets.

The difficulties increased day by day. It was no longer a mere question of hardships that must be overcome, it was a matter of life or death. Whoever found a shelter or lit a fire lived, whoever didn't find one perished. After a few days of marching it started snowing again, but this time there was nothing beautiful or pleasurable about it. It wasn't the big white flakes I'd seen dancing in the light of the hearth against the dark sky, looking out of a safe shelter. It was needles of ice that the ceaseless, vicious wind drove straight into our faces. No matter how you tried to defend yourself, the freezing air got the better of you: it stabbed your limbs like a dagger, stiffened your movements, blinded your sight, lashed at your clothes and at the cloaks that we tried to hold tight.

The hiss of the wind had grown deafening; it wounded your ears like a continuous, inhuman scream. We moved through a nebulous atmosphere where everything was uncertain, every figure a ghost, or a larva, that you could barely see in the driving sleet. Fatigue and cold eroded your will with every step you took, creating a sense of deadly prostration that it was almost impossible to fight off. The animals were exposed to the same harsh conditions. You'd see them, overloaded and exhausted, keeling over all at once in the snow. No one even tried to save the baggage, because no one had a drop of energy above what was required to place one foot after another.

The wolves came then, and devoured the mules and horses

while they were still alive. The animals' brays of pain and terror echoed through the valley below before coming to an abrupt end in the milky squall.

Towards evening the storm would seem to die down, but then there were ghostly presences that loomed all around us, frightening and disturbing. The long, mournful howling of wolves resounded from the mountains and the forests bowed under the snow. Sometimes at night we could see their red eyes glittering in the dark in the firelight. You'd often hear a brief, desperate yelp from the dogs who followed us and we knew that they'd fallen victim to a hunger more powerful and ferocious than their own.

I WAS ASTONISHED at Melissa's heroism: Melissa – the beautiful, irresistible girl who'd become a legend when she ran naked from Cyrus's tent to the Greek camp, the girl whom every soldier longed to possess at any cost, even perhaps that of his own life – walked through the knee-deep snow with incredible endurance, leaving the only protected place in the long column of warriors and women on the march to Lystra, the lowest of the low, the little prostitute struggling to bear her child.

There was no space any longer for love. When darkness overtook us we'd stop where we were to seek some sort of shelter so we could lie down and steal a few hours' sleep from the night. The guard shifts were very brief; few could resist the intense cold and it often happened that when one sentry went to relieve another he'd find him cold and stiff, a mummy of ice propped up against a tree with glassy wide-open eyes.

One day towards evening we arrived at a level clearing in the lee of high cliffs to the north that held back the snow. All around were dozens of charred stumps, perhaps the aftermath of a summer fire. Some of the soldiers began to chop them down with axes, others bundled together the dry branches and then those who guarded our most precious belongings – the clay jars holding embers buried under ash – lit the fires. Everyone

4">4">4">4">4">4">

immediately thronged around, and then they lit more fires, and still more, but by the time the tail of the column caught up, it was almost dark and the wood had been all used up. The men were loath to make room so that the newcomers could warm themselves around the fires already burning. At that point quarrels and shoving matches broke out. Some reached for their weapons, while others devoted themselves to an even more shameful business: selling a place by the fire. They demanded to be paid with wheat, wine, oil, blankets, shoes, anything that would guarantee their survival for another day or another couple of hours.

I realized that our soldiers were surrendering to the most terrible of enemies: selfishness. Cleanor of Arcadia, that bull of a man, saw this happening, saw one of his men refusing to give up his place to a comrade who had nothing to give him in exchange. He hurled himself at the soldier who had become so unprincipled, grabbed him by the shoulders and pushed him towards the burning fire. 'You want to be where it's nice and hot? You like the heat, you bastard? I'll help you get some, you son of a bitch!' The man tried to resist, but nothing could hold back Cleanor in a rage. He pushed him further and further until the cloak the soldier was wearing caught fire. At that point the commander let go and the man ran away screaming and burning like a torch. He threw himself onto the ground and rolled through the snow. He saved his own life, but he would always wear the scars of his shame.

Among the last to arrive was Xeno.

As always.

His place was at the rear, to gather those who fell, to encourage the weary warriors, to make a show of discipline and courage, to set an example. He never tired. With him were Lycius, Aristonymus and Eurylochus, daring, fearless fighters all, gifted with formidable strength and an indomitable will. But at times, even their resolve was not enough. Sometimes nothing they could do would get a man who had fallen back to his feet, no amount of shaking or slapping or punching. They'd even try to get their goat by yelling, 'Get up, you worm! You good-for-nothing coward! You bastard son of a whore!' Nothing would work. One of the surgeons said that the little they were eating was not giving them sufficient strength to fight the cold, the wind, their fatigue. They needed more to eat, or they would die. So Xeno pushed forward on his steed, searching among the pack animals until he found a little food to give to his exhausted boys.

Some of them got up.

Others crumbled and didn't rise again. A white shroud covered them and their last words were carried away on the howling wind.

22

WHILE SOPHOS was out on reconnaissance with his men, Xeno realized that the soldiers weren't going to make it unless he could convince them to rally. He had them draw up, there in the snow. The commanders called them to attention and the men stood like soldiers, despite their exhaustion, with courage and dignity, gripping the hilts of their spears with hands livid with the cold. Their knuckles white, fingernails dark.

Xeno reviewed the troops, and in his gaunt cheeks, his bristly beard and reddened eyes they could read all the suffering that he saw in their faces.

He inspected them one by one, adjusting their cloaks around their shoulders and looking away from the open sores and frozen limbs, the footwear and clothing that no longer protected them from anything. Then he spoke.

'Men, listen to me now! We have overcome countless dangers. We have routed the most powerful army in the world, we have defeated a savage, barbarous people who wanted to annihilate us, we have challenged river currents, climbed mountain passes, we escaped the clutches of two armies who both wanted us dead, but now we fight an enemy without a face and without mercy, an enemy against which our weapons are no help to us. Many of us have already fallen to this enemy and we've had to leave them behind without funeral rites and without the honours they deserved. We are in a hostile land under terrible conditions, but we must survive. Do you remember what Clearchus would say? "Survive, men! Survive!" This is the order I'm giving you now. The same order he gave you then.

'There are two things above all that torment us: the cold and the light. The cold is more dangerous; we can defend ourselves from the light.

'Never stop moving at night. When you're out on guard, don't stand still: stamp your feet and slap your hands on your body. Always look for a spot that's sheltered from the wind. When you're sleeping, loosen your shoes. I've seen that many of you have swollen feet. That's a bad sign. The surgeons tell me that swelling can lead to frostbite and that can lead to death. Under other circumstances, they could try to amputate. Here that would just be pointless torture.

'Many of you have lost your way because you've been blinded by the light, which is so strong here. When the clouds clear and the sunlight is intense, its reflection on the snow can impair your vision. I can see how red your eyes are. If you don't protect them, you'll lose your sight and then your lives. You must cover your eyes with a dark bandage, leaving only a small slit to be able to see. There's no other way.

'When you find shelter and can light a fire, you're safe. Those of you who lag behind and sleep in the cold and dark will die. It's not fair that those who protect you have to pay for it with their lives. Every day, the vanguard will switch with the rearguard and vice versa until we have a complete rotation. In this way, the probability of survival will be the same for all. One last thing: remember that as long as we stick together we have a good chance of pulling through. If we respect the rules and our code of honour we can overcome the worst difficulties. A man who saves the life of his comrade saves his own. If you only try to save yourself, you'll die and the others will die with you. And now, men, let's march.'

He moved his rearguard to the front of the column but he stayed behind. The rules didn't count for him.

How long would this ordeal continue? Would spring never

come? What month were we in, what day? A whole lifetime had passed since I'd left my five villages, and I'd often find myself longing for that desert dust that steals your breath and burns your throat. When we were marching I never turned round, because I didn't want to see the men falling one after another, the animals collapsing to their knees and not getting up, the ranks thinning out so rapidly.

Xeno found no time to write but I was sure that there was not a single event, an instant of this tremendous adventure, that he had not committed to memory, as I had myself. I didn't know where Melissa was, or what had happened to Lystra. Her time must be drawing close.

One night we were to join up with Sophos, who had gone on a scouting expedition with a group of peltasts and with the Thracians, who were used to harsh winters in their homeland and withstood the cold better than the others. When darkness had fallen, they'd taken up quarters in some villages, and four battalions were allowed to enter. Some of the men had found shelter, others were outside gathered around huge campfires. The end of the column, where I was along with Xeno and his men, was so far behind that we were surprised by nightfall in the middle of the high plain.

It was a clear, windy night. A very long night. And absolutely freezing. Millions of stars, made of ice themselves, glittered in the black sky. The milky way that crossed the sky from one side to another seemed a trail of snow raised by the wind.

The territory was bleak and barren, there were no trees or bushes and there was no place to seek refuge anywhere in sight. Xeno assembled the men and the animals, and had the soldiers search through the baggage to find some shovels. They cleared the snow from a wide area all around us, creating a kind of bank that would protect us from the biting wind. They lit a few lamps and distributed what little food there was, and a few sips of wine. Then all the animals were massed into the centre of the cleared area, with the men all around, as close as possible so no warmth would be lost. The last ones on the outside, who would serve as sentries, were wrapped in their cloaks.

That's how we spent the night, but in the morning we found a dozen men lying stiff in the snow, their eyes pearls of ice.

We resumed our journey along a ridge of low hills, and at a certain point the group walking at the top noticed something odd: a dark area in the middle of the whiteness, ground completely free of snow. They started to shout, 'This way! Come over this way!' and we all made our way up the hillside. From up there we could see the big, dark clearing from which a column of steam was rising, but this new vantage point also made us aware that we were not alone. There were bands of armed natives trailing us, intent on killing and plundering anyone who fell behind. They were in groups of about fifty men, dressed in skins, armed with pikes and knives.

But all of our attention went momentarily to the scene in front of us: there was a spring of warm water there, in the middle of that ice-covered wasteland! It filled a natural pool about two cubits deep. The land all around the pool was tepid as well, and the men tumbled to the ground to soak up its warmth: dry land!

They didn't want to leave. Xeno tried to get them back on their feet. 'I'll let you rest but then we're off again.'

'You can forget that! We're not moving from here,' said one of them.

'You can kill us, but we're not leaving,' added another.

'You're mad! There's nothing here, besides a little heat. What do you think would happen if you stayed? You can decide whether you'd prefer to starve to death or have those fellows over there chop you to pieces. It's your choice.'

He allowed them to rest, certain that they would soon be feeling better and be willing to resume the march. He was wrong. Many of them had been on their last legs when they reached the warm pool, and now they had stripped down and were lolling in the water, in a marvellous bath that consoled them for all the suffering they'd gone through. Their hardships, the frost, were a thing of the past. Xeno knew what they were thinking and so did I. Better to die sapped of all energy by this miraculous spring, this warm womb, than to face all the pain and privation that lay ahead.

Xeno managed to threaten and cajole most of them back to their feet, but there were about thirty who remained. They had become too feeble even to walk, let alone bear up under the weight of their armour.

He gave up. 'All right,' he said. 'But you were told that no one would be left behind and I intend to keep that promise. We'll go on until we find shelter then I'll send someone back to get you.'

I'll never forget the sight of those lads naked as babies in their bath, in that transparent water. They watched us leave with eyes full of infinite melancholy. Xeno muttered that they seemed like the companions of Odysseus among the lotus-eaters, but I don't know what he meant by that.

I think that it was the very air that was making us so tired. I'd never been up so high and neither had the others, but I realized that I had to breathe much more quickly than usual, and that every move cost immense effort.

We finally caught up with the army's advance guard and Sophos came to greet us. 'Come in! There's plenty to eat and drink here. You can sleep inside the houses and there's room for everyone. The people are not hostile.'

Xeno was cheered. 'Finally, some good news! Get me some mules or horses, food, dry clothes and some fresh troops: I need to leave right away.'

I kept thinking about those boys in their steaming bath. The sun was beginning to set. The night was advancing from the north like a black veil that covered part of the sky. They maybe had an hour of life left to them. Maybe two.

Xeno got his mules and horses. He left Eurylochus and Lycius in charge then headed out with a group of peltasts and Thracian skirmishers.

THE YOUTHS were still in the water, playing and splashing, but the air was getting colder by the instant. As the light dimmed, the steam became denser and turned to ice on some of the nearby bushes and a couple of dead trees, which loomed over them like skeletal creatures. The fantastic shapes formed by the ice burst into a myriad colours as they were struck by the last rays of the setting sun. The moon was still pale as it rose from behind the impassable mountain chain to observe the scene. The men's voices penetrated the vapour, but their forms had become indistinct and blurred.

Night was upon them.

Death was upon them.

The black divinity descended from the icy peaks without leaving a trace in the immaculate snow, cleaving the wind with the cutting edge of his naked skull. He guided invisible bands of marauders who swooped down the slopes, brandishing the tools of slaughter.

The young men could see them coming but did not react. What could they do? Their end would be rapid and warm: their tepid blood would mix with the tepid water and then darkness and silence would prevail.

XENO APPEARED at the top of a hill, rearing up on his horse, who neighed loudly, breathing steam from his nostrils like a dragon. Xeno unsheathed his sword and shouted, 'Alalalai!'

And right behind him were five hundred warriors, skirmishers and assaulters, no longer hungry now, and well armed. They drew up in a fan formation over the entire arc of the slope to cut off any line of escape for the marauders. Their gallop raised white clouds of powdery snow. Enveloped in rainbow light, they bore down on their enemies. They knew those enemies well:

they were the ones who waited for the cover of night to attack the stragglers, who preyed upon the desperate souls remaining alone and bewildered, who came to blows amongst themselves in the dark, howling as they fought over the spoils and the pack animals who could not get back to their feet.

The Thracians and the light infantry fought furiously and cut the enemy down, one after another, skewering them on their javelins, stabbing them with their daggers, carving them up with their long razor-edged swords.

The white expanse was stained with black and red and silence fell over all.

Xeno took no part in the combat; it wasn't necessary. He watched from Halys's saddle and only when it was over did he dig in his heels to urge the steed towards the centre of the snow-free valley. He jumped to the ground and neared the hot spring, from which no sound issued. He crossed the cloud of steam and appeared to his comrades who were still sitting there, dazed at what they had seen and heard.

Xeno counted them. No one was missing.

'Get out of there! Get dressed and take up your arms. At four stadia from here there's everything you need: shelter, food, drink and fire to warm you. You're out of danger now.'

Those young men stared at him as if he were a miraculous apparition, then they got out of the water without a word, put on their dry clothes, took up their arms and mounted the pack animals that Xeno had brought with him.

Death could wait.

Before morning they were at the village gates.

No one had ever seen such a place. There were at least ten large villages made up of houses with stone walls and thatched roofs, but under each house was another one, dug underneath. In those underground chambers were provisions of every sort and big jugs of beer. It was light and foamy, and quite delicious. There were chickens and geese as well, asses and mules, big barns full of hay and enough houses for all the men to find shelter.

It was warm there, finally. After so much suffering our men could curl up and sleep without alarms of any sort, without the midnight screams of marauders. Xeno began writing again, describing with the utmost precision the events that had taken place. He visited the villages one by one and took notes. Generals Cleanor, Timas, Agasias and Xanthi settled into the best houses with their women, and I went to visit Melissa, who was safe and sound and back with her Cleanor.

'Now you're a real woman,' I told her, 'a person who can face any trial in life. You've shown courage and compassion . . .'

'I had to,' she replied, laughing. 'You made me.'

'You're right, but I knew I was doing the right thing. And I'm still sure of it.'

'You called me a whore.'

'I'm sorry. I was beside myself.'

'I never had the chance to choose my own destiny, but I do have feelings and I always have. I'm a woman just like you are.'

'Now I know.'

'Don't ever offend me again or I'll scratch your eyes out.'

'All right.'

'How far are we from our destination?'

'I'm afraid no one knows.'

'You're telling me that no one knows where we're going? Xeno should know, and you're his woman.'

'The army takes its bearings from the sun. We're heading north. Xeno thinks we'll have to cross another big mountain chain before we reach the sea.'

'How long will that take?'

'Twenty days should do it. But none of our men has ever crossed this region. And what's more . . .'

'What?'

'I'm afraid, Melissa. I just can't shake all these doubts I have . . .'

'Doubts about what?'

'Maybe it's just a sensation, but there have been so many

coincidences. Too many. The way our commanders were
deceived. Whole armies that appear out of nowhere to bar our
path, traps that spring up suddenly. The turbulent river we had
to ford. The suicidal opposition of the Carduchi. Now that made
no sense whatsoever. I feel like our real enemies are invisible,
and impossible to defend ourselves against. I'm afraid we can
expect anything and everything.'

Melissa gave a disheartened sigh and dropped her head.

'No, take no notice,' I said. 'As I was saying, maybe I'm
seeing things that don't exist.'

Melissa raised her eyes. 'If something happens, stay close to
me. Help me, please. You're the only person I trust.'

'Cleanor will defend you at any cost,' I protested. 'Surely
you're safe with him.'

'Stay close to me anyway.'

I left her to find Lystra, who could be giving birth at any
time. I asked Xeno if one of the surgeons could help me, because
I had no idea what to do.

'Women have babies on their own,' he replied. 'The surgeons
are busy with other things.'

I'd expected that.

WE STAYED IN those villages for a while to recover from our
ordeal. Sophos often had dinner with us. He really was quite a
fascinating man: tall, athletic, with that teasing look of his and a
ready answer to everything. Nothing seemed to worry him. But
if you watched closely, there were moments when he seemed to
drift away. It was almost imperceptible, but his eyes would cloud
over at a sudden thought. He was a true Spartan, a descendant
of one of those three hundred who eighty years earlier had
stopped the Great King at the pass of the Fiery Gates, as Xeno
called it.

I listened as they discussed matters, evaluated possibilities,
itineraries, strategies.

'As soon as we reach a place that's known to the Greeks,'

Xeno said once, 'our suffering will be over. We'll know how to proceed and we'll quickly find a spot from which we can sail for home. We've always headed due north; we've never gone off course except for a slight detour here or there. We should be on the right track.'

Sophos smiled. 'I know a fellow who, after an evening drinking in a tavern, left because it was time to go home. He walked all night and the next morning he found himself at the same tavern. Either that was where he knew he'd find the best wine in town, or he'd wandered in a circle without realizing it.'

Xeno and the other officers who were present laughed heartily. The sense that our destination was not far off was becoming very strong. The food and the beer boosted their optimism, and the Armenians who lived in the villages seemed peaceful folk and willing to give a hand. There was reason to believe that the worst was behind us.

I went to Lystra before going to bed. 'Have this child now, here, where it's warm, girl. You've got everything you need here.'

Lystra answered with a tired smile.

We started our journey again on a grey, still morning. Sophos asked the village chief to be our guide, and he was forced to accept. He had seven male sons: they took one along to make sure he wouldn't betray them and turned the boy over to a soldier from Athens. But perhaps the chieftain would have accepted anyway: having ten thousand guests who ate three times a day was heavy going and he needed some way to get rid of us.

After several days of marching in thigh-high snow, Sophos lost his patience, because we'd seen neither a hut nor a village since we'd left. He began to insult the chief, who defended himself stoutly:

'There are no villages in this region. I can't give you what doesn't exist.'

'You bastard!' he shouted. 'You're leading us out of our way.'

'That's not true!'

'Confess that you're taking us in the wrong direction!'

The man reacted by shouting back even more loudly. Sophos took a stick and started to beat him. The village chieftain yelled and tried to defend himself, but he was unarmed and Sophos's blows fell with violent force. Xeno tried to stop him. 'Leave him alone, can't you see he knows nothing? We have his son as our hostage. If he knew something, he'd talk.'

Sophos paid no attention whatsoever and continued beating the man until he fell to the ground coughing up blood.

'You've broken his ribs, are you happy now?' Xeno accused him furiously.

'I did what I had to do! This bastard thinks we're idiots!'

Xeno lowered his head and walked away, muttering under his breath, 'It makes no sense, no sense at all . . .'

It snowed all night. The next morning the man was gone.

'What do you mean, he's gone?' exclaimed Xeno as soon as they had told him. He dressed hurriedly and rushed to Sophos's tent. 'How did he get away? Where were the guards? Why did no one stop him?'

'They must have thought that he was in such a bad way that he couldn't get far, and that he wouldn't have abandoned his son.'

'They must have thought?' repeated Xeno, incensed. 'What does that mean? Who's responsible for this? I want to interrogate the men who were on guard last night!'

Sophos snapped back, 'You won't be questioning anyone, writer. You have no authority to do so. You have no rank in this army.'

Xeno turned his back on him. He was seething; his friend had never treated him this way before.

'Where are you going?'

'Wherever I damn well please!'

Sophos changed his tone. 'Listen, I'm angry as well, but I can't punish men who spent the night out in the snow and have been living under such desperate conditions for months. We'll find our way without him.'

'If you say so . . .' Xeno replied, his teeth clenched. He left.

I'd never seen them arguing like that, and the other officers were taken aback as well. Xanthi called, 'Wait, come back. We have to talk.'

'Let him go,' said Timas. 'He'll get over it. We'll talk later.'

Xeno returned to the rearguard without saying a word. He was furious.

We started up again and we walked all that day and the next under the snow, which was falling quite heavily. Towards evening of the second day, we reached a river bank. Westward, the cloud cover was opening a bit, letting through the last rays of the setting sun which spread in bloody streaks over the water and the snow.

It seemed unreal, a magical spell. But it only lasted a few moments.

The river was wide and flowed full and fast from left to right. Eastward, I thought. There was no way to cross it but at least there were no other dangers in sight.

Sophos summoned his staff to a meeting. Xeno didn't want to go, but Agasias and Cleanor convinced him in the end, although they practically had to drag him there.

'What do we do now?' asked Sophos, scowling.

'A bridge,' suggested Xanthi. 'There are trees over on those hills.'

'A bridge?' repeated Timas. 'Yes, why not. We'll drive the stakes in the river bed two at a time, binding them together, and we'll build a footbridge, adding stakes as we go along, until we get to the other side.'

'Let's get started,' said Cleanor, 'and get one more obstacle out of our way. I'll bet you anything that on the other side of those mountains there we'll be looking at the sea.'

'Or we'll be looking at another mountain chain.' Agasias

dampened his enthusiasm. 'You know how deceptive appearances can be around here.'

'I say we'll see the sea,' retorted Cleanor.

'It's no use quarrelling over whether the sea is there or not,' Agasias commented.

Xeno hadn't said a word. He scrutinized the current and tried to understand.

'We have to figure out what river this is,' he said. 'Unfortunately, our guide has bolted.'

'I've heard enough about the guide!' Sophos burst out. 'And I don't want to hear any more!'

'Let's try to stay calm,' suggested Timas.

Xeno went on, 'This is a big river, an important river. It must have a name. Maybe it's a river we know. If we could find out, I think I could calculate fairly accurately where we are, and establish what direction we should take. It's essential that we avoid long detours and not waste time and energy in building a bridge if it's not necessary.'

Agasias dropped his head into his hands as if searching for an idea. 'We need to find someone from around here who speaks our language. I haven't seen a soul.'

'Then let's build this bridge,' concluded Xanthi.

'One moment,' interrupted Sophos. 'Look down there.'

Just then they glimpsed a man walking along the river bank with a dog, carrying a basketful of wood on his shoulders.

'Run, before he gets away!' shouted Agasias, as he set off full tilt in the direction of the man who'd appeared as if by magic. The others took off after him, and Xeno passed Agasias by running where the snow was less deep.

The man with the basket stopped, seeming more curious than afraid of the group of foreigners hurtling towards him, jumping like madmen through piles of drifted snow. The dog started to bark in alarm but didn't move.

Xeno got there first, panting. 'What is this river?' he asked, all in one breath.

The dog kept barking. The man shook his head. He didn't understand.

'The name of this river!' shouted Timas as he caught up to them.

Agasias started to gesticulate, trying to imitate the current flowing between the river's banks. 'The river, understand? What do you called this damned river?'

'He doesn't understand, can't you see that he doesn't understand?' said Xanthi.

The man gave a start, and finally seemed to intuit what they were asking. He said *'Keden? Keden gotchetsyal . . . Pase! Pase!'*

'*Pase . . .*' repeated Xeno. '*Pase*, that's what it's called. *Pase . . .* yes, of course! Of course! This is the Phasis! The river Phasis. I know where we are! I know exactly where to go. No bridge. We will follow the river and it will lead us to the sea and to a beautiful city. We've made it, boys! We've done it!'

Everyone started shouting and cheering with excitement, throwing handfuls of snow at each other like children.

I was the only one who still couldn't understand.

I couldn't understand why the water was flowing east, towards the heart of the Persian empire. Away from the sea, not towards it.

23

THAT NIGHT, in our tent, holding each other close under a ram's skin, we listened to the sound of the river running swiftly towards its destiny. All kinds of thoughts and questions were jostling in my head.

'How can you be so sure that the river is the Phasis? And why should the Phasis lead us to safety?'

As he'd done before, Xeno wrapped his arms around me and told me a story.

'The Phasis is the only big, fast-flowing river in this region. I've looked at the stars and I have no doubt about it. The name that man used, *Pase*, is certainly the original name that our Phasis comes from. Besides, Chirisophus is sure of it as well. He knows I'm right and he's backing my plan to follow the current.'

'But the water is flowing in the opposite direction to the way we should be marching,' I couldn't help but point out. 'If we follow it, we'll end up in a land even more distant and more unfamiliar than the region we're crossing now.'

'Water flows downward, and towards the sea. If the current is flowing east instead of west at this point, it's only because of the slope of the land. But it will change direction and descend towards the sea, and at the mouth of the river we'll find a city that one of our heroes visited many centuries ago.'

'Who was this hero? What was he doing in such a remote land?'

'His name was Jason and he was a prince. He was taken away from his kingdom as a young child on the night that his

294

father Aeson was killed by his own half-brother, Pelias, who seized power in his brother's place. The boy was raised in secret by a marvellous creature of infinite wisdom. When Jason was an adult he left the caves on the mountainside where he had grown up and returned to his kingdom. As he was crossing a river, he lost his sandal, and thus clad he arrived at the royal palace, frightening to death his uncle, who had been told by an oracle that he would be deposed by a man wearing a single sandal.

'So Pelias sent the young man to carry out what he thought would be an impossible task: to bring home the fleece – completely made of gold – of a gigantic magic ram. This fleece was considered the most powerful talisman on earth. The precious object was to be found in Colchis, the most extreme eastern region of the world, and was guarded day and night by an enormous dragon who breathed flames from his nostrils.

'Jason accepted the challenge and convinced the strongest heroes in Greece to join him. They built the first ship in human history, carved from a single towering pine tree from Mount Pelion, and left for Colchis. When he arrived there he asked the king for help, but it was the king's daughter, the beautiful Princess Medea, who fell in love with Jason and told him the secret that would enable him to defeat the dragon and return home.

'Jason captured the golden fleece, became king of his city, and married Medea.'

'So it all ended up well?'

'No, just the opposite. Their union turned into a nightmare and ended in blood.'

'I wonder why your stories always end badly.'

'Because they mirror reality. In reality, few things end up well.'

I felt the blood freeze in my veins. Was he trying to tell me that our relationship would end like Jason's and Medea's?

Xeno continued with his story. 'Centuries later other groups of Greeks reached the land of Medea and founded a city at the mouth of this river, giving it the same name: Phasis. I know exactly where that city is. It's on the coast of the Euxine sea, in a rich and fertile land. If we follow the river, that's where we'll end up, and our troubles will be over.'

'And when we've arrived at the city of Phasis, what will we do?'

Xeno sighed. 'We don't even know if we'll still be alive tomorrow, and you're asking me what will we do then? We'll try to survive, Abira, one day at a time. We'll think about the rest when the time comes.'

All at once the serene vision I'd had of our immediate future dimmed, like the sky above us. The silence between us weighed heavily and I tried to return to our conversation.

'So Sophos is happy with your idea?'

'He agrees with me. He's ready to support me in every way.'

'What about the others?'

'You want to know too much.'

'Well, what about the others?' I repeated.

Xeno hesitated, then gave in. 'They're against it. Not one of the other generals is convinced of this decision. We quarrelled about it, and a fight nearly broke out. Even Glous showed up, I hadn't seen him for a long time, and he was against it as well. But I was firm, and I've got Chirisophus's backing. We're going where I say. There is no river that doesn't lead to the sea. And this one goes to our sea.'

'May the gods hear you,' I said, and then fell silent. Down deep, I wasn't convinced either.

Next day we resumed our march, but there was no enthusiasm, no determination. Xanthi, Timas, Agasias and Cleanor must have spoken with their subordinate officers, who must have informed the men. We were heading east, and that was where the Persian empire lay, everyone was well aware of it. But perhaps we'd never left. Perhaps we were still within the territory of the Great King. Maybe the whole earth, except for the land of the Greeks, belonged to the Great King.

One evening we reached the foot of a pass swarming with warriors who were barring our way. It was happening again. The same thing that had happened over and over. In that mountainous land, every valley was a territory unto itself, a little homeland that had to be defended tooth and nail. And that we had to take by force. How many valleys lay between us and the sea? How many passes would we have to seize? How many villages would we sack? I forced myself to scan the endless sweep of mountaintops, of snowy peaks, of shimmering waterfalls and turbulent rivers, and I couldn't imagine the end. Not even Xeno, Xeno who knew everything, could tell me how many rocky cliffs we'd have to climb before we saw the glittering waters of the sea. That sea that I'd never seen, and that I was beginning to think I never would.

The river ... it was close at times, other times it would meander away, but we never lost sight of it. It was our guide, the liquid, wavy path that would one day lead us to flowery meadows caressed by the gentle breezes of spring, where Lystra would watch her child take his first steps.

I heard a shout, a curt order, and then the yelling of thousands of men and the deafening din made by the warriors' weapons as they charged. The commanders seemed to be running a game. They moved units from one area to another, made feint attacks only to withdraw and regroup the forces elsewhere, where they could deal the killing blow. It was like a hunting party, with the results taken for granted. I watched Xanthi striking with devastating power, Timas advancing at a run upslope, urging on his men, Cleanor dashing head-first behind his shield, overwhelming any obstacle, Xeno riding by with his spear held high, and all the others too, the heroes of that lost army: Aristonymus of Methydria, Agasias of Stymphalus, Lycius of Syracuse, Eurylochus of Lusia, Callimachus ... I recognized them all, from the timbre of their voices, the way they gesticulated, that way they had of charging into the fray, calling back and forth amongst themselves. They were lions set free in the midst of a flock of sheep. No one could withstand them.

Before night fell, the defenders of the mountain pass lay strewn over the slope, each man where the fatal blow had found him. Our men camped at the pass, to guard it.

The women and the baggage animals arrived later, only when the reflection of the moon on the snow allowed us to follow the path. On the other side of the pass, there were dark spots scattered over the white expanse: villages and fortified settlements, standing each one on its own craggy rise. The provisions we'd taken from the Armenian villages were almost gone: the army was hungry.

The next morning at dawn, Sophos ordered that everything that was left to eat be distributed among the men, and then had the trumpets sound the attack.

The army encircled the villages one by one. The skirmishers went first, testing the inhabitants' strategies of defence by attacking and withdrawing in waves, forcing the defenders into countering with arrows, darts and stones, primitive weapons and largely ineffective. Then they sent in the heavy infantry. I watched Cleonimus, Agasias and Eurylochus pounding in their heavy armour up the ramp that led to the village gate as if they were athletes running a mad race. Overtaking one another, pushing each other out of the way with shouts and laughter, crashing through the trellised gates with a mere shove of their shields, opening the way for their unleashed comrades.

It was there that I realized how far the love of liberty, the attachment to one's homeland, the terror of an unknown enemy, could push people.

I saw the village women hurling their own children over the city walls onto the cliffs below and then following them to their fate, dashed upon the sharp rocks. And I saw the men, having fought to the last moment, their weapons chipped and broken, every possibility exhausted, joining their brides and their children.

After getting their fill of plunder the army went beyond the villages, always continuing along the river, always heading east.

We advanced for days without ever stopping, passing close to the other mountain we'd seen so long ago, at dawn, sparkling on the horizon like a precious jewel. It was immense. Its peak pierced the clouds and its flanks, furrowed in black, rose majestically over the vast highlands crossed by the river.

Then it began to snow, in big flakes, over the boundless, silent plain, for a day and a night without pause. Or maybe it was two days, or three: those terrible days have become confused in my mind, lost to my memory. The only thing I recall clearly is that we lost a servant to the blizzard.

The next morning, Lystra went into labour. I was hoping it would all be over before the soldiers had finished eating, or while they were breaking camp and preparing to march. I'd had our surviving servant fix a pallet of woven straw between two poles that could be attached to one of the mules, thinking that the animal could tow it or drag it along so she'd have a place to lie with her baby when it was born. But things did not go as I'd hoped. Her pains were prolonged; the contractions were strong, and she cried out with every spasm, but the child would not come into the light. Xeno arrived already armed and holding his horse by its reins. 'What can you do? We have to get moving, you can't make the whole army wait.'

'I won't leave her behind in these conditions! The wolves would tear her to shreds. She's giving birth, can't you see that?'

'I'll have her helped onto the stretcher, but we have to go.'

'No! The baby is coming, she has to be able to lie down and be still. It won't take long. You go ahead, leave me the servant and the mule with the stretcher. We'll catch up to you. It won't be hard to follow your prints in the snow.'

Xeno was loath to leave me there, but he agreed in the end, knowing how strong I was and how used to adversity, by then. 'Don't do anything foolish, be careful!' he said as he waved

VALERIO MASSIMO MANFREDI

goodbye. He urged his horse alongside the column so he could
reach the head, where his scouts were.

It was still snowing, and the sounds of the army on the
march were fading. The servant was worried and tense. 'Let's go
now,' he kept saying. 'We can't wait any longer. If we lose
contact, we're done for.'

'It won't be long now, the baby will be coming soon, very
soon,' I answered with ever-lessening conviction. I tried to help
her. I pressed down on her belly. I shouted and pleaded. 'Push!
Come on, you poor little strumpet. Push out that baby, the child
of a thousand fathers!' With every passing instant I felt more
impotent and gripped by anguish. The realization that we were
not winning this battle against time made me feel like I was
suffocating.

I burst out sobbing as I begged her to push. 'Push out that
little bastard, damn you! Push!' At the same time, I started to
yell, 'Xeno! Xenoooo!' as if there were any hope of him hearing
me or helping me.

Lystra was pale, ice-cold and covered with sweat. Her eyes
were deep, dark circles. Her breath came in short painful gasps.

She looked deep into my eyes with a sad, lost, expression. 'I
can't,' she said in a tiny voice. 'Forgive me. I can't do it.'

'Yes, you can! Push, damn it. Look! I can see his hair, push
him out, you're almost there, you can do it!'

Lystra looked at me again with tears coursing down her
wasted cheeks. Her head rolled backward and then she was
perfectly still, her eyes open and staring at the flakes of snow
falling from the white impassive sky.

I grabbed her by the shoulders and shook her. 'Don't die!
Don't die, wake up, come on now, I'll take you away from here.
It's time to go now, we'll go together!' I didn't know what I was
saying, I was talking nonsense and shaking that limp body with
her arms hanging loose like a disjointed doll's. I covered her
body with mine as if I could pass on a little bit of my warmth,
and stayed that way weeping, I don't know for how long.

When at last I snapped out of that daze, I looked around to ask for help and I realized with terror that I was all alone. How much time had passed? Where was our servant? Which way had the army gone? The snow was falling fast and heavy, and the silence that surrounded me swallowed up every sound, even that of my own breathing. All I could see were small clouds of vapour.

I tried to get to my feet but I couldn't. The snow masked everything in a fluttery blur. The air was so dense with it, I couldn't see a thing. All of a sudden, I thought I saw dark shadows coming my way.

I started to scream at the top of my lungs, until my cries died in my throat. I tried to move, to find the traces of the army, but everything looked exactly the same in every direction. I was alone, next to a corpse already stiff and completely blanketed by the snow.

I would die too.

I was almost dead.

I would follow Lystra and her child.

I would never see Xeno again.

Or the dusty village of Beth Qadà. The well ... my friends ... my mother. Nothing.

I was overcome with weariness: heavy, sluggish ... sweet. I remember that I had a dream. As I was sinking into oblivion, I dreamed that I saw an indistinct shape advancing towards me. The shape took on the outline of a fantastic figure, a man. A horseman, white himself, on a white horse. His face was hidden behind the edge of the cloak that lay over his shoulders.

I dreamed that he jumped to the ground, light as a snowflake himself, and that he approached me.

'Who are you?' I asked when I saw him bending over me to lift me from the ground. Then his image dissolved in the swirling snow, vanished in the lethargy that locks out even dreams and visions.

I thought ... death.

XENO.

The face that appeared to me in the dim light of the evening was his.

'Where are we?' I managed to whisper.

'In camp. You're safe.'

The thought of Lystra immediately welled up and brought tears to my eyes.

'Lystra's dead.'

'I imagined as much. I'm sorry.'

'How did you find me?'

'The sentries found you outside, under a fir tree, nearly frozen to death.'

'That's not possible.'

'I can't understand it either.'

'I think I saw . . .'

'What? What did you see?'

'A man covered with snow, all white.'

'Maybe it was our servant. He hasn't come back. Maybe he found you and brought you here.'

'But where is he now?'

'Somewhere outside, maybe. It would be useless to search for him now. It will be completely dark soon. It's too dangerous.'

I slept all night. The morning after, a group of scouts found the remains of the mule and our servant. The wolves had left only their bones. Xeno bought another servant from the merchants who were still following the army, and we continued our journey.

Eastward. We continued eastward for many days, always alongside the river. Every evening when the staff met, the generals and battalion commanders insisted that to keep on in that direction was pure folly. We'd already covered a great distance, and there was no reason to think that we were any closer to the sea. One of them, whose name was so long that I couldn't pronounce it, but whom I called Netus, brought up a disturbing hypothesis. 'What if this river flows into the river

Ocean that surrounds the earth, and not the Euxine sea, as you're hoping?'

'What are you saying?' Xeno retorted.

'Prove to me that what I'm saying can't be true,' Netus insisted.

'We're suffering heavier losses than at any time since we've left Greece,' said Xanthi. 'We've lost more men to the cold and snow than in all our battles against the Carduchi.'

'And you're responsible, Xenophon!' Netus exclaimed.

'No,' Sophos broke in. 'I'm responsible. I have the high command. And I'm convinced that Xenophon is right. We have to stay with the river. It will take us to the sea, I'm sure of it. We've endured enormous hardship to make it this far. We can't turn back now.'

Xeno spoke up. 'I've never heard of anyone actually reaching the river Ocean except for one of the admirals of the Great King, a Greek from Caria, and as far as I know it is very, very far away, thousands of stadia away. Remember what Cyrus used to say? "My father's empire extends so far north that men can't survive there because of the cold and so far south that they can't survive because of the heat."'

'But he didn't talk about the east!' insisted Netus.

'That doesn't change anything. The extreme east is the same distance away from the sanctuary of Delphi as the extreme west, and therefore, if this river were to flow into the Ocean, it would be longer than the Nile!'

'I know why you want to follow this river,' fumed Netus. 'You think it's the Phasis and you want to found a colony at the mouth of the river!'

Many of those present turned to Xeno, yelling and cursing. Xeno drew his sword and hurled himself at Netus. He would have cut his throat if someone hadn't stopped him. 'What you're saying is slander!' he was shouting. 'A total lie, fabricated to discredit me. You're envious of all the good I've done for this army!'

'All right, I admit it,' replied Netus when both had calmed down. 'It's a rumour I've been hearing around the camp, but it makes sense. You're a man without a homeland, without a country. If you returned to Athens they'd have your hide, because you fought against the democrats at the time of the battle of Piraeus.'

Netus knew everything about Xeno's past. Or at least that he had been exiled.

'If you succeeded in founding a colony using these men you'd acquire eternal glory, they'd raise a statue to you in the main square of the new city with an inscription dedicated to the founder. That's what you're dreaming of, isn't it? These men don't know where to go, anyway. Doesn't it all work out?'

A furious argument broke out. Xeno managed to take the floor. 'Let's suppose for a moment that you're right: so what? What would be wrong with the idea? In any case, it would be the assembled army that would decide. I have no authority to make such an important resolution. Not even Commander Chirisophus could decide something like that on his own. But if you think I'm so blinded by ambition that I would endanger the lives of my comrades, who I greatly esteem and have grown very fond of, that I would risk sending them to their deaths in an icy wasteland, then you are a bastard and a cur, a contempt-ible coward hiding behind your smears. I'm trying to bring these men to safety in the best way I can, not lose them to adversity, one after another.'

'If you're accusing me . . .' shouted Netus, putting his hand on his sword.

'Enough of this!' exclaimed Sophos. 'We'll continue on our route. Xeno is right. This river can only be the Phasis, and it will only be a matter of days before it starts to descend towards the sea. We will follow the river until we reach safe shores. You must sustain the men's morale by setting an example. We have overcome a thousand obstacles and we'll overcome this one too.'

The meeting drew to an end amidst grumbling and accusations, but our march resumed and we went on for days and days. The perseverance of those warriors was truly remarkable: as well as the cold and the storms, there were continual raids from fierce local tribes who laid ambushes, attacked at night, hid in the deep snow and would burst out with no warning screaming their blood-curdling war cries.

Sophos adopted a new strategy to obtain what he wanted: he avoided calling his staff to council. He merely issued orders. This worked for quite some time, but then the discontent boiled up again.

Xeno had stopped writing, except for brief notes. Several times in our tent at night I saw him open the drawer with the white parchment roll, dip his pen in the ink, trace out a few words and then stop. I didn't dare ask him why. Actually, I didn't need to ask. He couldn't bear having to justify to himself a choice that was draining the men of their lifeblood, one drop at a time. What I couldn't understand was Sophos's unwavering support. It couldn't be that he simply agreed with the choice that had been made: there were certain moments when persisting with the choice was so manifestly mistaken that he had to have had doubts. I had doubts, and was anguished by them.

How I yearned to be able to read those signs that Xeno traced on his scroll the few times he chose to do so, to understand what he'd decided to commit to posterity and what he kept for himself. He was worried, that much was clear, always scowling, taciturn. It was growing harder to speak with him with each passing day. One evening we were confronted with a dire situation: the pass ahead was closed off by close lines of warriors who wore skins and carried big bows like those of the Carduchi. They were targeting us with constant volleys that the heavy infantry was blocking by drawing up in a tight formation with their shields overlapping. Then they attacked us from behind as well, and Xeno had to turn the front around to repel the onslaught from that direction. Once again, we were beset by enemies on all sides, but Sophos made the right decision. He left half of the army in plain view, simulating continuous attempts at frontal assault and, with Xeno covering both groups from the rear, he advanced with the other half of the army through a dense, dark wood which completely concealed his marching column.

They fell upon the enemy all at once, and scattered them in every direction.

From where he had been providing support, Xeno did not hear the cries of exultation that he expected from his comrades. What they had seen on the other side of the pass must have been so awful that it dampened any enthusiasm. Xeno urged Halys up the slope, and when he reached the top he leapt to the ground and saw the reason for their dismay: the river they had been following was no longer anywhere to be seen!

24

THE ARMY WAS locked in dejection. They had endured the harshest trials, the most unthinkable suffering. They had borne the loss of countless companions, dragged themselves through desolate territories in the hope of finding a safe path that would lead to the end of their pain. Salvation, the embrace of the sea. All this vanished in a single moment, just as they should have been celebrating another victory.

Netus came up with a mocking smile on his face. 'Your river is gone. What do we do now?'

Xeno didn't answer. He stood there in silence, contemplating the unbroken white expanse.

'Well?' goaded Netus.

'Well nothing. The river hasn't vanished. This valley is exposed to the north wind and it's very cold. The river iced up and the snow covered it. At first light we'll be able to locate it.'

'Oh, right. And what then? We wait for spring to come and thaw it? Not a bad plan, but by the time the river starts flowing again, there won't be a single one of us left to see it. There's no village here, not a single shelter, no place to get food.'

Sophos cut their quarrel short. 'We'll camp here and tomorrow in the daylight we'll come to a decision. Those dolts who attacked us did not rain out of the sky. Their villages must be around here somewhere. Now go find some wood in the forest and light fires. The sky is clear; it will be very cold tonight.'

And so the warriors who had fought their battle and won, tired and hungry now, set down their spears and shields, picked up their axes and set off in search of firewood.

Even Xeno, who had fought for hours and was bleeding from a couple of flesh wounds which I bandaged up, joined the others to fell trees in the forest.

Our servant cleared a big enough space and pitched our tent, packing snow around the base. I laid out the skins, blankets and cloaks and lit a lamp. Despite the difficult terrain and general weariness, a camp was established, tent after tent, sometimes with simple, makeshift shelters, fashioned by tying skins around three crossed spears.

Bundles of wood began to arrive and, as the men started to light the first fires, our will to survive kindled anew. I gathered some of the embers in a clay jar and brought it inside the tent to warm it. I was looking for a little barley to toast and grind in the mortar to make our dinner when my eye was caught by the drawer with the scroll. I'd give anything to know what Xeno had been writing during our long trek along the river . . . Melissa! Maybe she knew the signs of the Greeks and could translate them into words.

I went out and searched the camp for her until I found her in the Arcadian sector.

'I need you,' I said.

'What for?' she asked.

'Come with me, I'll tell you as we're walking.'

When he had reached the entrance to our tent, I stopped. 'Do you understand written signs?'

'You want to know if I can read? Certainly. A woman of my standing must be able to read, write, sing and dance.'

'Come in then. Read what's written here.' I took the scroll from the drawer.

'Are you mad? If Xeno shows up he'll break both of our heads.'

'No, don't worry. He's still chopping wood and then he'll go and talk to Sophos about tomorrow. He does so almost every evening. Anyway, I'll stay here at the entrance to make sure, and I'll listen as you tell me what you see on the scroll. If I see him coming, we'll have time to put it back in the drawer. If he asks what you're doing here, I'll say I invited you to warm yourself at the brazier.'

Reluctantly Melissa opened the scroll and read what Xeno had written since we'd arrived at the banks of the cursed river.

Almost nothing!

Just a few phrases. The distances and the stages of our journey, even skipping some. Nothing about the exhausting marches, the fallen, the wounded, the many comrades lost: a long trail of deaths along a path that led nowhere! There was not a word about the big pyramid-shaped mountain, nor even about the decision to follow the river. Not a mention.

'Are you sure that's all?' I asked incredulously.

'There's nothing else, I promise you.'

'Don't deceive me, Melissa, please don't.'

'Why should I? I swear to you that you've heard everything that's written here.'

I put the scroll back in its place and closed the drawer.

'Come on,' I said. 'Let me walk you back to your tent.'

I took her arm and went with her to the Arcadian camp. My head was spinning.

'Why are you so upset?' she asked me.

'Don't you understand? There's not a single word about the decision to follow the river and the terrible consequences it has had.'

'He's just written the important things. He certainly can't have found much time to write under these conditions. He'll do so later when we return. Then he'll have all the time to remember and reflect on what has happened.'

'So you think that all this is normal?'

'I don't see anything strange about it.'

'Well, I do. I can tell you that in even worse circumstances I would see him write for hours, until late at night. He's not writing because he doesn't want to.'

'I don't know what you mean.'

'Listen, I have to ask you to help me with something else.'

'Come on,' she pouted. 'Isn't what I've just done enough?'

'No. I have a terrible suspicion and I can't get it out of my mind. I absolutely have to understand what's happening and there's only one way.'

'What's that?'

'Going to Sophos's tent when he's not there.'

'Forget it. You're my friend, but I have to look out for myself, and I have no intention whatsoever of being thrown in with the whores hired out by that slobbering old pimp.'

'You're risking a lot more than that. Not only you, and me. All of us. We're risking . . . death.'

'Some surprise. What else have we been doing until now?'

'I don't have time to explain it now, but you'll understand when the time comes. You won't get into any trouble. All you have to do is convince Cleanor to invite Sophos and Xeno to his tent, along with some other officer that he trusts. Make him believe that he's the person most highly regarded by the chief commander and that he has to get Sophos to admit his true intentions and establish at what point he will agree to turn back.

'At first he'll tell you to stay out of it, that those are not women's affairs and that it's none of your business anyway. But then he'll think it over and in the end he'll claim that it was his idea to start with and he'll do as you say.'

'And if he does?'

'While they're meeting, they'll want you to leave anyway. You'll say that you're staying with me until it's over.'

'And then?'

'We'll enter Sophos's tent and we'll look for something that can explain this whole mystery.'

'I'm sorry, Abira. I can't do it. I'm too afraid.'

'But I can't read.'

'I'm sorry,' she repeated. 'I can't help you.'

'Then do as I've asked, convince Cleanor. I'll worry about the rest. I can do it all myself.'

Melissa let out a long sigh. 'But don't you understand that what you're planning is insane?'

'You still don't understand. You've got to believe me. We have to discover what's going on or we'll all die. Please, Melissa . . .'

Melissa hesitated, then said, 'I'm not promising anything. I'll see what I can do.'

'Thank you,' I replied. 'I know how brave you are.'

We parted in front of Cleanor's tent. By the time I got back to my tent, it was pitch-black outside.

Xeno arrived late and seemed completely done in. The fires that had been lit filled the camp with light and heat. Many of the soldiers had gathered around them to warm themselves, or to take some embers for their own tents.

I knew it wasn't the best time to ask questions, but I plucked up my courage and spoke to Xeno while I was changing his bandages.

'What will happen tomorrow?'

'I don't know.'

'They'll blame you for having brought them into a completely unfamiliar land with no destination in sight.'

'I have enough to worry about without you jumping in.'

'I'm saying that because I care about you.'

'If you care about me, shut up.'

'No. You have to be prepared for what is going to happen tomorrow.'

'Nothing will happen. In the daylight we'll be able to trace the river bed, and we'll carry on following it.'

'You know you can trust me. Are you really certain, deep down, that the decision to follow the river was right? You have no second thoughts, no doubts? Don't you feel badly about all the dead we've sown along our path, the comrades you've lost for refusing to stray from a road that goes nowhere?'

Xeno spun around to face me and the reflection of the brazier lit up his eyes filled with tears. 'Part of me has died with them,' he replied. 'But if I'm alive it's only because fate has spared me. I've never shirked my duty. I've always faced the same risks, suffered the same wounds, the same cold, the hunger. I've shared my food when I've had enough. I might have died a hundred deaths in all the battles I've fought. If the gods have spared my life it means that I have a job to do: bring this army back home. Or if that's not possible, find a new home for them.'

'Found a new city, then. So it was true what Netus was saying.'

'I've thought about it often, yes, but that doesn't mean I'd be willing to sacrifice my comrades to my ambitions.'

'But do you really think that the gods care about us, or about our fate? Is that what your teacher in Athens taught you? Hasn't it ever occurred to you that the destiny of this army was either to win, or die? Why do you think Sophos has supported your proposal with such conviction? Only him, among all the officers? And why aren't you writing any more?'

'I'm tired.'

'No. In your heart, you know that this road isn't taking us anywhere and you don't want to leave any trace of your error. You have made a mistake, Xeno, even if you've done it in good faith, but it was Sophos's unconditional backing that sealed your error.'

Xeno didn't answer me and I imagined that he was mulling over all of the strange events that had punctuated our long march: the way that Sophos had appeared so suddenly and mysteriously out of nowhere, the ambush of our officers and Sophos's immediate rise to the high command with that disturbing Neon character at his side, and finally this decision to persist in going in a direction that would end up scattering us to the winds.

Again, I couldn't help but interrupt his thoughts. 'You know that the soldiers and even the officers and the generals talk to their women after they've made love? And that we women talk to each other? You told me how you were approached by Proxenus of Boeotia, and how your comrades were recruited.'

'In secret. It was all done in secret.'

'Right, you and all the others. Xeno, tell me – this is where the key to this whole mystery lies – tell me why you were all enlisted covertly. Why was all this secrecy necessary to begin with?'

'So we could take the enemy by surprise.'

'How was that supposed to work? There were one hundred thousand Asians at Sardis with Cyrus, and we marched with them all the way to the battlefield. How was such a huge force going to be kept secret? Don't you think the Great King had spies in the territories we crossed? Cyrus must have known that. There must have been another reason, and I'm sure you know what it is. You must know! If you can get at that reason, the mystery will be solved, and we'll be able to understand what still lies in store for us.'

In the long silence that followed, in which every sound was swallowed up by the snow which had started falling again, I was reminded of my ordeal with Lystra, and of the dream I'd had of the misty white horseman who appeared when I'd already given in to death's intoxicating caress. Perhaps the gods had a mission for me as well? Perhaps it was a god who had descended from the sky and had transported me on his wings to the outskirts of camp, so I could be found? Sometimes . . . yes, thinking about it, I was sure that that mysterious horseman rode a winged steed.

Xeno never answered me that night. Perhaps his fatigue weighed so heavy on his eyelids that he was prevented from pronouncing a single word, or perhaps he could not accept that a simple girl, a little barbarian from the East, could have understood something that had escaped him or that, more probably, he had never wanted to admit to himself.

I let him sleep, in the tepid warmth of the brazier, on the

ram's fleece that made me think of Xeno's legend. But still I had one piece missing from the puzzle and I needed someone who could help me put it all together. Not Melissa, I didn't think she would have, or could obtain, the information I was looking for. It would have to be one of the officers, or a soldier, someone who wouldn't be able to refuse.

Nicarchus the Arcadian! The man whose belly had been slashed open by the Persians, on that sorry day our generals were betrayed. I had helped nurse him back to health. Surely he would help me now.

THE NEXT DAY the heavens split up into patches of broad blue sky, making the river banks discernible. A group of scouts found the sheet of ice that covered it, buried under the snow. But the moment of panic had not completely subsided. Once again Sophos's uncompromising will prevailed, strengthening my suspicions about him, especially now that Xeno seemed to be nursing doubts himself. I wasn't told what the staff officers said during their meeting with the commander, but there were rumours of a stormy, bad-tempered encounter that concluded only when Sophos threatened to go on alone with whoever wanted to follow him.

It was evident that such a solution would be a disaster: if the army divided in two, the part cut adrift would risk immediate annihilation, and the other soon after. Sophos claimed that if we went on until the ice on the river melted, we'd have no further problems. The worst would soon be over. This claim of his worried me even more.

We continued to follow the river for two days. At the end of our second day's marching we crossed a very narrow saddle between two sheer rock walls and we camped on an area of flat ground on the other side.

Looking for one man among a thousand who are marching in a column over a distance of half a parasang is a pretty desperate endeavour, but I knew where and how the Arcadians set up camp at every stop, and after asking around a little, I managed to find him.

'How's your stomach?' I asked him before he'd realized who I was.

'Is that you, girl? My gut's not in bad shape. Hurts me now and then, and bothers me a little when it's been empty for days and all I've had to eat is snow. But, as they say, it could have been worse.'

'I have to talk to you.'

'I was hoping you wanted to do more than talk.'

'If Xeno heard you, he'd rip you back open from top to bottom. But he'd cut your balls off first.'

'I'm all ears, then,' he said, with his wide smile.

'Tell me about the Great War.'

'The Great War? Why?'

'No asking why. Just answer me.'

Nicarchus shot me a crooked look, as if trying to fathom why I could be asking such a strange question. Then he said, 'I wasn't in the Great War. I was too young.'

Right. How could I not have known that?

'. . . but our commander is always filling our heads with his exploits. But you know, girl, that war lasted thirty years. There isn't anyone in the world who could tell you everything that happened, except maybe for . . . right, why don't you ask your Xeno, the writer? He knows much more than I do.'

'Because he has important matters to look after, and if he has any time left over, he writes.'

'That makes sense.'

'I'm only interested in the end of the war. What happened before this adventure began?'

'Well, the Athenians lost and the Spartans won.'

'But some time before that, weren't they fighting on the same side? At the time of the Fiery Gates?'

'That was then. Now they're fighting over who gets to be friends with the Persians. Funny, no?'

'Whose side were the Persians on?'

'Sparta's.'

'I can't believe it!'

'That's how it was. They couldn't have won at sea against Athens if they hadn't had money from the Persians. The Persians were happy to give it to them, because they wanted to destroy the Athenian fleet that had become their nightmare.'

'So who was giving Sparta the money?'

'Prince Cyrus. Everyone knows that.'

'Our Prince Cyrus?'

'None other.'

'I understand.'

'You do? What do you understand?'

'What I needed to know. Don't tell anyone I asked you these questions. Please.'

'I won't. But I haven't given away any secrets. Everyone knows what I've told you.'

'Everyone except me. Thank you, boy. Farewell. Try to make it home in one piece.'

'I'll try,' he said, with a smile that was more tired this time.

From the way he shook his head I could tell that he couldn't make sense of my visit, but the gleam in his eyes told me that he'd been happy to see me.

My heart was pounding with emotion. When I'd left my village, I never could have imagined the events that I would be witnessing, never would have believed that I'd be solving mysteries so much bigger than I was, reasoning through events that had changed the destiny of entire nations. Now everything suddenly seemed clear: Cyrus had wanted the throne, and to win it he needed the best soldiers in the world, the red cloaks, as many as he could get. Along with the soldiers that the Spartans had trained in the art of war. But the problem was that the Spartans were allied with Cyrus's brother, the Great King Artaxerxes, and this was the heart of the dilemma: if Cyrus had succeeded in his aim and defeated his brother, he would have owed his throne to the Spartans, and they would stand to gain enormous advantages from such a situation. But if Cyrus didn't succeed, Sparta would have to make the Great King think that she knew nothing about his expedition, that Cyrus had recruited the warriors on his own, without ever consulting them. This was the crux of the matter, and the reason why it had to remain secret! The Spartans wanted to play both games at once, and make sure that they came out on top, no matter who won.

But then, once the operation was launched, they must have started worrying: what if the situation slipped out of their control? What if the unexpected happened? There had to be a way to ensure that they would not lose the initiative. There had to be someone, someone who knew what he had to do, who would directly obey their orders. That's why, shortly before I met Xeno, Sophos showed up out of nowhere. That's why no one knew anything about him, or Neon.

The truth was that there was no second plan: the Ten Thousand had to win or die. Or better yet, disappear. No one could be allowed to survive and to reveal what was behind Cyrus's extraordinary, foolhardy expedition.

Things had not gone according to plan, however. Cyrus's army had lost but the Ten Thousand had won. They had survived, and this made them very dangerous: even though they were mercenaries, they were living proof that Sparta had betrayed her alliance with the most powerful empire on earth. They had betrayed the Great King by helping his brother to try to kill him.

I arrived at an inescapable conclusion, but I simply could not believe it. I sat on a stone to soak in a little of the sun's rays with my eyes closed and I let my mind dwell on this thought: Sophos had been sent to take any survivors somewhere they would not – could not – come back from, and Xeno's identification of the river had perfectly suited his purpose. All Sophos had to do was back him up. This obviously suggested something else: that Xeno was certainly mistaken, and that we were heading straight for the end, our end. Towards a destination from which we would never return.

There had to be a way to prove it. Any time I had tried to convince Xeno to see things my way, he had refused even to consider the possibility. Faced with such an enormity, there was no telling what he might do. Poor Xeno continued to think that the greatest danger came from the Great King. I needed proof to convince him that there was a danger that was even greater, born of double-dealing. The only place I could find evidence was Sophos's tent.

All that evening I pondered, waiting for Xeno and the others to return from a hunting party, an activity he always excelled in. As expected, they made a good haul: eight deer, four porcupines, two boars, half a dozen hares trapped in snares and some magnificently coloured birds. The males had a long pointed tail made of bronze-coloured feathers and incredible plumage on their necks and wings. The females' coats were less showy, but their meat was even tastier. In honour of the river that we were following and that he thought was the Phasis, he called those birds 'phasants', and he saved some of the feathers for me, so I could use them as ornaments.

The abundant meal put the men in a good humour and dissipated the sour mood of disheartenment and suspicion that was rife in the camp. The fact that their chief commander was so sure of himself started to seem like a good omen.

I had a lot to worry about. What would happen if I found nothing in Sophos's tent or, worse yet, was caught red-handed searching through his baggage? Would Xeno defend me or would he abandon me to my destiny? Would Melissa help me as I'd asked?

My thoughts turned to Lystra and her never-born child and I hoped that they could hear me and help me. I imagined the baby, with skin as wrinkled as an old man's, sitting in the endless Elysian fields and playing with the sterile asphodel blossoms. I'd become accustomed to the afterworld of the Greeks, even more wretched than our own.

I needed to dispel the anxious thoughts crowding my mind so that they wouldn't torment my dreams, and so I thought I'd take a walk at the edge of camp. I was holding my cloak tightly to defend myself against the chill evening air when a disquieting image stopped me short.

In the light reflected from the fires, at the end of a line of deep, black footprints, stood a man wrapped in a grey cloak whose back was turned to me. His head was hunched between his shoulders so I could barely make it out.

I approached until I was just a few steps away and with a courage that surprised me, I asked, 'Who are you?'

The man turned and my heart nearly jumped out of my chest: one of his hands held a quartered animal, a hare or a rabbit, while the other held its raw liver, which he was gorging himself on. Its blood was smeared all over his face.

I instantly realized who it was: one of the augurs whom I'd seen celebrating propitiatory rites at times of great difficulty.

'What are you doing?' I stammered.

The man replied with a dark, gurgling voice. 'I've sacrificed this animal to the divinities of the night ... I've inspected his liver to interpret their will ...'

'And?'

'I must devour it to learn the truth.'

'What truth?'

The seer's face twisted into a grimace.

'Death ... which death we are destined for.'

25

ALTHOUGH MY SEARCHING had brought me close to a conclusion, the next step, the one that would give me proof, seemed to be drawing further and further away.

The following morning dawned even clearer than the day before, so the sun in the cloudless blue sky revealed the snaking presence of the river bed under its snowy blanket. It wound from one side to another of a vast snowy basin of flat land completely surrounded by mountain crests. Like a 'crater', Xeno said, seeing that its shape was similar to a type of Greek vase of that name. At the end of the plain, directly opposite the point from which we had entered, was another pass, probably crossed by the river which could then flow on towards an unknown sea.

Sophos remained convinced of his plan and the clear view of the river seemed to give Xeno new faith in his hypothesis. The rest of the army acquiesced patiently, certain if nothing else that the heavy stride of the warriors was unstoppable and would take them to their final destination. All that was needed was perseverance, courage, energy, discipline. The winter would end, that much was sure, and the land would soon be free of its icy grip.

But how many comrades had fallen in the meantime, during the long march, thinning out our ranks day by day? Many girls – like Lystra, who was always on my mind – had lost their lives as well, laid low by one crisis after another. But what was really bothering me that morning was that beyond the edge of the crater you could see more mountains in the distance, with peaks even taller than those surrounding us. The sight threw Xeno into a state of consternation, and made me realize that the time to act had come. If I succeeded in finding something in Sophos's tent, I could convince Xeno to call a meeting and call on the assembly to turn back. The soldiers still thought highly of him and not even Sophos could oppose a decision taken by the whole army.

That evening I found Melissa off on her own, leaning against one of the wagons we'd requisitioned from the last village we'd occupied, her head between her hands. She was crying.

'What's happened?' I asked.

She raised her face and I could see that her perfect features were marred with signs of fatigue and lack of sleep.

'I can't bear it any longer. Cleanor doesn't love me like he used to. There's never a moment when we can be alone together. All of this tension is making him irritable, even towards me. All he wants me for is to keep his tent in order, to cook and look after his things. He's too tired for anything else. I'm afraid that soon he won't even want me around any more, and he'll trade me for a mule or a sack of barley. May the gods help me then!'

The time was right. The gods were helping me, I was sure of it, and by helping me they would save her as well.

'Melissa, do you believe me now when I tell you we're all going to die, and that there will be no hope for anyone, if we persist in going east? Can't you see those mountains on the horizon? They don't even look that tall from here, but that's only because they're far away. You'll learn otherwise when we get close. How much longer can we survive under such harsh conditions? How will the warriors find the strength to keep fighting for ever? They've already accomplished the impossible; they've faced and overcome more than what a human being can endure. Sophos is leading us to our doom. I'm sure of it. Xeno is starting to listen to me, although he still has doubts. Help me, Melissa! I'll try to convince Xeno to set up a restricted meeting with Cleanor and Sophos to discuss the itinerary and to examine the possibility that the mountain chain rising on the horizon will make it impossible for us to push on any further in that direction. You'll just tell Cleanor that Xeno wants to see him together with the high commander for a very important meeting. It won't be difficult. And in the meantime, we'll decide on a plan of action. I've learned that Neon, the commander's field adjutant, is very susceptible to the charms of a beautiful woman. He'll be easily distracted by one of our girls.'

Melissa got up and hugged me. 'I'm not like you, Abira. I'm afraid. I'm sure I'll give myself away.'

'No, you won't. I'm sure that you'll be perfect, and everything will go as planned. You've been magnificent until now: you've prevailed over obstacles that you could never have dreamed of. You're a survivor. Now let's get to work!'

'What if we don't find anything?'

'Then I'll convince Xeno to call an assembly. But I need you now, Melissa. You can read, and I don't have time to learn.'

'All right,' she said, seemingly resigned. 'When?'

'The sooner the better. We're running out of time.'

'I'll talk to Cleanor. I'll let you know what he says.'

The area we were camped in was so rich in game that it was decided that we would stay for several days so that the men could regain their strength and we could put by some provisions if possible. Melissa arranged the meeting for two days later, and I got hold of some meat for her so that the dinner would be prolonged, even in our absence. At the first opportunity I told Xeno that Cleanor had agreed to hold a meeting in his tent and had invited Commander Sophos.

My crazy plan was ready to be put into effect. I was well aware how fragile and unprotected I was, and what consequences I was exposing myself to. The thought made me tremble. Anxiety filled my throat and my chest and my heart beat so loudly at night that I couldn't sleep. As the hours passed and the moment for action neared, my fear grew into something like panic. It bubbled up inside of me until I was afraid I wouldn't be able to control it, and I felt like giving up and letting events take their course.

The first day passed, and so did the second.

Dusk was approaching, and so was the moment in which Melissa would come and we'd set off together to search Sophos's tent.

Xeno put on his cloak and, without taking up any arms, said that he was going to Cleanor's tent and that the idea of a restricted meeting had been a good one. Only if they came to any important decisions would the entire war council be summoned.

Things started well. After he'd left I allowed a little time to pass and then went out myself. It was snowing but the sky wasn't completely covered and every now and then you could see the moon appear in a wide rent between the clouds. I headed for Sophos's tent and stopped at a certain distance, hiding behind a line of mules tied to stakes driven into the ground.

The commander came out a few moments later, without armour but wearing his sword at his side. He headed towards Cleanor's quarters. He caught up with Xeno before they reached their destination and the two men greeted each other and hugged. The faint light of the moon made it possible to distinguish their figures.

I kept the mules company for a while until I saw the girl who was supposed to be distracting Neon arrive on my left. She was one of the young prostitutes accompanying the army and I could see that Melissa had taught her well. Her gown was elegant, light but clingy in a way that accentuated her curves. She was probably freezing, but she was carrying out her task with great aplomb.

She had spotted him, and slowed her step but didn't stop. Neon said something to her that I couldn't understand and she answered, continuing her slow walk. Neon turned around and tried to take her hand. The girl let him embrace her, but then wriggled away and kept walking.

He stopped.

So soon, and my plan was already failing! Neon was too chilly, too controlled. I felt faint. What would we do now?

Neon seemed to change his mind. The girl darted glances back at him until he took a quick look around to make sure no one was watching and decided at last to follow her. I could soon hear their voices, and the girl's laughter, coming from one of the tents.

Now it was up to me, but I had to wait for Melissa. What could I do alone? And for how long would my pretty friend be able to keep the young officer occupied? Certainly not for very long. As soon as his thirst was quenched, he'd be out of there.

Melissa was nowhere to be seen. I glanced towards Cleanor's tent, hoping to see her emerge at any moment, but nothing happened. Perhaps she couldn't get away or perhaps Cleanor had asked her to serve his guests, despite the reserved nature of their meeting. I'd have to attempt it on my own.

I approached my objective. I could make out the entrance to the command quarters thanks to the faint light of a lamp inside. I checked again for Melissa and, not seeing her, went in. Strangely enough, the nerves that had been gnawing at me disappeared. Having taken action, I finally felt calm.

There wasn't much there to search. The ground was covered by a wicker mat. At the centre of the room was a little table and a couple of chairs, and to one side a hanger which bore the commander's armour. Directly opposite was a closed chest which was latched, but not locked. I drew the bolt.

The chest contained a blanket, an extra cloak, which seemed brand new, and two grey woollen tunics. At the bottom of the chest were the most precious items: a silver cup and . . .

'What are you doing here?' a voice rang out behind me. Joined straight away by other voices. I was shaken by a violent jolt, a feeling I'd never experienced in my whole life: the sensation of having committed an illicit act and having to pay the consequences. I turned, trying desperately to think of something to say, but I could pull nothing out of the tumult inside my head. There was no way out: I would have to face my punishment.

It was Neon who was facing me, but I could see Sophos approaching as well, along with Cleanor and Xeno, and behind them an indistinct figure that might have been Melissa: she who had certainly betrayed me.

Two soldiers soon joined them, holding the young girl who had tried to seduce Neon by her arms. She had been beaten hard enough to draw blood. She was half-naked and livid with the cold. For several moments all I saw was the snow, an infinity of white flakes swinging tranquilly through the still air. My mind tried to escape the rest, to remove myself from what was happening.

Another two warriors arrived with lit torches and the vague figure moving in the background took on the guise of Melissa. I felt my heart stop.

But the heart of a woman has many resources and, in a flash, before surrendering to my destiny, I saw an image in my mind's eye. I had caught a glimpse of something, just before the rough voice of the commander's adjutant had rung out behind me. There had been a skin on the bottom of the chest. A skin with a drawing, and a word.

At the top of the drawing was a sequence of triangles of differing heights that perhaps were meant to represent mountains, and between them a wavy line that possibly stood for a river. The four signs traced there were so clear that they will remain for ever fixed in my mind as if they had been carved into a piece of wood.

ΑΡΑΞ

Along the wavy line was another, interrupted by a series of small vertical strokes, each one distinguished by one or two signs.

'What were you looking for in my chest, girl?' asked Commander Sophos with an icy voice.

Just then Melissa ran in, past the small group of men, before anyone could stop her. She was shouting, 'I didn't want to! They forced me!'

An ugly welt crossed her flawless cheek. She fell to her knees, weeping hysterically, and one of the soldiers dragged her away. Cleanor didn't lift a finger.

'What were you looking for?' Sophos repeated harshly.

I didn't know what to answer, so I said nothing.

'You must know something,' he said, turning to Xeno, who looked as if he'd been turned to stone.

Xeno didn't answer Sophos, but turned to me. 'Why did you do this? What did you want to take? Why didn't you tell me anything?'

Neon slapped me hard and made my lip bleed. 'They asked you a question!' he snarled.

Xeno grabbed his wrist before he could hit me again and squeezed it forcefully, then started to twist it. A glance from Sophos and his adjutant stepped away.

I covered my head with my shawl because I didn't want to see or hear anything and I burst into tears. Xeno made me stand up straight, uncovered my face and repeated in a firm voice, 'Tell me what you were looking for. You have no choice.'

I stared at him through my tears and then looked around: Sophos was still and scowling, Neon's face seemed a stone mask, the little prostitute was livid and about to faint, Melissa was in the back sobbing, the two armed warriors had their torches in hand, there was the commander's armour, red in the torchlight, red as blood. And the snow . . . the snow was covering everything. I forced myself to speak.

'I was looking for an answer.'

'An answer?' asked Sophos, and I could read a sudden disquiet in his eyes.

'Yes, but I'm only a poor girl and I can't bear the force of your presence or the look in your eye. I'll speak with Xeno and if he likes, he'll speak to you.'

Sophos fell silent in surprise.

'Leave Melissa and that other poor wretch out of this. They know nothing. I asked them to help me and they agreed. You'll know everything from Xeno, once I've spoken to him.'

'I can have you tortured,' said Sophos icily.

'I don't doubt that, but I couldn't tell you anything you don't already know.'

I looked him straight in the eyes as I said those words and somehow I got across what I wanted him to understand.

Xeno was badly shaken but he was beginning to figure things out. Words that I'd said, suspicions I'd had, were re-emerging into his consciousness.

Neon had lost his imperturbability and the look on his face was grim. Melissa seemed uncertain and bewildered. Cleanor, standing further back, had not had any particular reaction, except for curiosity about what was happening.

Sophos spoke. 'Take these women away,' he ordered Cleanor. 'And you two can go as well,' he added, addressing the warriors. 'I don't need you any more.' Cleanor led Melissa out of the tent.

Sophos turned to Xeno. 'How could you? How could you violate my tent? And you didn't even have the courage to do it yourself. You sent a woman, and she had to get help from other women . . .' He added sarcastically, 'Since when does a secret among three women stay secret for longer than an hour?'

'I had nothing to do with this,' Xeno retorted. 'If I tell you I had nothing to do with this, that means it's true. You know well that I never lie and that I'm a man of my word. Look into my eyes: do you see shame, or fear? Let me talk to her. She'll tell me everything.'

Something had broken. Something had wormed its way into Sophos's iron spirit. He drew a long breath and his gaze seemed lost in the swirling snowflakes falling from the sky.

VALERIO MASSIMO MANFREDI

We walked away and I could not believe that Sophos didn't
stop us.

'You want to know what I was looking for? Here's what!' I
said to Xeno as soon as we arrived in our tent. I didn't want to
give him the time to unleash the rage that must have been
building inside him.

Before he could say a word or make a gesture, I took a stalk
from the wicker mat and used it to draw the image I'd seen,
there on the hard dirt: the sequence of triangular shapes, the
wavy line, the second line broken up by short vertical strokes
and then, over the wavy line, the four signs from the Greek
language: ΑΡΑΞ. It came out very sharp and clear, and I could
see the astonishment on Xeno's face.

'What is that?' he asked.

'Signs that I saw on a skin inside Sophos's chest. I think they
represent the place we find ourselves in: these are mountains,
this is the line of our march. Those vertical marks are the stages
of our journey. And this is the river. Sophos knows exactly
where we're going.'

Xeno's look of amazement and incredulity grew as he
observed my drawing.

'Are you certain that it was exactly the same as what you've
drawn here?'

'Identical.' I knew I would have to prove it to him, so I'd
memorized all the tiniest details. 'There's just one thing I don't
understand: what these mean,' I said, pointing at the four signs
written in the language of the Greeks.

Xeno bowed his head. His voice cracked with emotion. 'They
mean that you were right. That Sophos is deceiving us, or much,
much worse . . .'

'Why?'

'Because these signs say that he knew full well that the river
was not the Phasis as I believed, but the Araxes.'

'What difference does that make?'

'The Phasis leads to the Pontus Euxinus, which is a sea

surrounded by Greek cities. No one knows for sure where the Araxes leads, but I'm afraid to the Caspian, an unknown sea at the edge of the world.'

'What will you do now?'

'I'll confront him.'

'When?'

'Now.'

'Don't do it now, please listen. Wait until tomorrow. Take time to reflect.'

My words were to no avail. Xeno headed towards Sophos's isolated tent.

I told myself I would wait it out, but my anxiety was choking me. I strained my ears, but couldn't hear a sound. I couldn't just sit and wait until Xeno came back; I was too worried about what would happen to him. I hadn't been this upset when I'd seen him fighting hand-to-hand against fierce warriors or throwing himself into the thick of the battle. In the end I decided to follow him and I sneaked up on Sophos's tent. I hid behind the bellies of the mules tied up in back, behind a bush. I heard Sophos's voice first.

'If anyone else had dared to slander me with such a claim, I wouldn't have given him the time to regret it. But you . . . you are my friend, you've risked your life time and time again for these men, although you aren't even part of the army. I'm grateful to you for this, but do not provoke me further or . . .'

'Or what? Chirisophus, can you honestly tell me you have nothing to hide? Listen to me, and listen well. Abira, the girl you caught here, did everything completely on her own. That may seem impossible to you, but it doesn't surprise me. She's been trying to force me to face the truth for some time now, but I wouldn't listen. She evidently felt she needed proof of what she suspected, and she found it. If it was here that she saw the word she traced out for me, I must admit that she was right.'

'What are you blathering on about?'

Xeno repeated my whole line of reasoning, all the strange

and inexplicable coincidences, and even though the situation I found myself in was hardly ideal, it made me feel proud.

Xeno added, 'But what really struck me was the symbols she scratched out on the ground in my tent: they clearly represented a river, and Abira wrote me the name of that river – A-R-A-X. That was the proof she was looking for: you are fully aware that the river we are following is not the Phasis, as I had believed, but the Araxes, which doesn't flow into the Euxine Sea but very, very far away. To the ends of the earth.'

'You've gone completely mad,' Sophos broke in him. 'You're raving!'

'I am? Then why don't you show me the map that Abira saw and drew for me so exactly? Her drawing proves to me that you've always known full well that the river we are following is not the Phasis. But you have continued to back up my mistaken assumption, with all the weight of your authority. And you know why, Commander! Because your job was to make this army disappear; dissolve into nothingness without leaving a trace. That's why! Conveniently, you didn't even need to stick your neck out; you laid all the responsibility on me: "Xenophon's right, he knows where we are, all we have to do is follow this river and we'll reach the sea!" Weren't those your words, Commander?

'But that little girl that you found searching through your things had guessed your game! Precisely because she isn't one of us, she's not a soldier sworn to obey without asking the reason for an order.

'This army had to win, or be wiped out. Otherwise we are the living proof of Spartan treason, proof that Sparta was an accomplice in the plan to assassinate her greatest ally, the man who had allowed her to win the war against Athens: the Great King!'

I would have given anything to see the expression on Sophos's face and I wanted to hug Xeno, to thank him for what he was doing. I was trembling with the cold despite my cloak, but I wouldn't have left for all the gold in the world.

His voice rose up again. 'That's why the recruiting for this operation was done in secret, in out-of-the way places, signing on small groups of men. Not to keep the expedition a secret from the Great King – that would have been impossible, seeing that Cyrus had his own army of one hundred thousand men. But to keep secret the involvement of the government of Sparta in an endeavour aimed at defeating and assassinating the Great King himself. What exactly did Cyrus promise Sparta? And the Queen Mother? What did she vow?'

Silence. A silence more eloquent than a thousand words. Then Sophos's voice, colder than the wind whipping at my face. His words pierced my heart. 'You've put me in a very difficult situation, Xenophon, and I imagine that you're well aware of this. Let's admit for a moment that you're right: what do you expect me to do at this point?'

Xeno spoke calmly, as if his words did not concern him personally. 'I imagine that you mean to kill me, and to kill the girl. The latter would be pointless: who would ever listen to her? She'd never run another risk like the one she took. She's already terrified. She doesn't represent a danger for you.'

'You're wrong. She does. As does Melissa, who she confided in, and I can't exclude Cleanor, either. He's quite dependent on her for his physical and mental well-being . . .'

I can imagine his mocking look. Sophos never shed his sarcasm, even in the most dramatic situations.

Another long silence followed. Although I could see very little, it seemed to me that Sophos had taken a seat. Perhaps he needed a more comfortable position to say what was coming. But Xeno spoke first. 'I'm unarmed. Do it now. I won't fight you . . .' I felt a sword of ice plunging into my heart. '. . . but spare the girl. Leave her in the first village you come upon. She'll never find a way out on her own, and even if she did

331

she'd end up in her dusty little village and fall into oblivion. I'm asking you, Commander, in the name of our friendship, in the name of everything we've suffered and been through together. If you allow me to speak with her, she'll obey me. I'll order her never to speak a word of this to anyone.'

Xeno loved me. That was enough for me to face whatever awaited me without regrets.

I saw Sophos's shadow leaning forward and I thought I heard a sigh, before he spoke. 'Have you asked yourself what destiny I've carved out for myself, if I manage to execute the task you attribute to me?'

'You'll die with them,' replied Xeno. 'I do not doubt that. I have never thought you would survive your soldiers.'

'This comforts me, in a certain way.'

Xeno's voice was trembling now, with emotion, with disdain. 'But this does not absolve you of disgrace. How can you lead them to their deaths? How can you bear it?'

'A soldier knows that death is part of the life he has chosen.'

'But not like this, Commander. Not this death. Not being led like sheep to the edge of a cliff. A soldier has the right to die on the battlefield, and you who are Spartan know this better than anyone else.'

'And I who am Spartan know that I must obey the orders of my city, at any cost. I know that our lives can be spent so that the nation can survive and prosper. What do you think Leonidas did at the Fiery Gates? He obeyed!'

'But these soldiers are not all Spartans, to my knowledge. You cannot decide for them. They have the right to choose their destiny.'

'Ah . . . democracy!'

'Don't you see them? Come out of this den, Commander, and take a look at them!'

Xeno had walked outside. I could hear his voice distinctly now. Sophos came out as well. A sea of campfires stretched out before them, pockets staining the white blanket of snow with red.

'Look at them! They've always obeyed you, they have fought like lions in a hundred battles. They've lost their comrades, they've seen them sinking under the snow, tumbling into rocky chasms, falling into the cold sleep of death while they were out on guard duty, protecting the sleep of the others. They've been wounded, maimed, but they have never stopped. They have never given up. Like mules, they've climbed the mountains bearing the weight of their arms, their shields, their baggage, their wounded or sick comrades, with never a protest or complaint. When they could they buried them, dry-eyed, shouting out their names, raising them to the sky on the points of their spears. And do you know why? Because they have faith in you. Because they trust you to take them to safety. They knew – and they still believe – that at the end of this endless march they would find salvation!

'Do what you want with me. Blame me for everything. It's true, after all, that I'm to blame. I'll face the punishment that I deserve, but Commander, let them go back. Take them back home.'

A long, tense silence ensued. In that suspended atmosphere, I heard the distant rumbling of thunder – how distant? – and saw sudden flashes of light on the horizon. Gods in heaven! Somewhere, who knows where, a storm was raging and the power of the lightning had reached all the way here to me, penetrating the mute dance of the snowflakes. Somewhere, spring was coming. But would we ever see it?

I curled up and cried, under the bellies of the mules, wept with all my heart. I felt overwhelmed by such violent emotions that I was sure I would never be able to gain control of myself again, until I heard sudden shouting. 'Look! Up there! Look!'

More shouts followed. 'What is it?'

Then Xeno's desperate voice. 'Oh gods, gods of all the

heavens! What's happening? Did you do this? Answer me, by all the demons in Hades, are you responsible for this?'

The shouts had died down, giving way to widespread, despondent muttering, and then to utter silence. I came out of my hiding place and what I saw left me speechless and took my breath away. On the mountain rim that completely surrounded the valley we found ourselves in, a multitude had gathered. Each man held a burning torch. An immense snake of fire coiled around the edge of that immense crater, casting a bloody glow onto the snowy slopes below.

Warriors.

Tens and tens of thousands of warriors. Still more behind them, like a cascade of fire, descending to block the passes at the entrance and exit of the valley.

This time it was truly all over. This time there was no way out.

Xeno grabbed Sophos by his shoulder and shouted again, 'Did you do this?'

'If I said no, would you believe me?' Sophos replied.

'No.'

'Then think whatever you want to think. It makes no difference.'

'What do we do now?' Xeno demanded, as all the other officers showed up at a run: Cleanor, Timas, Agasias, Neon.

'We'll die,' replied the commander darkly. 'As warriors.'

'Die?' replied Xeno with a strange expression in his eyes. '. . . I have a different idea.'

26

IT SNOWED ALL NIGHT. The torches went out up above, and so did the campfires down below. The world was swallowed up in darkness and silence. At dawn, the chiefs of the army gathered at the rim of the great crater had the war horns sounded and began to descend into the valley. Soon the man who seemed to command them all, a blond giant, ordered them to stop, to wait until the light grew stronger. He must not have believed what he saw before him.

The great basin was empty. The army of invaders had vanished. All that was left on one side was a group of wagons, covered by the tent canvases, joined in a circle.

Where had they disappeared to? What magic was this? The way in and the way out of the crater were firmly in the hands of his own forces. A whole army couldn't have just melted away.

Gripped by superstitious terror, the chief decided not to order the entire army forward, but to send a column of his best fighters in reconnaissance. He lined up more than five thousand men in full battle gear, wearing conical helmets and carrying big oxhide shields, in a column formation in ranks of one hundred men. They advanced slowly, gripping their long double-edged swords. They had already covered the slope and were entering the level area in the middle. They were only about two hundred paces from the wagons. Silence reigned over the entire valley because their steps made no sound in the snow. When they were exactly at the centre of the basin, a trumpet blared and, as if by some miracle, an army of ghosts rose up to the right and to the left of the column. They emerged from the snow, shaking its white mantle off their backs. They swiftly drew up side by side and formed ranks, shouldering the shields that had covered them through the night and brandishing their spears. In no more than a few moments the two formations, looming on both sides of the enemy column, were ready for battle; at the second trumpet blare they lowered their spears and charged. Trapped between them, the natives didn't know which way to turn; they ended up slaughtered between two forests of steel points, crushed between two walls of shields which closed in with irresistible power.

The others, still at the top of the mountain crest, were so startled and horrified by this vision that they didn't even attempt to regroup, or to go to the aid of their comrades. They watched dumbstruck as those superhuman beings emerged from the bowels of the earth. They could not begin to imagine what had happened that night.

Xeno had recalled how some time earlier the soldiers who'd been punished for setting fire to some huts in one of the villages they'd occupied had survived outside the circle of sentries by sleeping under their shields, covered by their cloaks and protected by the snow falling from the sky.

A roar of triumph burst from the bottom of the crater. The Ten Thousand uttered a victory cry so loud that it rang through the entire valley. At the sound of their cry, the girls who had been hiding in the wagons up until then, myself among them, responded with passionate cheers.

Xeno ran up to Sophos. 'See? We can do this. We've cut them to pieces. We can break through the circle and get away. We've already dealt them a harsh blow.'

Even in the midst of all that enthusiasm, Sophos was unmoved. He was eyeing the rim of the crater. 'Look,' he pointed out, 'more are coming, the gap has already been filled. They're laying siege to our camp. Even if they don't move from where they are, we'll die of hunger and exposure.'

'I don't believe this!' exclaimed Xeno. 'Can you seriously be thinking of leaving these men – who have given you everything – with no hope? All they want from you is a reason to fight, even if it's to the last breath. A man can't live without hope, but you can't be thinking of letting them die that way!'

'I'll be with them,' replied Sophos gloomily. 'I'll be the first to descend to Hades.'

Xeno spun his gaze around the generals who'd gathered near him: Timas, Cleanor, Xanthi, Agasias, along with the captains like Neon, Lycius, Aristeas, Nicarchus and Eurylochus. They were standing there, covered in blood and ice, staring in shock at their commander who was incapable of saying another word.

They were shaken from their stunned silence by the voice of Aristonymus, one of the boldest and most fearless warriors. 'There's no use talking,' he said. 'They're coming this way.'

Everyone raised their eyes to the top of the crater: there were warriors from many tribes and nations, perhaps some of those we'd defeated, perhaps others that the Great King had sent in pursuit of us. Maybe they were those whose villages we'd sacked. Who knows, perhaps we'd never met up with them before and they simply wanted to stop us from entering their land.

Or maybe Commander Sophos had called them there somehow, from somewhere, so that we could finally be wiped out.

But there they were, joined in a ring of iron that was shrinking with their every step and tightening around us.

Without waiting for anything else, Cleanor and Timas shouted out, 'Men! In a circle! Closed formation, line up!' Each went to join his own unit. Agasias and Xanthi did the same, and so did Sophos, each standing firm at the head of his own battalion, outside the curved line of the army, which had closed into itself for the last battle.

Sophos beheld that close formation, the warriors' shields high and overlapping, the spears jutting out between them, and his features twisted into a strange expression. His eyes seemed to be looking into a different reality, in another time and another place.

'Careful!' shouted Cleanor. 'Archers!'

'Fast,' urged Sophos, 'shields up, retreat behind the wagons.'

The soldiers held their shields high as swarms of arrows were loosed upon them without pause. Many of the men were struck and fell, because the arrows were coming from every direction and at every angle. The others pulled back towards the circle of wagons. They tipped them over and used them as protection against the lethal barrage of missiles. Those who were unable to reach cover behind the wagons protected themselves with their shields. The attack stopped only when the enemy had run out of arrows. Moments of spasmodic tension followed. In the silence of the battlefield the cries of the wounded rang out acutely. Some time passed without anything happening, then, all at once:

'Look!' shouted Agasias.

A group of warriors on horseback, perhaps ten in all, had detached from the rest of the army and were slowly riding towards them, including their chieftain, the blond giant. The rest of the immense army had stopped at a distance of about one hundred paces from our formation. Were they coming to check how many of us had survived their rain of arrows, or did they want to negotiate?

Their horses sank up to their fetlocks in the snow, and the freezing wind that was blowing in from the north ruffled their manes. They stopped within hailing distance.

The blond giant hurled his spear at the ground and it stuck deep in the ice. He shouted a few harsh, menacing words.

'What does he want?' asked Cleanor.

'What did he say?' repeated Agasias.

I stepped forward, to the stupor of all those present. 'I understand his language.'

'Well?' demanded Xeno.

'He said: "Surrender your weapons!"' I repeated those words

again, shouting at the top of my lungs so everyone could hear: 'Surrender your weapons!'

The unthinkable happened. Sophos gave an abrupt jerk, as if he'd been hit by lightning. Distant images danced in his suddenly infuriated gaze. He looked back at his men crouched behind the wagons with their spears posed to strike, then turned around and stared his gigantic adversary straight in the eye. He raised his spear and his shield and thundered out in his sharp Laconian dialect, 'Molòn labé!'

I knew what that meant: 'Come and get them!'

His words spread like wildfire. The five commanders strode out with their battalions from behind the circle of wagons and repeated, 'Molòn labé!'

'Molòn labé!'

'Molòn labé!'

And then they began to bang their swords against their shields.

All the warriors stood straight as their spear shafts and started to beat their swords against their shields, yelling out those words, each blow, each shout swelling them with energy, with frenzied rage.

The blond giant and his guard were struck by the shriek of bronze as if by the blast of a tempest.

Sophos shouted, 'Wedge formation. Five spokes, each proceeding straight forward, one battalion per spoke. We'll breach the enemy line at five points, then advance to the crest at the double. We'll join up at the top. Ready for action! Xeno, with me! Cleanor, Timas, Xanthi, Agasias, ready to move. Trumpets, pipes. Forward!'

I knew then and there that for us women it was all over; we'd surely be left behind. Instead Xeno's voice rang out as loudly as Sophos's had. 'Women inside the wedges. Don't miss a step. Keep up or you're dead!'

The trumpets sounded and the five battalions charged into the attack. Each general was at the head of his unit, each unit splitting from the others like the spokes of a wheel diverging from their hub. The generals were joined by the most powerful warriors in the army: Eurylochus of Lusia, Aristonymus with his long, slender legs, Aristeas with his flaming red hair, Lycius of Syracuse, Nicarchus of Arcadia. They were calling all the time for more trumpeters and flute-players. This meant one thing: heads down for an all-out attack, no stopping until the enemy front was fractured beyond repair. The pipes began to sound the marching cadence in unison, the drums rolled, making you feel as though your heart would burst, and the five wedges shot out like rays of light from a star. Their shields were as close as overlapping tiles, with only the massive ashwood spears protruding. Their worn red cloaks still stood out dramatically on the snowy expanse. The enemy continued to loose arrows which stuck into their shields, weighing them down, but not slowing their inexorable advance. When the clash with the enemy was imminent, the trumpets burst out, louder than I had ever heard them. The blast prevailed over the pipes and drums and exploded over the entire valley. At that point the five battalions led by their commanders struck the enemy front with such violence that one line after another of combatants fell and the formation was ruptured.

The enemy fought back with rabid fury, but even though their front was hundreds of men deep, it was breached at five points as the combatants were overwhelmed and pushed out of the way. But even as they were forced to give ground, they reacted with such savagery and frenzy that a great number of our men were wounded or killed. The Greek war cry sounded continuously, in waves of hundreds, thousands of voices, and that cry throbbed with a miraculous energy that no one had thought they possessed. As our forces showed no sign of relenting, the enemy began to break off in small, panicked, disorderly groups. Their resolve began to flag and they started to collide with each other, soon losing their cohesion and courage.

When the war cries, the trumpet blasts and the penetrating

sound of the flutes had died down, the enemy circle had been broken into five segments. The battalions of Sophos and the other generals were climbing to a dominant position at the rim of the crater. Our Thracian skirmishers in the rearguard were loosing missiles of every type in fast succession on the remaining enemy, backing uphill behind our men, closer and closer to the top of the crest.

The incredible endeavour had been successful. From the rim of the crater the Ten Thousand raised a cry of victory. No one would ever dare to attack them again, after what they'd accomplished.

Xeno, exhausted and panting, approached Sophos. 'Did you see your men? Did you see what they did? Don't they deserve to be saved, whatever it takes?'

Sophos remained mute, looking around dumbstruck and dazed, without believing what he was seeing, like a dreamer shocked into wakefulness. Then his voice pierced the silence. 'You're right, my friend. Whatever may happen, writer, we're going back home. I'm taking them home.'

No one turned, because they wouldn't have been able to bear the sight of their comrades remaining on the bottom of the crater or strewn over its slopes, dead or dying, nor the sight of the women who had been engulfed by the chaos of blood, iron and ice. On their backs, on the bloodstained snow.

When it was all over we started on our way again, dragging along until we came upon a group of villages that had been abandoned by their inhabitants where we could stop and rest.

When night had fallen Xeno came close and held me tight. Then he pulled away and looked me in the eye.

'Tell me the truth: did you really understand the language of that barbarian?'

'No. But I knew those were the only words that would stir up the courage of Sophos and all the others. You were the one who told me the story of Leonidas at the Fiery Gates, remember?'

Xeno couldn't take his incredulous eyes off me.

27

WE STARTED OUR JOURNEY back the next day. The officers in charge of devising a new route decided that it would be best to go north for ten days, and then head west again. They hoped that path would bring us somewhere close to the sea. Perhaps we'd find guides along the way, since we would be passing through areas where the natives did not know us and would, we hoped, be less hostile.

The order of march was the same as always. The lightly armed peltasts in front, followed by the more heavily armed infantry, then the pack animals with our baggage and the remaining women. Last came the mounted rearguard, led as always by Xeno.

Melissa had survived, or so Xeno told me. That made me very happy, but days went by before I found her. She was clearly avoiding me because she was afraid I was bearing a grudge against her. I let her know through one of the girls that I'd be waiting for her one evening at the centre of the camp.

I watched her come towards me, hanging her head. Her hair was covered with a scarf, her feet bundled up in pieces of sheepskin secured by leather straps. Whatever had happened to those precious, elegant sandals of hers? What had she done with her beauty creams, her eye shadow, the ointment she used on her eyelashes and the pomade for her hair? When she lifted her eyes to meet mine her cheeks and nose were ruddy with the cold, her hair was tousled, her lips cracked and her hands swollen. And yet her beauty shone through, in her luminous eyes, in the sensual curve of her lips and even in the tone and inflexion of her voice.

'You'll never forgive me . . .' she began.

'Don't be ridiculous. I never expected you to be a hero. You did what you could. In the end we got what we wanted. We're going back, Melissa, and sooner or later we'll reach the sea. Soon it will be spring. We'll feel its warm breeze on our face and arms and we'll breathe in the scent of flowers. All we need now is strength and courage. We've been through so much! The worst is behind us . . . I hope.'

Melissa threw her arms around me and cried and cried. Then she dried her eyes and left.

I wasn't at all sure that what I'd said was true. Were we over the worst? Our march was just beginning, and there was no telling what difficulties we'd find. In fact, we struggled on in waist-deep snow and the skins we wore on our feet were quickly sodden, sending a chill straight up our spines. We'd often have to stop to dry them, or when possible change into different footwear.

The baggage animals foundered so deeply that they often couldn't take another step. They would rest all their weight on their bellies and refuse to go forward. We'd have to remove their packs and clear the snow all around them to make room, then push them into action, replacing their loads after they'd started moving.

Sometimes the sun would peep through the clouds, some-times it would shine blindingly in the middle of a cobalt-blue sky and its reflection on the vast white expanse was so strong that we had to bandage our eyes with scraps of dark gauze so that we wouldn't lose our sight. Then, towards evening, it would start to snow again, thin needles of ice that pricked at our faces, driven by a cruel wind that wouldn't let up for hours. Many of the women fell ill, with high fevers and continual coughing. Many died, and many of the men suffered the same fate.

Never did we abandon a body to the wild animals. Xeno

would not permit it; he respected his comrades, and had deep religious feelings. Each body was buried, and funeral rites celebrated. The women got tears and wailing and a last kiss from their sisters. The men had a warrior's farewell, with a war cry, spears raised against the dark clouds, their names shouted ten times, hurled at the immaculate, indifferent peaks. The soldiers' voices echoed, only to be swallowed up by the immense solitude of that hostile, desolate land.

When we found villages we would take food for ourselves and forage for the animals and seek shelter from the cold to regain our strength. I remember the time we were carrying one of the young warriors who had been wounded by a bear while hunting. He was stretched out on a makeshift litter. His right shoulder had been maimed by the bear's claws and the wound had festered, causing a high fever. He was delirious and would certainly have died if we hadn't found refuge.

His name was Demetrius. A handsome boy, blond, with intensely blue eyes and dark eyelashes and brows. The daughter of the village chief nursed him herself, changing his bandages and applying ointments the locals had made. I think she was in love with him, and when it was time for us to leave again, she asked if he could stay behind. Sophos called a meeting of his generals to decide; many of them felt it was a betrayal to leave a Greek in the hands of barbarians. In the end they decided that the only way to save his life was to leave him there, and we went on without him.

I've often wondered what became of that boy. If he survived and if he grew to love the chieftain's daughter. She was pretty and had a nice figure, with firm, full breasts, deep black eyes and the look of a woman who enjoyed making love. I hoped that the story had had a happy ending, that the young warrior had lived to marry the girl who'd nursed him and that their children would grow up brave and strong in that land of ice and blinding light. But I knew well, after what I'd lived through, that a man's fate hangs by a thread and that, at any moment, the whims of fortune can raise him to the heights or dash him into the blackest misery, or even death.

As WE PROCEEDED NORTH, the mountains which had loomed up ahead of us while we were following the river that led nowhere began to shrink out of sight behind us, until we could barely make them out on the horizon. But in front soared another vast range, full of towering peaks and deep valleys, covered by black forests of trees as pointed as the mountain peaks.

Xeno said that was a good sign, and that we'd soon be turning west, where we'd find inhabited villages and guides capable of leading us to our destination.

I realized that unless some big changes were coming, we could expect more trouble, more hardships and perhaps a bitter end.

The truth was hard to swallow. What I had intuitively suspected, without understanding the reasons behind it, had proved to be accurate. Now I knew that what was left of the army would still have to fight against the Great King, but also against the power of Sparta, who wanted them dead or scattered to the four corners of the earth, so far from their homeland that they'd never be able to return.

Sparta had expected them to win or to disappear, never considering a third eventuality: that the army might win and lose at the same time. And now, against any imagining, they were returning.

Xeno said we'd soon encounter inhabited places, and by his calculations spring was not far off. He wasn't mistaken. I had the first sign one clear and freezing morning when I got up to collect snow so I could melt it over the fire and have water to drink and wash with. I found myself standing in front of a forest of enormous trees with huge bare branches. As soon as the sun rose, the air was filled with screeching cries. I raced back to camp as fast as my legs would carry me, but I soon discovered there was nothing to be frightened of. No one was chasing me, no one was threatening me. It wasn't human voices I was hearing.

It was birds.

I'd never seen such animals before, but I'd heard them described by travellers who'd passed through our villages. I turned back, one step after another, and I took a good look. There were dozens of them on the branches and even on the ground, and they suddenly froze at my approach. They looked like painted images, barely real: the males' necks were covered with feathers so blue they glittered like gold, and the same impossible colour adorned their tails, which looked like royal cloaks, dotted with big bronze and gold eyes. They were wondrous creatures. Their elegance and incredible beauty contrasted with their voices, capable only of that raucous, monotonous shrieking.

At first I thought they were our comrades who'd fallen in battle or been carried away by the current, screaming out their despair at a life cut short too soon, filling the air with their laments. But then one of them lifted its tail and opened it in a brilliant arch of bronze, blue, gold and silver, and I was so moved that tears came to my eyes. No, it wasn't a howl of death I was hearing, but a song and dance of love. They must have been the sacred birds of some divinity, and with their gracious courtship they were announcing the approach of spring!

This only confirmed what I'd always been firmly convinced of: nature never gives all of her gifts to one creature alone. To some she gives one thing, to some she gives another. The nightingale is tiny and insignificant, but he sings with the most melodious harmony ever created. If there was a paradise on earth, I thought, every creature there would be perfect, and there would be birds like those of such extraordinary beauty gifted with the voice of a nightingale.

After several days' march, we arrived at another river which raced along in the opposite direction to the one we'd been descending before, and we began to follow it. The locals called it the Harpas and it coursed rapidly down-valley, which is where we wanted to go. Even the weather was changing: the rivers and torrents ran fast and full of crystalline water, and in the bends and deep coves you could see beautiful silvery fish splashing. And down below us, a vast fertile land opened out, with flowered meadows and shining emerald grasslands. As we went on, villages began to appear, and towards evening you could see smoke curling up from the roofs in slow whorls rising towards the pink sky of dusk.

Down there it was springtime.

THE VOICE OF the army returned to what it had once been: deep and powerful. It had been so long since I'd heard it that I'd forgotten all about it. For months the men had been moving in near-silence, oppressed by an immense fatigue that weighed more heavily on their hearts than it did on their shoulders or legs. They had seen their comrades dropping one after another at the hands of a powerful enemy, and they were prostrated by it, by the ghost of winter, shrouded by mist or by storm, opaque and transparent at the same time, icy and blinding. They had no voice, because winter's voice drowned out all the others or swallowed them up in the dazed silence of the heights, in the dark, endless nights. But then had come the day of the great battle, the impossible victory that had given them and their commanders the strength to start the long journey back.

It was truly exciting to descend towards the valley, to leave the snowy slopes behind us and enter green pastures and fields covered with flowers. To see the men discarding the pelts that made them look like beasts and regaining, day by day, the vigour and sparkle of youth. Muscular arms and legs were bared and faces shed their grimness, as long, unkempt beards disappeared with the aid of scissors and razor, instruments of a nearly forgotten civilization.

And their weapons! Dulled and discoloured by damp and

neglect, they were restored to their original sheen. The bronze gleamed, iron and silver flashed. The crests of their helmets were washed in the pure water of the brooks and swayed red, blue, white and ochre in the wind. The trumpets announced danger or called the men to their ranks with silvery clarity, blaring out with a voice as sharp as a sword.

We reached the foot of the valley one evening after sunset and I turned around to look for one last time at the frozen world we were leaving behind us. For a moment I thought I saw a horseman, a hazy shape that blended into the snow in the last reflected glow of dusk: one of the many memories that refused to leave me . . .

THE COMMUNITIES scattered over the valley were peaceful, more given to trade than to war, to barter rather than to battle. Some of the villages were large enough to be called cities. The passage of the army aroused more interest than fear, more curiosity than hostility.

One of the larger villages we came upon had houses of stone or wood and a market square where you could buy anything: livestock, wheat, barley, poultry and eggs, beans and vegetables. It was there that I realized that Sophos's chest must have had a double bottom, or a secret compartment, because I saw him spending an amount of gold darics, the imperial coin which pictured Darius the Great in the act of shooting an arrow. The generals also had Persian money to spend. The army could finally buy everything it needed, and the abundant fresh food improved everyone's conditions.

Xeno spent a lot of time at the market seeking information with the help of an interpreter who spoke Persian. He was even invited to the house of the man who governed the city. Evidently, the word was out that the empire had its eye on these foreigners. Xeno's host spoke fluent Persian and the interpreter had no problem making himself understood. His house was spacious and had an interior garden. There were many servants and maids dressed in their local costumes.

'We don't often see an army of this size in the city. From your weapons and the sound of your language I'd say you're Greek. How did you get here?' he asked.

'We serve the Great King. We lost our bearings during a blizzard up in the mountains and we were about to give up. Now that we're here we need your help to return to our bases on the sea.'

The nobleman had his servants bring roasted meat and pigeon's eggs boiled in salted water to honour his guest, and he pretended to believe the lie that Xeno had told him regarding the nature of the military mission. He said, 'I will be happy to help you. Before evening, I will send a guide to your camp who can show you the best route to take. In exchange I'd like a small favour.'

'Consider it done,' replied Xeno. 'How can I help you?'

'The guide will tell you. I prefer to have my guests enjoy my hospitality without personally discussing such details.'

Xeno noted all the local habits and customs and returned to camp after lunch to report on his meeting. The guide arrived in the late afternoon. He was a robust man and carried himself with a certain dignity. He was dressed and outfitted for a mountain journey. He evidently assumed that the response to the governor's request would be positive. He was received in the tent which was being used as the camp headquarters, in the presence of the generals and battalion commanders.

'We are grateful to you for offering such invaluable help,' Sophos began. 'First of all we would like to know how far we are from the sea.'

'In five days' march, I can take you to a place from which you can see the sea. Is that what you seek?'

Neither Sophos nor the other commanders, much less Xeno, managed to hide the enormous emotion his words aroused in them. Sophos replied, 'It certainly is. And how may we repay you?'

'After the second day's marching, we will enter the territory of a tribe which is hostile to us. They make continuous raids into our territory, sacking and destroying everything in their path. They are wild, fierce highlanders. You must destroy them. Burn their villages and take everything you want, even the women.'

Sophos eyed the other commanders and saw determination in their gazes. He answered simply, 'We can do that.'

'Then let us leave at once,' said the guide. 'Time saved is time gained.'

We did leave at once, even though it was late. We headed towards the northern flank of the valley where the track we'd taken on our approach to the city took a turn towards the mountains. We travelled up a long, narrow gully with a torrent at its centre, moving in a column formation, as always, with the scouts at the head accompanied by our guide and with Xeno's mounted rearguard at the back.

The days had grown longer; we realized this the next day as we were climbing the mountain slope because the sun stayed with us, on the right side of the valley, until it set. We stopped for the night in a clearing, a sort of grassy terrace spacious enough to contain the whole army.

Xeno and the others climbed to the crest of a ridge that rose above our camp, and they could see a group of villages on another terrace. In the dim light, they could make out some campfires, where food was being cooked, and light coming from lamps as well.

'Why don't we attack now?' demanded Agasias. 'Let's get it over with and then we can eat in peace.'

'No,' Sophos replied. 'I don't want to attack at night in the mountains. Tomorrow we'll have breakfast before the sun rises and then we'll attack.'

The guide approached them. 'You have to wipe out the women and children, too,' he said, 'unless you want to keep some for yourself.'

'No,' replied Sophos. 'That wasn't part of the agreement. We'll take on anyone who offers armed resistance and we'll burn the villages. Don't ask for more.'

Millions of stars were teeming in the sky that night. The white veil that crosses the firmament from one side to the other seemed to rise and fall as if a mysterious wind were setting it aflutter and the air was full of the perfume of unfamiliar flowers.

After dinner Sophos went up to the ridge, dressed only in his cloak, gripping his spear in his hand. Xeno joined him.

'I can't believe it. Four days from now we'll see the sea,' he said.

'You shouldn't believe it. Not until we've seen it.'

'You're right. We've had our share of complications.'

They stood there in silence, until Xeno spoke again. 'What will you do when we get back?'

'Me? Nothing. I'll never get to Sparta.'

Xeno didn't comment. Sophos was pronouncing his own death sentence and there was nothing that Xeno could say to counter it. They sat on the ridge for some time, looking at the villages that they would put to fire and sword the next day.

As the men were pitching camp I had discovered a spring of clear water under a big rock covered with green moss. When it had grown pitch black I went there, stripped off my clothes and slowly immersed myself in the icy water. At first it was so cold I couldn't even catch my breath, but at last I was able to wash and purify my body and my hair in the uncontaminated waters. It was like being born into a new life, and as soon as I lay down, I plummeted into a deep sleep.

I WAS AWAKENED by a chorus of screams and cries of terror, and the sinister crackling of fire. I ran outside and saw that the camp was empty; only a small unit had been left behind to garrison it. I climbed up the ridge and watched our soldiers paying the price to see the sea: slaughter.

The men of the village were fighting with all that they had, but there were few of them left standing because the assault had taken them by surprise, before sunrise. Many lay sprawled on the ground, transfixed. Some of the women were running off with babes in their arms, seeking refuge in the forests, while others wept over the bodies of their slain husbands. The children tried to take up the arms of their fathers who had fallen fighting off an implacable enemy that had pounced out of nowhere on their sleeping village. The huts with roofs of wood and straw burned like torches, raising swirls of dense smoke and sparks to the heavens. Before long, the crackle of the flames was the only sound to be heard. The army formed ranks again, led by the guide, and one by one destroyed every village on the mountain-side, leaving a wake of smoke-blackened ruins. The ravages lasted three days, and only when our guide declared himself satisfied did we move on, towards the crest of the mountain range we were crossing.

As we climbed, the snow reappeared, but only in patches, here and there. In the pastures we saw fleshy white flowers which were very beautiful and, a little higher up, carpets of purple blossoms with thin, long petals arranged in a star shape. It was a splendid sight. I saw some of the girls gathering them up and I picked one too, and put it in my hair. I hated to see them crushed under the warriors' heavy feet.

The head of the column had nearly reached the crest, but we still lagged far behind with the pack animals. Xeno and his men were on foot, leading their horses by the reins. Finally even we women arrived at a high plain which was wide enough for two battalions to pass side by side. Towards the west it shelved gently upward.

All at once, confused shouting could be heard from the head of the column, getting louder and louder. Xeno was just a little way behind me with Lycius of Syracuse and the others of his squad. I heard him shout, 'Mount your horses, men! The vanguard is under attack! Be quick! Move!'

In an instant they had vaulted onto their horses and were racing alongside the column, which had ground to a halt. The officers were fanning out their units so as to reach the battle line more quickly and come to the aid of their comrades. The shouts were getting even louder.

But something in that sound struck me as strange and I had a sudden realization. I ran like mad towards the front of the column.

It was a prolonged, powerful cry, like the rolling of thunder, and the closer I got the more the cry grew in intensity, till my heart felt it was about to burst.

It was a word they were shouting, one word, the same I'd heard pronounced as a hope and an invocation during the freezing nights, in the endless marches. I'd heard it in the melancholy songs that rose from the camp when the sun was dying behind the grey winter clouds.

The sea.

Yes, that's what they were shouting, 'The sea! The sea! The sea! The seeeeeeeaaaaa!'

My heart was pounding by the time I got to the top, panting and covered in sweat. Xeno saw me and shouted: 'Look! It's the sea!'

Delirium surrounded me. The warriors were beside themselves; they couldn't stop repeating that cry. They embraced each other, they embraced their officers as if in thanks for not giving up on them. Then, brandishing their swords, they began to beat them on their shields without ever ceasing their cry, making the air tremble with the deafening roar of bronze.

For a long while they stood there dazed by that vision. The thick cloud cover that hid the foot of the great mountain chain was opening and with every passing moment, with every renewed cry from the warriors, the break was growing wider, and there before us lay an intense and splendid stretch of blue, a sparkling, translucent blue, rippling with a thousand glittering waves, edged with white foam. I'd never seen it before.

The sea.

28

THEIR ENTHUSIASM AND JOY showed no signs of diminishing. The sight of the sea was not only the end of a nightmare, it was a vision of home. It meant familiar shores, places studded with the settlements, villages and cities that the motherland had founded on the continent.

Someone abruptly yelled something that I didn't understand, but everyone in earshot began to gather stones. Soon the entire army and many of the girls as well were joining the soldiers in adding rocks and pebbles, each as many as he or she could carry. They found a great number of them in a depression in the ground about two or three hundred paces away, and they built up several huge mounds to mark the spots from which they'd first seen the sea. It would serve as the reminder of what they had achieved, a trophy that would stand for centuries and perhaps for millennia in memory of their victory over their enemies, over hunger, thirst, cold, wounds, illness and betrayal. It would celebrate their impossible endeavour for all time.

They were so excited that the pile of stones grew before my eyes, taking on huge dimensions. The guide, standing off to the side, said nothing. He watched with a puzzled look, not realizing what they were doing, not understanding, I believe, the meaning of such behaviour. He didn't move, didn't bat an eyelid, as the totally spontaneous and monumental project took shape, growing by the hour.

By dusk their task was complete. Each mound was more than twenty paces wide and about ten cubits high, rising at the rim of the clearing, looming over the steep slope that descended towards the sea. The clouds in the meantime were crowding the sky again and obscuring the sight of the boundless blue expanse. When the monument had been completed, the soldiers tossed onto it the weapons that they'd taken from their enemies, and only then did the guide react. He broke some of them in pieces and asked our men to do the same. His hate for those who had carried them must have been extreme.

It was time to reward him for having guided us to that point. He was given a horse from those the men used in common, a beautiful Persian robe and ten gold darics, a fortune and a sign of the army's unending gratitude. But the guide had set his eyes on their rings and pointing at the soldiers' fingers, he asked to be given those as well. Many turned them over happily. Even Melissa: I saw her take a ring off her little finger and give it to the guide, who put it in the sack with the others. Then, without saying a word, he turned on his heel and melted on horseback into the shadows of the night.

A sense of calm fell over the army then, in the silence, and an infinite sadness. The euphoria, the wild, irrepressible enthusiasm, the crazed yells, the furious raising of a symbol of their salvation, all faded, giving way to reflection and memory. They had somehow survived an undertaking that had cost continual sacrifice and struggle, a battle one thousand battles long, a war against everything and everyone. Their eyes saw the scenes that would never leave them as long as they lived: comrades fallen in battle, dying slowly amid atrocious suffering, youth maimed, wounded, doomed to wander for ever in a blind, dark world.

That's who those mounds were dedicated to: to the ones who hadn't made it. Their heroism, their valour, their courage. No other monument like them existed in all the world. This was no work commissioned by great wealth from a renowned artist and lavished with gold and bronze and precious marbles. No, those mounds had been raised by those who remained, each man adding a stone or two stones or a hundred, without the design of any architect, inspired only by their hearts.

At dusk I saw more than one of those young warriors off on his own, weeping. Others had gathered around the biggest mound and were raising their voices in a sad, majestic song that rose to the sky, where the first star was already shining.

The next day we started to march again, downhill this time. The Ten Thousand were leaving the world of the heights that they had crossed from one end to another. Solitary peaks, unending chains of mountains furrowed by turbulent rivers roaring through rapids and exploding into foaming falls, all behind them now. They were going back to the sea, from where they had started.

We crossed a wood of shrubs not much taller than a man, laden with purple flowers. Beyond them were green fields dotted with other marvellous blooms, stretching as far as the eye could see.

Here and there ran dozens of little brooks that carried down to the valley the water of the glaciers and the snows that had melted in the heat of what had become late spring. They splashed from one rock to another, releasing a fine mist that shone in sunlight with the colours of the rainbow. The sound of all this rushing water, of each little fall, the gurgling and bubbling that changed in tone and intensity at every stone, formed a single, indefinable, magical voice, joined by the chirping of the birds and the rustle of the leaves in the breeze.

This is how paradise on earth must have been, in the golden age, I thought. The bright reflection of the sun penetrating between the branches, glistening dewdrops, fragrances carried on the warm wind that blew in from the sea, redolent with other scents.

Our suffering truly seemed behind us, hardship and hunger a mere memory, but we soon were forced to realize that not everything would be so easy. A local tribe barred our path at a river, and only after long negotiations were we allowed to cross unscathed. When Xeno asked the young skirmisher who had stepped up to offer himself as an interpreter how he had learned the language of a people living so far from Greece, he replied, 'I don't know . . . I suddenly realized that I could understand them when they were speaking.'

It was a kind of miracle, with no easy explanation. Then the youth said that, as a child, he had been sold as a slave in Athens and so it was possible that he was a son of that people. His mother tongue had stayed buried in his mind, neglected for years and years, until his memory was awakened by an unexpected contact with his forgotten origins.

They were forced to fight further on, at a mountain ridge where a line of soldiers was drawn up: the Colchians, the people of the golden fleece!

I felt that I had stepped into a wondrous universe where truth and legend were mixing constantly, in which real visions were transfigured in fanciful settings.

This time Xeno led the charge, urging the warriors to seize this last pass. He rode up and down the ranks encouraging them, joking, cursing in his military jargon, until I heard him yell, 'Let's get on with it, we're going to eat them alive!'

The men responded with a roar, launching themselves into the attack with fury and overwhelming power. The Colchians were swept away at the first assault and the army camped in several villages that we came upon before evening. Here something very strange happened. Hundreds of our men showed signs of poisoning: they grew exceedingly weak and feverish, with cramps and vomiting. It was said that they'd eaten honey that had intoxicated them, but I'd never heard of bees that could produce poisonous honey. Could they be immune to their own poison? I suspected other causes, and so did Xeno, I think, because he knew that the army had its enemies and that the reasons for wanting it annihilated had not gone away.

Fortunately, those who had fallen ill managed to get better

fairly soon, and this helped to allay my suspicions that our persecution would have no end.

We set out again, and at last we reached the coast, which stretched out a long way before us. On the second day, the city of Trapezus appeared. A Greek city.

It had been over a year since our men had been able to speak their own language with a community of people, and their joy was immense. We camped outside the city, and while our commanders made contact with the authorities and tried to secure the help we needed to continue our journey, the men organized games and contests to thank the gods.

When the celebrations were over, it was time to make decisions. The assembled army, with all the ranks taking part, did not leave their officers much of a choice. No one wanted to march any further, face more combat, risk more losses. Their mission was concluded, as far as they were concerned, and they wanted to find a ship that would take them home. One of the soldiers even made a speech that seemed inspired by the mono-logues of the comic actors at the theatres, performing a parody of the soldier as hero. As if to say: we've had enough.

Sophos tried to obtain warships and cargo ships from the city authorities, but the results were disappointing. Only a couple of ships and ten or so smaller vessels were found. On top of everything else, one of the men who was an expert in navigation had been put in charge of the ships, but during the night he weighed anchor and set sail with one of the two warships. His name was Dexippus and he would be for ever remembered as a traitor.

The remaining vessels would certainly not suffice to transport the army, who were thus forced to make forays into the interior so that they could raid and plunder the villages of the native peoples, who defended themselves with tooth and nail. I didn't witness any of those raids, because I stayed back at camp with the other women, the wounded and the convalescents, but I found out more than I wanted to know from the stories we'd listen to after dark: cruel tales of havoc and destruction, women and children jumping in flames from their houses only to have their bones crushed in the fall, fighters on both sides turned into human torches, ferocious hand-to-hand combat, massacres.

Did they have any choice? They would have preferred to buy what they needed in the markets, but they had little money left, and nothing precious to barter. Even I had begun to think like them, and I knew the law of survival was not something you could ignore. The horrors of war were a sad consequence of that law. Once the battle had begun, the pain, the blood, the agony of body and mind did the rest, and any semblance of decency was cancelled, any restraint overwhelmed. I was fortunate I didn't have to watch it.

After we'd been camped in the same place for a month, the army had created a void all around us. There were no villages left to be sacked in a range of one or two days' march. We had to move on. The inhabitants of Trapezus had long had enough of us, and would have done anything to see us gone. At that point it was decided that the non-combatants would board the ships and the available vessels would put to sea: in this way, the amount of food we needed would also be greatly diminished. The command of the fleet was entrusted to Netus, the officer who'd often had differences of opinion with Xeno. It seems that he is writing his own story of the expedition; I'd love to know what he has written.

So the wounded and the sick, the older men and the remaining women left by sea. Yes, the girls were leaving. The girls who had cheered on the warriors at the turbulent river as if they were athletes at the stadium, the girls who had held them in their arms when they returned from battle, curing and salving their wounds, consoling them and alleviating the hardships of living, of fighting, of facing death every day and every night. The girls who had kissed them and loved them because the next day might be their last. The girls who had followed them to the end of the earth and who had mourned them on their funeral pyres as if they were their brides, sisters, mothers.

They were leaving.

I stayed with Xeno. Melissa stayed with Cleanor, and so did a few others who had become the constant companions of some of the officers. The march resumed again, along the coast. We never lost sight of the sea. For a while we could see ships and boats sailing in convoy and sometimes I thought I could see the girls waving to us with brightly coloured cloths flying in the wind. I'd get a lump in my throat and I couldn't hold back my tears. I couldn't stop thinking about Lystra. About her striving to deliver her baby in the freezing cold, about my own desperation and solitude. Death had demanded his due: a poor slave and a child who would never be born. And in the bright sunshine that reflected off the sea in a million sparkles, I thought of the mysterious divinity of the storm who had taken me into his arms and flown me to the outskirts of the camp so that I could be found. Perhaps he was made of snow and had melted with spring's return, perhaps his spirit now surged through the fast-flowing torrents that rushed down the valleys and plunged into the sea.

We reached the first important city after several days of marching and, I'm not sure why, the bitter moment of counting up the survivors arrived. Officially, to know how many mouths were left to feed. The army was drawn up in full order, and the officers commanding each unit loudly called out the roll. When the name of one of the survivors was called, you'd hear 'Present!', but often the call was met with a long silence. Although the officer knew he was calling a dead man, he'd repeat the name because that was what the military tradition demanded, and only after prolonged silence did he go on to the next name. As the roll continued, the expressions of those present darkened, because each silence corresponded to a comrade, a friend, a brother who had lost his life, and brought up memories of blood and suffering.

I remembered that although I'd always called them the Ten Thousand there had been considerably more to start with, about thirteen thousand five hundred. Of these only eight thousand six hundred answered the call. Almost five thousand men had died of the cold, hunger, wounds. Most of them in the last grievous battle of the crater.

The soldiers also divided up the booty that had been plundered in all of the assaults conducted during the expedition. The tenth part was offered to the gods, and the rest was divided according to rank, among the generals, the battalion commanders and the soldiers.

I was really struck by the fact that Sophos refused his due. He left his whole entitlement to his field adjutant, Neon of Asine. I was watching Xeno when the supreme commander gave up his share: his initial expression of surprise changed to one of sad realization. Sophos had told Xeno he would never return to Sparta, and his actions revealed how convinced he was of this.

After we'd left that city we arrived at the border of a territory inhabited by savages who had divided into two factions. We allied with the faction that agreed to let us pass and attacked the other. They called themselves 'tower-dwellers' in their language because their chiefs lived in wooden towers that loomed above the huts in their settlements.

It was another bloody battle that resulted in many losses, but our men were victorious once again. When the Greeks formed up, obedient to their commanders, when they made a wall with their shields and shouted out their terrible war cry in unison, no one could resist them. No one could even bear the sight of their ranks advancing in compact order to the sound of flutes and drums.

After our victory, our allies showed us their villages and the chieftains introduced their children, extraordinary creatures, I must say. They fattened them up on certain nuts that grew in their territory that were inedible if you tried them raw, but delicious if you roasted or boiled them and peeled off their leather-coloured shell. Those children were broader than they were tall, barded with layers of fat. Their flesh was very pale and completely covered with colourful tattoos. They looked something like talismans that you'd offer to the gods to appease their wrath. They wouldn't have been good for anything else.

The men were very active and even quite intrusive. They would try – in plain sight! – to mount the girls who had remained among us, as if they were animals. Melissa was hotly contended for, and a brawl would certainly have broken out had the interpreters and local guides not interceded and made appropriate explanations on both sides.

Xeno told me that he thought those were the most barbarous of any of the barbarians we had encountered. In fact, they did in public what the Greeks did in private, like have intercourse with a woman or perform their bodily functions, and in private what the Greeks did in public, like talking or dancing.

I saw them myself, dancing or carrying on a conversation, all alone. It was fascinating. They were a people who lived in a natural state, without cunning or hypocrisy, but that didn't make them any less fierce. It made me think that ferocity was a part of being human, especially for men, although women were certainly not immune to it. I recalled what Menon had told me about the tortures inflicted by the Queen Mother on those who had boasted of killing her son; they'd left me sick with horror.

We had ample provisions now, and plunder, and pack animals. The situation had changed greatly. I couldn't help but notice, however, that Sophos, that is, Commander Chirisophus, had grown detached. He occupied himself with marginal tasks, like looking for ships. He no longer appeared in public meetings, you'd never see him inspecting the troops. He seemed to want to melt away, as if he were no longer needed or no longer had a role to play. Who knows, maybe he was planning on slipping away as suddenly as he had appeared. Maybe one morning he just wouldn't be there any more.

I would have liked to ask Xeno what he thought, or what he knew, but since I'd been caught searching through Sophos's things, the topic was out of bounds. Strange, from a certain point of view, if you considered that it was that act of mine that brought everything to a head and forced Sophos to take a decision that I think he may have been already convinced of, deep down. I could understand, though. I had interfered in a delicate, secret, dangerous situation – I was well aware of that! – and no one could be allowed to learn what I had done. Anything I might say could only add to the risk.

We arrived at another city by the sea inhabited by Greeks. It was called Cotyora, as I recall, and like the others we'd visited by then, it was subject to the authority of another city to the west of it called Sinope, which had been founded by yet another city, perhaps one of those on the Greek mainland.

Here at last Xeno openly revealed the intention he'd long nursed of becoming the founder of a colony. After all, he'd often told me that he could never go back to his city, Athens, because he had fought on the side of the losing faction. Even if he were allowed to return, and his safety guaranteed, he would never be able to assume any important role in the government or in the army, nor would he enjoy respect or consideration. I knew him well: he would prefer death to such an existence. On the other hand, to found a colony meant becoming the father of a new homeland and a legend for his descendants, commemorated in statues and public inscriptions, not only in the new colony but in his land of origin as well. Thus, a total redemption of his name and reputation. As I understood it, the homeland was ready to forget any negative aspects of a native son if he managed to establish himself in a distant place, overseas, and no longer represented any problem for them. He could create a new community that would enjoy a special relationship with its mother city, and he would be long honoured in both.

A plan like that would benefit the soldiers as well. Many of them were rootless men who trusted in providence and sold their swords to the highest bidder. Those who had families could send for them, those who didn't could marry a native girl. They would be the privileged founders of the most important families, of a new aristocracy. They would be forever remembered in popular stories and songs that would be handed down for generations in the new city.

I admit that his project fascinated me as well, although I couldn't even confess this to myself at the time.

If Xeno had become the hero of a new homeland I could have become his wife. I – the little barbarian from a dusty, forgotten village – would become the mother of his descendants, and my name would be honoured along with his. My long and adventurous journey would have a happy ending, like the stories told by the old men in Beth Qadà, as in the dream I'd embraced the first time I met him at the well.

Was that why Commander Sophos was pulling away? He was not a common man. Perhaps he wanted his friend to remember him for ever as the man who had paved the way for his glorious destiny and then faded into the shadows to allow him to be the sole protagonist. I could think of no other explanation. Or maybe I didn't want to.

Our tent hosted repeated meetings of the officers so that they could weigh the various options. They counted up the men who might be willing to join them, to gauge how big the colony might be. They spoke of the Phasis and of returning to Colchis, ruled by a descendant of the king who had possessed the golden fleece; a rich and magical land where our city would enjoy flourishing trade, an ideal base for creating ties, alliances and treaties with other cities and states.

They were dreaming.

But there was no saying that this time dreams could not become reality. Xeno continued to offer sacrifices to the gods, assisted by an augur who had followed us during the entire expedition. He wanted to know whether to tell the entire army or to keep his plans to himself and his fellow officers for the moment. It was rumoured that many men were favourable to founding a colony. Many wanted to stay where we were, others were inclined to follow Timas the Dardanian, who proposed they settle in his native land or somewhere nearby.

When Xeno finally made his move it was too late. The project was completely compromised. No one wanted to return to Colchis, and so many different opinions had sprung up that it was impossible for any of the alternative projects to get sufficient support. The only thing that everyone agreed upon was accepting the proposal from the government of Sinope to transport us by sea to the limit of their area of influence. This would save us yet another long march through the territory of yet another warlike tribe. Xeno accepted, but only on condition that all of the army be transported together at the same time. He wanted no part in splitting them up.

Xeno had earned such esteem from the soldiers that they called an assembly and decided to offer him the supreme command.

Xeno refused. He was sure that the army's choice was the result of a passing whim. He was afraid that sooner or later old resentments would re-emerge, vestiges of the Great War, and that he, as an Athenian, could not hold sway for long over an army made up almost completely of men from the territories and cities of the enemy coalition that had won the war. He said that the only man worthy of the position was Chirisophus the Spartan.

Thus Sophos, who had gradually withdrawn, perhaps to allow Xeno to emerge, was forced by Xeno's refusal to undergo an official investiture which confirmed him in the position he already held through a formal act of the assembly.

I wondered whether they had spoken beforehand, if there was any agreement between them, but Xeno never mentioned it to me. In any case, Sophos's attempts to manipulate events according to a precise plan had not succeeded. In the light of what happened later I can say that his plan was to ensure the survival of the army by allowing Xeno to assume command. Not because there weren't other officers courageous and charismatic enough to hold the army together, but because Xeno was the only one who was aware of the grave danger that still threatened the army and the only one capable of taking adequate measures to hold it off.

Our journey continued by sea. We travelled west until we reached another of the Greek cities dedicated to their greatest hero, Heracles. The city was called Heraclea, in fact, and the authorities welcomed us as friends. They gave us flour, wine and livestock, which we knew, however, would not last us long. We needed much more than that. Some of the officers proposed that we ask the city for a large sum of money. The authorities would certainly not dare to refuse, seeing the size of our force. Sophos rejected the idea resolutely. 'We cannot tax a city of Greeks that has already spontaneously given us all it could. We have to find another solution.' But his words were not heeded. A group of officers including Agasias, one of the heroes of the army who had distinguished himself in many bold acts, went nonetheless to the city to demand an exorbitant sum in gold. The inhabitants' only answer was to gather all the provisions they had harvested, bar the gates and post armed sentries along the entire circuit of the walls.

Discontent exploded among the troops. The common dangers we'd faced were behind us, making way for negative and disruptive forces, rivalry and jealousy. No one realized that the most terrible threat was still looming over us. Placing all the blame on the incompetence of their commanders, the most numerous ethnic groups – the Arcadians and the Achaeans – decided to break away from the rest of the army and go off on their own. Cleanor was an Arcadian, and he left with Melissa. She and I parted with a long and tearful embrace, thinking we'd never see each other again.

The army was split in two.

Xeno and Sophos were dismayed. The unity of the army had

been, until then, the supreme prize that was never lost sight of, and conserved at any cost.

Xeno decided he would attempt to join the contingent that had left, taking with him the men who had remained loyal to him. He was still trying to prevent the army from dispersing, and he thought Sophos would do the same. He was wrong.

Xeno learned, I'm not sure how, that Neon – Sophos's field adjutant, the one he had left all his booty to – had made the commander a proposal. It turned out that Cleander, the Spartan governor of the most important Greek city of the east, Byzantium, who was responsible for relations with the empire of the Great King, had already been informed of our presence and had made a proposal: if Sophos and his men showed up at the next port, he would send ships to pick them up.

Sophos was completely demoralized. Not because he was certain this meant that there was no way out for him, but because the source of that proposal was his own field adjutant, a man he had always trusted and to whom he had bequeathed all his worldly goods. Yet it was Neon who was pushing him into the hands of those who were longing to eliminate him.

Yes, they must have wanted very badly to be rid of him, Commander Chirisophus, the only regular Spartan officer, the hero who had led his men through a thousand dangers. The only man who knew the secret of Spartan involvement in the plot to dethrone and assassinate the Great King, officially their most powerful ally. The man who should have died or disappeared along with the rest of the army, he who had wilfully disobeyed his orders at the sight of his men's desperate courage. He who had sworn that he would bring them back, knowing that he was signing his own death sentence.

Perhaps Sophos thought that at this point all his efforts had been in vain. That Dexippus, who had fled Trapezus with one of the warships, had done so not to save himself but to report to Sparta that the army was returning. Sophos must have thought that he had no choice but to face his destiny, and so he did.

No one heard Neon's conversation with Sophos, but I imagined it, imagined the look in Sophos's eyes when Neon asked him to leave. I'd wager that not even then did he resist making a sardonic remark. It made me want to cry. I'd never forgotten how he stayed by my side and protected me on the day of the battle of Cunaxa, when Cyrus confronted his brother the Great King on the banks of the Euphrates.

Xeno met with him the evening before his departure, at one of the harbour taverns.

'You're about to leave, then.'

'So it seems.'

'Why? Together we can still achieve great things.'

Sophos curled his lip. 'Who told you that? One of your seers? Did he read it in the guts of some sheep?'

'No, Commander, I'm convinced that if we want to we can . . .'

'. . . found a colony? Hard to let go of your dream, isn't it, writer? Do you seriously believe that a dream can become reality? Are you truly convinced that in a world divided between two dominant powers it's possible to found an independent city? In an important, strategic location, where it could thrive and become prosperous? I'm afraid you're deceiving yourself. The days when a handful of men, guided by the prophecy of a god, weighed anchor in search of a new home in a wild, faraway land where they would grow free and strong . . . those were other days, my friend. The days of the heroes are gone for ever.'

Xeno was silent, his heart heavy. Sophos buckled the sword that he'd laid on the table onto his belt and threw his cloak over one shoulder.

'Farewell, writer.'

'Farewell, Commander,' Xeno replied, and sat there listening to the sound of his hobnailed boots fading away in the night air.

29

AFTER NEGOTIATING WITH the city authorities, the Arcadians and the Achaeans had left by ship. The city had agreed to transport them to a village called Calpe, a few days' sail to the west.

Commander Sophos set off a day or so later on foot, followed by over two thousand men who had refused to leave him.

Xeno was torn by doubt over what to do. So deluded was he that he thought for a while that we should set off alone, find a boat somewhere and set sail for Greece. But the remaining two thousand men gathered around our tent, saying that they considered themselves at his orders. He was profoundly moved, especially since among them was Timas of Dardania, one of the five generals, who immediately offered to be his field adjutant. That meant a lot to Xeno: the men recognized his role as their leader and he rose to the occasion. That same day he convinced the inhabitants of Heraclea to transport them west as well, but only as far as the border of their territory. The army which had been such an impenetrable block was now divided into three parts, each of which was drifting off on its own. If nothing else, Xeno's decision to leave straight away meant that he still wanted to join forces with the biggest contingent.

In the meantime, the Arcadians and the Achaeans had reached their destination as night was falling. They decided to set off at once so they wouldn't be seen and marched towards the interior. Just before dawn, they swooped upon a number of inland villages, seeking to raid their livestock, plunder their homes and take a great many of the inhabitants as prisoners, to be sold as slaves.

They had left Greece in the hope of returning with immense riches, and they didn't want to show up empty-handed. This was their last chance.

They had split up into a number of units and planned to meet on a hill that overlooked the territory so as to share out their plunder and return all together. But they hadn't anticipated that the reaction of the natives would be so fierce. The smoke of the fires and the alarm that passed from village to village over the whole region rallied a host of mounted warriors who attacked each of the Greek marching columns. Overloaded with booty and held up by the livestock and prisoners, they were overwhelmed by an incessant rain of arrows shot from a distance, sowing panic and death. One of the units was trapped in a ravine and annihilated. Another, surrounded by crushing forces on the plain, was almost completely destroyed. The others, after suffering heavy losses, managed to regroup on the hill, and there they spent the night without closing an eye.

Commander Sophos, unaware of any of this, proceeded along the coast in the direction of Calpe, he and his men all ready and willing to die hard.

After we disembarked, Xeno decided to travel by an inland route, and every so often, when we met a shepherd or peasant, we would use our interpreters to ask whether there was any news of an army passing through. On the evening of our second day's marching, two old men told us that there was an enemy army being blockaded on a hill that could be seen about twenty stadia away. They were besieged on all sides.

'Have you seen them yourself?' Xeno asked the younger of the two.

'Certainly. I passed yesterday on that path down there,' he said, pointing to a pale line that cut across the green plain, 'and if you ask me, I don't think they'll see the sun set tomorrow.'

The news was confirmed when night fell and we could see a

number of fires burning at the foot of the hill. Xeno summoned all the available officers.

'There are only two thousand of us,' he began. 'There were more than four thousand of them, and see how they've ended up. If we wait and attack tomorrow, even with the aid of our cavalry I don't think we'll have any chance of breaking through the encirclement.'

'I'm afraid you're right,' nodded Timas. 'What are you thinking?'

Xeno meditated in silence for a while, then said, 'Listen. We must create the impression that we are ten, twenty times stronger than we are. Those barbarians down there must be made to think that the Arcadians and Achaeans they're surrounding were only the advance guard, that we're the bulk of the army. Oh, if only Commander Chirisophus were with us!'

'Well, he's not here,' replied Timas. 'We have to get out of this one on our own. What's the plan of battle?'

'I know it's dangerous, but we have to split up into groups. Yes, that's what we'll do. Each group will set fire to anything and everything on its path that can burn: huts, shepherd's shacks, straw, bales of hay, isolated houses, fences, granaries, stables, anything and everything. Not trees or bushes or stubble, though. We don't want them to think it's a wild fire. It has to look to them like an act of ruthless military retaliation.'

'That's right,' approved Timas. 'We'll scare the crap out of them. They'll think we're putting the whole country to fire and sword.'

'Exactly. The fires will allow us to keep track of where each of the groups is, but remember to leave any area in flames behind you as soon as possible; the wind can change direction and you don't want to become trapped. Come on men, let's get going.'

The men formed groups of about fifty, lit torches from the braziers we always carried with us and, fanning out over the countryside, began to set fire to anything that could burn.

The flames burst out all over the fields and spread rapidly until the whole plain was ablaze. In keeping with Xeno's instructions, the individual fires increasingly converged on the area around the hill, giving the impression of a huge army come to break up the siege.

When dawn broke and the hill was finally visible there was no longer a soul there. Neither the besiegers nor the besieged. Only ash and smoking campfires and a number of fallen soldiers from both sides strewn over the hillside.

'What in Hades has happened here?' yelled Timas as he cantered back and forth. 'Where did they all go?'

Xeno's eyes were darting all around, trying to grasp how the place had come to be completely deserted, until one of the interpreters arrived, saying he'd spoken to a shepherd. 'He saw soldiers descending the hillside and moving quickly out towards the coast, just before dawn, as soon as the fires had gone out.'

'It's them,' said Xeno. He summoned Timas and ordered him to lead the infantry while he rode ahead with the cavalry to make contact. It wasn't long before he caught up with the Achaeans and the Arcadians, and there was great shouting and jubilation, as though they'd awakened from a nightmare.

'I'm sure you've realized that splitting off from the rest of the army was ill-advised. You've certainly paid for your mistake, with the lives of many of your comrades,' said Xeno. 'I hope the ones who had the idea in the first place were among those we lost.'

Xanthi was the first to step forward. He was grimy and wild-eyed with fatigue and tension. 'You're right, we were idiots. I don't know what got into us . . .'

Agasias ran towards Xeno and embraced him. 'You saved us from being completely wiped out. We couldn't have held out for long on that hill.'

'What happened last night, then?'

'As soon as we saw the fires, we knew it was you and the enemies realized it too and they cut and ran. But since you hadn't come forward, and we were afraid those barbarians might come back, we thought it best to get away as fast as we could. And here we are.'

'All right. But enough is enough. We won't split up again. Let's wait for Timas with the heavy infantry and then we'll march to the coast. The natives won't trouble us again.'

We camped on the beach at Calpe. It was a beautiful place, a peninsula that extended into the sea with a magnificent natural harbour, and I was able to embrace Melissa again, to my great joy. She was still with Cleanor, thank the gods. We also saw Aristonymus of Methydria, one of the mightiest warriors of the entire army, who spoke up as soon as he saw me. 'You know, girl, your writer really saved our arses this time. If it hadn't been for him, we all would have ended up impaled.' Xeno would have been proud to hear that, but at that moment he was off scouting the territory: the soil was rich and fertile and there was a spring gushing with pure water. The vast, almost circular peninsula was connected by an isthmus to the mainland.

I knew what he was thinking: that this would have been an ideal place to found a colony. Halfway between Heraclea and Byzantium, it was guaranteed a future of prosperity. Before the sun had begun to set, he started making plans to go back the next day and bury our dead, organizing a unit headed by the skirmishers and escorted by the cavalry.

I overheard Timas asking him, 'Where's Commander Chirisophus?'

'He'll be at Chrysopolis by now,' replied Xeno. Chrysopolis, as I would see later, was opposite Byzantium on the Asiatic side of the straits.

'Chrysopolis? I hardly think so,' protested Timas. 'It's too far.'

Cleanor walked up. 'I heard one of our scouts say that he's not far from here.'

'Here? Where?' asked Xeno.

'Down there,' replied Cleanor, pointing west. 'About thirty stadia away.'

'So close? Why doesn't he head back and join us?' asked Xeno again.

'I don't know,' said Cleanor, and off he went. The matter did not interest him, or perhaps he just didn't want to get involved.

Xeno had his horse made ready and set off in the direction Cleanor had indicated.

I found myself standing alone in the middle of the camp, and I was suddenly seized by an impulse so strong I could not help but act on it. I wanted to know what was happening to Commander Sophos, where he was and why he hadn't met up with us here at the beach of Calpe. I felt bound to him; I somehow sensed that his destiny was mine.

I entered our tent and put on one of Xeno's tunics, wrapped myself in a cloak that reached down to my feet and covered my head with a helmet. I found a horse tied to a fence and mounted him as best I could, dug in my heels and urged him down the road that led west. I'd never ridden a horse but I'd watched Xeno plenty of times. The animal was good-tempered, and I reached Commander Sophos's camp quite quickly. I stopped the first officer I came across and said, 'I'm Commander Xenophon's attendant. I must speak to him immediately.'

'He's in Commander Chirisophus's tent,' the man replied. 'That dark one, down there.' He seemed preoccupied, burdened by some gloomy thought. Then he added, 'The commander is quite ill.' I gave a nod, tied my horse and made my way towards the tent. As I was walking I noticed a small twenty-oar warship, its bow pointing at the beach. A red standard at the stern had a strange symbol: two lines that met at the top and opened wide at the bottom. It looked like a sign of the Greek alphabet.

There was a sentry in front of the tent. I approached and said in a low voice, 'I'm Commander Xenophon's attendant. I know he's inside. I have a message to deliver, so I'll wait here.'

The sentry nodded.

I recognized the two voices I knew so well and could hear

them distinctly because we were isolated from the rest of the camp.

Xeno's: 'How is that possible?'

Sophos, in a weary tone: 'I don't know. I haven't been well for days and I was taking a medicine. It wasn't the first time. It had always helped me in the past. But this morning it made me feel ill. Quite ill.'

I could picture his face clammy with sweat, his hair pasted to his forehead, his chest rising and falling as he struggled to breathe.

'Where did that ship at anchor by the beach come from?'

'Cleander. He sent it. He's the Spartan officer who governs Byzantium.'

'Did you meet with them? What do they want?'

'Yes, yesterday ... They were waiting for me here. They wanted to know a lot of things ... about the battle, about our long march.'

'What exactly did they ask you?' insisted Xeno, as if Sophos's answer hadn't satisfied him.

'You know,' replied Sophos's voice, ever more wearily. 'They asked me why ... why we're here.'

A long silence followed. But I could hear the soft whistle of Sophos's breathing.

His voice, again. 'I told you. I'll never see Sparta. Never again ...'

'You've won so many battles ... you'll win this one as well. The army needs you.'

'You'll command them. They want you all dead ... but you, Xenophon, you'll take them home. Take them all back home.'

Then, the silence of death.

I slipped away as the sentry protested, 'Hey, didn't you say you needed ...'

'I'll be back,' I replied as I set off to where I'd left my horse. I mounted him and led him slightly off the path so I'd be hidden by the vegetation that fringed the beach.

I didn't see Xeno until more than an hour later, when the sun had already begun to set.

I was preparing dinner in front of our tent over the embers of some pine branches I'd gathered in the wood. He came up and sat next to the fire as if he were cold.

'Commander Chirisophus is dead,' he said in a flat voice.

'Sophos . . . dead? Was there a battle?'

'No. He was poisoned.'

I didn't ask anything else. He must have thought I could draw my own conclusions.

Xeno began to eat in silence, but after two or three mouthfuls he pushed his plate away. There was a sound: flutes, their tune carried by the evening breeze blowing from the west. The same that had accompanied our long march, across deserts and mountains, for months and months. But this time the music was slow, tense, full of despair. Xeno listened, thoughtfully. The sound of the flutes was soon joined by a chorus of voices.

The loud buzz of the men going about their evening chores in the camp suddenly hushed, then died down completely. One after another, the soldiers turned towards the sound and one after another they rose to their feet. Xeno looked at me, then turned towards the soldiers and shouted, 'Commander Chirisophus is dead!'

He grabbed his spear and set off at a run towards his horse.

'Wait!' I shouted. 'I want to come with you!'

Xeno was mounted already, but he leaned down and stretched out a hand. He hoisted me onto the horse's rump behind him and raced off towards the west.

As we got closer, the sound of the flutes grew more distinct and we could soon make out a line of warriors carrying a litter on their shoulders with the body of their commander, completely dressed in his best armour. At his side was the great crested helmet that symbolized his rank. A pyre had been erected at the eastern edge of the camp, made of pine trunks and branches. Four warriors stood around it, holding their torches high. Just as an officer was approaching to order them to lower their torches, another music rose in the distance: the warbling of flutes and a powerful drum beat, sounding a marching cadence.

Xeno turned in the direction of the sound and saw a long line of warriors bearing lighted torches advancing along the coast towards us. The flames were reflected in the still waters of the gulf, shedding a scarlet reflection that lapped at the keel of the beached warship. The last rays of the dying sun were swallowed up by the sea. Xeno turned to me. 'Our men,' he said, his eyes veiled with tears.

The warriors continued to arrive: Arcadians, Achaeans, Messenians, Laconians, all decked out in their armour, gripping their spears. They silently took their places in the ranks, filling in file after file, behind their comrades already in formation around the litter.

The entire army was present. All the survivors of the long march. When Chirisophus's body was placed on the pyre, when the four warriors set fire to the branches and the flames flared up in the sea breeze and illuminated the clearing, Agasias the Stymphalian shouted, 'Alalalai!'

He unsheathed his sword and started to beat it against his shield. The same shout erupted from thousands of mouths, thousands of swords glinted in the vermilion light of the blaze and were pounded hard on their bronze shields, with inexhaustible energy, until at last the flames began to subside.

The commander's sword was seared in the fire and ritually bent. His ashes and bones were gathered in an urn and then his name was shouted out ten times so that the echo would never die.

The army began to file out, one man after another, each making his way back to his own tent. Darkness settled over the field and the flames were slowly extinguished. We returned as well, our horse walking at a slow pace along the deserted beach.

'Now what will we do?' I asked, to break the unbearable silence.

'I don't know,' answered Xeno. He said nothing else.

XENO DID NOT forget the comrades who lay unburied on the hill where the army had been besieged, abandoned there after the battle in which the Arcadians and Achaeans risked annihilation. He couldn't stand the thought of leaving them to the mercy of predators and of the elements. He left the next morning with a sizeable force to see them to their final rest.

They circled around to approach the hill from the direction of the villages. It was a painful task that they faced: the bodies had been left there for more than five days and were already decomposing. Dogs and wild animals had ravaged the remains. Many of the men were no longer recognizable. Xeno had expected something of the sort, and had taken the veterans with him, knowing they would be better able to bear such a harrowing sight. Each of the fallen was buried with a short and simple rite, as the situation demanded, but not without tears. Seeing the comrades who they'd lived side by side with reduced to those conditions was heart-breaking. The men who had shared that endless adventure with them, run all the same risks, protected each other to the death. The friends whose voices they could still hear, singing, joking. An unspeakable torment.

The closer they came to the hill, the worse the sights they saw. There the fallen warriors were still clinging to one another in the last throes of hand-to-hand combat, one on top of another, weapons protruding from their chests, necks, stomachs. Strangely, not even the natives had been back to gather their dead, perhaps still fearing the reprisal of an army much greater in size than the one that actually remained.

It took all day to bury the fallen, but in the end many of the men were still missing. A mound of stones was raised to commemorate them, crowned with rings of braided oak and pine branches. Then each of the men gave his comrades a last farewell, in the way he felt best: a phrase, a wish, a memory, in the hope it would reach them in the dark houses of Hades. They returned to the camp in silence, with heavy hearts.

In the days that followed the army reunited in a single camp, but the situation we found ourselves in became nearly unbearable, even grotesque. Over time, Xeno's religious convictions had grown so strong that they had prevailed over any other considerations. The army wanted to move on, but Xeno insisted on offering a daily sacrifice to the gods, asking a priest to examine the entrails. An ill omen emerged every time. And the days passed without any decision being made. Some insinuated that the augur was secretly conspiring with Xeno to found a colony there and was trying to prevent the army from moving on, so that the project could take root. Xeno was indignant and asked the soldiers to choose a seer they trusted who would oversee the inspection of the entrails. Since the outcome continued unfavourable, provisions began to run low.

After this had gone on for some time, Neon, Sophos's lieutenant – perhaps meaning to demonstrate that he was worth as much as the late commander – led his unit on a raid inland without consulting the others.

It was a disaster. Neon was attacked by the troops of the Persian governor of the region as his men were intent on sacking some villages, and suffered heavy losses. A few of the soldiers broke ranks and returned to the main camp to report the news of the rout, and Xeno flew off to assist the survivors of that sorry expedition. They returned all together as evening was falling, defeated and depressed. It seemed that the army was doomed to lose one man after another until there were no more left to lose.

Dinner hadn't even been prepared yet when the enemy troops attacked the camp, forcing our men into an impromptu counter-attack, with yet more losses. The generals ordered a double circle of sentries to stand guard all night.

Xeno was shattered.

'It's the end, isn't it?' I asked him.

No answer.

'Who were those men who attacked us?'

'The troops of the Persian governor.'

'So there's no way out for us. You don't have to explain anything any more: I understand what's going on. The closer we get to your homeland, the more the noose tightens. The Persians and the Spartans want the same thing, for different reasons: to see the army destroyed.'

Xeno didn't even try to deny it. 'That's why I wanted to keep the men here. I would have saved them by founding a colony. But they still want to go home.'

'And they'll walk straight into a trap.'

'I don't know about that. The last word hasn't been said.'

'So you think there is a way out?'

'I trust in the gods and in the spears of my men.'

'The gods? Their responses have kept us nailed to this place, putting us on the verge of starvation, with this disaster as a result. How many men did Neon lose?'

'If we'd moved despite the ill omens the result would have been far worse. The gods have always assisted us. No one would have bet a penny that we'd get this far. So close to home.'

'But you don't want to go home. You want to stay here and found your colony.'

'That's not true. And anyway, you have no right to meddle with my plans.'

'All right then, I won't. I can only hope your gods will help you.'

I realized that I had spoken with a tone of complete disbelief and I immediately felt sorry. Hadn't the gods saved me when I was completely alone and lost in that blizzard? I should have been the first to believe in them. But the growing toll of dead and wounded distressed me no end. I was afraid we were heading to our ruin. The army was being bled by nearly daily losses and would be completely demoralized and exhausted by the time they would, inevitably, find themselves up against the most difficult test: win or die.

And yet Xeno continued to worry about his men, and not only those who were still alive. Next day he mounted another mission to bury the bodies of the fallen.

This time he brought the young warriors with him, because in case of attack their reaction would be more vigorous, but it turned out to be bitter work indeed. The path they travelled was strewn with corpses, but only when they reached the inland villages did they realize the scale of the massacre. There were hundreds of bodies, so many that they had to dig a common grave.

And the worst was yet to come. The Persian governor had been holding his troops in check, but they suddenly appeared in full battle order on a rocky ridge that blocked the Greeks' way back. Our men were greatly outnumbered, and caught in an exposed position. Timas was at the head of the cavalry, while Xeno took command of the rest of the force.

I wasn't there, so what I know I heard later from the soldiers and from Xeno himself, and perhaps I've added something from my imagination, but what happened then was nothing short of miraculous. Maybe it was the sight of their comrades slaughtered and left to the dogs that made them understand how desperate their situation was and that they had nothing to lose. Maybe it was Xeno's battle plan that made the difference, or maybe it was the gods rewarding him for all those animals he'd sacrificed in their honour, but the army seemed to be possessed by some superhuman force when Xeno yelled out, 'It's them! They are the ones who butchered your comrades and now they want to cut you to pieces as well. Show them what you're made of, my lads, they're all yours! Forward!'

The young warriors ran straight up the slope, protected by their shields, shouting the war cry that had routed the left wing of the imperial army at the gates of Babylon. They overran every obstacle and overcame all resistance, slicing into the enemy formation like a sword into living flesh. They charged like angry bulls, massacring those who dared to fight back. Shoulder to shoulder, shield to shield.

When Timas unleashed his horsemen there was neither order nor rank among the enemy: each man was bent on escape and they were mown down by the hundred.

I saw them only when they returned to camp, drenched with sweat, filthy with dirt and blood, marching in step to the sound of flutes. The eyes behind the sallets of their helmets were still flaming.

They were singing. Their song throbbed and thundered in the bronze that covered them.

THE THREAT OF further attacks on the camp convinced the commanders it would be best to regroup on the peninsula. They barricaded the isthmus with a trench and a palisade. Everyone was saying that the Spartan governor of Byzantium, Cleander, would soon arrive in person to get them out of that fix, and so it was thought best to stay at Calpe and wait.

This situation dragged on at some length, and Xeno's old dream came to the fore again. He was the man whom all the other commanders came to when they had a problem: he always gave the right counsel, the best mix of prudence and courage. The place they occupied was ideal for a settlement: the peninsula that widened out into the sea could host a city which would be easily defended in case of attack, the port was well protected and in the lee of the most dangerous winds, a spring at the base of the isthmus would guarantee their water supply, and all around was a vast, fertile area with fine red soil.

A rumour spread that a colony was to be founded there. Although Xeno always denied it, I think it was him, or someone close to him, who put the word out. Native chieftains began to show up to get information and establish contact. The soldiers were antagonized by this; they'd long been suspicious of Xeno and afraid that they would be tricked or forced into staying there against their will.

Cleander's arrival with a mere two warships was a great disappointment. It certainly wasn't the fleet they were expecting to take them home. The situation worsened when a quarrel broke out between one of Cleander's men and one of our soldiers, who was promptly arrested and was being taken to the naval camp of the Spartan commander. The soldier was one of Agasias's men, and his commander recognized him, as well as the man who was dragging him off.

Agasias flew into a fury. 'You fucking bastard of a traitor! What hole did you crawl out of, you son of a bitch? How dare you show your face around here? Take your hands of that boy right now!'

Agasias had recognized Dexippus, the man who had fled with one of the two ships the inhabitants of Trapezus had lent us. In a flash, Agasias was on top of him and he would have run him through had not someone pulled them apart. Dexippus slipped away and took off towards the ships, but Agasias charged after him like a bull, knocked him to the ground and started to pummel him with his fists. He would have beaten him to a pulp if the Spartans aboard the ships hadn't heard the din. Their commander came out. 'That's enough!' he shouted. 'Let that man go!'

But at that point Agasias's men had come to their commander's aid with their swords drawn. The Spartans unsheathed theirs as well and for a few moments the tension ran incredibly high. Anything might have happened.

Xeno was close to me and I looked into his eyes without saying a word, but his expression told me that he'd finally caught on: the Spartans in Byzantium had been alerted to our presence by none other than Dexippus, thief and traitor. Perhaps he'd always been a spy! So that was why the Spartans were ready and waiting at the beach when Sophos arrived with his men. And soon after that, our commander – the only man in the entire army to know all the details of the enormous plot to let the Ten Thousand win or dispatch them to die – was dead himself.

Other officers intervened and so did Xeno. The brawl was halted.

Next day our generals began to negotiate with the Spartans. In the end they decided that the army would resume their march in the direction of the straits.

I wept that night. Xeno's hopes had been dashed and the army was setting off for the last march.

Towards death.

30

I HAD ALWAYS IMAGINED that the adventure of the Ten Thousand, of the heroes who had fought and won against all opposition, even the forces of nature, would end in an all-out battle.

We were together again, under Xeno's command, and no one had ever defeated the united army. It was only when groups had cut loose from the whole that they had ventured off on rash initiatives and suffered losses. This would not happen again. Agasias himself, with the support of Xanthi, had proposed and passed a resolution imposing the death sentence on anyone who tried to split up the army again.

Maybe we'd be attacked on open ground; perhaps we'd find ourselves surrounded by an overwhelming host and buried beneath thousands of arrows. Maybe hordes of barbarians would be hired to wipe us out in a night-time attack, or perhaps our ships would be sunk as we tried to cross the sea. But none of this happened. Once we reached Byzantium, the army – what was left of it – left the heroic space of vast battlefields, sky-high mountains, turbulent, unknown rivers and savage tribes so fiercely jealous of their liberty, to return to the space where ordinary mortals dwelled.

The Great War between the Athenians and the Spartans had swallowed up the best of their energy and cut down the bravest and most intelligent men, leaving the field to mediocre players, to petty schemers bearing high-sounding titles like admiral and governor. Where had the red cloaks gone who fought at the Fiery Gates against the innumerable forces of the Great King?

Not even their memory remained. Their descendants had only been capable of plotting intrigues, secretly conniving with their old enemies to approve unavowable agreements. All they were interested in was power. The control of their little world. Ideals were lost.

What happened then was so confused, so baffling, uncertain and contradictory, that it's even difficult for me to remember it. Cleander and his admiral, Anaxibius, played a vile and dirty game, tricking and deceiving us, promising without delivering. Perhaps their strategy was to make the army lose cohesion and break apart without leaving any traces. They certainly didn't have the courage to challenge us on the battlefield. Six thousand warriors who had marched thirty thousand stadia, overwhelming any force that opposed them, still commanded an awed respect. Better not to risk it.

The army was forced to remain outside the city walls, without money or supplies, and told to wait. Only those who were sick or wounded were allowed to enter.

The person who disappointed me most was Xeno, and I'm still saddened by it. He simply wasn't himself. He acted as though this situation were acceptable, and nothing untoward had happened. He even told me that things had changed; the army was no longer a threat to Sparta and our lives were no longer at risk.

'My mission is over,' he said to me one evening while we were camped outside the city walls. 'I'm leaving the army.'

I couldn't believe my ears. 'Leaving the army? Why?'

'The governor has told me that if the army doesn't move on, the government of Sparta will hold me personally responsible.'

'And that's enough to make you abandon the men you've shared everything with, life and death, for so long? The men that Sophos entrusted to you before he died?'

'I have no choice. I can't fight alone against the power that dominates all of Greece.'

'You're not alone. You have an army.'

'You don't know what you're saying. Do you know what the governor means when he says he's holding me responsible? That if we don't leave, he'll call in Spartan forces and they'll slaughter us. This city is in an incredibly important strategic position. It's the link between Asia and Europe, between the Aegean and the Euxine seas. Do you really think that Sparta would leave it in the hands of a mercenary army? This story is over. At least for me.'

I thought I'd die. The moment had come for me to pay for the choice I'd made that night at the well of Beth Qadà. How much time had passed? A year? Ten years? It seemed to me that a whole lifetime had passed. But I still wasn't sorry. I'd learned from the Ten Thousand that every obstacle can be overcome, every battle won. I'd learned never to surrender.

'Where will you go?' I asked him. 'And where will I go?'

'I don't know yet. Someplace where Greek is spoken, and you'll come with me. I've collected great experience in this expedition, I could become a good military or political adviser, perhaps in Italy or Sicily. There are wealthy cities there where a man with my knowledge is welcomed, and well paid.'

I didn't know what to reply. I was torn. On the one hand, his words consoled me: he wouldn't leave me and I'd see new lands with him, beautiful, faraway cities; perhaps I'd have a house, and servants. On the other hand, to abandon the army seemed shameful to me, and I was troubled by his decision.

'They're not alone,' said Xeno. 'They have their commanders: Timas, Agasias, Xanthi, Cleanor, Neon. They'll be all right. I've done everything I could, no one can blame me. How many times have I risked my own life? How many of their lives have I saved?'

He was right, but that didn't change things for me. I couldn't give up.

We moved into a house in the city that was quite comfortable, with a kitchen and a bedroom, and we had our servant with us to take care of our needs. Xeno continued to meet with important people, but he never told me anything.

One day a man with an unpronounceable name showed up. He was from Thebes and he wanted to take command of the army. He said he would pay their salaries and buy their supplies. He wanted to lead them on raids into an area inhabited by native tribes, but when he returned several days later with only a few cartloads of flour, garlic and onions, they gave him a kick in the backside and started throwing the onions at him until he disappeared. That was the last straw. They'd had enough.

It was what happened next that pushed events to a head. The governor sent his closest collaborator and political adviser to talk to Xeno; they met at our house. I can't remember his name, but I'll never forget his face or the look in his eyes.

'The city authorities are well aware of all the trials you have been through,' he began. 'We'd like to do more for you, but the governor has his hands tied. All the same, he wants to make a gesture of good will on your behalf. He has managed to find enough provisions and money to enable all of you to return to your homes, and wishes to host a celebration in your honour. A farewell party, as it were. You'll be welcomed inside the city and there will be food and wine for all. Your men will be the guests of our citizens; if there is not enough room for all of them, they will be allowed to sleep under the city porticoes. All of the officers and their bodyguards will be the personal guests of the governor.

'After this celebration, the army will be given a full month's worth of provisions – more than enough time for you to dismiss the men and send them on their way. There are several ports along the coast. With the money you'll be given, it won't be difficult to book passage on ships setting sail for a number of destinations.'

Xeno felt that this was much more than a simple gesture of good will; he believed that he had finally made peace with the

Spartans, and this filled him with relief and joy. But he wanted to take no risks, and before accepting, he said, 'My men will never agree to part with their weapons. Is that a problem?'

'Certainly not,' replied the messenger. 'We are friends, aren't we? And we share the same blood.'

These words reassured Xeno, and he accepted. The army would at last be moving on. He parted with Cleander's associate on good terms.

Xeno spread the news that things had finally taken a turn for the better. He convened the men and gave them instructions. 'There will be no disorders, nor quarrels, no violence of any sort. You will not use your weapons except in self-defence if someone should attack you, otherwise you will take no initiatives. When the celebrations are over, you'll find a number displayed on the houses of Byzantium; this will indicate how many of you can be accommodated there. Those who do not find room will sleep under the porticoes or the temple colonnades. The next morning, I want you all out of there and ready to leave. If all goes well, in a few days' time you'll have food and money enough to return to your homes.'

A burst of enthusiasm greeted his words. The men began to prepare their best garments and to polish their armour so as to make a good show at the festivities. There was even a rumour going around that there would be a parade.

Two days later they entered the city and the celebrations began. Xeno and most of the officers took part in a banquet hosted by the governor. I accompanied Xeno.

The sounds of laughing and good-natured joking that filtered in from outside let us know the men were having a good time. Beautiful dancers entered the banquet hall, and elegantly garbed girls who went to sit with the officers. I caught a glimpse of Melissa, standing next to Cleanor. The look she shot me led me to understand that she had something to tell me. She gave me a little wave and I walked over to join her.

'What is it?' I asked.

Melissa was all smiles, answering with the most frivolous of tones and punctuating her words with silly little giggles as if she were repeating some risqué titbit. But what she had to tell me was deadly serious. 'Listen, I met a girlfriend of mine from Lampsacus who's the companion of one of Cleander's officers. She has overheard some very interesting conversations. This party is a complete sham.'

It was what I'd suspected, but I'd never dared share my worries with Xeno. He was so sure that the Spartans had good intentions that I didn't want to ruin things for him, or maybe, for once, tired as I was of all those continuing threats, I wanted to believe it myself.

'When the partying is over and all the men have split up and found a place to sleep, the Spartan contingent here is going to conduct a massive round-up operation. Our men will be scattered all over the city in small groups and won't be able to fight back. The plan is to kill them all, or take prisoners and sell them as slaves.'

I felt my knees buckling and I had to lean against the wall.

'Smile!' ordered Melissa. 'Pretend I'm telling you some entertaining little story. We can't let on we know anything.'

'Have you told Cleanor?'

'No. But if Xeno agrees to pass word on to the other officers, give me a signal and I'll tell him straight away.'

'All right,' I replied.

While Melissa was rejoining Cleanor, I told Xeno everything. He paled, then started to get to his feet.

'No, wait,' I said. 'Don't move. I've already agreed with Melissa that when I give her a signal she'll tell Cleanor and he'll pass the word on. Everyone will be alerted.'

'All right. As soon as you can, get another message to Melissa, and tell her to pass it on. When I get up from the table, the others should all follow me out, acting in the most natural way possible.'

'I will.'

'Someone should inform the men before they begin to scatter. Better for you to go; you won't be missed here. Agasias is outside. Find him and tell him.'

'I can do that. I'll leave as soon as I'm sure no one will notice.'

In the meantime, I'd nodded to Melissa, who whispered something to Cleanor. He glanced at Xeno with a significant look.

'Wait,' continued Xeno. 'Listen carefully. Tell Agasias that when they see an incendiary arrow shooting into the sky all the men should gather in the main square. All of them, understand?'

I left.

It wasn't easy to find Agasias, who was outside with his men, but I managed to pass on the order. While the festivities were at a peak, the entire army began to assemble, under the surprised and worried eyes of the onlookers, in the city's main square. Shortly thereafter, a flaming arrow rose into the sky and a war cry broke loose. Xeno and the others ran up, arms in hand.

The men were infuriated.

This time the city would hear the roar of the Ten Thousand.

At Xeno's order, they stormed the citadel, overran the city's defences and occupied the fort. The garrison was taken by surprise and the men who staffed it were forced to surrender.

The governor and his admiral were notified of what was happening, and they promptly escaped, putting out to sea on a ship.

The soldiers lifted Xeno onto their shoulders and carried him to the general headquarters of the Spartan garrison. The commanders flanked them, decked out in their best armour. The city was at their feet!

'Byzantium is ours!' they were shouting. 'And ours it will remain!'

'Yes, we'll tax and levy tolls on all the goods in transit for the straits and we'll grow rich. With the money we get we'll enlist more soldiers – we know where to get them – and no one will be able to drive us out.'

'We can form alliances with the tribal nations inland. We'll become a great power, and everyone will have to reckon with us!'

They were right. That's what they should have done. But to carry out such a project they needed a leader who was capable of dreaming the impossible and turning it into reality. Xeno was not that man. He had courage, and had proved it, he could devise clever strategies, but not build dreams. He could only conceive of doing what was realistically possible, and only after consulting the gods to make sure they agreed. The army spent the night in the square.

Before dawn, a messenger from Cleander, who had entered the city in disguise, informed Xeno that seizing the citadel would be considered an act of war by Sparta. If Xeno didn't resolve the disastrous situation, the affair would end in a bloodbath.

That morning, Xeno convinced the assembled army that it was necessary to leave the city. He asked them to trust him, and promised that he would negotiate acceptable conditions with the Spartans. If they wanted to avoid the most dire consequences, they would have to surrender the city. Only then would the Spartan governor agree to help them.

Crestfallen and dissatisfied, the Ten Thousand, or what was left of them, abandoned Byzantium.

THE RUNAWAY RULERS returned, furious at having been exposed as cowards, but they continued to stall any real solution, and to provide just enough supplies for the men to survive.

The soldiers became despondent. They saw no future in store and many sold their armour and scattered. Many officers as well. Some of the most valiant, including Aristonymus of Methydria and Lycius of Syracuse, vanished without saying goodbye. Glous, whom I'd continued to see every now and then, disappeared as well.

They probably couldn't bear the wretchedness of the situation and the pain of so bitter a parting. A new governor arrived in the city. He arrested all the wounded and ailing soldiers who had been allowed to remain within the walls and sold them off as slaves. Xeno knew about it but did nothing; I suppose he thought it was the lesser of two evils.

In the end, after further unnerving and exhausting delays and negotiations, the conclusion was that nobody wanted a band of uncontrollable and dangerous mercenaries hanging around. The solution finally arrived, whether by chance or strategy I couldn't say. A barbarian prince from Thrace called Seuthes offered to engage the entire army and to pay the soldiers, officers and generals in coin, each in proportion to his rank. Xeno put the proposal to a vote and it was accepted.

A sign of the times: just under a year ago they had departed under the orders of Prince Cyrus, and now they were in the pay of a man dressed in fox hides, with a fur hat on his head instead of a tiara.

Fortunately, Timas and Neon agreed to come along, as did Agasias, Xanthi and even Cleanor, so I could be with Melissa.

Seuthes's plan was to reconquer his lost kingdom in Thrace by attacking in the middle of winter, when no one expected it.

A harsh, horrible winter, perhaps even colder than the one we'd spend in the mountains of Asia. Many of our men suffered frostbite and lost their ears and noses, remaining disfigured their whole lives. Handsome young men, who would never be able to look at a woman again without feeling ashamed.

I couldn't help but weep when I found myself on my own. An infinite sadness weighed on my heart. I cried because I could not adapt to such a wretched life, to such a narrow horizon, to men who seemed like mice. But I had no choice.

And I cried when Xeno agreed to marry one of the daughters of Seuthes. Necessary for political reasons, he told me. Fortunately, the wedding never took place. We had more important things to think about. Like surviving.

Xeno had started writing again. He wrote more than ever. This irritated me. What was so interesting that it deserved to be marked down on that white parchment, in such a freezing, barbarous land, among those hairy creatures, where squabbles between villages became wars?

On those evenings when Xeno was at dinner with the other high officers in Seuthes's hut, I would invite Melissa to have dinner with me. Talking with her felt good for my soul.

'I don't understand you,' she would say. 'Xeno did the best thing! What did you expect? That he'd raze Byzantium to the ground and stand up to the most powerful force in Greece on his own? This life is tough, I'll grant you that, but at least we have food and shelter. Once the winter is over we'll look for a solution. Don't lose heart.'

I didn't know what to answer. I would prepare a little warm milk with honey by the fire, the only thing that gave me some joy, a small luxury I could share with my friend. And Melissa had wonderful stories to share, stories that would always make me smile, in the end. About how she'd seduced important personages: heads of state, governors, philosophers, artists, all at her feet. She had used them. By giving them the single thing they wanted she'd obtained countless things from them: houses, jewels, gowns, perfumes, delicacies, parties and receptions.

'You know,' she'd tell me, 'to tell you the truth, I never held on to any of that stuff. You know, to live the life I did, you always had to be elegant, stylish, made up, sweetly scented, and all that cost a pretty penny. Sometimes I think, what if Cyrus had won . . . can you imagine? I would have been his mistress and he would have covered me in gold . . . But that's life, right? Too bad. Anyway, Cleanor is a real man. A real bull, I should say! And he treats me well. He gives me everything he can. But when this disgusting war is over, I'm going to go to some nice city on the coast where there's money to be had. I'll find a nice little place to receive special guests and I'll be good as new again in no time. It's easy, you know? You put on a little transparent something, a pretty pair of sandals, and let yourself be admired as you go to the temple to offer a couple of doves to Aphrodite. Then you let out what baths you like to visit and . . . that's that! Once they've caught a glimpse of you naked they'll pay any sum. If you have the body, obviously. You know, Abira, you're not so bad yourself. If Xeno ever leaves you, you'd have a future with me. We'd do well together!'

'Oh, right,' I'd say. 'You know, I'd come with you gladly, but I don't know how to seduce a man. I could be your maid, though. We'd have lots of laughs together, wouldn't we?'

And we'd giggle away the melancholy of those long nights.

One evening I gave in to temptation and asked her to do something I never should have asked: to read me what Xeno had written.

'Why would you ask me to do that? We did it once and it got both of us in trouble. Xeno cares about you, he's always wanted you with him. His writing is something he never shows to anybody, right?'

'Yes, you're right. But I must know what's written on that scroll.'

'Most likely nothing of what you're expecting. He's probably writing down his thoughts on life, the principles, virtues and vices. He was a student of Socrates, you know.'

'Socrates the Achaean? I didn't know they knew each other back in Greece.'

'No. Another Socrates, his teacher. The greatest thinker of our time.'

'I don't think you're right. Xeno is writing the story of this expedition. Just read me the last part.'

'But why?'

'Because I'm looking for the answer to a question I've been wondering about for a long time.'

'It's not a good idea. You know why? What a person thinks and writes when he's alone might not be the truth. The truth is what you do in reality, the way you act. It's facts, not words, that count.'

'Please. I've always been your friend, even when . . .'

'. . . I betrayed you?'

I hesitated a moment before I said: 'No, that's not what I meant.' But it was too late and Melissa had understood.

'All right,' she said. 'As you wish. I owe you and I'll do as you ask, but it's a mistake and it could ruin your life.'

'I know,' I answered. And I opened the drawer.

'Where should I start?' asked Melissa. 'Each stage of the expedition has a number.'

'From where we left off.'

'From when we were still at the river?'

'Yes, from there.'

Melissa started reading and I listened from the entrance to the hut with the door half-closed so I could warn her if I saw Xeno or anyone else arriving. I had my back turned to her, and she couldn't see the expression in my eyes or my face as she continued.

The story narrated what had happened, from Xeno's point of view, and the events flowed rapidly through my mind, sometimes as vivid images of facts that I'd witnessed myself personally, dialogues that I'd heard myself or had him repeat. He spoke of himself as if he were speaking of another person. He didn't say 'I'; he said 'Xenophon.' Perhaps he found it embarrassing to speak well or badly of himself. There was no mention of the battle of the crater. That day of glory, worthy of being remembered for all time, would leave no trace, and it was because all those deaths weighed too heavily on his conscience. Because his mistake, even though involuntary, lay at the source of that trail of blood. The story ended with what had happened five days earlier. He'd been very busy in the past few days and hadn't had time to update his account.

Melissa replaced the scroll in the drawer and said, 'It finishes here.' I turned without thinking, to thank her, and she glared back at me.

'You have tears in your eyes. I told you so.'

'I'm sorry,' I answered. 'I didn't want . . .'

'I knew this would happen. If it had been up to me . . .'

'He didn't say a word about anything that happened on our journey down the Araxes river, that much we'd already seen. But not a word about the battle of the crater, about all those who fell there . . . I suppose I could have expected that. But it has saddened me terribly. Forgive me, Melissa, I'll never ask you to do this again. Next time we'll talk about other things. I promise.' I gave her a kiss and she walked back to her lodging as it began to snow.

THE ARMY FOUGHT from mid-autumn until nearly the end of winter: night assaults, raids, exhausting marches, combat on the open field. They were spared nothing, and yet they continued to do battle, as they had always done, to survive, as Commander Clearchus had ordered them to do when he addressed them for the first time. But there was no future, no one knew what would happen at the end of that small bloody war. A destiny of slow, steady destruction seemed to be playing out day after day.

Sometimes the thoughts that tormented me seemed to be the fruit of my imagination. I tried to marshal all the coincidences, the many tragic events, the ambushes, the betrayals, trying to find the logic that tied them all together. Had the ambush at the crater been planned or did it happen by chance? And then? After that? Had the Spartans ever really wanted to completely wipe out the Ten Thousand? Or had they simply given up along the way? After all, the final massacre that I was expecting – and that perhaps Xeno was expecting, although he never told me so – never took place. Ever since Heraclea, when the army had split up and Xeno first mentioned us going off on our own and leaving everyone behind, a terrible thought had been worming its way into my mind. Had Xeno wanted to abandon the army to its destiny out of fear? So as not to share its fate when the day of reckoning finally arrived?

He'd said the same thing again in Byzantium. But then he changed his mind: he assumed his responsibilities with courage and wisdom. Yes, wisdom was the right word. In my mind's eye I always saw the young hero I'd met one spring evening at the well of Beth Qadà, and now I felt I couldn't accept the prudent person who carefully took stock of his experiences and was capable only of realistic calculations. The religious man who, having been saved so many times by chance, now depended on the gods to ensure his survival. But most of all, I couldn't accept what Melissa had read to me; it was difficult for me to separate the man from what he wrote. I kept hoping that the man I loved would win me over again and dissipate my doubts by making a gesture of true generosity.

ONE DAY at the end of the winter the situation had become dire. The army hadn't been paid in some time and Seuthes, the Thracian prince who had hired them, was avoiding Xeno when he asked to be received. In a stormy assembly, Xeno was accused by some of his men of having pocketed the money destined for the army.

Nothing like that had ever happened to Xeno; he had never received such a grievous insult. I expected him to whip out his sword to make the man who'd spoken swallow his words, but Xeno gave an impassioned speech instead on everything he had done for his men, a heartfelt defence of his deeds and his decisions.

We'd touched bottom. The plotting of those who meant to destroy an extraordinary army of invincible warriors was revealed now as it played out according to plan.

Everything had an explanation, its own glaring logic. Since the army had succeeded in returning more or less to the world it had departed from, and the word of what it had achieved had leaked out, a violent end would only serve to multiply their glory beyond measure and would dangerously draw the whole world's attention. Better, then, to confine the army instead to this mean, narrow, hopeless existence and to wait until exasperation, disappointment and frustration corroded the monolith of bronze that had forced the soldiers of the Great King to their knees. Whatever remained of its decomposed body would be washed away with the mud of the spring thaw.

That's exactly what was happening. I looked at Agasias, Timas, Xanthi, Cleanor. No one spoke up to defend him. I looked at Xeno. His eyes were glittering with tears, with pain more than indignation. He had once been left disaffected and drifting, a man with no hope of making an honourable name for himself in his homeland. But then he'd made the army his homeland and his city, and each time he'd thought of leaving it, he'd never succeeded. He'd always stayed where his honour and his affection had placed him.

Xeno asked his officers if they had nothing to say. Some of the men defended him, others hurled insults. Scuffles broke out, and some drew their weapons.

There. That was to be our miserable end. An unworthy end that would obscure the glory of the Ten Thousand. Dying at each other's hands in some lonely place in Thrace, abusing and cutting each other to pieces over some sheep and a handful of coins.

But just when all seemed lost . . .

The sound of galloping hoofs!

A band of mounted warriors.

Red cloaks!

The fighting stopped abruptly, the men regained their composure. The officers, shouting and cursing, hustled their soldiers into formation. Xeno mounted Halys.

I was trembling. What could be going on?

Two men on horseback stopped in front of Xeno and saluted him. It was a formal, fundamental gesture. It acknowledged him commander of the army.

'Welcome,' said Xeno. 'Who are you and what has brought you here?'

They were Spartan officers. 'We've been sent by the city and by the kings on an important mission. We ask to address the army in the name of Sparta.'

'You are authorized to do so,' Xeno replied, and ordered the men to present arms. Their shields were lifted to their chests, their spears thrust forward with a sharp metallic sound.

The first of the two officers spoke. 'Men! The news of your exploits has spread throughout Greece and filled the Hellenes with pride. The valour you have shown is beyond all imagining. You arrived where no Greek army had ever gone, you held the armies of the Great King in check, you have overcome insurmountable obstacles, and at the price of enormous sacrifices, you are here. We wish to render honour to your commander, Xenophon, whose devotion and dedication to duty has no equal.'

Many of the officers and soldiers were looking at each other with thinly concealed amazement: what was happening? Wasn't it the Spartans who had sold their wounded and ailing comrades as slaves in Byzantium, who had plotted to kill them all? Wasn't it a Spartan governor who had threatened to wipe them out if they didn't leave his territory?

'Warriors,' the officer's voice thundered on, 'Sparta and all of Greece need you! The Great King seeks to take over the Greek cities of Asia, just as Darius and Xerxes did eighty years ago! We said no then, and we rallied at the Fiery Gates. We are saying no now, and we have landed in Asia. The man we face is Tissaphernes, your sworn enemy, the man who fought and betrayed and persecuted you in every way. In the name of Sparta I ask you to join us in Asia, there where your great adventure began under the orders of Commander Clearchus. You will be fed and paid according to your rank, and you will be able to take revenge on those who inflicted such suffering upon you. What do you answer me, men?'

The warriors hesitated for a moment, and then exploded into a roar, raising their spears to the sky.

THE RED CLOAKS went back to wherever they had come from.

Xeno managed to get Seuthes to pay the army, partly in money and partly in livestock, and we set off again at the beginning of spring. When we arrived in Asia, Xeno found himself so badly off that he had to sell his horse. He was not a man easily moved, but this time he was truly anguished. He stroked his steed's long mane, laid his cheek against the magnificent animal's head. He couldn't stand to be parted from Halys. He was selling a faithful, generous friend. He was suffering, and ashamed.

Halys seemed to understand that this was their farewell. He snorted and whinnied, and pawed at the ground. When Xeno handed the reins to the dealer, the horse reared up and hammered the air with his front hoofs.

Xeno bit his lip and turned away to hide his tears.

I felt sorry for him. Why was it all ending this way? His fervent love of adventure, his wild dreams of greatness and glory, the torrid nights of love we'd shared. It had shattered, all of it; day by day it was crumbling away.

Xeno was increasingly obsessed by religion. His biggest concern was always where to find animals he could sacrifice so as to learn the will of the gods. He would try to interpret the omen himself, his hands fumbling through the steaming bowels of the victims, or would enlist the aid of seers and soothsayers.

The dream was dying slowly in the grey, monotonous fog that smothered our hearts and minds.

But the army was hungry.

There would be no pay until we reached the assembly point and so, to survive, the army began again to do what it had always done: raiding and plundering. This time it was the properties of Persian noblemen who lived in the inland villas and castles.

During one of those attacks, Agasias of Stymphalus, the fearless warrior, hero of a thousand battles, inseparable companion, was mortally wounded. Xeno wasn't with him when it happened, and anyway there was nothing to be done: an arrow had pierced his liver. Cleanor ran to him under a rain of darts, and covered him with his shield. I saw what was happening and tried to bring them some bandages, but I had to crouch behind a boulder just short of where they were to avoid getting killed myself. I could hear the arrows crackling like hail against the stone that protected me and against Cleanor's bronze shield.

'Leave me,' I could hear Agasias telling him. 'Save yourself. It was bound to happen sooner or later.'

'No,' replied Cleanor, sobbing. 'Not like this ... not now ...'

'One arrow is like another, my friend. What difference does it make? We sell our lives to the highest bidder, but in the end ... in the end, we're all hired out ... by death.'

Cleanor closed his eyes and ran off to rally the men for a counter-attack.

Xeno wasn't there for the counter-attack either. He was back in camp. His main worry had become preserving the booty. He knew that every time the sun rose he had to feed his boys, like a father, and to feed the gods with the victims of his sacrifices.

As WE NEARED our destination, a couple of officers from the invasion force arrived to make contact with us. They were Bion and Nausiclides of Sparta, and they became quite friendly with Xeno. A few days later, having learned that he had been forced to sell the horse that he was so fond of, they managed to buy him back and they brought him to Xeno. That was another scene I shall never forget. Xeno saw his horse at a distance and knew him at once; he started shouting, 'Halys! Halys!' With a sharp tug of his proud head, the horse jerked the reins free of the hands of the servant who was leading him and set off at a gallop, neighing and whipping the air with his tail.

I think they were both crying as they got closer, as Halys's master stroked his velvety muzzle and fiery nostrils.

Finally, late that spring, we reached our destination and Xeno delivered the survivors of the Ten Thousand to the Spartan commander, Thibron. After two years of incredible adventures they were once again waging war against their old enemy.

I said goodbye to Melissa and she sobbed in my arms. Xeno bade farewell to his remaining friends: Timas whose eyes were black as night, Cleanor the bull, Xanthi of the flowing locks, and Neon, the enigmatic heir of Commander Sophos, and then all the others as well.

And then he was alone.

YES, ALONE. Because I was no longer the same person that I'd been for him until then. Alone, because he had lost the army, his only homeland, and I could certainly not fill that huge void. His heart had been broken, and was full of despair. I knew that soon I would not be enough for him.

My story with Xeno was ending, I could feel it. The story that started when I met a young warrior at the well one spring evening long, long ago.

Despite this we continued to journey together, the two of us and our servant, barely talking, until we reached a city on the coast where Xeno thought he would get news from home.

And so he did.

There was a letter for him, held by the priest of the temple of Artemis. He sat on a marble bench under the colonnade and read it intently. I stood in silence, awaiting my verdict.

In the end, I couldn't stand the tension that was wringing at my heart, and I spoke.

'I hope there's not bad news,' I said.

'No. My family is well.'

'I'm glad.'

He seemed to hesitate.

'Is there something else?'

'Yes,' he replied, lowering his gaze. 'I have a wife.'

I felt my heart exploding in my chest, but I forced myself to speak. 'I'm sorry ... what does that mean, "I have a wife"?'

'It means that my parents have chosen a bride for me and that I will marry her.'

The tears were pouring down my cheeks now and I was futilely trying to dry them with the sleeve of my tunic. There would be no Italy, no Sicily, no beautiful cities that I'd dreamed of seeing with him. For me there would be nothing. No adventure, no journey, nothing.

He looked at me with a gentle gaze. 'Don't cry. I won't send you away. I can keep you with me ... you can stay with some relatives of mine, and we'll be able to see each other now and then.'

'No, I won't come,' I replied with no hesitation. 'That's not a life I could live. But don't worry. When I left with you, I knew it wouldn't be for always. I've been preparing myself every day for when this moment would arrive.'

'You don't know what you're saying,' he replied. 'Where could you go on your own?'

'Home. I have no other place to go.'

'Home? You don't even know how to get there.'

'I'll find it. Farewell, Xeno.'

He looked at me with a deeply troubled look and for an instant I hoped with all my heart that he would stop me. Even as I was already walking down the temple steps I was hoping that he'd call me back and that we'd find a ship and sail to Italy ... I finally heard his voice. 'Wait!'

He was running behind me and I turned to embrace him.

He was holding out his hand. 'At least take this,' he said. 'You'll have to buy yourself food, pay for your passage ... Please, take it.' He gave me a bag full of money.

'Thank you,' I said. And I ran away in tears.

Epilogue

ABIRA ENDED HER STORY one early winter night in the hut by the river. She'd left the city on the coast in the late spring and headed east, paying for passage with a caravan of Arabs bound for Jaffa. It took her thirty-two days to reach and cross the Cilician Gates. And another fifteen to arrive, on foot, at Beth Qadà.

When she stopped talking, there were hundreds of questions we were dying to ask her. We were curious about all sorts of things; so much of what she had told us had sparked our imaginations. We'd fantasized about them on our own but we'd never wanted to interrupt her tale, which was made even more fascinating by her enchanting voice, which trembled and shook and sighed as she narrated the stories of men and nature. But there were some questions we simply couldn't stifle.

'How did you feel,' I asked her, 'after Xeno disappointed you so terribly?'

'I thought that in any case I'd lived a life that was worth a thousand lives. I travelled through lands that none of you will ever see, I met extraordinary men and women. I bathed in rivers whose waters came from mountains as high as the sky, rushing into seas so distant their waves had never been ploughed by a ship, and into the river Ocean that encircles the earth.

'I felt suffocating heat and bone-chilling cold and I saw more stars in the night sky than I'll ever see again in all my life. I saw solitary fortresses perched on peaks covered with snow and ice, steep chasms and golden beaches, promontories carpeted with forests thousands of years old, peoples I never knew existed, garbed in strange and fascinating costumes. And I was loved . . .'

'What did you think when you returned here, to the village? What did you think you'd find here?'

'I don't know. I thought that my family would have welcomed me back and that with time they might even have forgotten what I'd done. I thought that I'd ask for the forgiveness of the boy I had been betrothed to, and try to explain the reasons for my irrevocable choice. Not that I thought he, or anyone, could understand. Or maybe, without realizing it, I was journeying towards death. Towards those who would kill me.'

'They didn't kill you,' said Abisag.

'Yes they did. That's what they meant to do, kill me. And intentions are stronger than actions. I'm alive by pure chance. A trick of fate and a gift from your hearts.'

'Abira,' Mermah broke in, 'what was it that wounded you so deeply when Melissa read you the words that Xeno had written? Was it only that he didn't mention those who had fallen in the great battle, or was there something else?'

Abira looked at us distractedly, wondering perhaps if it was right to reveal something that was never meant to be divulged, but then she answered: 'Yes, it was that, but there were other things as well . . .' and she stopped. Was she thinking of Xeno? Yes, she must have been, because her eyes were shiny.

The wind was blowing again. It rattled the hut's reed matting and slipped inside our clothes, giving us an uneasy chill, as the evening held its dark hands out over the rooftops of Beth Qadà.

'Other things,' she said finally. 'The first is how he remembered the death of Commander Sophos – "Chirisophus by this time was dead as a result of taking a drug while he was feverish" – that's all he wrote, nothing else. So few words that I can remember every one of them. So few words for the man who had chosen obedience over all else, scrapping every bit of humanity, and had accepted a horrifying mission: to lead Ten Thousand soldiers into a void. The man who always remained at their head, ready to

407

sacrifice himself, to endure the same pain, to suffer as much as a human heart can possibly suffer, ready to be their commander to the bitter end. The man who at the end let himself be convinced to rebel and to accept the penalty of his disobedience, to pay with his life for his decision of passing the command to him, to Xeno, so that Xeno could lead the army to safety.'

'But Xeno did his duty,' I said. 'He did save the army.'

'Yes. But, not to grieve for a man like Sophos, his best friend, the man with whom he shared every instant of that desperate march, not to commemorate his greatness, the light and the dark in his soul ... that is simply mean-hearted. There's no other explanation. And there is no greater pain than to have to admit such a thing to yourself about the man you love.'

We really couldn't completely understand what she was saying because she had grown accustomed to a closeness with men who were demons and gods at the same time. Beings whom we found it hard to imagine and would never have met. That's why we let the wind speak for long, endless moments, the rasping wind with its hint of the winter chill.

'And then?' piped up Abisag, finally.

'And then,' replied Abira, 'something about me.'

We watched her, holding our breath, waiting to hear what she would say.

' "From here, Xenophon entered Thrace; he had nothing with him but his servant and his horse." I was there, too,' she said. 'I was there with him.' And she burst into tears.

BY TELLING US the story of her journey and her experiences, it was as if Abira had emptied out her soul. Her vital energy had dissipated and dissolved into the air. Our care and food and affection had restored her to life, but now it seemed as if she didn't know what to do with it. She didn't want us to see her in such a melancholy mood because she didn't want to appear ungrateful. But if it was true that she'd come back to die, I wondered whether our saving her just meant that her fate had been postponed, but not changed. After her dreams and her reason for living were destroyed, she had decided to act like the Ten Thousand who had left a place only to wander at great length and then to return to that very same place. She wanted to close the circle.

My friends and I spoke of nothing but Abira when we brought the flocks out to pasture. Abira, and the people she'd told us about. It almost felt as if we knew them, and would recognize them if they appeared in front of us. Sometimes Abisag, who was the most naive of all of us, imagined that Xeno would return for her. Maybe he would realize that he couldn't live without her and maybe at that very moment he was tracing Abira's steps along the route that led to the Cilician Gates and to the Villages of the Belt. She liked to imagine that he would show up one evening at the well, dressed in shining armour, on a horse that pawed at the ground, as he waited for Abira to come to draw water. She could just see them running into each other's arms and promising never to part again.

Sweet, silly Abisag.

The days passed and the sky was always darker. The days grew shorter and sometimes the storms raging over the peaks of Mount Taurus would push their way to our villages, the wind an angry whistle.

Then one night, after we were already curled up under our covers, thinking of her so sad and alone in that little hut by the river, we heard the wind that roars! The wind that announces an extraordinary event.

Towards morning, a little before dawn, we heard the dogs yelping and then barking furiously. I got up and went on tiptoe to the window. The clustered houses of the other villages stood out against a pearl sky.

What was happening? The atmosphere was just like that day when Abira had been stoned. I could feel a strange, mounting excitement, growing stronger and stronger, out of control, while the dogs howled at invisible presences crossing the steppe.

I went outside dressed as I was, in my nightgown, wrapping a blanket around me, and went to wake up Mermah and Abisag. I met them along the road. They couldn't sleep either.

Together we left the village and went, arm-in-arm, towards the well. We were guided only by an indefinable sensation, following a kind of premonition that they say can come to young virgins when they first discover the mystery of their lunar period.

The roaring suddenly stopped, giving way to a dry, continuous wind, taut as a bow-string. A dust storm was advancing across the steppe. In no time, the outlines of things were lost. Real shapes became no more than shadows in the swirling dust. We pulled the blankets up to cover our heads and mouths and walked on until we could make out the figure of Abira. It was unmistakably her, standing straight and still outside the hut, her gown glued to her shapely body by the desert wind. She wasn't facing us, but seemed to be watching something ... We crouched down in the shelter of a thicket of palm trees so we wouldn't be seen, and looked in the same direction.

'Look!' gasped Mermah.

'Where?' asked Abisag.

'Over there, to the right.'

A nebulous shape was advancing towards us in the direction of Abira's hut, a ghostly figure that was becoming gradually more distinct as it approached and emerged from the dust. We heard the soft snorting of a horse and the jingle of armour.

He passed so close that we could have touched him: a horseman, wearing a polished suit of armour covered by a white cape, mounted on a powerful stallion, black as a crow's wing. Abira was coming towards him, her step uncertain as if she were trying to understand what kind of an apparition was materializing before her. Then we saw astonishment fill her eyes as she stood stock-still, watching him dismount from his horse and take off his helmet, freeing a head of blond hair as fine as silk.

Mermah moved and inadvertently snapped a twig. The noise made the warrior spin round and we saw his face. As beautiful as a god, with penetrating, blue-grey eyes. His sword already flashed in his hand.

'It's Menon!' whispered Abisag, her voice full of admiration and wonder. 'It's him.'

He was the snowy god who had appeared in the middle of the raging storm and had saved her from a frozen death, he the indistinct apparition that fluttered over mountains and forests, always too far away to see, he who everyone had thought dead together with the other commanders, the only one of them who could have survived: Menon, blond and fierce.

Abira came closer and they stood facing each other for a long time, both enveloped by his huge wind-whipped white cloak. We heard no words, saw no gestures. I had to imagine their deep, intense looks. Then the warrior helped her onto his stallion, leapt up behind her and touched his heels to the horse's flanks.

We came out of our hiding place with tears in our eyes as we watched them ride away and slowly disappear into the dust.

Author's Note

This story is based on one of the most famous works of Greek literature, the *Anabasis*, written by Xenophon of Athens. It is the diary of the expedition of ten thousand Greek mercenaries hired by the Persian prince Cyrus the Younger, who was plotting to overthrow his brother Artaxerxes, the Great King of the Persians, and seize his throne. One hundred thousand Asian soldiers joined them in the endeavour, but the Greeks were considered the spearhead of the entire army, those who would enable Cyrus to fulfil his ambitions.

Cyrus's army set off in the spring of 401 BC from Sardis, in Lydia, and reached the village of Cunaxa, at the gates of Babylon, towards the end of the summer. This is where the battle with the army of the Great King – whose forces greatly outnumbered theirs – took place, on a desert plain on the banks of the Euphrates. The Greeks charged the left wing of the enemy and overwhelmed them, then took off after them in close pursuit. But at the end of the day they were greeted by a bitter surprise: Cyrus had been defeated, his body impaled and decapitated.

Thus began the Greeks' long retreat through the desert, the mountains of Kurdistan and finally the desolate, icy expanse of the Armenian high plain in the middle of winter, all lands defended by savage tribes fiercely attached to their territory. What is most surprising is that an army of heavily armed infantrymen, accustomed to fighting on open ground and in a close formation, managed to survive the attacks of native warriors who would have benefited from all the advantages of guerrilla warfare, moving with extreme agility and speed over a harsh, mountainous land whose every aspect they were completely familiar with.

In the end, after unspeakable suffering and massive losses, due mainly to frost and starvation, the survivors of the Ten Thousand arrived within view of the sea. Their triumphal cry 'Thalassa! Thalassa!' ('The sea! The sea!') has become part of our collective imagination as the symbol of an unthinkable triumph over unbeatable odds.

This long march of over six thousand kilometres amidst every kind of danger and natural obstacle filled Xenophon's contemporaries and later generations alike with wonder and admiration, but has been considered largely insignificant from a historical point of view, if not in view of the fact that it demonstrated the substantial weakness of the greatest power of that time, the Persian empire, and probably inspired the conquests of Alexander the Great. It has in fact been demonstrated that the Macedonian sovereign was greatly influenced by the *Anabasis* and followed Xenophon's itinerary scrupulously during the early Anatolian and Syrian stages of his own expedition into Persia in 331 BC.

I have long been fascinated by Xenophon's account and set out, beginning in the 1980s, to reconstruct the itinerary of the Ten Thousand on the actual terrain, undertaking three separate scientific expeditions on which I was able to map out the route with considerable accuracy and at times with complete certainty. In 1999 I joined British scholar Timothy Mitford for a close inspection of the territory. Mitford had already localized the circular bases of two huge stone cairns on the Pontian mountains south of Trabzon, and identified them as the trophy erected by the Ten Thousand when they came into view of the sea. Our joint reconnaissance fully confirmed Mitford's thesis and his meticulous topographical survey.

But the novel does not stop here. It narrates the long march in an emotional key and hints at the existence of a huge international plot at the end of the fifth century BC, based on several discoveries which emerged during my field work and were later published in a scientific volume. My studies suggest that the Spartan government played a direct – yet covert – role in the expedition, officially organized by Cyrus alone.

First of all, it is likely that the original commander of the Ten Thousand, Clearchus, who was allegedly wanted for murder in Sparta, was actually a Spartan secret agent.

Chirisophus, the only regular Spartan officer to take part in the expedition – who became the commander of the Ten Thousand after Clearchus fell in an ambush along with all his general staff – was most probably poisoned by his own compatriots as a reward for bringing the army all the way back to Byzantium.

Xenophon himself almost certainly cut three months out of his account, precisely at the point in which the army gets lost in northern Armenia, perhaps even ending up in Azerbaijan.

Disturbing hints, these, that the expedition had not gone wholly according to plan. I hypothesize that Sparta – which had earlier won the Peloponnesian war against Athens with the help of Persian gold – learned about Cyrus's intentions and decided to play two hands at once by allowing the rebellious young prince to enlist the Ten Thousand while keeping the entire operation absolutely secret. If he succeeded in winning the throne, Cyrus would be in debt to Sparta, whereas if he failed, the Spartan government could claim that they had had no part in the scheme and continue to enjoy good relations with Artaxerxes, guaranteeing their hegemony over all of Greece. In other words, the Ten Thousand were truly meant to win or disappear. But the outcome of the venture foiled Spartan expectations. Unimaginably the Ten Thousand succeeded in surviving their long march through a region from which no army had ever returned: two years after Cyrus's luckless attempt, they were back at the gates of the Greek world.

Although what Xenophon seems to have deliberately left out

of his account – the details of these events and their repercussions – can only be surmised, the mystery can be explored through fiction, crafting an imaginary, but quite likely, scenario.

Valerio Massimo Manfredi